Heartland

VOLUME ONE

by Lauren Brooke

SCHOLASTIC INC.
New York Toronto London Auckland Sydney
Mexico City New Delhi Hong Kong Buenos Aires

Coming Home, ISBN 0-439-13020-4, copyright © 2000 by Working Partners Ltd., London

After the Storm, ISBN 0-439-13022-0, copyright © 2000 by Working Partners Ltd., London
The poem "The life that I have" copyright © 1958 by Leo Marks.

Breaking Free, ISBN 0-439-13024-7, copyright © 2000 by Working Partners Ltd., London

Heartland series created by Working Partners Ltd., London.

12 11 10 9 8 7 6 5 4 3 2 1   5 6 7 8 9 10/0

Printed in the U.S.A.   23

ISBN: 0-439-85552-7

First compilation printing, February 2005

Contents

Heartland

Coming Home

*For Craig Walker — who listened
and understood*

With thanks to Monty Roberts, who first wrote about the "join-up" technique and whose work has made the world a better place for horses.

And with special thanks to Linda Chapman.

Chapter One

As the school bus disappeared into the distance, Amy Fleming shifted her backpack onto her shoulder and headed up the long drive leading to Heartland. On both sides of the dusty path were fields filled with horses and ponies grazing lazily in the afternoon sunshine, their tails swishing away the clouds of flies that buzzed around them. Amy smiled. It was a sight that always made her glad to be home.

She hurried on up the curving drive toward the weather-boarded house and brick stable block with its whitewashed doors. As she drew near, a stall door opened and Ty, Heartland's seventeen-year-old stable hand, came out leading Copper, a chestnut gelding.

Amy waved, but Ty was concentrating on the horse and didn't see her. He led him past the turnout paddocks and toward the circular training ring at the top of the yard. Amy shaded her eyes. She could just make out the slim, blond figure of her mom waiting at the gate.

Amy hurried past the farmhouse and up the path after Ty. There was nothing she loved more than watching her mom work, and it looked like she was about to start a session with Copper.

As Ty drew the horse to a halt near the gate, the gelding threw his head up to shake off the flies settling on his face. Instinctively, Ty raised his hand to brush the flies away. With a sudden loud whinny of alarm, Copper shot backward.

"Copper!" Amy gasped as the horse reared, his front hooves flailing in the air.

"Whoa!" Ty cried as he lost grip of the lead.

Copper's front hooves clattered down to the ground. The whites of his eyes showed his panic. Ty managed to grab the lead rope, but the sudden movement sent the terrified horse rearing up again, his lethal hooves whisking through the air, inches from Ty's head.

"Here!" Marion Fleming's voice rang through the air. The next instant she was by Ty's side, grabbing the lead rope from him. "Steady, now! Steady!" she called to the horse.

Momentarily landing on the ground, Copper reared straight up again. Holding the end of the lead rope lightly, Marion let him go. Amy watched intently as her mother calmed the frightened creature, her lips moving in soothing words.

Copper came down with a snort and then reared again but not as high. Still, Marion talked. Copper's hooves came crashing down again, but this time he kept all four feet on the ground. He stood there, trembling slightly. For a long while Marion didn't move, her eyes fixed on his, her voice calming and reassuring. As he relaxed, she turned her body at a slight angle to his and moved slowly toward him, her eyes looking toward the ground. Amy held her breath. As Marion reached for Copper's halter, he snorted and lowered his head.

Amy let out a huge sigh of relief.

Ty's face was pale. "I can't believe I was so stupid," he said under his breath, pushing a hand through his dark hair.

Marion looked around. "It's OK, Ty," she said. "It was just a mistake. We've just got to remember that Copper still doesn't like hands around his head." She patted the horse. "And with good cause," she added.

Amy knew what she meant. Copper had come to Heartland four weeks ago, a ruined show horse whose owners had been reported for whipping him on his head and neck whenever he knocked a jump down or made a mistake in the ring. Slowly, under Marion's care, Copper was regaining his trust in humans.

For what seemed the first time, Amy's mom noticed

her. "Hi, honey," she said, a smile lighting up her blue eyes. "Had a good day at school?"

"Sure," Amy said. She didn't want to talk about school. "Is Copper OK?" she asked, looking from her mom to the tall chestnut horse.

"He'll be fine," Marion said, leading him into the ring. "I'm going to try to join up with him. Want to watch?"

"Of course!" Amy answered eagerly. She went and stood beside Ty at the gate. "Hi," she said, dumping her bag on the ground.

"Hi, there," Ty replied. His hair flopped down across his forehead as he looked at her, his green eyes filled with self-disgust. "I guess you saw that."

Amy knew he was talking about Copper's panic. She shrugged.

"I can't believe I tried to brush those flies away like that, Amy," Ty said, shaking his head. "How dumb could I be?"

"Don't worry," she said reassuringly, putting her arms over the top of the gate and nudging him. "Look at him now."

Amy watched eagerly, momentarily lost in what she was seeing. Copper was cantering freely around the ring in smooth circles, his hooves thudding rhythmically on the sand surface. Marion Fleming stood in the middle of the ring. No rope or line attached horse to human, but it was as if they were bound by an invisible thread. As her mom took a step forward, Copper slowed down — as she moved back, he quickened up. Copper's outside ear was pricked forward, but his inside ear was pointing toward where Marion stood in the center. He stretched out his head and neck as he cantered, his nostrils blowing at the ground. He was saying that he trusted her.

Amy glanced at Ty. He met her gaze and they exchanged smiles. "There's nothing like seeing your mom work," he said quietly. "If I could be just one tenth as good with horses, I'd be happy."

"Me, too," Amy sighed.

Marion urged Copper on. And then, after two more circles around the ring, Copper started to open and shut his mouth as if he were chewing. Amy knew that it was the signal her mom had been waiting for. Amy watched as her mother turned her body sideways, so she was angled away from the horse. The gelding slowed and stopped. He looked toward the center where Marion waited patiently. Amy held her breath. This was the point when Copper would decide if he wanted to join up with Marion. There was a second's pause, and then Copper walked confidently over to Marion's shoulder. Stopping beside her, he snorted softly. Marion rubbed him gently between the eyes.

Amy felt happy tears pricking at the back of her eyes. She knew that the moment had come — her mom had found a way to connect with Copper. He had been so frightened of people, but now he was willing to trust Marion. It was the first step to his recovery. It was a big step.

As Marion sent Copper out again, Ty turned. "Come on, we should let your mom work," he said in a low voice. Amy nodded and quietly picked up her bag. They walked down past the turn-out fields, past the twelve-stall back barn, and around to the front stable.

Ty had started helping at Heartland three years ago, at first working on weekends and after school to earn money to help his family. Then at sixteen he had dropped out of high school to work full-time. It had always been his ambition to work with horses. Amy thought it was a good decision. Ty had a great way with the horses, and it was fun to have him around more.

"I have to groom Chester," said Ty, stopping to pick up a halter and grooming bucket as they passed the tack room.

Amy headed for the stall where a large bay hunter was looking out over his half door. Chester's owner had sent him to Heartland so he could overcome his fear of loading into horse trailers. "How are you, gorgeous?" she murmured, stroking him on the nose as Ty walked up with the halter.

"I didn't know you cared!" Ty grinned.

Amy hit him on the arm. "Like I meant you!"

Ty went into the stall and patted the big bay. "He's going home tomorrow. Your mom says he's ready."

"Tomorrow?" Amy said, her heart sinking slightly at the thought of saying good-bye. Having to say good-bye to the horses when they went to a new home or, as in Chester's case, returned to their owners, was one of the worst things about living and working at Heartland. "I'll miss him," she said softly.

Ty nodded. "Me, too."

For a moment they both stood, stroking Chester in silence.

"Hey, cheer up," Ty said. Amy realized he was looking at her downcast face. "At least it means —"

"That another horse can come and be helped," Amy finished Ty's sentence for him. She grinned as she saw the surprise on his face. "We were thinking the same thing."

"Oh, no, I need help!" Ty said. He dodged as she tried to hit him again.

"Do you know if Lou's called?" Amy asked as he picked up a body brush and started to groom Chester.

Ty shook his head. "Nope. Why? Are you expecting to hear from her?"

Amy nodded eagerly. "Yeah. She's coming for my birthday. She said she'd call and say what time she's arriving." Amy's gray eyes sparkled with the thought of seeing her sister. "I can't wait to see her again. It's been ages!"

"And she's definitely coming?" Ty said questioningly.

"Yes." Amy saw his slightly skeptical expression. "Yes!" she insisted. "This time she's promised!" Grabbing her bag, she let herself out of the stall and went down to the white-painted farmhouse that stood at the end of the stable block. She couldn't blame Ty for being doubtful. Ever since Lou had moved back from England to take a high-powered banking job in New York a year ago, she had been promising to come and visit. But so far, something had always seemed to come up at the last minute to prevent her.

Amy pushed open the back door, kicked off her sneakers, and went into the kitchen. "Hi! I'm home," she announced. ·

The kitchen was large but cluttered. In one corner there was a bookcase crammed and overflowing with books on horses and copies of horse magazines. The battered old table was littered with odds and ends — a hoof pick, a snaffle bit, one odd glove, a pot of keys.

Jack Bartlett, Amy's grandfather, was fixing a wooden grooming box at the kitchen table. "Hi, honey, how was your day?" he asked, putting down his screwdriver with a smile.

Amy rolled her eyes and grabbed a soda. "Better, now that school's over! Has Lou called?"

Jack Bartlett shook his head. "Not yet. I guess she'll call after work."

Amy nodded and took a couple of cookies out of a jar. "I'm going to get changed, Grandpa."

She went up the winding stairs to her bedroom, taking them two at a time. As usual, her room was a mess. Dog-eared horse magazines littered the floor. The bed was unmade. Half a grooming kit was scattered on her bedroom table. As she pulled on her work jeans and a T-shirt, she looked out at the front stable block. Chester was looking out over his door, and Ty was going into Pegasus's stall. Amy scraped her long brown hair into a scrunchy and hurried back down to the kitchen.

Just then the phone rang. "I'll get it," she said as she grabbed the cordless phone off the cradle. "I bet it's Lou."

It was. "Telepathy," Amy exclaimed. "I knew it was you."

"Yes, it's me," said Lou. "Hi."

"What time are you getting here tomorrow?" Amy asked eagerly. "We're having dinner at seven, but Mom said you'd probably come earlier. I can't wait to see you!"

"Well . . ." Amy heard the hesitation in her sister's voice. "You're still coming, aren't you?" she demanded.

"I'm sorry, Amy," Lou said awkwardly. "But something's come up at work. . . . I just can't put it off."

"But you promised!" Amy protested. "And it's my birthday!" She knew she sounded like a six-year-old, but she didn't care. She couldn't believe that Lou was canceling again.

"I know it is and I'm sorry. I really am." Lou's voice suddenly brightened, "Look, why don't you come and visit me again? There's so much to do in New York. We can go shopping or go to a show. We can do whatever you like."

"Yeah, sure," Amy said flatly.

"Can you tell Mom and Grandpa I'm sorry?" Lou said. "I've sent you something in the mail. And Carl sends his love."

Amy didn't say anything. Carl Anderson was Lou's boyfriend. Amy had only met him once, but she hadn't liked him. When she had told him about their mother's work, he had laughed, "Horse shrinks, what will they think of next?" She didn't know *what* Lou saw in him.

Lou seemed to sense the uncomfortable pause. "We'll catch up soon," she said quickly. "Promise. But I must go now. Bye!"

Amy put the phone down with a bang. She should have known! She met Grandpa's eyes. He looked at her in concern. "Isn't Lou coming?" he asked.

"No!" Amy said angrily. "She has work to do. As usual!"

Jack Bartlett sighed. "You know what Lou's like about her job, honey — it's very important to her."

"My fifteenth birthday's important, too!" Amy exclaimed. "And anyway, it was just an excuse. She just doesn't want to come here. You know she doesn't. She makes an excuse every time."

Grandpa didn't deny it. "She finds it difficult," he said with a sigh. "You know she does."

Amy scowled and threw herself down in a chair. Grandpa squeezed her shoulder and disappeared into the hall. "Here's something that might cheer you up," he said, coming back in and handing her the new issue of *Horse Life*.

"It's come!" Amy exclaimed, temporarily forgetting about her sister. She opened the magazine and scanned down the contents page. Yes! There it was — "Life at Heartland," page 23.

She flipped through the pages. What would the article say about them?

In the rolling hills of northeastern Virginia, Marion Fleming, "the horse lady," works her magic at Heartland, a rescue home for horses, ponies, and donkeys. Horses come here to be healed and to have the scars of the past lifted away.

Amy grinned. She liked that line. She read on:

Marion Fleming, once one of the world's finest female show jumpers, started Heartland following the breakup of her marriage twelve years ago. A fall at the show-jumping World Championships left her husband, British show jumper Tim Fleming, in a wheelchair and unable to ride again. The couple separated soon after.

Frowning, Amy quickly read over the rest of the paragraph. It was about her father's accident. He had been the favorite to win the gold medal. Racing against the clock, he had steered his horse, Pegasus, too sharply to the last fence. Unable to take off properly, Pegasus had caught the top rail of the jump between his legs and had come crashing down, landing on his rider. Tim Fleming had been temporarily paralyzed in the fall.

Uncomfortable feelings prickled through Amy. She had only been three at the time and didn't have any clear memories of the accident or the aftermath when her father, unable to cope with his injuries, had abandoned them. Her first real memories were at Heartland, her grandpa's home, where she and her mom had eventually come to live with Pegasus. Her eyes skipped over the words in front of her. It was a relief to read that the next paragraph focused on Heartland again:

With its thirty stalls, Heartland is a recovery center for horses that have been rescued from dreadful neglect or

physical cruelty. Horses that have been deemed dangerous and unridable or that have nowhere else to go have a
chance at Heartland. In treating these horses, Marion uses
a mixture of conventional veterinary medicine and other
remedies she learned while nursing the great Pegasus
back to physical and mental health. With patience and
compassion, Marion Fleming finds ways to reach these
horses. When they get better, concerted efforts are made
to find each horse a new and permanent home.

The article went on to explain that Marion also
treated privately owned horses with behavioral problems. Amy raced through to the end.

"What do you think?" Jack Bartlett asked when she
looked up.

"It's great!" Amy exclaimed, her bad mood forgotten.
"It makes Mom sound totally amazing. We'll have loads
of people who want to bring their horses here!" She
jumped to her feet.

"Now, Amy, don't go counting your chickens."

But Amy shrugged off his practical words. Excitement bubbled through her. "Has Mom seen it?" she
asked eagerly.

"Not yet," Grandpa replied.

"I've got to show her!" Amy said.

She pulled on her sneakers and raced to the yard,
hoping that her mom would have finished with Copper

by now. Her mind was buzzing with ideas. The article was bound to bring them a lot more paying clients and that meant more money, which meant they could afford to help more horses. Her imagination took over. She saw a new twenty-stall barn and another horse trailer and pickup. Maybe even an indoor ring for the winter when the outdoor riding rings were often hock-deep in mud. Her biggest ambition was for Heartland to be as successful as possible. This could be just the way for that to happen!

She reached the ring. Her mom was standing in the middle, patting Copper. "Come on in," she called to Amy.

Amy climbed over the gate. "The article that *Horse Life* did on us has come out! Look!" she said, hurrying over.

Marion took the magazine from her and began reading the article, while Amy carefully stroked Copper's warm neck.

"I like this line," Marion smiled. "'Healing the scars' — that's good."

"Me, too!" grinned Amy. She fed Copper a mint from her pocket. He snuffled it up, his warm breath grazing her palm. "You're a good boy," she told him, very gently rubbing his face.

Marion smiled, momentarily distracted from the magazine. "You couldn't have done that to him four weeks ago."

Amy nodded and looked over her mother's shoulder. "Isn't the article good? I bet lots of people will want to bring their horses here for us to help. Heartland will make loads of money!"

"We're not doing too badly at the moment as it is," Marion pointed out. "We've got almost more paying clients than we can deal with." Since she had started Heartland, Marion's reputation had grown. There was now a steady stream of owners who hoped Marion might cure their horses of behavioral problems.

"But if we get even more, we can build a new barn and help lots more rescue horses," Amy said.

Marion smiled. "Let's wait and see what happens." She handed the magazine back to Amy. "Come on, let's take this boy in."

They led Copper through the gate and down the yard. As they reached his stall, Amy suddenly remembered her other, less exciting news. "Lou called," she said. "She's not coming."

"Oh," Marion said, her face falling.

Amy told her about the phone call. "It's the same as always," she said, quick anger rising inside her again. "She never comes. She says she will and then she doesn't. She doesn't care about us; all she cares about is her stupid job and Carl!"

"Amy, you know that's not true," said Marion, picking up a body brush and starting to brush Copper. "Lou loves you, loves all of us. She just finds it difficult coming here."

"But that's so crazy!" Amy exclaimed. "This is her home!"

"No, it isn't, Amy." Marion said. "You know it isn't."

Amy wanted to resist what her mom was saying, but deep down she knew it was true.

After her father had left, Lou had refused to move to Virginia. Convinced that he would one day come back, Lou had begged to be allowed to stay at her English boarding school. Marion had agreed because she couldn't bear to put Lou through any more emotional stress. During vacations, instead of traveling to stay with Marion and Amy at Heartland, Lou had almost always found an excuse to stay with friends in England. When she had come over, she made it clear that she blamed horses for their father's accident and sudden departure, and that she felt Marion and Amy had been wrong to leave England. With her English accent it was sometimes hard to believe Lou was American at all, let alone Amy's sister.

Amy sighed. Despite their differences, they were still sisters. "I just want to see her, Mom."

"I know you do, honey," Marion said sympathetically. "And you will. She'll come back one day."

"Yeah, maybe when I'm sixty!" Amy retorted. "Why

can't she just forget about Daddy's accident? It happened so long ago."

Marion shook her head. "I know it seems like that to you," she said. "But Lou was older, and she was really close to Daddy. They were inseparable." She half smiled. "He was so proud of her when she was little. He used to put her on all our horses, and she would ride anything. She's a lot like him — brave and practical. You know, Lou was amazing after his accident." She sighed and Amy saw the sadness in her eyes. "She was so strong and helped me with so many things. I don't really know how we would have managed without her."

Marion looked down and there was a pause. Amy swallowed, suddenly feeling a pang of guilt. She never thought about how much her mom must miss Lou, too.

Marion carefully stroked Copper's forelock and then forced a smile. "Lou will come to terms with it all in the end," she said to Amy. "You'll see." Giving Copper a final pat, she walked out of the stall. In the next stall, Pegasus was looking out. He nickered a soft welcome, his dark eyes lighting up as Marion walked along to greet him. She placed a hand lovingly against his great gray head.

Amy followed her. "Am I like Daddy, too?"

For a moment, Marion didn't answer.

"Mom?" Amy persisted. The older Amy got, the more

she found herself wondering about her father, but her mom rarely wanted to talk about him.

Marion looked at Amy's tall, slim frame, her brown hair and thickly lashed gray eyes. "On the outside, yes, you look like him," she said quietly. "But inside I think you're a lot more like me — emotional, intuitive." She smiled. "I guess that's why we make such a great team. Lou — now, she's practical, feet firmly on the ground."

"Like Daddy?" Amy said.

"Yes," Marion said, nodding. She stopped, her eyes darkening with sadness, and she looked down. "Well — like I always thought he was," she whispered, her voice so quiet that Amy hardly caught the words. Marion didn't say anything for a long moment. Then she looked into Amy's worried face and seemed to force herself to smile. "Come on, don't look like that," she said. "Hey, I tell you what, why don't you take one of the ponies out for a ride after we've fed the horses? It's such a perfect afternoon. Ty and I can finish off the work."

Amy was surprised by her mother's offer. It was rare she got to go trail riding on school days — pleasure riding always came second to getting the work done. "OK," she said, brightening up.

Marion smiled. "It *is* almost your birthday, after all."

"Soraya's coming around later," Amy said. "I'll see if she wants to come." Soraya Martin had been Amy's best friend since third grade, and she loved horses almost as much as Amy did.

Marion nodded. "Good idea. You two go and enjoy yourselves."

Just then the back door opened and Jack Bartlett looked out. "Marion! Telephone!" he called.

With a quick smile at Amy, Marion hurried off down the yard. Amy moved closer to Pegasus. He nuzzled her, and she leaned her head against his comfortingly strong neck. As far as she was concerned, loving and caring for Pegasus seemed to bring her father closer. She wished Lou could feel the same way. "When do you think Lou will come home?" she said to him. Pegasus snorted quietly in reply. Amy hugged him. At least she always had him to talk to. "I love you," she whispered.

As she waited for her mom, she let her fingers work on Pegasus's ears with light, circular movements that helped release tension, fear, and pain. It was one of the many alternative treatments that Marion used on the horses that came to Heartland. In response to Amy's skillful touch, Pegasus lowered his enormous head, obviously enjoying the attention.

A few minutes later, Marion came back from the house. "That was Wayne Taylor," she said, "wanting to make arrangements for picking Chester up tomorrow morning." Two of the horses farther down the stable block, Jake and Tarka, kicked impatiently at their doors. Marion smiled. "Come on," she said, "let's get these horses fed."

In the feed room, the sweet smell of beet pulp filled the air. Cobwebs hung off the beamed ceiling, and the floor was made of old, cracked flagstones. Marion started scooping bran, barley, and alfalfa cubes into the battered yellow feeding buckets. "When you're out, would you ride up to Mrs. Bell's for me?" she asked. "I promised her I'd drop off some herbs to help with Sugarfoot's sweet itch."

"Sure," Amy said. Mrs. Bell was an old lady who lived in a tiny house on a lonely road up the mountain. She owned a little Shetland pony named Sugarfoot. He followed her everywhere, more like a dog than a pony. Amy sometimes dropped by to give Mrs. Bell a hand looking after him. "Then after we've seen Mrs. Bell, we can go over to Clairdale Ridge," she said, starting to add a scoopful of the soaked beet pulp to each bucket. "Soraya hasn't seen the Mallens' new horse yet."

Her mom frowned. "Grandpa heard a rumor in town that the Mallens were moving."

"Already?" Amy said, surprised. "They haven't been there that long." The Mallen family was renting a dilapidated old house on Clairdale Ridge. They had an odd assortment of skinny animals — hens, dogs, and a couple of cows. But just recently, a beautiful young bay stallion had joined the cattle in the sparse field at the front of the house. Amy liked to ride past and admire him whenever she could. "Where are they moving to?" she asked.

"No one seems to know," said Marion, picking up the dusty cod liver oil can and adding a dollop to each feed bucket. "Hopefully somewhere with better grazing for those poor animals. But it could just be a rumor that they're going."

"I'll check it out," Amy said.

Marion looked warningly at her. "Don't forget to stick to the trails. That road up to Clairdale Ridge is far too dangerous to ride on."

"OK, Mom," Amy sighed. Her mom had warned her about that road about a thousand times. Shaking her head, she picked up a pile of feed and set off for the front stable block.

Chapter Two

After finishing the feeding, Amy went down to the ponies' field. A pretty black pony standing by the gate whinnied a greeting. "Hi, Jaz," Amy said, pulling a packet of mints out of her pocket and offering one to the mare. Jasmine gobbled it down greedily, her soft muzzle immediately nudging at Amy, asking for more.

Alerted by the rustle of the paper, the other ponies in the field looked up, ears pricked. They crowded over to the gate, and Amy began distributing the mints between them as fairly as she could. Suddenly, the little group scattered as a buckskin pony came barging through, ears back, teeth snapping.

"Sundance!" Amy exclaimed as the buckskin stopped dead and thrust his head hard against her chest. He rolled his eyes threateningly at the other ponies, warning them to keep back. "You're a bully!" she told him severely.

Sundance looked up adoringly at her. *Who me?* he seemed to say as he nuzzled her and snorted happily. Amy kissed his golden head. Sundance looked up at her cutely and then spoiled the expression by kicking at Jasmine, who was edging next to him. Amy sighed. Nothing was ever going to change Sundance's bad temper, but she didn't mind, she loved him anyway.

She had fallen in love with him the first moment she saw him in a pen at a horse sale two years ago. With his small ears back and his head high, he had defied the world, attacking anyone who dared try and enter his pen to inspect him. "He'll go for glue," Amy heard two men say. But he hadn't. Amy had persuaded her mom to buy him and had worked with him, slowly gaining his trust and affection. Much to everyone's surprise, Sundance had proved to have an exceptional talent for jumping. Now there were lots of people who wanted him. But Marion had promised Amy that he would always have a home at Heartland.

"Amy!"

Amy turned. Soraya was running up the track with a halter in her hands, her black curls bouncing on her shoulders.

"Hi!" Amy called.

"Hey!" Soraya panted. "I just got here. Your mom said we can go for a trail ride."

Amy nodded. "Who do you want? I'm going to ride Sundance."

Soraya only had to think for a second. "I'll take Jasmine." She knew the horses and ponies at Heartland almost as well as Amy did.

An ex-dressage pony, Jasmine was another long-term Heartland resident. Before Marion had rescued her, she was about to be put down because she was lame in her front legs. And now, after successful treatment of the swelling around her fetlocks, Jasmine was sound enough for light work and she loved to be ridden. She was a pretty pony, half Arabian with a dished face, a white star, and two white socks. In contrast to Sundance, she had the sweetest of natures. Although it would be hard to part with her, Amy hoped that one day they'd be able to find her a new home.

It didn't take Amy and Soraya long to bring the ponies in from the field and groom and tack up. Before setting off, Amy picked up the herbs for Sugarfoot from her mom and put them in her saddlebag. They rode on the sandy trail that led up Teak's Hill, the wooded slope that rose steeply behind Heartland. As they headed toward Mrs. Bell's house, the trees on the slope cast a welcome shade.

"So, do you know when Lou's coming yet?" Soraya asked.

"She's not," Amy replied. "She called and canceled."

"What — again?" Soraya said.

"Yes, again."

Soraya looked at her sympathetically, and then, sensitive as always, she changed the subject. "What do you think you'll get for your birthday?"

"Well," Amy replied enthusiastically, deciding not to think about Lou anymore, "I want that blue jacket in the window of Cooper's — you know, the waterproof one. I've shown it to Mom about ten times now."

"Oh, yeah," Soraya nodded. Cooper's was the local tack shop. They visited it every time they went into town.

"And some new gloves and show breeches," Amy continued.

Soraya smiled. "Do you think Matt will get you a gift?"

Amy thought about Matt Trewin, tall with sandy hair, brown eyes, and a lopsided grin. She shrugged. "I don't know."

"I bet he will!" Soraya said. "It's so totally obvious he likes you. He's always hanging around with you at school or coming by Heartland."

"That's because he comes with Scott," Amy interrupted. "Not to see me." Matt's older brother, Scott, was

the local equine vet, and often when he visited Heartland, Matt would be in the car and would hang out with
Amy while Scott checked on the horses. "He says he
wants to find out about being a vet."

"Like that's true!" Soraya said, rolling her eyes.
"Everyone knows Matt wants to be a doctor."

"Well — maybe he's thinking about changing his
mind," Amy said.

"Amy!" Soraya exclaimed. "Quit acting stupid! You
know Matt wants to go out with you. Why don't you just
admit it and say yes? I would!"

Amy struggled to find the words. It wasn't that she
didn't like Matt. He was fun to be around and they got
along just fine, it was just . . .

"I wish he liked riding more," she said. "He's not exactly into horses, is he? Not like Scott," she added,
thinking about Matt's twenty-nine-year-old brother,
who was devoted to horses. She saw Soraya's incredulous expression.

"Amy!" Soraya cried. "I don't get you sometimes! The
cutest boy in school totally adores you, and all you can
think about is that he isn't really into horses. Nearly
every girl in our class would give anything to go out with
Matt! He's cute, smart, caring. I wish I could meet
someone half as nice. I only attract jerks!" Her face
brightened. "Still, who knows, maybe I'll meet someone
at camp."

"I bet you will!" Amy said.

At the beginning of July, Soraya was going to a riding camp for a month. It was a camp where you rode the same horse the whole time and then entered in competitions. Soraya's parents had organized it for her as a special treat. Amy thought about having a whole month without her best friend. "I'll miss you," she said wistfully.

"Sure," Soraya stroked Jasmine's neck, "and I'll miss you, too — and all the horses. But I'll be back in August."

Amy grinned at her. "And maybe with a new boyfriend."

Soraya's face lit up. "I hope!"

They giggled and pushed the ponies into a canter. It was cool in the shade of the trees, and as they rode along side by side, the wind rushing by, Amy felt she could have gone on forever. However, they quickly reached the dirt track that led to Mrs. Bell's small clapboard house with its rickety fence.

"Whoa, boy." Amy eased Sundance to a halt. "I wonder where Mrs. Bell is," she said to Soraya.

Just then, Jasmine neighed, and an answering whinny came from the other side of the house. Amy and Soraya looked at each other, dismounted, and led the ponies around the back to the garden, where they saw Mrs. Bell kneeling in the vegetable patch. She was slowly digging up carrots and putting them in a basket next to her on the ground. Each carrot seemed an enormous effort. Beside her stood a tiny Shetland pony. As Mrs. Bell worked, she sang in a cracked, quavering voice.

"Hello, Mrs. Bell," Amy called out, but the old lady didn't hear. She continued singing. Sugarfoot stood happily beside her, his ears pricked.

"Let's leave Sundance and Jasmine here," Amy said to Soraya. They hitched the ponies to a fence post and then went up the path to the vegetable patch.

Every time Mrs. Bell finished digging an area of soil, she moved farther along the row of carrots, and Sugarfoot, the little pony, followed her. Mrs. Bell was wearing a torn apron and an old hat, but Sugarfoot looked in excellent condition. His chestnut coat gleamed. His blond mane and tail were lovingly combed, and from underneath his bushy forelock, his eyes peeped out, dark and bright.

Mrs. Bell turned to pat the little Shetland and murmured, "What do you think, Sugarfoot — the squash aren't doing so good this summer, are they?"

Sugarfoot pushed against her hand and nickered softly.

"He is so cute!" Soraya said.

"Mrs. Bell," Amy called again.

The old lady started in surprise at the sound of her voice, and then, seeing it was Amy and Soraya, a smile lit up her face. "Hello, there," she said, straightening up slowly and smiling broadly. "How nice to see you both." Sugarfoot trotted over to Soraya and nuzzled against her, searching for a treat. "Would you girls like a drink?" Mrs. Bell asked them.

"I'm OK, thanks," said Amy, looking at Soraya, who also shook her head. "We just came to see how you were and to give you some herbs for Sugarfoot. Mom said they're for his sweet itch. How are you, Mrs. Bell?"

"Oh, me, I'm fine and dandy."

Amy didn't think Mrs. Bell looked fine at all. The old lady was breathing heavily, with a strange wheezing sound.

"Do you want a hand?" Soraya offered.

"That's kind of you, honey. If you could carry the basket indoors for me, that would be a big help."

The girls followed Mrs. Bell into the house, Soraya carrying the vegetable basket and Amy bringing the bundle of herbs. Mrs. Bell leaned against Sugarfoot's withers for support. Amy was amazed at how the little pony seemed to understand exactly how to help his owner. He came right into the kitchen, letting the old lady support herself on him until she was able to sink down into a chair.

Amy looked around at the ancient, cracked sink, the single chair at the table, the threadbare blue rug on the wooden boards and breathed in the stale air that smelled of boiled vegetables. Sugarfoot helped himself to an apple from the fruit bowl on a low table beside the door.

"Is he allowed to do that?" Soraya asked, surprised.

"Oh, he only takes one," said Mrs. Bell. She stroked Sugarfoot's neck. He slobbered apple appreciatively onto her apron and then rested his head against her shoulder. "And he knows he's only allowed in the kitchen," said Mrs. Bell. "He's something else."

"How long have you had him?" asked Soraya, who didn't know Mrs. Bell as well as Amy.

"Twelve years. I still remember that first day I saw him." Mrs. Bell shook her head fondly at the memory. "Just weaned, and the tiniest foal ever. I had to buy him. He's been with me ever since." Sugarfoot nuzzled her shoulder and Mrs. Bell put a hand on his neck. "Well, better get on," she said. "There's the housework to do."

"Are you sure you're OK, Mrs. Bell?" said Amy, concerned. She always worried about the old lady, all alone up on Teak's Hill. No one ever seemed to visit her apart from herself and Eric Beasley, the mailman.

Mrs. Bell smiled at her. "Of course I'm OK, honey. I've got Sugarfoot to look after me."

❧

As they rode back down the hill, Amy turned to Soraya. "I think we should go to see Mrs. Bell more often."

Soraya nodded in agreement. "She sure doesn't look too great, does she?"

Amy shook her head. "I'll tell Mom when we get back." She looked across Teak's Hill to where Clairdale Ridge rose up, dark and craggy against the blue sky. The sun was still beating down on them, but in the distance, near the ridge, a group of dark clouds seemed to be gathering. "Do you want to go over to the Mallens' house?" she said.

Soraya grinned. "Yeah! I want to see this horse you keep talking about."

"He's gorgeous!" Amy said.

The trail widened and they pushed the ponies into a canter. Amy tightened her reins. Seeing two fallen tree trunks lying to one side, she steered toward them and nudged Sundance on. As always at the sight of a jump, his ears pricked up, his head rose, and his stride became full of energy. As he reached the logs, Amy felt his muscles bunch and gather. He cleared the jump by at least two feet and threw in a buck for good measure as he landed. Grabbing his mane, Amy laughed.

They slowed down. "He's jumping well!" Soraya said, patting Jasmine's black neck. "Are you taking him to any shows over the summer?"

Amy nodded. Sundance was a natural in the large Pony Hunter classes. With Amy riding him, he just seemed to sparkle in front of an audience, meeting each jump perfectly, never touching a pole, and jumping with such athletic ability and style that judges could rarely resist him. In the ring he was a picture of good manners and obedience. *It was just lucky the judges never saw him at home,* Amy thought dryly as he swung his head grumpily at Jasmine, his ears pinned back.

Soraya grinned. "Ashley better watch out."

They both laughed. Ashley Grant was in school with them. Beautiful and wealthy, she was also a talented rider. Her parents owned a distinguished hunter/jumper stable called Green Briar, where her mom, Val Grant, was the trainer. Ashley rode in all of the shows and had won lots of prizes with her expensive push-button ponies. When she had first seen Amy arrive at a show with Sundance, Ashley christened him the Mule because of his unfavorable buckskin coat and displays of bad temper outside the ring. She had laughed less, however, when Sundance cantered into the ring, ears perfectly pricked, and had jumped his way to being Large Pony champion.

"Did I tell you that Ashley's mom wanted to buy Sundance?" she said.

"You're kidding!" Soraya replied, surprised. "After all those things they've said about him?"

"She called last week." Amy grinned. "She offered a lot of money. Mom said no, of course." She patted Sundance's neck. "As if I'd ever let you go somewhere like Green Briar!"

Green Briar's training methods were very different from those used at Heartland. Val Grant believed in force and very firm discipline. She schooled ponies to respond to the commands of any rider — her horses learned to excel in one area and would complete a course to win. Val Grant considered it a waste of time developing relationships with them. And many of the riders she trained felt the same way. It made Amy angry that anyone could treat horses with anything less than the respect and understanding they deserved.

At that moment, Jasmine stepped too close to Sundance. He squealed and snapped his teeth. "On second thought," Amy said, shaking her head, "maybe Ashley's welcome to you!" She laughed and patted Sundance quickly to show that she didn't mean it.

She wondered how many shows they would get to that summer. She had a secret ambition to try him in Junior Jumper classes as well as doing Pony Hunter. The problem was finding the time. If Heartland was busy, then Mom couldn't take her. But she didn't really mind. As much as she liked competing, it wasn't the most important thing in her life — that was helping out with the horses at Heartland.

"Let's trot," Soraya said. Amy nodded.

The nearer they got to Clairdale Ridge, the rougher

the terrain became. The steep sides of the mountain were covered with tufted grass and rocky outcroppings. A few lonely buildings huddled on its slopes.

They reached the trail that led to the Mallens' house.

"Look!" Amy said, halting Sundance. Three strands of barbed wire were stretched across two posts on opposite sides of the trail. They were at chest height to the ponies and too dangerous to jump. Besides, Amy thought, usually the trails were only blocked if they were impassable.

"Maybe there's been a rock slide or something," Soraya said, stopping Jasmine beside Sundance. She looked up — the black clouds that had been in the far distance were getting closer now. "Maybe we should just go back. The weather's not looking so good."

"But we're so close!" Amy protested. She wanted to see the bay stallion again. "We can take the road instead."

"But your mom's always telling us not to use that road," Soraya said doubtfully.

"It'll be OK." The thought of the stallion drove Amy on. "We'll only be on it for five minutes. Come on!"

Amy urged Sundance forward. Looking back over her shoulder she saw her friend hesitate for a moment before following. The road was narrow and winding, and on either side there were crumbling stone walls topped with old wooden posts and rusty barbed wire.

"It doesn't look too safe," Soraya said, looking ahead at the sharp bends.

"Look, it'll be OK," repeated Amy impatiently.

They trotted up the road, the ponies' hooves clattering loudly on the worn asphalt. As they came around the second bend, the road plunged into a dark tunnel of trees. Sundance snorted uncertainly and stopped.

"It's all right," Amy urged him. "Walk on," she said, clicking her tongue.

Sundance stepped forward into the darkness, high footed, cautious. The air felt suddenly cold, the leafy canopy overhead blocking out the warmth of the sun. With a wild squawk, a jay flew out of a nearby tree. Both Jasmine and Sundance shied violently, losing their footing on the smooth surface. Amy glanced back at Soraya. Her face was tense.

"Let's trot again," Amy said quickly. She was beginning to have the uncomfortable feeling that her mom was right. It was a dangerous road to ride on. It would take just one car to come around the corner too fast . . .

Clicking her tongue, she pushed Sundance on. He was agitated and skittish, but she soothed him and he settled into a steady trot. Amy was glad when a couple of minutes later they emerged from the tunnel of trees. Ahead of them was the track that led to the Mallens' house. She turned down it in relief. As they drew closer to the house, Amy frowned and slowed Sundance to a walk. "They're gone!" she said in surprise.

The house was undoubtedly empty. The bay horse and the scrawny cows were missing from the field, the rusty pickup had disappeared, and the windows were bare and curtainless. Only a few bags of garbage by the door suggested that there had been people living there recently.

"Oh." Soraya sounded disappointed.

Amy's heart sank. She had really wanted to see the stallion again. "I guess we *should* go home, then," she said despondently.

They rode around the side of the house, heading for a trail that led back to Teak's Hill and Heartland. They passed a collection of dilapidated wooden outbuildings. The air had become heavy and still, dark clouds pressing down overhead.

"This is spooky," Soraya said in a low voice.

Suddenly, Jasmine put her head in the air and whinnied shrilly. Both girls jumped. "Jaz!" Amy exclaimed. The words died on her lips as an answering whinny echoed through the still air. She and Soraya stared at each other in shock.

"Where did that come from?" Soraya gasped.

"I — I don't know!" Amy stammered. She looked around wildly, almost believing that she must have heard a ghost. And then a second whinny came.

This time Amy caught the direction it was coming from. "That barn!" she said, pointing to one of the sturdier looking outbuildings. She grabbed her reins as Sundance sidestepped, his head up and his cream ears pricked. Soraya was struggling with Jasmine, who was whinnying excitedly again. Amy dismounted quickly and, leading Sundance over to Soraya, thrust his reins at her. "Here, hold him!"

As she ran the short distance over to the shed, a large raindrop splashed down onto her arm. She ignored it, her fingers fumbling with the door's rusty metal bolt. She could hear a hoof pawing at the floor on the other side. Why was a horse shut in this barn? What sort of condition would it be in? The bolt jerked back, but the door was stiff and heavy and stayed in place.

"Be careful!" Soraya called anxiously.

Amy had been about to throw all her weight into heaving the door open, but she checked herself. Soraya was right — the horse would be terrified from being shut in the dark, and fear could make any horse dangerous.

Amy cautiously slid the door open a crack and peered in. For a moment she couldn't see anything, but then her eyes gradually adjusted to the dim light. She gasped.

At the back of the barn, eyeing her suspiciously, was the Mallens' beautiful bay horse.

Chapter Three

"It's the stallion!" Amy called, motioning frantically to Soraya. She tugged the door farther open, bumping it heavily along the ground. Once the door was ajar enough to let in some light, she could see the stallion clearly — and he could see her. His eyes rolled in fear as he stood at the back of the barn, his muscles bunched and tense, his shoulders and flanks quivering.

"It's OK," Amy said to him as soothingly as she could. "I won't hurt you." Her eyes swept around the shed. The floor was bare, and there was no water or food. However, the stallion's physical condition looked good, which meant he couldn't have been shut in there for more than a day or two.

The horse called out shrilly. Amy's mind raced. If she opened the door farther, he might try to break free. That could be disastrous — he would either escape into the wild of Clairdale Ridge or end up on the narrow road. They had to help him somehow. She swung around to Soraya. "We've got to do something!"

Soraya had her own problems. Excited by the stallion's whinnies, Sundance and Jasmine were whirling around. Sundance tried to bite Jasmine, causing the mare to rear backward. Soraya barely managed to keep her seat.

Amy looked up at the dark sky. It had begun to rain heavily. Large drops were splashing down. Her heart pounding, she turned again to the barn and started squeezing through the gap in the door.

"Easy now," she called to the frightened stallion. He half reared and she jumped back. "Steady!" But the horse wouldn't be calmed. He kicked out, his back hooves crashing against the barn wall.

"Amy!" Soraya called from outside. "I can't hold onto Sundance much longer!"

Amy hesitated. She knew Soraya needed help, but what about the horse? The rain was pelting down now, bouncing off the roof and forming puddles on the ground. Her mind was in a whirl. Even if she could get near the stallion, how was she going to get him back to Heartland without a halter or bridle?

"Amy!" Soraya's voice was higher, more desperate now.

Amy made up her mind. She squeezed back out of the

shed and dragged the door shut. "I'm sorry!" she whispered through the crack as she rammed the bolt home. "But I'll be back soon."

The stallion cried out frantically as he found himself in the dark again. Trying to shut out the sound, Amy turned away. Sundance had reared up and Soraya was struggling to hold on to him.

Amy raced over to her friend. She grabbed Sundance's reins and pulled him down. "Quick! We've got to get help!"

Steadying Sundance, Amy swung herself up into the saddle, and the two girls set off down the trail at a gallop.

❧

By the time they got back to Heartland, Amy and Soraya were soaked to the skin, their jeans clinging to their legs and T-shirts plastered against their bodies.

They clattered into the yard at a tremendous pace that brought Marion Fleming hurrying out of the tack room. "What on earth are you doing?" She looked at Amy's wide eyes and pale face and her tone changed. "What's happened?" she asked anxiously.

"The Mallens' horse!" Amy gasped, sliding off Sundance. "They've gone, but it's shut up in a barn outside their house. Mom! You've got to help!"

"It's been abandoned?" Marion said.

Amy nodded. "We've got to go and get it!"

Marion looked at the rain pouring down around them. "We can't take the trailer out in this, Amy! The roads up on Clairdale Ridge are so steep and narrow. It would be too dangerous."

Amy pushed away the picture of the forbidding tunnel of trees high up on the ridge. "But we can't leave that horse shut in for another night!" she cried. "It hasn't got food or water or anything!"

"Nothing?" Marion said quickly.

Amy shook her head. "He's terrified, Mom! If a storm starts, he might try to break free!"

Marion paused as she made up her mind. "OK, we'll go get it," she said decisively. Her voice became brisk and efficient. "You put the ponies away and get a bucket of food for the stallion. I'll get the trailer out." She hurried off. "See you in a minute."

"Here!" Soraya said, reaching to take Sundance's reins off Amy. "You go. I'll put Sundance and Jasmine away. I'd better not come with you. Dad will be here to pick me up soon." Amy hesitated for a moment. "Go on!" Soraya urged. "You can call me tonight and tell me how it goes."

"OK! Thanks!" Amy gasped. Turning, she ran after her mom.

❧

As they drove out of Heartland, the weather seemed to get even worse. The sky was heavy and dark gray. The windshield wipers squeaked rhythmically back and forth, barely making a break in the sheeting rain. The tires splashed noisily through the water on the road.

Amy shivered in her damp clothes. "Why do you think the Mallens left him, Mom?"

Marion shook her head, her eyes glued to the road. "I guess he might have been stolen, and before they'd found someone to sell him to, they got scared. Maybe the police had been asking around."

"I can't believe they could just abandon him like that!" Amy exclaimed. "He could have starved to death."

Marion looked grim as she turned the trailer onto the steep, winding road that led up Clairdale Ridge. "Some people don't care about things like that." The engine clunked as she lowered it a gear to negotiate the sharp bends. Water was running in streams down the road.

They headed into the gloomy tunnel of trees. The truck and trailer crawled around the tight bends. A branch cracked loudly and thudded onto the roof. Amy jumped. She didn't like this dark passageway one bit. A tree creaked alarmingly as they passed. Amy gripped the seat and concentrated on rescuing the horse.

At last they emerged into the open. "I can hardly see a

thing," Marion said as heavy rain hit the windshield again.

Amy peered through the blur, searching the drive that led up to the farmhouse. "There! There's the turn. Not far now, Mom."

The truck splashed along the rutted driveway. Marion stopped it outside the house and, leaving the headlights on to illuminate their way, she jumped out. Amy grabbed the halter and lead rope from the seat beside her while Marion put the trailer ramp down. "Which building is it?" she called to Amy.

"That one!" Amy shouted, raising her voice above the wind.

They staggered through the rain to the barn. After Marion had pulled back the bolt, they heaved the door open together so it stood slightly ajar. Amy looked in. The bay stallion stared at them, head up, nostrils flaring, eyes wild. Marion looked at him for a moment and then, turning her back into the wind, took out a small container from her pocket. From it she took a pinch of dark, gritty dust and rubbed it into her hands. "Stand back a bit," she said softly to Amy.

Amy did as she was told, and Marion squeezed through the gap in the door. The horse moved uneasily on the spot, his ears back. Turning herself sideways toward him, Marion looked at the floor, knowing that eye contact could agitate horses. The stallion regarded her warily. Very slowly she held out her hand. The bay began to jerk his head back, but then he seemed to catch the scent of the powder. His nostrils flared and he inhaled, his ears suddenly pricking up.

Amy held her breath. The powder was made from trimmings of chestnuts — insensitive, callous growths found on the inside of horses' legs. An old horseman had once taught Marion that the scent could calm nervous and frightened horses. Now, shivering in the doorway, Amy watched to see what would happen.

Very cautiously, the horse stretched out his head. Marion stayed absolutely motionless, still looking down. *I am no threat,* her body language seemed to be saying. The horse took a step forward, all the time breathing in. His delicate muzzle touched Marion's hand, his nostrils dilating. He took another step forward and lifted his head to her hair, breathing in and then out.

Very slowly, Amy saw her mom turn, and as the stallion breathed in again, the fear left his eyes. His muscles relaxed, and lowering his head he nuzzled Marion's hand. She stroked him. "Pass me the halter," she said quietly to Amy.

Without the slightest objection, the horse let Marion slip on the halter. She patted him. "Come on, boy, let's get you into the trailer."

Amy heaved the door open. The horse obediently followed Marion out into the sheeting rain. Amy patted him and he nuzzled her arm. Now that his initial fear was gone he seemed friendly, even affectionate.

When they reached the trailer, she stood on the ramp and rattled a feed bucket. The horse stretched out his head and neck and gobbled a mouthful. Then, with no more prompting, he walked calmly into the box. Amy put down the bucket to let him eat, and then, leaving her mom to tie him up, she slipped out of the side door to heave the ramp up. Her wet fingers slipped as she fastened the bolts. The wind and rain lashed down. At last Marion emerged. "Home," she said, coming around to check the bolts. "And fast."

Their faces were streaming with water as they climbed back into the truck. Marion turned the key and the engine spluttered to life. Amy shivered and squeezed water from her hair. Marion turned on the heater. It roared noisily, competing with the sound of the rain. They could hear the stallion move uneasily in the back as the rain battered the roof of the trailer.

Outside there was an ominous rumbling. Seconds later, a jagged fork of lightning split the sky, and the rain started to sheet down with a new intensity. As they turned onto the steep downhill road, a crash of thunder broke over them.

The horse began to panic. His feet thudded against the side of the box, causing it to rock alarmingly. Amy glanced anxiously at her mother. The truck was gathering speed as it headed down the hill. Marion was concentrating hard, braking slowly and steadily to keep the trailer under control on the wet road.

"This is insane," muttered Marion. "We should never have done this, Amy. Not in this storm." Her eyes showed her anxiety as she gripped the steering wheel tightly.

Amy jumped as lightning forked straight down through the sky, accompanied by an immense clap of thunder. The stallion's hooves crashed into the walls of the trailer again and again as he struggled to escape.

The tunnel of dark trees loomed ahead. As they entered, branches closed over the top of the trailer, banging and scraping against it. Every muscle in Amy's body was tense. Her heart was pounding. Her breath was short in her throat.

The trees on each side of them swayed as the unrelenting wind and rain bent them against their will. The road seemed pitch-black beneath the tree canopy. Then there was a brilliant flash of lightning and a clap of thunder so loud that it sounded as if a cannon had gone off overhead. Amy screamed and jumped. The horse let out a shriek as a cracking noise echoed through the tunnel.

Straight in front of them, a tree started to fall.

Marion braked violently, but the tires failed to grip on the flooded surface. The truck skidded down the road, straight into the path of the falling tree.

Time slowed down. Powerless to do anything, Amy watched as the tree fell toward them in horrifyingly slow motion. For one wild moment she thought they were just going to get past it, but then, with a final creaking, crashing noise, the tree collapsed.

With startling clarity, in a single second that seemed to last forever, Amy saw every little detail, every vein of every green, damp leaf. "Mom!" she screamed.

There was a bang, a sickening feeling of falling, and then nothing.

Chapter Four

Amy's eyes fluttered open. White. Everything was white. Where was she? She blinked and then focused on a figure sitting at the side of the bed.

"Lou?" she said in surprise.

"Yeah, it's me," her sister replied with a smile. She looked the same as ever, with her short corn-colored hair and forget-me-not blue eyes. But her face was pale, her eyes strained.

Amy sat up. A sharp pain shot through her head and chest, and she caught her breath. "Ow!" she gasped.

Lou put a hand gently on Amy's shoulder. "Careful," she said, "don't try to move too quickly."

"Where am I?" Amy asked, looking around in confusion.

"In the hospital." Lou gently encouraged Amy to lie

back against the pillows. "You've been unconscious for eight days. We were so relieved when you woke up briefly yesterday." Her eyes searched Amy's. "Do you remember?"

Amy shook her head. She looked around the room. "Where's Mom?" As soon as the words were out, her eyes widened as the memories returned. The road. The tree. She stared at Lou. "We crashed!"

Lou nodded hesitantly.

"Oh, no. Is the horse all right?" Amy gasped as she shot upright again, ignoring the pain in her chest and head. "And Mom?" She saw Lou look down, and her heart suddenly somersaulted with fear. "Lou?" she demanded, her voice catching as she looked at her sister's half-hidden face. "Lou! Where's Mom? Is she in the hospital, too?"

Lou took a deep breath and reached out for Amy's hand. "The horse is with Scott Trewin," she said, looking deep into Amy's eyes. "He's injured but not too badly; he's mostly in shock." Lou paused. "But Mom . . ." Lou's voice shook, and her eyes dropped to where she held Amy's fingers in her own. ". . . We lost her, Amy."

The blood drained from Amy's face. "No," she whispered. She stared at Lou. It couldn't be true. Lou nodded helplessly. Amy's voice rose. "She can't be. Mom can't be dead!"

"I'm sorry," Lou said, swallowing hard, her eyes filling with tears. "We had her funeral three days ago."

Amy stared, her breathing getting deeper and deeper.

"You were in a coma. We didn't know what to do," Lou said desperately. "Grandpa and I didn't know when you were going to wake up. I'm so glad you did. I wish we had known." Her eyes searched Amy's. "Oh, Amy, I understand. I'm so —"

"No!" Amy cried, the pain erupting out of her. Her cry turned into a scream. She couldn't stop it; she didn't want to stop it. She screamed and screamed, only vaguely aware when Lou ran to the door and a nurse came hurrying in. She didn't even feel the prick in her arm. Her screams faded to a whimper and then sleep closed in on her, dragging her back into the blackness.

❧

For the next few days, Amy lay in her hospital bed and cried as if her heart was going to break. She had broken two ribs and her head ached constantly, but she welcomed the physical pain, wanting desperately to block out the anguish she felt inside. It had all been her fault. If she hadn't made Mom go out in the rain, then there wouldn't have been an accident and she'd still be alive. Over and over again she heard her mother say, "We can't take the trailer out in this." But then she had persuaded her to go. It was her fault.

Even seeing her grandpa didn't help. "I've brought you some magazines," he said sitting down beside her. "How are you feeling?"

Amy couldn't answer.

"The horses are fine," he said. "Ty and I have been looking after them. I think they all miss you. And Lou's taken leave from her job to run the business side of things. She's been marvelous. She's so driven — just like your mom." He swallowed. "And you're like your mom, too, honey." He put his hand on her chin and lifted her face. "I'm so lucky to have the two of you," he said, looking into her eyes.

Amy stared back down at the white sheets on the hospital bed.

Jack Bartlett looked at her. His eyes could barely conceal his own grief. "Come on, sweetheart," he said, putting an arm around her and drawing her close. "We'll manage. We have to. You, me, and Lou, we've still got one another."

Amy shut her eyes. Pain seared through her brain. How could they manage? Her mother was dead, and she had killed her. She pulled away, the words bursting out of her all at once. "It was my fault, Grandpa!"

Jack Bartlett looked confused. "What do you mean?"

"I killed Mom," sobbed Amy. "I made her go out in the rain. She didn't want to. I made her go."

Her grandpa gripped her shoulder tightly. "No, stop

that!" he exclaimed intensely. "Amy, you mustn't think that way."

"But it's true!" she cried. "I told her we had to go."

Her grandpa pulled her close. Tears were streaming down his face. "Your mother knew it was dangerous, but she wanted to go because she knew a horse needed her. Your mother never did anything she didn't want to do. It was her decision." He hugged her fiercely.

"She wouldn't have gone if it weren't for me," Amy said, her anguished voice reduced to a croak. "And I'll never forgive myself."

❧

As the days passed, her eyes ran dry of tears. A terrible numbness stole over her. She couldn't feel, she couldn't think. It was as if everything that was happening to her was happening to someone else. Grandpa and Lou visited every day. Ty came by and so did Soraya and Matt. But she found she had nothing to say to them. So much had happened that they would never understand.

And then one day her grandpa and Lou came together. Jack Bartlett stood by the window, looking at Amy. Lou perched on the side of the bed and took Amy's hand. "The doctors think it's time for you to come home," she said.

"Home?" said Amy bleakly. "I don't have a home anymore."

"Of course you do."

Amy looked into Lou's resolute face and slumped back against the pillow, hot pain like needles behind her eyes. How could she go back to Heartland if Mom wasn't there? She turned her head away.

Grandpa stepped forward. "Please, Amy," he said gently, his voice wavering. "Come home."

🙊

Going back to Heartland was worse than she could have imagined. As they turned into the driveway, Pegasus and Copper were looking out over their doors. Ty was filling a water bucket at the tap. Everything looked so normal. Amy felt her stomach lurch, and for a moment she thought she was going to be sick. She flung open the car door and ran into the farmhouse, ignoring the ache from her broken ribs.

She refused to leave the house again. She wouldn't go to see the horses. She sat in the kitchen, staring at the floor, wrapped in bleak misery.

"Why don't you come and help me?" Grandpa said the next morning, but Amy stayed put, hunched over in the easy chair.

She watched as Lou tried to make sense of the office that their mother had run. There were papers, notes, and cards everywhere, and even the phone numbers for people like the feed merchant and the blacksmith were all kept in different places. Lou was practical and efficient and appeared to have a system for everything. She did the paperwork and made the phone calls, but she left the horses to Grandpa and Ty. Amy sat in the kitchen, feeling drained and hopeless.

Sometimes she caught Lou glancing in her direction. Sensing the barely hidden frustration in her eyes, Amy always looked away. She knew Lou thought she should be helping, but she couldn't — she couldn't go out to the yard and act as if nothing had happened.

Three days after Amy had come home, Lou turned to her. She had been busy, and her eyes were looking strained. "Amy," she said, "can you go and check with Ty which horses need to see the blacksmith? I can't leave the phone. I'm expecting a call from Bob Shaw, Tarka's owner, any minute now."

Amy shook her head.

"Please, Amy," Lou said pleadingly. "I need to wait for the call."

Amy dug her nails into her palms. "I'm not going out there," she said coolly.

"Oh, for goodness sake!" Lou said, visibly annoyed. Pulling on some boots, she hurried out through the door.

A few minutes later, the phone started ringing. Amy stared at it. The shrill bell cried out in the silence of the kitchen, but it was as if her legs were frozen. She let it ring and ring.

Suddenly, the door burst open. Lou came dashing in and seized the receiver. "Hello? Heartland," she gasped, her face flushed from running back from the barn. There was a second's pause and then she slammed the phone down. "He's gone!" She turned to Amy. "Why didn't you pick it up?" she exclaimed.

Just then, Jack Bartlett came in. Obviously sensing the tension in the air, he cleared his throat. "Uh, Lou. Have you called to confirm the feed delivery?" he asked. "It's just that we're getting rather low."

"The feed delivery!" Lou ran a hand through her short hair and stared at him. "What feed delivery?"

"We have a feed delivery every three weeks."

"Well, why didn't someone tell me?" Lou's voice rose angrily. Seeing the surprised expression on their grandpa's face, her eyes immediately softened. "Sorry, Grandpa. I didn't mean to snap at you," she said quickly. "I'll straighten it out. Don't worry."

"You're doing a great job, Lou," Jack Bartlett said softly.

Amy felt a sob rising in her throat. Feed deliveries! Phone calls from horse owners! How could they both carry on as if nothing had happened? She got up from her chair and hurried upstairs to her bedroom. Once there, she slumped to the floor, and surrounded by a jumble of magazines and clothes, she wrapped her arms around her knees and began to sob. What was the matter with them? Mom was dead. Was she the only one who cared?

げ

Amy stayed in her bedroom and didn't go downstairs until the middle of the next morning. When she walked into the kitchen, she found Grandpa and Lou sitting at the table. They abruptly stopped talking as she came in.

"Hi, honey," Grandpa said, standing up. "How you doing this morning?"

Amy didn't answer. She just walked over to a chair and sat down.

There was a silence. Amy saw Lou and Grandpa look at each other, and then Lou spoke. "Amy," she said quickly, "Grandpa and I have been thinking — it's about time you started to see your friends again."

Amy felt her stomach sink. Soraya and Matt and her other friends from school had been stopping by and phoning ever since she had gotten back from the hospital, but she had refused to see or speak to any of them. They'd only try to make her feel better.

"I don't want to," she said.

"Amy!" Lou said. "They're your friends and they want to be here for you." She paused. "Please, Amy. We've organized a belated birthday party for you tonight. We thought that way you could see them all together. It could be fun."

Amy felt as if she had been punched. "I've told you already," she exclaimed in horror, jumping up, "I don't want to see them."

Grandpa came over to her. "Hold on, Amy, Lou's right," he said gently. "You need to start getting on with your life again."

Amy stared at him. *Get on with my life again!* How could she, when Mom was dead?

"We haven't invited lots of people," Lou said. "Just Soraya, Ty, Matt, and a few of your other friends whom Soraya suggested."

"Well, cancel it!" Amy cried, an awful gnawing feeling growing in the pit of her stomach. "I don't want to see anyone!"

Lou's voice rose. "Amy! You can't just opt out of life like this!" Grandpa laid a hand on Lou's arm, and biting her lip, she turned sharply away.

"Grandpa, please . . ." Amy said.

But much as she argued and pleaded, Lou and Grandpa would not listen. They told her it was for her own good. Exhausted, she ran upstairs to her bedroom and refused to come down again for the rest of the day. She was still there at seven o'clock when the guests started to arrive.

Grandpa knocked on her bedroom door. "Amy?" He pushed the door open. "Come on," he said gently. "Come downstairs." Amy shook her head miserably. "Please,"

Grandpa said, holding out his hand. "For me, honey. I hate to see you keeping to yourself so much."

Amy looked up and suddenly realized how tired he looked. The skin around his eyes was sagging, his brow was furrowed. Very slowly, she took his hand and stood up.

He smiled. "It'll be OK. You'll see."

Amy followed him downstairs, her heart beating fast. As soon as she stepped into the kitchen, she knew that it had been a mistake. Her friends stopped talking and stood in silence around the room, awkwardly holding brightly wrapped presents. There were Soraya and Matt, Matt's friend Danny, and Ellen and Robyn from her class. Ty stood next to Lou by the sink.

There was a pause. Soraya stepped forward and broke the silence, her brown eyes anxiously searching Amy's face. "Hey, Amy," she said, giving her a hug. "Happy belated birthday."

As they separated, Amy tried to manage a smile, but inside she just wanted to be swallowed up, to escape.

"Hi." Matt came forward. "How you doing?" Amy looked up into his handsome face. His eyes were deep with concern.

"Can I get anyone a drink?" Lou asked. "Amy, what would you like?"

"Nothing," Amy whispered.

There were a couple more seconds of silence. "Drinks, anyone?" Lou said quickly. "Soraya? Ellen? What can I get you?"

As her friends murmured their responses, Amy's eyes strayed to the table.

"Come and sit down, honey," Grandpa said.

Moving as if in a dream, Amy walked over. She looked wordlessly at the pile of presents there.

"Help yourselves to food, everyone," Lou called out. But it seemed as if no one was hungry. The pizza and potato chips remained untouched as they all sat down, looking at Amy with worried eyes.

"Here's something for you," Matt said as he handed her his gift, unmistakably a wrapped-up soccer ball. He smiled. "Bet you can't guess what it is."

Amy swallowed. "Thanks," she said, trying to force a smile as she took it from him. She stared at the present in her hands. Had it really been only three weeks ago that she and Soraya had laughed about whether Matt would get her a gift or not? It felt like a lifetime ago. She looked down, not wanting people to see the tears filling her eyes.

"Here," Ty said suddenly, seeming to sense her distress. He handed her a flat, oblong package. "Open mine next." Grateful to have something to concentrate on, Amy fumbled with the paper. She pulled out a framed photograph of Pegasus. "Oh, Ty, I love it," she whispered, her fingers gripping tightly onto the frame. She glanced up. Ty's eyes met hers, full of understanding.

One by one, Amy unwrapped the other presents. They were just what she had wanted — a new longline, breeches, riding gloves. Only now they didn't seem to matter anymore. Finally, Grandpa handed her the last one. It was large and bulky. "This one was from your mom," he said. "She bought it before the . . ." his voice trailed off.

Even before her fingers touched it, Amy knew what it was. Trembling slightly she tore back a strip of the wrapping paper. Some blue material showed through. It was the waterproof jacket she had wanted so badly. It was just too much to bear. A sob tore through her as she shoved the unwrapped present away, turned, and fled from the room.

A few seconds later, Amy's grandpa appeared in her bedroom doorway. "I'm sorry," he said, coming and sitting beside her on the bed. He put his arm around her shaking shoulders. "I guess we got it wrong. It was too soon, wasn't it? Too much, too soon," he said softly.

Through her tears, Amy heard a soft tap on the door. She looked up. It was Soraya.

"Come in," Jack Bartlett said. Getting up, he looked from Soraya to Amy and then walked over to the door. "I'll be downstairs," he said, leaving the room.

As soon as he was gone, Soraya rushed forward. "Oh, Amy," she said, sitting down and hugging her. "I'm so, so sorry." She leaned her head against Amy's so that their hair mingled. "I've been wanting to see you so much, but you just kept saying no," she said. "I'm supposed to be going to camp tomorrow, and I had to see you before I left. But I'll stay if you want me to."

"No, you should go. I just want to be left alone," Amy said, staring down at her hands.

There was a pause. Realizing how her words must have sounded, Amy looked up. Soraya was looking at her, her eyes brimming with sympathy. "It's OK," she whispered. "I guess I'd feel the same."

The next instant they were hugging each other desperately. "I'll write lots," Soraya said through her tears. "If you need me, just call, I'll come straight back. I'll always be here for you, Amy."

"I know," Amy whispered. "I know."

When Soraya left the room, Amy started to cry even harder. She was on her own. There was no one who knew how she was feeling, no one who could understand, except maybe Mom. And she wasn't here anymore.

❧

The next afternoon, Lou watched the feed truck arrive. "I hope Ty and Grandpa manage all right," she said, sounding worried. "I'd go and help, but the accounts are so behind." She glanced at Amy as if hoping for a response, but Amy stayed silent. Lou opened her mouth but then seemed to stop herself. She turned sharply away and, collecting a big ledger and a pile of papers from one of the drawers in the dresser, she sat down at the table. "I cannot believe these aren't computerized," she said.

She quickly leafed through the papers, sorting them into piles. She seemed agitated, slapping the papers down on the table and glancing every so often at the door as if wondering how the delivery was going. Her mouth looked strained, and the areas beneath her blue eyes were shadowed with gray rings of old makeup and exhaustion.

After a few minutes, Lou threw up her hands. "This is impossible! How can I tell who we owe money to? There's no system at all, and there're so many invoices missing!"

"They're probably on the bookcase," Amy said flatly. "Or under the easy chair."

"You've got to be kidding!" Lou looked at her incredulously but got up anyway and started rummaging around under the easy chair. She pulled out a stack of papers. "I don't believe this!" she exclaimed. "Look at them! They're covered in coffee stains."

"So?" said Amy.

"So!" echoed Lou. "So, it's dreadful! It's the worst set of accounts I've ever seen." Her voice rose. "Mom was completely and utterly disorganized. How could she have kept things in such an awful mess!"

"Because she didn't know she was going to die!" Amy cried. She was overwhelmed by her emotions. Anger, pain, and misery exploded like a volcano inside her head. "Mom's dead!" she screamed, jumping to her feet. "Don't you get that? She's dead, and all you're worried about is this stupid paperwork! You don't care — do you? You've never cared!"

Lou slammed her fist on the table and stood up. Her face was ashen. "How can you say that?" she gasped, her voice shaking. "Have you any idea how hard it is for me to try and carry on? You're so selfish, Amy!" Amy tried to interrupt but Lou wouldn't let her. "Yes, you are!" she cried. "You don't think about Grandpa or Ty or anyone else. The only person you think about is poor Amy Fleming. And all you want to do is mope around, feeling sorry for yourself. Well, moping around isn't going to bring Mom back, and I can tell you one thing. If Mom were here now and you were dead, she'd be out there looking after those horses! You say I don't care. Well, take a look at yourself, Amy! Just take a look at yourself!"

For a moment they stared at each other. Amy felt all the color drain out of her face. Lou suddenly looked appalled. "Amy —" she said, quickly stepping forward. "Amy, I'm so —"

"Leave me alone!" Amy hissed, jumping away.

"Try to understand," Lou begged.

"You try to understand!" Amy howled. "Just leave me alone!" Turning, she raced out of the kitchen and up the stairs to her bedroom. Slamming the door, she flung herself onto her bed and gave way to her grief.

Lou came up and knocked softly on the door. A little while later Grandpa did the same, but Amy refused to let either of them in. "Oh, Mom," she sobbed wildly, "Mom! Why aren't you here?"

℉

It was just getting light outside when Amy woke up. Her eyes were sore, her face felt rough with tears. She stood up and looked out the window. All was silent. She felt empty inside, and she knew this emptiness would never leave because there was no one who could take her mom's place. Her life seemed to stretch out bleakly ahead. No one understood her anymore.

Then she noticed Pegasus looking over his door. Amy's heart gave a leap as she saw the big gray head, the half-pricked ears — watching, waiting. And suddenly it hit her like a thump in the stomach. Of course — why hadn't she thought about him before?

She crept downstairs, silently opened the back door,

and hurried across the yard. Pegasus pricked his ears and snorted with delight at the sight of her. She eased back the bolt on his door and let herself in. The warmth of his familiar stall enveloped her. Pegasus bent his head inquiringly, breathing out love and trust.

She wrapped her arms around his neck. "Oh, Pegasus!" she said desperately. "What am I going to do?"

Pegasus's neck was warm and solid. His mane scratched against her face. "We've lost her," Amy whispered, her voice breaking. "Things will never be the same again. It's just you and me now."

Pegasus snorted softly.

"Just you and me." As Amy painfully repeated the words, she thought about everything she and her mom had done together, about everything they had meant to each other. And as she drew comfort from Pegasus's presence, she thought about Lou's words. Was she right? Was she being selfish?

Her hands started to work absentmindedly, massaging Pegasus's neck. Small circles, light pressure, just like Mom had shown her. Pegasus liked that. Amy smiled as she felt him relax beneath her touch, and as her hands moved, she felt her own tension start to ease.

The time passed. The sun rose. Amy heard her grandpa's old-fashioned alarm clock ring in the house. Amy kissed Pegasus on the nose and slipped out of his stall. Unnoticed, she hurried back to her room.

She lay on her bed, feeling much calmer. It had started to rain. She heard Grandpa and Lou get up. She heard the clank of feed buckets and the stamping of hooves. Moving to the window and standing at the side of the curtains, she watched as her grandpa began to feed the horses. She saw Ty arrive. It was a dull day, the clouds were gray, and a fine drizzle was falling. Downstairs Lou was getting breakfast ready. Another day at Heartland had begun.

A few minutes later, she saw Lou come outside and go over to chat with Grandpa. Turning slowly, Amy walked out of her room and down the winding staircase. As she reached the hall, she stopped. Someone had put her birthday present from Mom on the hall table. It was still wrapped, with the gift card on top. Amy swallowed and then slowly moved toward it. She paused before reaching out with trembling fingers to lift the card.

Just at that moment the telephone in the kitchen rang out shrilly. Amy jumped and turned. Should she answer it? She was about to go through to the kitchen when she heard the back door opening and stopped herself.

"Hello, Heartland," she heard Ty say cheerfully. She smiled at the sound of his voice, but as she listened, his tone changed dramatically. "Yes . . . I know the place," he said, sounding quick and serious. "That doesn't sound good. . . . OK. We'll be there as soon as possible." There was the click of the receiver and then the sound of the back door being thrown open. "Jack!" he shouted. "You'd better come here!"

Amy hesitated in the hall. What was happening? There were running footsteps and the sound of Lou and Grandpa entering the house. "What's up, Ty?" she heard her grandpa demand.

"That was the sheriff!" Ty exclaimed. "They've just been up to old Mrs. Bell's house. They broke in and found her inside." He paused. "She's been dead for over a week."

Dead! Amy's hand flew to her mouth.

"Oh, no!" she heard Lou gasp. "That's awful!"

"Eric called them after he went up there this morning on his mail route," Ty continued quickly. "I guess no one had been up Teak's Hill in a while."

"Of course, ordinarily Amy or Marion would have stopped by," Grandpa said. "Oh, my — what a way to go."

"It gets worse." Ty said grimly. "It's not just Mrs. Bell. They were calling because of Sugarfoot." Amy's heart somersaulted. Sugarfoot!

"The little Shetland?" Grandpa said.

"Yes. He's been shut in his stable," Ty said. "No food and very little water. The police say he's in really bad shape, half starved and very frightened. They've called Scott but wanted to know if one of us could meet him up there."

Amy felt a trembling sob rise through her. Oh, poor little Sugarfoot! Her heart ached for the tiny pony — alone, starved, frightened.

"Can you go?" she heard Grandpa asking Ty.

"Sure," Ty said. "Sugarfoot doesn't know me, but I guess that can't be helped."

"I'll take you up there," said Lou.

Amy imagined how Sugarfoot would feel when Ty, whom he didn't know or trust, tried to put him in a trailer and take him away from the only home he had ever known. Her heart began to beat fast. She looked around the hall desperately, and as she did her eyes fell on the present again. *Mom,* she thought, *Mom, what would you do?* Almost without thinking she lifted the card and read:

To my dear Amy,

    Keep trusting those instincts and together we'll reach our dreams. Happy Birthday!

                              Love and hugs, Mom

The words seemed to hit Amy with the force of a sledgehammer. *Together.* Tears sprang to her eyes as she thought about the dreams she and Mom had shared, the plans they had made.

"I guess we'd better get going," she heard Ty say in the kitchen.

Suddenly, Amy knew what she had to do. Swiftly, she tore the wrapping paper off the coat and slipped the coat on. The card lay on the table. Touching it, Amy swallowed her tears. "I'm doing this for you, Mom," she whispered, "for our dreams."

Grandpa, Lou, and Ty all jumped slightly as Amy appeared in the kitchen doorway. She paused for a second, seeing their faces, and then started snapping her jacket.

"Sugarfoot knows me," Amy said. "I can go."

Chapter Five

Lou and Amy walked around the house to where the pickup and trailer were parked. Neither of them spoke. Their angry words from the day before seemed to hang in the air between them like an invisible barrier. Ignoring Amy, Lou picked her way cautiously through the long, damp grass in her open-toed shoes and unlocked the door. Amy suddenly stopped. The side of the truck was freshly repaired and painted.

Lou looked around. "What are we . . ." Her words trailed off as she followed the direction of Amy's gaze. "Oh," she said, her face instantly softening. "I'm sorry. I didn't think." She closed the door to the truck and pocketed the keys. "Look. You don't have to come," she said. "I'm sure Ty can manage."

Amy swallowed and shook her head. She dug her

hands deeper into the pockets of her coat. "No," she said. "I have to help Sugarfoot."

She walked slowly up to the truck and got in, her heart pounding in her chest. Still looking at her anxiously, Lou started the engine. Every bump and jolt as they drove down the driveway flashed another scene of the accident in Amy's mind. The windshield wipers swept across the glass, and she gripped the seat tightly, forcing herself to think about Sugarfoot.

As they made the turn out of the driveway, Lou spoke awkwardly to Amy. "I'm really sorry about yesterday," she said. "I shouldn't have said those things."

Amy looked out the window into the sideview mirror. There was a weighted silence. The words that had passed between them couldn't be unsaid. She could try to reassure Lou now, but although the gap that separated them was only the width of a seat, emotionally it felt as vast as an ocean. Apart from the few whispered directions that Amy gave, they drove the rest of the way in silence.

"Where's the stable?" Lou asked as she parked the trailer outside Mrs. Bell's house.

Amy pulled the door open. "At the back," she said, jumping out into the drizzle and running behind the house. As she ran up the path to the barn, a strong smell of manure and urine hit her. She hesitated for a moment a short distance from the half door. What would she see when she looked inside? Biting her lip, she stepped forward.

"Oh, Sugarfoot!" a horrified whisper escaped her. The little Shetland stood in the center of the stall, his head drooping low to the ground. His ribs stuck out, his flanks were hollowed, and his coat was matted with clumps of mud. The stench of ammonia in the stable was almost unbearable.

With trembling fingers, Amy unbolted the door and pulled it open. The pony's chestnut ears flickered, and with the greatest of effort he raised his head. His dull, glassy eyes fixed on Amy, and with a glimmer of recognition he nickered hoarsely. Ignoring the muck, she crouched beside him, her hands reaching up to gently touch his head and neck. He moved his ears slightly as if to acknowledge her. She could hardly believe the change in him.

"Amy?" It was Lou, calling from the garden.

She stood up and went to the stable door. "Over here!"

Lou walked gingerly up the overgrown path. "Should I turn the trailer around before you put him in or should I —" Her voice stopped abruptly as she focused on Sugarfoot. She stared at the emaciated little pony and drew in her breath sharply. "Oh, no!" Lou stepped closer, and for a moment the two of them said nothing. "It's dreadful!" Lou eventually gasped, tears filling her eyes.

Just then there was a shout from the bottom of the garden. "Amy — are you there?" Amy and Lou turned.

"Scott!" Amy said, seeing the tall figure of Scott Trewin, striding up the garden toward them. He stopped in front of her and looked down at her with concern in his eyes.

"How are you doing?"

"I'm fine," Amy brushed off the question. She wanted to put her own problems on hold and deal with the immediate situation. "It's Sugarfoot we have to worry about." She moved to let Scott look in the stable, and then realizing that Lou was still standing there, Amy hastily introduced them. "Oh, this is Lou. My sister."

Scott and Lou acknowledged each other. "We've met," Scott said.

Amy suddenly realized that Scott was still looking after the stallion that she and her mother had picked up in the trailer that night on Clairdale Ridge. Of course, Lou and Scott would have met before. He would have gone to their mother's funeral. She pushed the thought away. It was something she didn't want to think about right now.

Scott went into the stable and glanced around. "OK, let's try to get him out of here. Amy, get ready to support Sugarfoot on that side and gently encourage him to move. Remember, he'll be very weak."

Amy and Scott stood on either side of the little pony's head and encouraged him forward. Painfully, step by step, he slowly left his stable. Lou watched for a moment or two and then disappeared down the garden path. Amy hardly noticed her go; she was too busy concentrating all her attention on Sugarfoot. "OK," Scott said as they got him out onto the grass. "Let's check him over." He gently ran his hands over the pony's body and then took his pulse and heart rate.

Amy caressed Sugarfoot's tiny ears to soothe him. All the time Scott was examining him, the pony stood still, staring straight ahead. Amy was amazed that he didn't seem interested in the lush grass all around him.

Scott looked inside the stable again. "Well, he's had water," he said, pointing to a drainpipe that ran from the side of the roof and emptied into a pail in the stable. "If it hadn't been for that . . ." He shook his head. Amy knew what he meant. No horse could survive without water for more than a couple of days in the heat of the summer. "I think the best thing we can do is to get him back to Heartland and see what you guys can do for him. There are no signs of secondary problems at the moment. As long as we can get him eating, his chances are good."

"I'll get him eating," Amy said confidently. She stroked Sugarfoot's head. She was going to make him better.

"OK, then," Scott said with a smile. "Let's get him to the trailer."

Lou was waiting for them. She had lowered the ramp and watched as Amy and Scott tried to coax the little Shetland into the back.

Sugarfoot took a few tentative steps and then hesitated, only going in when Amy pulled on his halter and Scott encouraged him from behind.

"Can you do anything for him?" Lou asked Scott anxiously as the pony stepped the last of the way inside.

"Well, other than being undernourished, there seems to be nothing else wrong with him," Scott answered, coming down the ramp. He sounded restrained. "Leave it to Amy. She knows what to do." Amy frowned as she lifted the ramp. She appreciated Scott's support, but it wasn't like him to be so reserved. He turned to her as she started fastening the bolts. "Give me a ring if you're worried about anything, OK?" he said, sounding more like his normal self. "Otherwise I'll stop by in the morning."

Amy nodded. "OK. See you tomorrow, then."

"Yeah, tomorrow." Scott nodded briefly at Lou and then strode off to his car.

🐾

When they arrived back at Heartland, Amy was relieved to find that Ty had put a thick bed of straw down in one of the stalls in the back barn. With his usual patience he helped Amy get Sugarfoot down the ramp and into the stall. The little Shetland walked in and then lay down immediately, his nose resting on the straw and his eyes half closed.

"Looks like he could use some fattening up," Ty said,

running his eyes over Sugarfoot's ribs. The concern on his face belied his casual words.

Amy nodded. "I'll go and make him a bran mash to start him off. Is there any beet pulp soaked?"

Ty nodded. "In the feed room. I'll get some hay."

Amy smiled at him gratefully. "Thanks, Ty." She was relieved that he hadn't made a big deal about her being out of the house and in the barn again. He simply seemed to accept it, immediately concentrating on the task of getting Sugarfoot better.

She went to the feed room and filled a bucket with bran and put the kettle on the stove. As she waited for it to boil, she chopped up some carrots and mixed them, with a scoop of beet pulp and a handful of barley, into the bran. She knew it was essential not to overfeed a horse in Sugarfoot's condition. Having not eaten for so long, his stomach wouldn't be able to cope with a large amount of food. The progress had to be slow and steady, the quantity gradually increased over a period of time.

She went to the cabinet in the corner of the room. It contained books on herbal remedies, dried herbs, flower essences, ointments, and aromatherapy oils. It was so familiar to Amy. Marion had carefully taught her all she knew about natural remedies.

Ignoring a lump rising in her throat, Amy consulted her mom's notebook and then added fenugreek seeds to the feed to make it more appetizing for the little pony, some garlic powder to help his digestion, and a handful of chopped rose-hip shells, rich in vitamins.

At last the feed was ready and Amy carried it down to Sugarfoot's stall, placing it on the floor by his nose. He lifted his head slightly when she came in. "Here you go, boy," she said, crouching down beside him to stroke his neck. He sniffed at the bucket and then looked away.

"Come on, Sugarfoot," she said, feeling surprised that he needed any encouragement. It was rare that a horse refused a bran mash. She picked up a handful of food and held it out to the little pony. His lips snuffled at her hand as he ate a piece of carrot. She reached for another handful. Sugarfoot nibbled a bit more, but after the third handful he turned his head away again.

Amy sat back, feeling perplexed. Maybe it was just too soon after his journey, maybe he needed more time to settle in. Leaving the pail beside him, she fetched a grooming bucket. Sitting next to him on the straw, she very gently started to comb through his coat and unknot the tangles in his mane and tail.

🐎

By the evening, Sugarfoot's appearance was better, but he still had not eaten more than a few handfuls of food. Amy was beginning to feel concerned.

"Still no luck?" Ty asked, poking his head over the stall door before he left for the day. Amy shook her head.

"Maybe he just needs a good night's sleep," Ty said.

"Maybe." Amy stood up and looked at the little pony. He was resting his head on the straw, his eyes half closed. "I hope so," she said, brushing herself off.

"Guess we'll find out tomorrow," Ty replied as he turned to leave. But then he looked back and smiled at Amy. "You know, it's nice to have you back," he said, and headed out the door for the night.

Chapter Six

Amy woke up earlier than usual the next morning. As soon as she opened her eyes, she immediately thought about Sugarfoot. Would he be better today? Pushing back the covers, she jumped up, hurriedly got dressed, and ran down the stairs and out into the yard. The horses pricked their ears and whinnied in greeting as she passed.

But Sugarfoot was still lying in his stall, his legs curled up underneath him, looking tinier than ever. Amy unbolted the stall door. Her heart sank when she saw that he still hadn't touched his feed or hay. His appetite obviously hadn't returned.

She knelt down beside him. His eyes flickered on her for a moment and then dropped dully. Amy gently stroked his mane and smoothed his thick cream-colored forelock away from his eyes. With a sigh, Sugarfoot leaned his muzzle on her knee. Her fingers started to gently massage his ears with tiny, feather-light circles, moving from the base up to the tip and back. Focusing entirely on her work, Amy didn't hear the footsteps coming toward the stall.

"Hi."

Amy jumped. Lou stood on the other side of the stall door looking in.

Amy's gray eyes widened in astonishment. "Lou!" Lou never came into the barn.

Lou sighed. "I couldn't sleep," she said. "And then I saw you head over from the house." She looked at Sugarfoot. "How is he?"

"He still hasn't eaten," Amy said, trying not to sound surprised.

Lou frowned. "But why not? He must be starving."

Amy knew Lou's reaction was logical — she was confused by Sugarfoot's lack of hunger as well — but she tried to explain it to Lou as best she could. "Horses are a lot like people. Sometimes, when a horse is in shock, he won't eat. Sugarfoot's traumatized. He doesn't know why he was locked in his stall for so long or why he was brought here. He's only known his life with Mrs. Bell. She treated him just like a pet, she used to talk to him and let him in the house. Now she's gone, and I guess that's the only thing he's really aware of."

"He's probably totally disoriented," Lou said softly. She looked at Sugarfoot for a moment and then her gaze turned to Amy, a certain respect showing in her eyes. "You really have a great connection with horses, don't you, Amy?"

"It's from Mom," Amy said. She swallowed and struggled with the emotion that suddenly threatened to engulf her. For a long moment she was lost in her own thoughts.

"He'll get better, won't he?" Lou asked, eventually breaking the silence.

Amy looked at the little Shetland. She desperately wanted to believe he would, but at the same time she couldn't deny the foreboding feeling that seemed lodged in the deepest corner of her heart.

Lou saw her hesitation and that was enough. "Why do horses always cause so much heartache?" she said bitterly, stepping back from the door.

"They don't always," Amy said, looking at her quickly. "Most of the time they give so much to the people they love."

"Maybe, but in the end they take away a lot more," Lou replied coldly, and walked away.

Lou would never understand, Amy thought. Shaking her head, she went back to massaging Sugarfoot's ears.

🙰

At seven o'clock, Amy left the little pony and set to work getting the breakfast feeds ready. She added a handful of dried mint to the top of Sugarfoot's bran mash, hoping that it might tempt him to eat, but when she put the pail in his stall, he turned his head away. Amy sighed and finished feeding the other horses. She would just have to try something else.

After filling the water buckets and giving Sundance — who was whinnying frantically every time he saw her — some attention, she went into the house for breakfast. Lou was talking on the phone. Grandpa was sitting at the table finishing a mug of coffee. Amy kicked off her sneakers at the door and padded across the floor in her socks, starting to talk about Sugarfoot.

Lou put her hand over the mouthpiece. "Can you be quiet?" she hissed. "I'm trying to have a conversation!"

"It's Carl." Grandpa winked at Amy.

"Oh," she said, unimpressed. She poured herself a glass of orange juice and sat down.

"Yes, I know," Lou was saying. "I miss you, too."

Amy made a face at her grandpa. He frowned at her, but she could see the twinkle in his eyes. She guessed that he hadn't taken to Carl any more than she had.

"I know. It's difficult," Lou said. There was a pause. "Yes, soon. I promise." Looking over her shoulder, she met Amy's gaze and turned her back. "Look, I can't talk now. But I promise it won't be long." She paused and said softly, "Yeah, me, too. Bye." She put the phone down, and her gaze fell on Amy's sneakers in front of her on the floor. "Amy, do you have to leave everything lying around for other people to pick up?"

"I'm going out again in a minute," Amy protested.

"And how was Carl?" Grandpa asked as Lou moved the offending sneakers.

"Fine, thanks." She smiled. "Anxious to know when I'm going back."

"Going back?" Amy echoed, the glass of orange juice stopping halfway to her mouth.

"Yes." Lou frowned. "You didn't think I was going to stay forever, did you? My life's in Manhattan. I've got my job and Carl and my apartment."

Amy didn't know what to say. She hadn't really given it much thought. She had just assumed that Lou would be staying with them.

Seeing the expression on her face, Lou's eyes softened. "Don't worry. I'm not just going to desert you," she said. "I'll keep in better touch, and I'll still do all the paperwork — I can do it in the evenings. And I'm working out a business plan for Heartland." She folded her arms. "You and Grandpa will have to be a lot more practical in the future."

"Practical?" Amy echoed, shooting a look at Grandpa.

She had a horrible feeling that she wasn't going to like Lou's plan.

"Yes, practical," Lou said firmly, collecting the breakfast dishes from the table and carrying them over to the sink. "Things are going to have to change around here. We can talk about it once I've got it all figured out." She paused by the window. "There's someone coming up the drive. I think it's your friend Matt."

Immediately pushing Lou's "practical" plans for Heartland to the back of her mind, Amy hurried to the window in surprise. Lou was right, it was Matt! Forgetting breakfast, Amy went out the back door.

Seeing her, Matt waved. "Hey, stranger!" he said.

"Matt!" Amy exclaimed. She hadn't seen any of her friends since her disastrous birthday party. "What are you doing here?"

Matt jogged over. "I came to see you. I thought you were probably missing me by now." He grinned, then his voice softened, and he looked at her with concern in his eyes. "How've you been?"

"OK," Amy said quickly. For a moment she thought Matt was going to hug her. She hurriedly started to tell him about Sugarfoot.

"I know. Scott told me," Matt said. "Can I see him?"

"Sure. He's in the back barn." Amy said.

Matt followed her up to the Shetland's stall. He whis-

tled softly under his breath when he saw the pony's emaciated state. "He looks pretty bad."

"I've been trying to get him to eat, but he just won't,"
Amy explained. "I think it's time to have another look
through Mom's books."

Taking a pile of books down from the shelf in the tack
room, Amy said, "I want to try wormwood. It's supposed
to encourage appetite, and we've got some in the herb
patch."

"Well, if you want to go and pick some, I'll read
through these and see what else might work," Matt said,
opening the first book.

"Are you sure?" Amy asked.

"Sure," Matt said, flicking through the pages. "I like
books like this. Alternative therapies are interesting."
He grinned up at her. "Anyway, I'd like to help."

By the time Amy came back, Matt already had a page
of scribbled notes. "There's quite a few different treatments for increasing appetite," he told her. "But a wormwood infusion seems to be the most popular."

"Then let's hope it works," Amy said, filling up the
kettle. She tore up a handful of wormwood leaves and
put them in a bowl with the boiling water. They let the
infusion stand for fifteen minutes and then carried it to
the back barn.

Sugarfoot didn't even raise his head when they came

in. Amy knelt down beside him on the straw, but no amount of coaxing could persuade him to drink.

"If only he'd take even a tiny bit," Amy said. "Come on, Sugarfoot." But the little pony wasn't interested.

"We could get a syringe and squirt it into his mouth," Matt suggested.

Amy shook her head. "If he won't eat it, then he's telling us that it's not what he needs."

Matt frowned at her. "But if it's going to help him, shouldn't you try to get some of it down him?"

Amy shook her head. "You have to trust the horse — listen to him." The words caught in her throat. She could almost imagine her mom standing there, saying the same thing. *Listen to the horse,* her soft voice spoke in Amy's thoughts, *they know what they need.* Looking at Matt's puzzled face, she could see he didn't understand.

"Come on," she said, forcing herself to get to her feet, "let's go and find something else to try."

But no matter how many other herbal remedies they tried, Sugarfoot simply turned his head away. Amy had never known a horse to refuse absolutely everything. She was becoming more frustrated with every failed attempt. There had to be something they could do.

Just before lunchtime, Scott arrived. One look at the full feed bucket told him the news. "So he hasn't eaten anything yet?" he said to Amy and Matt.

Amy shook her head and described the herbs she had

been trying. "He won't eat any of them," she said. "What else can we do, Scott?"

Scott gently rubbed Sugarfoot's neck. "Just keep on trying, I guess." His eyes looked grave. "But if he's going to recover, he has to start eating. His immune system will have weakened. Soon, we'll be dealing with secondary problems — pneumonia, other respiratory infections." He stood up and brushed the straw off his clothes. "Come on, let's leave him to rest."

"You want something to drink?" Amy asked as they walked down the yard.

Scott nodded. "Sure."

They headed into the house. Amy dropped her sweatshirt by the door. "Soda OK?" she asked, going over to the refrigerator.

"Fine," said Matt.

Scott nodded. "Yeah." He looked at the table covered with forms and files arranged in neat piles. "Somebody's busy."

Amy handed Scott and Matt a can each and opened one for herself. "Sit down," she offered, pushing the papers to one side with her arm, just as Lou came into the kitchen.

"Watch those papers!" she cried. "They're for work." Amy had placed her drink on a pile, and a damp ring had already spread around the bottom of the can. "Amy!" Lou exclaimed, snatching the can up. "These are important!" She saw Amy's sweatshirt. "And do you have to leave your clothes in the middle of the floor?"

"Sorry," Amy said.

Lou sighed. "I hope you'll be a bit neater when Carl comes to stay."

"Carl!" Amy echoed. "He's coming here?"

"Yes. He told me this morning. He's coming in two weeks."

"Oh, great," Amy muttered.

Lou ignored her and turned to Scott, who was still standing by the fridge. "Hello," she said brightly. "How are you, Scott?"

"Fine, thank you," he said in an oddly formal way.

"Maybe you can help me. I'm trying to think of a decent restaurant that Carl and I can go to. I mean, if I were in Manhattan I wouldn't have a problem." She laughed. "There you're never five feet from one, but here! Well, I don't know how you manage!" She looked at Scott. "Is there anywhere you would suggest?"

"Not really," Scott said indifferently. "I don't eat out much." Amy looked at him in surprise. Scott was usually so talkative.

"Oh, right," Lou said, looking rather taken aback. "Well. I'll just look in the phone book or ask Grandpa."

Scott turned to Amy. "I'd better get going. I'll stop by again tomorrow." He looked at Matt. "Are you coming with me or staying here?"

"I'll come," Matt said. "I promised to help Dad this afternoon." He looked at Amy. "But I'll come back again soon. OK?"

"OK," she smiled.

Scott nodded briskly to Lou and strode out to the car with Matt following. Amy frowned as she stood in the doorway and watched them get into the car. What was up with Scott? He had been so cool to Lou that he'd almost been rude. It wasn't like him at all. She shrugged and went back inside. Maybe he just found it difficult relating to people who didn't love and understand horses the way he did.

🙢

Amy made herself a sandwich and headed toward the barn, eating as she walked. There was so much to do — stalls to be mucked out and grooming to be done, and that was just the start of it. There were also horses to be exercised as well as the ones that needed work in the ring. Sundance, who was so delighted to have her back that he galloped to the fence every time he saw her, always wanted extra attention. She stopped to feed Pegasus the crusts from her sandwich, and for the first time began to wonder how she, Grandpa, and Ty would cope with all the work involved with looking after all of the horses. Thank goodness she had summer vacation to concentrate on Heartland.

The boarded horses — those whose owners had sent them to Heartland so Marion could treat their behavioral problems — had all been returned to their homes after the accident. But that still left eight horses and seven ponies needing attention, many of whom required substantial work if they were going to be successfully rehomed.

Amy patted Pegasus. How would they manage? She worked out a plan. The only thing to do was to keep more of the horses out to pasture full-time, rather than stabling them. That way, less time would be needed on cleaning the stalls. Then she and Ty could spend more time working with the horses that needed it. But what would happen when she went back to school in the fall? And what about in the winter when it would be too cold to keep the horses out all the time? They needed more help, but they would never be able to afford another paid stable hand. If only Lou would stay.

"We'll manage," Amy thought aloud. After all, things had always worked out in the past. They'd been through tough times, and they always made it through.

She gave Pegasus one last pat and went to find Ty.

He was filling hay nets in the barn. Amy told him about her plan to keep more of the horses out in the paddocks.

"Mm, that's a good idea," he said, stopping and folding his arms. "We definitely need to do something to cut down our workload. Which ones do you reckon?"

"I thought Jake, Moochie . . ." She was interrupted by the sound of the phone ringing. "I'll get it!" she said. She raced down the yard and into the kitchen. Lou and Grandpa had gone out together to get groceries.

"Heartland," she gasped.

"Hi." It was a man's voice on the other end. "My name's Nick Halliwell. I'm calling about a horse of mine. I was hoping you could help. . . ."

🐎

Ten minutes later, Amy returned to the barn. Ty had finished the hay nets and was sweeping up the loose hay from the aisle.

"Anyone interesting?" he asked, leaning on the broom.

"Umm — yes." She looked down at her hands. "It was a man about a horse."

"A rescue?"

"No, a horse that won't go in a trailer."

"Oh," Ty started sweeping again. "Did you suggest anyone else? There's Ridgeway Farm. They're a little far, but they're supposed to be reasonable." When she didn't say anything, he looked at her. "Amy, you didn't —"

She nodded rather sheepishly. "I said he could come here."

Chapter Seven

It didn't take Amy long to convince Ty to come around
to the idea. "It's not going to be that much work. It's only
getting the horse to go in a trailer. The owner sounded
really desperate — I couldn't turn him down. And anyway, it will bring in some money."

Ty sighed with resignation. "Well, I guess you're
right," he said, picking up the brush again to finish off
the sweeping. "So how old is this horse?"

"Five. He's a show jumper. The man had seen the article in *Horse Life*. I told him about Mom, but he still
wanted us to have a try," her voice wavered. She looked
at Ty.

"So when's it coming?" Ty asked quickly.

"Tomorrow."

"Tomorrow!"

"I'll go and get a stall ready now," she said.

As Amy shook out the fresh straw, she wondered if she had done the right thing. Yes, she was sure she had — Heartland needed as many paying horses as they could get, and the man had sounded so grateful when she had said yes. "He's a very special horse," he had told her. Amy smiled to herself. Everyone always thought their horse was the most special horse in the world. Still, she had liked the sound of his voice. She would go with her gut on this one. And saying yes to Nick Halliwell had definitely felt like the right thing to do.

🙰

She waited until suppertime to break the news to Lou and Grandpa. "A new horse is coming tomorrow," she said when they were all sitting around the table.

"A new horse?" Grandpa echoed.

"Yes. Its owner called today; he said that it wouldn't go in a trailer and asked if we could help." Amy paused. "I said yes." She looked around at them both. Grandpa was shaking his head in amused exasperation, but Lou was staring at her as though she had grown two heads.

"You told someone that we could take on another horse?" she exclaimed as if Amy had just said she could fly.

Amy nodded. "I thought we could use the money, and it's an easy problem to cure."

"But Amy, what about the time and work involved?" Lou lifted her hands incredulously, her voice rising. "There are already fifteen horses out there that aren't getting the attention they need. Ty's worked off his feet as it is, and Grandpa has no time to himself these days!"

"We'll manage," Amy said, feeling optimistic. "After all, we're going to have to start taking in horses again at some point."

"No we aren't!" Lou cried. Amy stared at her in disbelief. Her face was burning with emotion. "Amy! Heartland can't carry on as it did before. I'm amazed that you can't see that! Things have to change."

"Lou," Jack Bartlett interrupted warningly.

Lou swung around. "We have to tell her, Grandpa. She's not figuring it out by herself."

"What?" Amy asked, looking inquiringly from one to the other. As she saw them nod in agreement, her heart started to speed up. "Tell me what?" Her voice rose. "What are you talking about?"

Lou looked at their grandpa. He grimaced slightly as if giving her permission to go ahead. "I told you this morning that I'd been making some plans," she said to Amy. "I've been discussing them this afternoon with Grandpa. Heartland can't continue to be run the way it was; it's just not possible without Mom."

"Why not?" Amy demanded.

"Time, Amy. Time, money, and manpower. You,

Grandpa, and Ty can't possibly manage all the horses by yourselves."

"We can!" Even as she said the words, Amy knew that Lou was right, but she was determined to try to defend her side. She couldn't bear for things to change anymore than they already had. "Well, I know Soraya would help, and you could promise to stay!"

Lou frowned. "I've told you, my life's in New York. Not here. And anyway, Amy, it's the money as well. Most of the money coming in was from the problem horses Mom dealt with. Without her, that line of income is closed. People aren't going to bring their horses here anymore."

"They are!" Amy cried. "What about this one that's coming tomorrow?"

"That's just one horse. Let's face it; people brought their horses here because of Mom."

"So what are you saying?" Amy stared at her in disbelief. "We close Heartland?"

"Well, not exactly," Lou appeared to be choosing her words carefully. "No. Think of it more as downsizing. We'll rehome each of the horses as they become ready, and then we won't take any new ones in. By autumn, we're left with the six or so permanent residents that can't be rehomed. You get to keep Heartland, but on a much smaller, more reasonable scale."

Amy jumped to her feet. "No!"

"Amy, be sensible," Lou said. "You have to admit it, it's the practical solution."

"Heartland isn't about being practical," Amy argued.

Amy turned to her grandpa for support. "Grandpa, do you agree with this?"

"Lou has a point, Amy," he said, sighing. "When fall comes, you'll be in school all day. Ty can't cope with fifteen horses on his own. We can rent out the extra land, and that should bring in enough money to pay for the keep of the remaining horses."

Amy stared at him. She felt as if a knife had just been twisted into her heart. "How could you?" she whispered, her voice full of hurt and bewilderment. She looked at her grandfather and then at her sister. "How could you do this to me? And how could you do it to Mom?"

"Amy —" he began.

"I thought you loved this place as much as I do!" she yelled accusingly.

Lou jumped to her feet angrily. "Don't you dare speak to Grandpa like that!"

Amy swung around. "I hate you!" she screamed. "Why don't you just go back to your fancy job in New York and stay there! Your business here is finished!"

With an agonized sob, Amy ran out the kitchen and slammed the door. She ran blindly, tears streaming down her face as she headed for Pegasus's stall. She flung her arms around the horse's neck.

A few minutes later, quiet footsteps stopped outside the stall door. "Amy?" It was Grandpa.

"Go away," she sobbed.

But Jack Bartlett let himself into the stall and laid a hand on her shoulder. She flinched at his touch, but then seeing his face, so concerned and hurt, she couldn't help but seek the shelter of his arms. "Oh, Grandpa, I can't bear it. I really can't!"

Grandpa held Amy close, letting her cry, gently stroking her hair. Beside them, Pegasus nickered softly into the warmth of the night.

🐍

Amy came downstairs the following morning, her eyes red and her face pale. She found Lou in the kitchen, sitting at the table, listlessly stirring a spoon around and around in her mug of coffee. Their eyes met.

"Amy," Lou said, standing up.

Ignoring her, Amy walked through the kitchen and out the back door. She just couldn't deal with Lou first thing in the morning.

Amy went straight to Sugarfoot's stall. As soon as she saw the little pony lying so quietly in the straw, his bucket of food untouched, she pushed her own troubles to the back of her mind. He looked so weak. She hurried to fetch some more wormwood from the garden and offered him a few of the fresh leaves. His lips grazed over her palm, scattering the leaves onto the ground. "You're supposed to eat them, Sugarfoot," Amy said, feeling her desperation start to grow as she collected the leaves. "If you tried them, they might help you get your appetite back." Sugarfoot looked at her with dull brown eyes.

She paused for a moment, the truth suddenly becoming clear. Sugarfoot didn't want to get his appetite back. He didn't want to get better. He was missing Mrs. Bell so much that he wanted to die himself. If Amy was ever going to get him to eat, she had to find a way of easing his grief first.

Ignoring the other horses that kicked on their doors and whinnied hopefully as she went past, she hurried to the feed room and went to the corner cabinet. She opened one of her mom's books and found the chapter on emotional problems. It recommended the use of flower remedies and aromatherapy oils. Deciding to start with rescue remedy, which was supposed to help with emotional shock, Amy found the dark brown bottle in the cabinet and hurried back to Sugarfoot's stall. She placed two drops from the bottle on the back of her hand and offered it to him. He sniffed and then listlessly licked them off.

Amy let out a sigh of relief. It was a start at least. Adding ten drops to his water bucket, she left his stall. Now all she could do was wait and see what happened.

❧

Ty arrived soon after, and they got to work, mucking out the stalls. As Amy shoveled, she couldn't stop thinking about Sugarfoot — would the rescue remedy help? Her thoughts were interrupted by the sound of hooves coming up the drive. A chestnut horse clattered into the yard, ridden by a young man.

"Hey!" Amy said curiously, going to meet the rider.

"Are you Amy?" he asked. She nodded. The man dismounted and held out his hand. "Taylor Ellis. This is Star. Mr. Halliwell sent me over with him."

Star! The horse that needed to be cured of its problem with trailers. "Oh, right," Amy said, looking at the horse's warm neck. "How long did it take you to get here?"

"A couple of hours." Taylor obviously registered her surprised expression. "But it would have taken twice that to get him into a trailer. He goes crazy. He'll rear and throw fits, or he'll just lie down and refuse to move. We're really hoping you have some luck with him."

Amy looked at the Thoroughbred horse. His head was finely chiseled, his eyes large and calm. She dug in her pocket and produced a mint that he gracefully accepted. "Oh, we will," she said, gently touching Star's face and noticing how he pushed against her in a friendly way.

Taylor raised his eyebrows slightly and looked as if he was going to say something, but just then a car came up the drive. "Here's my lift," he said. "Nick said he'd call you tonight." He gave Star a quick pat. "He's got great plans for this horse."

Amy helped unload Star's tack and blankets from the car and then put the horse in the stall next to Pegasus. She would leave him to settle in before starting to work together.

❧

After lunch, she got Ty to drive the trailer out into the yard. "We'll just see what he does," she called as she went to fetch Star's bridle. She noted that it was made from the best-quality English leather. Mr. Halliwell, Star's owner, obviously wasn't short on cash.

Star snuffled her pockets as she slipped the bridle over his ears and fastened the throatlatch. "He's a good-looking horse," Ty said appreciatively.

Amy guided Star toward the trailer. But as soon as he saw it, she felt him stiffen. "Walk on," she encouraged. Star stopped still and laid back his ears. "Walk on," she repeated insistently, clucking her tongue to encourage him.

The Thoroughbred took another few hesitant steps and then threw up his head and plunged sideways.

"Whoa, steady!" called Ty. "Take it easy, Amy."

Amy nodded, concentrating all her effort on hanging onto the bridle as the horse threw himself about.

"It's OK — calm down, boy!" But it was as if he was possessed. He reared up, his front feet lashing through the air, inches from her head.

"Amy!" There was a scream from the kitchen, but Amy only vaguely registered it. She jumped out of the way of the angry hooves, and the second his feet touched the ground, took the opportunity to grab his reins close to the bit and pull him around in a tight circle before he could go up again.

Keeping him circling, she moved him swiftly away from the trailer and brought him to a halt. "OK," she said, looking him in the eye. "So you don't like trailers. I get the message."

"Amy!" Lou came running out of the house. Her blue eyes were wide with fright. "Are you all right? I thought you were going to be killed!" She stopped a little way off, her face ashen.

Amy looked at her in surprise. "He only reared." Suddenly she remembered that she wasn't talking to Lou. She scowled angrily. "Anyway, why would you care?"

Lou looked as if she had just been slapped in the face. Two spots of color sprang to her cheeks. Turning abruptly, she marched back to the house.

Amy noticed Ty's astonished look. She didn't feel like explaining. She turned her attention back to Star. "All right, boy," she said soothingly. "Let's take things slowly." She clicked her tongue and led him back to his stall. *That's what they all needed to do,* she thought. *Take things one step at a time.*

❧

By the time Amy had brushed Star over and settled him in his stall, she was beginning to feel guilty. She kept thinking about the look on Lou's face and the way she had stormed back into the house. As Amy put Star's halter away, she glanced toward the kitchen. She could see Lou through the window. Impulsively, Amy hurried to the house.

Lou glanced around as she heard the back door open. Seeing Amy, her face became rigid.

"Lou —" Amy said uncomfortably.

"What?" Lou snapped. Her eyes were cold.

The words rushed out of Amy. "I'm sorry about what I said — out there, with Star." She looked at Lou, expecting to see her expression soften, but it didn't. Lou just stood there, color mounting in her cheeks. "I — I didn't mean it," Amy said.

Anger and humiliation darkened Lou's eyes. "But that's the problem, Amy — I really think you did! You seem so sure of yourself, maybe you're right." Turning on her heel, she strode out of the kitchen, slamming the door behind her.

The sound echoed around the kitchen. Amy stared at the door in shock. Lou had rejected her apology! She was being so unfair. Amy angrily threw back her shoulders. *Well, if that's the way Lou wants it,* she thought, *then fine — just fine!* She didn't know why Lou had even come home.

🐎

Amy spent most of the day sitting with Sugarfoot in his stall, working on his ears and grooming his coat in a desperate attempt to make him feel better. Ty stopped by every so often and sat with her for a while. To Amy's relief he didn't bring up the subject of Lou but simply talked about Sugarfoot and what else they could do to help the little Shetland.

Late in the afternoon, Sugarfoot drifted off to sleep. Amy kissed him on the nose and crept out of his stable. She would let him rest and use the break to start her work with Star.

Putting a halter and a longline on the Thoroughbred, she led him into the small ring. "Now you and I are going to do some bonding," she told Star, rubbing his forehead. She unclipped the longline, and stepping back, gently flicked him with the end of it on his hindquarters. "Out you go."

Snorting in surprise, Star shied slightly to the side. Amy clicked her tongue and swung the rope in his direction. Star set off at a trot around the ring. He broke into a canter as she pitched the line at him. She kept him going by clicking her tongue and raising the longline in his direction every time he looked like stopping.

Amy knew she had to get Star to trust her. To do that, she had to show him that she would listen to him and that she understood him. She was going to join up with him. Amy had watched Marion do it a hundred times, but this was the first time she had tried it on her own. She took a deep breath and concentrated on Star.

Her eyes on his eyes, her shoulders square with his head, she drove him around the ring. After six times around she let him slow down and by moving her left shoulder got him to change direction before setting him off again. She watched his inside ear. When she noticed that his ear had stopped moving and seemed to fix on her, she knew she had his respect. His head tipped slightly, and he started to lick around his mouth, making chewing movements. With a flick of the line, Amy kept him going a while longer, and at last he gave her the signal she had been looking for. Stretching out his neck as he cantered, he lowered his head until it was near to the ground. Amy felt a shiver of delight. That was his way of saying that he wanted to be a team with her.

She dropped her eyes, and coiling the rope, she stood at an angle to him. Star slowed down. From out of the corner of her eye she could see that he had stopped and was looking at her. She held her breath and then let it out as he started walking toward her. When he reached her, he stretched out his neck and touched her shoulder with his muzzle, snorting gently. Amy turned around slowly and rubbed him between the eyes. She felt an electricity buzzing through her. He had joined up. By coming into the center, Star had told her that he trusted her.

Just to check, she walked away. Star followed her. She walked in a circle to the right and then a circle to the left. Star stayed right beside her. She tried running and he trotted. When she halted, he halted, too. At last she turned and stroked his neck and rubbed his forehead again. She clipped his line back on. A couple more times and she would try to load him in the trailer again.

When Amy went into the house for supper that night, she took some books with her. Sugarfoot's condition was getting worse. Although he had continued to accept the rescue remedy from her hand, he was showing no real signs of improvement. She knew that natural remedies took time to work, but a horrible thought kept repeating in her head — how much time did Sugarfoot have?

She sat down in the empty kitchen and opened one of the books. Maybe there was something else that might be more effective, something she hadn't tried yet. She flipped through the pages. Just then Lou walked in. Seeing Amy, she paused rather uncertainly by the door. Amy ignored her.

"Are — are you still searching for something to help Sugarfoot?" Lou asked, looking at the books.

Amy shut the book she was reading with a thud and got to her feet.

"How is he?" Lou's eyes hesitantly searched Amy's face.

"Don't pretend to care," Amy said bitterly, heading for the door. "You've made it perfectly clear how you feel about the horses — and me."

"Amy!" Lou exclaimed. She ran a hand through her hair. "Look! This is ridiculous. I'm just trying to be sensible." Her voice rose. "Someone around here's got to be!"

"Sensible!" Amy cried. "If we were sensible all the time, Mom would never have started this place!" Glaring at Lou, she turned and stalked out of the room.

Chapter Eight

"He's not looking any better." Ty shook his head and looked at Amy with worried eyes. They were kneeling side by side in Sugarfoot's stall, staring down at the Shetland.

With every breath he took, Sugarfoot made a wheezing noise, and a thick discharge ran from his nostrils. This was the very sign they didn't want. "He's getting too weak to fight," Amy said anxiously. "I'm going to call Scott."

She hurried to the house to make the phone call. Although it was still early in the morning, Scott was already up and about to start his rounds. "I'll be with you within the hour."

Amy returned to the barn. "He's on his way." She looked down at Sugarfoot, and as she watched his labored breathing, she felt her eyes fill with tears.

"I'll feed the other horses," Ty said, squeezing her arm. "You just stay here."

Amy nodded and sat down next to Sugarfoot. He sighed and coughed and rested his head listlessly on the straw.

❧

When Scott arrived, the expression of concern on his face deepened. He shook his head when he listened to Sugarfoot's strained breathing. "It's bronchopneumonia," he said, straightening up after his examination. "As I suspected, his immune system is severely weakened." He rubbed his forehead with his hand. "Amy," he sighed, "there's a strong chance we're going to lose him."

Amy stared at him in dismay. "But there must be something you can do!"

"I can give him the appropriate drugs," Scott said, "but they aren't going to be enough to keep him alive. Not if he's lost his will to live."

Amy looked at the little pony. It was so hard to watch him languish. "Oh, Sugarfoot, I won't let you give up." Determination filled her. She didn't care what it took. She was going to keep him alive.

After Scott had injected Sugarfoot with antibiotics and painkillers and had taken a sample of mucus for laboratory analysis, he and Amy left the stall. "Keep him warm and quiet and keep encouraging him to eat. Call me if there's any change. Otherwise, I'll come again to-morrow." He looked curiously at Star as they passed the front barn. "New horse?"

"Yeah, Star, he came yesterday. He's just a boarder — he has a fear of trailers," Amy explained.

"He's a looker," Scott said. He walked curiously up to the stall. "You know, he seems familiar. Who does he belong to?"

"A man named Nick Halliwell," Amy said, patting Star.

"Halliwell!" Scott exclaimed. "You mean *the* Nick Halliwell?"

Amy shrugged.

"Amy," Scott said, looking at her as if she were crazy. "Nick Halliwell — the famous show jumper?" Scott saw Amy's eyes widen. "Yes, that one. He moved into the county a couple of months ago. His main stable is still in Florida, of course, but he wanted some privacy while he trained, so he came here. I've been to his place a few times. I thought I recognized Star. He's the talk of the stable — a future Olympic horse, or so Nick says."

Amy stared at Scott in amazement. She had one of Nick Halliwell's horses here in front of her. Nick Halliwell, show-jumping champion. "He said Star was special, but I just thought he meant special to him," she said in amazement.

Scott shook his head.

"Wow!" Amy said, looking at Star with new eyes. "Wow!"

Scott grinned. "So, how's it going with him?"

Amy explained about Star's reaction to the trailer and then her joining-up session. "It went really well. I was going to try again today but —" she thought about Sugarfoot, "well, with Sugarfoot being so bad, I think I'd better stay with him."

"Sugarfoot just needs to rest," Scott said. "Go about your other work as normal." He glanced at his watch. "I don't have to be anywhere for another hour or so. Can I watch you work with Star?"

"I guess," Amy agreed. "I'll go get the longline."

Scott leaned against the fence as Amy went through the process of joining up again with Star. It was a relief in a way to be able to focus so entirely on Star and escape from her anxiety about Sugarfoot for a short while. Star only cantered around twice before lowering his head and chewing and licking his mouth. Amy turned to let him come to the center. He nuzzled her shoulder and then followed her around the ring as he had done the day before.

She stopped and stroked his neck. He lifted his face to hers. It tickled as he blew warm air against her ear.

"What do you think?" she said proudly, clipping the longline on and leading Star over to Scott.

He climbed over the fence and stopped beside her. "I think you've got your mom's touch," he said, his eyes warm.

Amy felt tears well at the back of her eyes, and she looked down. Scott hugged her. "She'd be so proud of you," he said softly.

Amy swallowed the hard lump in her throat. Sensing her distress, Star nudged her — rubbing his face on her arm — his dark eyes looking at her with surprise and concern. She smiled through her tears and patted him.

"So what's the next step with him?" Scott asked.

Amy brushed the tears away from her eyes and focused on Star. "I guess now I need to see how he reacts to the trailer," she said. "Hopefully, he'll trust me this time around."

She checked her pockets for treats. It was important that if Star did trust her enough to go into the trailer or even to go near the trailer that she could reward him and make it a pleasant experience.

As they walked Star down the yard to the trailer, Scott said, "I'll have another patient for you soon — if you want him."

"Who?" Amy frowned.

"Spartan." Scott saw her puzzled expression. "The

bay stallion from the Mallens' farm?" A look of anxiety crossed his face as he saw her start. "Of course, if you don't want him here," he added quickly, "I'm sure we can find somewhere else."

Amy didn't know what to say. That horse had been the reason for her and Mom going out that day. Would she be able to help him? Would she be able to handle the memories he would conjure?

"You don't have to decide now," Scott said, responding to the bewilderment in her eyes. "Just keep it in mind. OK?"

Amy bit her lip and nodded.

When they reached the trailer, Scott let down both the rear and side ramps and then stood back. Amy let Star follow her around in circles, his head almost touching her shoulder. He looked like a toddler trailing his mom. When she was convinced that he was happy and relaxed, Amy started moving closer to the trailer.

Star snorted, stopped, and stepped back. It was his way of saying that he wasn't comfortable. Amy listened to him and turned away from the trailer. She glanced at Star. He had stopped and was watching her movements with a surprised expression in his eyes. *You listened to me,* he seemed to say. *You actually listened to me!* She walked on and he came trotting after her, slowing to a walk when he was by her shoulder again. This time he stayed even closer than before. After a few more circles, Amy tried again.

This time, Star trusted her enough to follow her around the trailer. After circling it in both directions, Amy walked up the ramp and took a couple of steps into the trailer. Star stopped at the bottom, his front hooves square with the ramp. He lifted his head with a jerk. "That's fine," Amy showed him by sitting down on the edge of the ramp, taking a carrot out of her pocket, and biting a piece off the end. He could take his time. Star's ears pricked at the sound of the crunch. Looking slightly to the side of him, Amy munched on the end of the carrot. Star snorted and, lowering his head, walked up the ramp and blew into Amy's face.

"Decided to join me, have you?" she smiled, snapping the carrot in two and giving him half. She tried to appear as calm as possible, but inside she was jumping up and down with delight. She fed Star the rest of the carrot and then stood up and walked straight through the trailer and out the other side. With just the slightest hesitation, Star followed her.

At the bottom of the ramp, she stroked his neck and immediately led him through again. This time he did not hesitate at all.

As she brought Star to a halt a good distance from the trailer, Scott came striding over. "Nice work!"

Amy put her arms round Star's neck and hugged him hard. "He's brilliant!" she said, her eyes shining with happiness.

Scott smiled. "He's not the only one."

🙟

After Scott had left, Amy put Star away and hurried to find Ty to tell him the good news. He was mucking out one of the stalls in the back barn. "Of course, he's not properly cured yet. I want to go through it lots more times with him, and then he's got to learn to go in with other people, but isn't it good?" Amy chatted excitedly.

Ty nodded, grinning at her. "I bet his owner will be pleased."

"And guess who that is?" Amy said with a hint of pride in her voice. She paused. "Nick Halliwell!"

Ty was just as astonished as she had been. "The show jumper?"

"Yes!" Amy said. "It didn't occur to me — he sounded really normal on the phone." Suddenly she heard a dry, rasping cough coming from Sugarfoot's stall. The excitement that had been bubbling through her dried up instantly. "Sugarfoot," she said, rushing to the stall and looking over the door.

There was no apparent change in the little horse's condition. With every breath, he struggled and wheezed.

Ty joined her in the stall. "Some tea-tree oil might help

clear his passages," he said. "That worked on Topper last winter. And if we could get some garlic or black sampson down him, they would help the infection."

"I'll see what I can do," Amy said.

She dropped a few drops of undiluted tea-tree oil on a cotton ball and held it just under Sugarfoot's nose, being careful not to let it touch his muzzle in case it irritated his skin. After a few minutes, she took it away and offered Sugarfoot some of the herbs Ty had suggested, but Sugarfoot turned his head. Amy sighed with frustration. The herbs would help him fight his infection, but not if he didn't eat them. Amy stayed with Sugarfoot all morning, massaging his ears and face. Every so often she would stop to offer him something to eat, but with no luck.

At lunchtime, Ty came into the stall. "You need a rest," he said.

"I'm fine," Amy replied. She was determined not to leave Sugarfoot.

Ty frowned. "You're not fine," he said firmly. "You need something to eat and some fresh air. Come and have lunch." Ty gave Amy's arm a tender pull. Amy looked at him in surprise. She wasn't used to him ordering her around. But Ty's tone was adamant, and Amy reluctantly gave in.

"Are you going to work Star again later?" he asked as they went into the kitchen and made lunch.

"Umm . . . I don't know." Amy's thoughts were still on Sugarfoot.

"I think you should," Ty said. "You should reinforce what he learned this morning."

Amy knew Ty was right. "I guess so," she said.

He raised his eyebrows. "You know so."

After they'd eaten, Amy got Star out of his stall to repeat what she had done that morning. Soon the chestnut horse was following her quite happily in and out of the trailer.

Ty watched. "He's looking good!"

Amy smiled. "Do you want to try?"

With Ty leading him and Amy walking on his other side, Star walked up into the trailer again. By the time Amy called a halt to the session, Star would happily allow Ty to lead him in and out of the trailer on his own. Amy was thrilled. It was a major step. Her work would have been useless if Star would only go in the trailer for her. The next move would be to start putting the ramp up when he was inside.

"I think that's enough for today," she said, anxious to get back to Sugarfoot. "Let's stop on a good note."

However, just as she had put Star away in his box, a large silver car came purring up the drive. "Who's that?" Ty said.

Amy frowned. "I don't know —" She broke off. "Oh, yes, I do," she said, her heart sinking as the car drew nearer and she caught sight of the girl with long, platinum blond hair sitting in the front passenger seat. "It's Ashley and her mom."

"Ashley Grant?" Ty asked, recognizing the name of Amy's show-jumping rival. "From Green Briar?"

Amy nodded. "I wonder what they want?"

The car drew to a halt. Val Grant, a tall woman with short blond hair and legs clad tightly in navy breeches, got out. Amy swallowed and went over. "Hello, Mrs. Grant."

Val Grant smiled. It was a smile that seemed to contain too many perfect white teeth. "Amy," she said. "How are you?"

"OK," Amy said, wondering what she wanted.

Ashley got out of the car, too. She leaned against the door frame, her shining hair falling over her shoulders. "Hi, Amy."

"Hi," Amy said briefly.

"We were so sorry to hear about your mom," Val Grant said solicitously. "We thought we'd stop by and see how you are. How have you been coping?"

"Fine, thank you," Amy replied politely, thinking they were the last people she would share her problems with. Mrs. Grant didn't seem to be listening, though; she was glancing around the yard as if looking for something.

Val Grant turned her attention back to Amy. "There's a rumor going around that you've got one of Nick Halliwell's horses here." She sounded casual but her eyes were needle sharp.

So that's why you're here! Amy thought to herself. She took great pleasure in nodding and seeing Ashley's and Mrs. Grant's facial muscles tighten. "Yes. He's in the stall over there." With perfect timing Star put his head out over the stall door.

"Oh," Ashley said, surprised. She walked around the car door and over to the stall to stroke Star. As she did so, she smiled at Ty, who was standing a little way off. "Hello," she said.

"So, who's treating him?" Mrs. Grant questioned Amy.

"I am," she replied.

Val Grant looked as if she couldn't believe what she had just heard. "I see." She cleared her throat. "Well, if you need a hand, just let me know. Ashley!" she called. "Let's not bother Amy any longer!"

With a last lingering smile at Ty, Ashley sauntered back to the car. She got in without even saying goodbye. *So much for caring how we are,* thought Amy cynically.

Val Grant paused as she opened the driver's door. "How about your other horses? Are you managing to cope with all of them?"

Amy nodded. "Yes, thanks. We're just fine."

Val Grant nodded thoughtfully and then got into the car. Amy watched them drive away. Shaking her head, she went back to Ty.

"Mm, nice family," he commented, raising an eyebrow.

"I don't think so!" Amy said.

❧

Amy sat with Sugarfoot for the rest of the afternoon. At the end of the day, Ty came to find her. "I'm off now," he said. "Is there any change in him?"

Amy shook her head. Sugarfoot's breathing was still heavy, and his temperature was high. "But I'm not going to give up." She rubbed her eye; her hand lingered over her face as she thought. "There has to be something we can do."

Ty looked at her with concern and understanding. "Don't stay in here all night. You look worn-out."

"I won't." Amy sighed. "See you tomorrow."

When he'd gone, Amy set to work again, gently massaging Sugarfoot's face with neroli oil. As her fingers worked, she focused her mind on willing him to get better. "I'm going to keep trying," she told him. "I'm determined to get you through this, Sugarfoot." But his head remained resting on the straw. It was as if he had put up an invisible barrier and nothing that Amy did would reach him.

Amy was so absorbed in her work that she hardly noticed the lengthening shadows on the stall floor as late afternoon turned to evening. Her temples began to throb with the effort of concentrating for so long, and she rested her head against Sugarfoot's neck.

"Amy." She looked up. Grandpa had come home. "I think you should come in now, honey. You've given it your best shot."

Frustration welled up inside Amy. "What good is my best shot if it hasn't made Sugarfoot better?" she said with a sigh.

"Amy. Come on." Seeing her grandpa's unwavering expression, Amy reluctantly got to her feet and left the stall without saying a word. On her way to the house, she collected an armful of battered books from the feed room. Maybe she had missed something. There just had to be more she could do.

Chapter Nine

"Amy! Phone!" Ty called from the house.

Amy started. It was early afternoon the following day. Apart from a brief session with Star, she had hardly left Sugarfoot's side. The Shetland coughed, his whole body shaking with the effort. *He's getting worse,* she thought with a dreadful sinking feeling in her heart. She felt his ears. The sky was overcast outside and the air was cool, but Sugarfoot's ears were damp and hot.

Ty came up to the stall door. "Nick Halliwell is on the phone."

Amy got to her feet. Her head ached and her eyes were hurting. She had read far into the night, desperately searching for some remedy that might help Sugarfoot, but she had found nothing. She went down to the house.

"Hi," she said, picking up the receiver. "Amy Fleming here."

"Hello, Amy," said Nick. "I was calling to find out how Star is doing."

Amy leaned against the wall. Account books were spread out across the kitchen table — pages of tiny figures and columns with calculations. "Fine." She forced herself to concentrate. "Good, actually. He went into the trailer and let us put the ramp up this morning. Tomorrow, I'm —"

Nick interrupted. "You got him into a trailer?"

"Yes," Amy said. "He's walking in quite happily now. He was reluctant at first, but he's much better now. He's still not completely cured — that will take a little more time — but he's definitely on the way."

"You've had him two days and you say that he's already walking easily up a ramp?" Nick sounded incredulous. "With no problem?"

"Yes," Amy repeated patiently.

"This I have got to see!"

"Well, as I said, he's not really ready to come home just yet," Amy said quickly. "We need to get him used to being in the trailer while the van's moving and for longer periods of time."

"But can I come and see him walking up the ramp?"

"Sure," Amy replied.

"This is great news. I'll be over in half an hour."

"What? Now?" Amy's eyes widened. "It's not really a good time," she began hastily. "You see —"

But Nick Halliwell didn't seem to be the sort to take no for an answer. "I won't stay long," he interrupted. "I just want a quick look. Right. Half an hour. See you then."

Amy replaced the phone. This was just what she didn't need. Star hadn't even been groomed! At that moment, Lou came into the kitchen, a calculator in her hand. "Hi," she said.

"Hi," Amy said absentmindedly.

"We've had some good news," Lou said, smiling. "Val Grant just called. She's offered to help us with a couple of the horses until we get things sorted out. She's going to take Pegasus, Sundance, and Jasmine."

Amy gasped in horror.

"What's the matter?" Lou said, frowning as she saw her reaction.

"No way. She can't have them!" Amy cried.

"Why not?" Lou looked confused.

"Because of the way she treats her horses! No way, Lou! Absolutely not!"

"Oh, Amy, she can't be that bad," Lou said, raising her eyebrows. "It would be the sensible thing to do, and then she might want to have them permanently — buy them, maybe — which would be a real help."

"Lou!" Amy couldn't begin to explain all the reasons

why Val Grant shouldn't get Pegasus and the ponies. "How can you even consider letting Daddy's horse go?"

"But Amy —"

Amy ran from the kitchen, slamming the door as hard as she could behind her.

Ty was waiting for her by Sugarfoot's stall. "Hey! What's up?" he said in alarm as she stormed down the stable aisle.

Suddenly, Amy couldn't help herself. She was too tired, too full of emotion. Covering her face with her hands, she burst into tears. Ty stepped forward and put his arm around her shoulder. "Hey, what's the matter?" he asked.

Amy sobbed out Lou's latest plans. "I hate her, Ty! I really do hate her! She's going to ruin everything!"

Ty stroked her hair. "Come on, now, that's crazy. Lou just has a lot to learn about Heartland. Everything will be OK."

"How can it be?" Amy cried. "Grandpa, you, and I can't cope on our own! Lou just wants to go back to New York! What are we going to do?"

"Something will turn up," Ty said, still stroking her hair. "You'll see." He held her until her sobs quieted. At last, she sniffed. "I've made your T-shirt all wet," she said, stepping back and feeling slightly embarrassed.

"That's all right," Ty said softly. He looked at her with a concerned smile. "So what did Nick Halliwell want?"

Amy's eyes widened as she remembered. "He wants to come and see Star now! Can you give him a brush over for me, Ty?"

"Well, actually," Ty shifted his feet, looking a bit embarrassed, "I was kind of on my way." Amy suddenly noticed that he had changed out of his yard clothes. "It's my half day today," he said as if to remind her. "I know I haven't been taking them recently, but I need to get some groceries and things."

Amy immediately felt dreadfully guilty. She'd completely forgotten that Ty normally had a half day once a week. He'd been working so hard.

"I'll stay if you want," he offered.

"No, of course not," Amy said quickly, her hand flying to her temples as they resumed their throbbing. "You've been great, Ty. Go home."

"Everything's done. The horses are all watered and the stalls are clean." He stepped toward her, his eyes anxious. "Now, you're sure you'll be OK?"

"Sure." Looking up into his worried face, she smiled, words leaping impulsively out of her. "Thanks for everything, Ty," she said. "You've been a real friend."

There was a pause. Ty's eyes searched hers and then suddenly, without warning, he reached out and brushed his hand against her cheek. At the tender touch of his warm hand, Amy felt a shock run through her. It was over in a couple of seconds, and Ty stepped back.

"See you tomorrow," he muttered as he strode quickly away.

Amy stared after him for a few seconds, not knowing how to react.

"Amy!" she vaguely heard her grandpa calling her from the house. "Soraya's on the phone!"

Still in a daze, Amy headed toward the house.

🙚

"That is amazing!" Nick Halliwell had an expression of astonishment on his face as Amy led Star out of the trailer for the third time. He looked just like he did on TV — blond hair, suntanned face, and sharp blue eyes. When she had first seen him get out of his car, she had felt a sudden rush of butterflies in her stomach, but now, with Star to concentrate on, her nerves had left her.

"Well, like I said on the phone, he's still got a little way to go, but it's a good start," she said, leading Star over. The horse quickened his pace as he approached his owner and then nibbled his outstretched palm.

"A good start? It's more than I ever hoped for." Nick vigorously patted the horse's chestnut neck. "You've worked a miracle," he said to Amy. He looked her up and down. "How old are you?"

"Fifteen," she replied.

He shook his head. "Well, you've done more than any-one else has ever been able to do with this horse, and like

I said, he's a special boy." He smiled at her. "By the time I've gotten the word out about this, you're going to be overwhelmed with horses." He smiled. "You'd better start building another barn."

Amy's throat tightened at the unfairness of it all. Build another barn! Not if Lou had her way. A sudden aching depression filled Amy as she looked at the barn, the rings, and the fields. If Lou went through with her plan, then all this would change. The fields and barns would no longer be full of horses. Heartland wouldn't be there for the horses that needed their help most. Horses like Copper, Sugarfoot, and Star. Amy didn't know what she would do if she couldn't work with rescue horses anymore.

Nick didn't seem to notice her reticence. He patted her on the shoulder. "Well, I don't want to hold you up. Thanks for letting me have a look. When can I expect him home?"

Amy forced herself to focus. "In about ten days," she said. "I'll let you know."

"OK. Keep up the good work!" Giving Star one last pat, Nick Halliwell strode down the yard to his car.

Amy watched him drive off. "Star," she whispered, burying her face in the horse's neck and giving way to the wave of tiredness that swept over her. "Why is life so complicated?" She heard the back door open and looked to see who was there.

Lou was coming out. She hesitated for a moment and then walked over. "I was watching from the kitchen window," she said, stopping a distance away from Star. She looked uncomfortable. "I just wanted to say that I'm impressed. You've — you've done a really good job."

For Amy, it was the last straw. "Well, thank you, Lou!" Hot anger shot through her. "I'm glad you're impressed!" she said sarcastically. "But that really doesn't matter, does it? If things turn out your way, Heartland will never help another horse again!"

Lou took a step forward. "Amy, I didn't mean it that way."

"Don't!" Amy yelled. Her misery consumed her. "If you cared, you'd stay and help us save Heartland instead of trying to close it down. But you don't care about anything that really matters!" Amy was shaking with emotion now. "You don't care about Grandpa or me or the horses! This is what I have left of Mom. She cared for all these horses. I'm not about to give them up. I can't lose them, too." Acting blindly, without thinking, she grabbed Star's mane, and the next instant she was on his back.

"Amy!" Lou's voice rose with alarm. "Amy, stop! What are you doing?"

"Getting as far away from you as possible!"

With a sob, Amy dug her heels into Star's side. He leaped forward and with just the lead rope to guide him, she galloped him bareback up past the fields and onto the trail leading to the woods. The trees ripped by her, her mind blank except for the desperate need to escape, to run away. She didn't stop until she had put several miles between her and the house. Only then did she notice Star's labored breathing and sweating sides.

She let him slow to a walk and then to a halt. Suddenly, Amy became horribly aware of what she had done. Star didn't even belong to her. Her heart pounding, she slipped off his back. He was breathing heavily, his nostrils moist and flaring. She crouched down and quickly checked his legs. Relief flooded through her as she realized there was no obvious damage. She didn't even like to think how valuable Star was. If she had injured him in any way . . .

She threw her arms round the chestnut's hot, damp neck. "Oh, Star, I'm so sorry." He nuzzled her and snorted. She rubbed his head and looked around. Where were they? They had come off the trail a long way back. The trees towered overhead. From high above she could just hear the first pattering of rain falling. She shivered. Her bare arms felt cold.

She remounted and, clicking her tongue, turned Star and headed back through the trees the way they had come. But after a few minutes it was impossible to tell which path they had taken. There were so many forks in the trail. When they passed what looked like the same fallen tree for about the fourth time, Amy felt panic starting to set in. How were they ever going to find the way back home?

As they reached yet another fork in the path, Amy looked from left to right. She dropped the lead rope on Star's neck in despair. Which way? She dragged her hands down her face trying to decide. She didn't have a clue. Star stepped toward the left track, his ears pricked. Amy was about to stop him but then stopped herself. Was it possible that he knew the way back? Sitting very still, without directing him with the lead, she let Star pick his way through the trees.

She was just beginning to give up hope that Star could find the way when, suddenly, he stepped out of the trees onto the trail. Relief and hope rushed through her. Leaning forward to throw her arms around Star's neck, Amy burst into tears, and Star continued to take her home. Afternoon was fading into evening, and rain drizzled from the sky, soaking Amy's T-shirt and jeans, but she didn't care. They were almost there.

As she neared the gate, Lou came running up the yard. Amy's heart sank. Now she was going to get it. "I'm sorry," she burst out, jumping off Star and clutching onto his lead rope with her cold hands. "I'm really sorry, Lou." She looked at Lou, expecting her to explode with anger. Instead she saw that Lou's eyes were wide and frightened.

"Amy!" she gasped. "It's Sugarfoot — I think he's dying."

Chapter Ten

Hastily shutting Star in his box stall, Amy raced to the back barn, her heart pounding. She looked over the half door. "Oh, Sugarfoot," Amy sobbed. The little pony was lying flat out on the straw, his eyes closed. Lou had covered him with a blanket. Opening the door, she crouched beside him and very gently stroked his neck and face. "Please don't die. Please get better." And then, no longer able to control herself, she collapsed in tears.

"I've called Scott," Lou said. She stood uncertainly in the stall doorway. "He's on his way."

Amy nodded in recognition.

"What about Star?" Lou said.

"Star?" Amy suddenly remembered that Star was standing cold and damp in his stall. "He needs rubbing down." She half stood up, wiping the tears from her face, and then knelt down again to stroke Sugarfoot's neck once more. She couldn't bear to leave him.

"I'll do it," Lou said suddenly. "You stay here."

Amy turned, shocked. But Lou was already hurrying down the yard. Just then, Sugarfoot coughed. Amy's eyes raced back to him. Stroking his neck, she started to shiver in her damp clothes.

A little while later, she heard a motor engine and the sound of a car door. Quick footsteps strode up the yard. She looked around as Scott entered the stall. "Amy," he said in a hushed voice, kneeling down beside her. He didn't say anymore as he checked Sugarfoot over. Amy felt her eyes fill with fresh tears.

Lou appeared in the stall doorway. She was carrying a mug of coffee, a fleece top, and a blanket. "Here," she said to Amy. "You're soaked through." Amy's fingers were so cold that she could hardly pull the top over her head. She gulped at the hot coffee, barely tasting it.

"I found him like this about half an hour ago," Lou said to Scott. "I put down some fresh straw and tried to keep him warm."

"You did just the right thing," Scott said, looking her square in the face.

"Is there anything you can do?" Lou asked.

Scott stroked Sugarfoot's neck. "Well, I could give him more injections to fight infection and stop the pain, but that's about all." He stood up and sighed. "He's in really bad shape," he said, rubbing a hand over his eyes. "It might be for the best if we put him to sleep."

"What?" Amy said through trembling lips.

"We can't let him suffer," Scott replied. "He's been through a lot."

"You said you could give him painkillers. He might still get better!" Tears choked Amy's voice as she looked down at the little Shetland stretched out in the straw.

Scott crouched down beside her and put a hand on her shoulder. "More medicine is not the answer. Amy, you know science doesn't always have a cure. He just doesn't want to get better," he said gently. "He's not fighting to stay alive anymore. If he was, then there would be hope."

"Just one more night!" Amy begged frantically. "Just give us one more night!"

Scott looked at her for a long moment. "OK," he said at last. "One more night." He got up to prepare an injection for Sugarfoot. A few minutes later, as he left, he turned to Lou. "I'll be by first thing tomorrow morning. Give me a call if there's any change."

She nodded. "I will." She smiled gratefully at him. "Thank you for coming so quickly, Scott. It means a lot — to both of us."

"No problem." Scott looked at her again, his voice warm. "See you tomorrow."

❧

Amy sat in Sugarfoot's stall, gently stroking the little pony's neck. If only he could tell her what he needed. She felt as if she had failed him. As the evening turned to night, his breathing became more shallow. She touched his face. "Sugarfoot," she whispered, tears trickling down her face. "Please tell me. What do you want?"

The stall door opened. It was Lou. Both she and Grandpa had come by regularly through the evening to see how Sugarfoot was doing. "Amy, it's getting late," she said softly. "You should go to bed."

Amy shook her head. "I have to stay with Sugarfoot."

Lou knelt down beside her. "Let me stay with him."

Amy looked at her in surprise. Her sister looked calm and determined.

Lou nodded. "You need some sleep. Go on in. You can always take over later." She was insistent in a gentle way, and Amy gave in, too exhausted to argue anymore. She walked numbly back to the house. Her grandfather was waiting in the kitchen.

"How is he?" He understood the expression on her face. "No better?"

Amy shook her head. Grandpa came forward and hugged her tightly to him. Tears spilling from her eyes, she let her head rest against his chest.

🖋

Amy bolted upright — what time was it? She checked her bedside clock; she had slept for several hours. What if Lou had left the barn, left Sugarfoot on his own to die? She could never forgive herself for falling asleep.

Amy scrambled out of bed and rushed over to the window. With relief, she saw a light shining out from the back barn. She hoped Lou was still there.

Going downstairs she looked into the kitchen. The radio was on and Grandpa had fallen asleep in the easy chair. She crept quietly past him and went outside. The night air was cool on her face as she hurried through the yard. When she reached the barn, she slowed her pace to a walk. Treading as quietly as she could, she approached Sugarfoot's stall.

She could hear Lou's voice but couldn't quite make out the words. She looked over the stall door. Lou was sitting beside Sugarfoot, talking to him. Amy was about to push the door open when she realized that Lou's face was streaming with tears.

She paused, shocked. She couldn't remember ever seeing Lou cry. She stepped back uncertainly, not knowing how to react.

"Oh, Sugarfoot, what am I going to do?" she heard

Lou say, her voice low and despairing. A sob burst from her. "I don't think I can take it anymore. I've tried to be strong, but I miss Mom so much."

Lou started to cry in earnest. Amy stood frozen, wondering what to do. She thought about saying something, but somehow, something held her back.

Lou started speaking again. A sob caught in her throat. "I've lost Dad and I've lost Mom. Amy thinks I don't care, but she doesn't understand. I'm just trying to keep a brave face. It's just so hard, and now I could lose Amy, too."

Amy crept forward to look through a chink in the stall wall. Lou was cradling Sugarfoot's head on her knees. Her voice choked with tears, she started to sing softly to the little pony.

After a few seconds, Lou's voice trailed off. "Sugarfoot, you could be happy here," she said softly. "We'd take good care of you, I promise." She kissed him gently. "I know you lost Mrs. Bell. And it hurts a lot. But Amy and I understand. We really do." She started to sing again.

Through her own tears, Amy suddenly noticed that Sugarfoot was stirring, his eyes were flickering. She stared. The singing somehow seemed to be getting through to him. That must be it. Mrs. Bell had always sung as she worked — maybe it reminded Sugarfoot of home and comforted him. At that moment, the little Shetland weakly lifted his head.

With a breath of anticipation, Lou stopped singing. "Sugarfoot!" she whispered. The tiny pony looked at her for a long, long moment. Then slowly and with a great effort, he reached out to touch Lou's arm with his muzzle. "Hello, boy," Lou whispered shakily. She touched his head and he snorted gently. "Did you like that song?"

Lou picked up the herbs that Amy had left in the stall earlier. She held out a few stems, and to Amy's amazement Sugarfoot started to eat. Picking up a handful, Lou started to sing softly again and as he finished the herbs, she reached for his feed bucket. Handful by slow handful, she fed him the contents — the bran, the barley, the carrots and apples. At last, Sugarfoot turned away.

Lou put down the pail. "That's a good boy," she said softly. "Get some rest, little horse. We can face tomorrow together."

Sugarfoot rested his muzzle on the straw and closed his eyes, and Amy slipped quietly into the stall. "Lou?" she said softly.

"Amy!" Lou started. Her expression immediately became alarmed and defensive. "How long have you been there?" she asked in a low voice.

Amy hesitated for a moment, wondering whether she should lie, but she had heard too much. She knew that

Lou really missed Mom, too. She met Lou's eyes, and tears welled up in her own. Putting her arms around Lou's neck, she started to cry. "I'm sorry for all those things I said. I'm sorry I said you didn't care. I just didn't understand."

Lou hugged her back. "It's all right," she soothed. "Amy, it's all right."

Amy pulled away. "No, it's not all right. I should have realized. I never gave you credit for all your help. And you've made Sugarfoot better, too," she said, looking at the little Shetland, sleeping at last. "I saw you with him. You got him to eat."

Lou's eyes were bright. "He just suddenly seemed to wake up. I didn't do anything. Not really."

"But you did!" Amy said passionately. "Don't you see? You understood what he was going through. You sang to him like Mrs. Bell used to and reminded him what it's like to have a happy home. You gave him a reason to start fighting again." For a moment, Amy and Lou both looked at the little pony. "And I thought you hated horses," Amy said.

"I've never hated them," Lou said quickly. "I've just blamed them for all the hurt they've caused — for losing Dad and Mom. But being with them brings back so many good memories. I'm beginning to see that you can't run away from your past." She smiled as Sugarfoot snorted into the straw. She laid a hand on his head.

"Some pretty amazing things happen here, don't they Amy? Heartland is a special place. I'll miss it when I go back to New York," she said softly. She turned to Amy. "And I'll miss you, too."

"Then don't go back," Amy said impetuously. "Stay here. Stay here and help us keep it going. You could help Ty and me. I could teach you all Mom's techniques. You could even look after Sugarfoot. Together we could make it work."

"Oh, Amy, I can't," Lou said, shaking her head. "I live in New York."

"But this is your home!" Amy exclaimed. "With Grandpa and me! We can be a real family again." She saw the truth of this sink in. "We could all live here together."

Lou wavered. "But my life isn't here. What about my job? Where will the money come from? No one will bring horses to Heartland without Mom here."

"But they will!" Amy quickly told Lou about Nick Halliwell and what he'd said that afternoon. "He'll tell everyone he knows!" She grabbed Lou's hands. "We can do it, Lou!" she said. "We really can!"

Lou was silent for the moment. "We'll never get along. We're too different. We'll fight all the time. It just won't work."

"We'll argue, but we'll make up again," Amy said. "I'll be practical. I'll be sensible."

Lou laughed. "You couldn't if you tried."

"Well, maybe not," Amy admitted with a grin. "But at least I will try." She looked eagerly at Lou. "Just please say you'll stay. Please."

They heard the straw rustle behind them. They both turned. Sugarfoot had lifted his head and was looking at them. The light had come back into his eyes, and Amy could see he'd turned a corner — he wanted to live again.

Lou returned her gaze to Amy. She took a deep breath. "I'm not making any promises," she said. "But for now, I'll stay." She squeezed Amy's hand tightly.

Amy gasped, "Oh, Lou, this means so much to me. You've been away for so long." She wrapped her arms around her sister's shoulders. "Thank you for coming home."

Heartland

❧

After the Storm

*For Jane, who taught me everything
that is true about horses*

Chapter One

Amy tried to scream as she saw her mom open the driver's door to the pickup. But no words would come out. She wanted to stop her, but she couldn't move. She could only watch, horrified, as her mother put the key in the ignition and started the engine.

And then the dream sped forward.

Now they were both in the pickup. Rain pounded against the windshield, blurring Amy's vision. And the trailer behind them was shaking violently as the bay stallion kicked out in fear. Amy tried hard to wake herself up, but the dream tightened its hold on her. She was trapped in the same nightmare she had been having over and over again for the past month.

Her mother's hands gripped the steering wheel tightly.

"This is insane," she muttered, her blue eyes looking into Amy's. "We should never have come out in this."

"Stop!" Amy sobbed desperately. "Stop, Mom, please stop." But Marion didn't hear her.

A flash of lightning split the dark sky, and the clattering of hooves in the trailer was drowned out by a huge crash of thunder overhead.

Amy started to scream when she saw the tall, swaying trees that loomed on the road ahead. Branches closed over the top of the pickup, banging and scraping along the roof of the trailer. A long, drawn-out creak of breaking wood was followed by a clap of thunder so loud that it sounded like a cannon had been fired. Straight in front of them, a tree started to fall slowly into the road.

"No!" Amy screamed. "Please, no!"

"Amy! Amy! Wake up!"

Amy suddenly felt her shoulder being shaken. She opened her eyes. She was lying on a hard wooden floor. Her grandfather was bending over her, his forehead creased in concern.

"Grandpa," Amy said, sitting up in confusion.

She breathed in a faint, familiar smell of perfume. Photographs of horses stared down at her from the walls. She was in her mother's room. A coat was slung over a chair just where her mom had left it the day of the accident. The hairbrush on the dressing table was coated in a fine layer of dust, a few blond hairs caught in the bristles. Nothing in the room had changed for six weeks, not since the night of the storm when Marion Fleming had died.

At the sight of all the familiar things Amy felt her stomach twist. "What am I doing here?"

Jack Bartlett must have seen the shock on her face. "It's OK, honey," he said reassuringly. "You were sleep-walking."

"It was that dream again," Amy stammered, getting to her feet. The air in the room felt still and quiet. Sweat prickled through her long hair as she looked around.

"Come on, it's over now," her grandpa said soothingly. "Let's get you back to your own room." He put his arm around her shoulders.

Just then her mom's bedroom door opened. Lou, Amy's older sister, stood in the doorway. "Are you all right?" she asked, her short blond hair tousled from sleep. "I heard screaming."

"It's OK," Jack said quickly as he steered Amy toward the door. "Amy had a nightmare and was sleepwalking."

"Oh, Amy," Lou said, moving swiftly to Amy's side.

"I'm OK," Amy said, pulling away from Grandpa and pushing past Lou to the door. She just wanted to get out of the room. She could hardly breathe. It was too much to bear — knowing that Mom was never coming back.

The sheets on her bed felt cool. She pulled them over her. Grandpa and Lou came to the doorway. Out of the corner of her eye she could see Grandpa say something to Lou in a low voice.

Lou nodded. "Sleep well, Amy. See you in the morning," she said softly, and left.

Grandpa came over and sat on the edge of Amy's bed.

"I'm OK, Grandpa," Amy told him. "You should go to bed now, too."

"I can stay for a bit," Grandpa said.

Amy felt too exhausted to argue. She lay back against the pillows. As her eyes began to shut, the nightmare flickered around the edges of her consciousness. She shuddered and blinked.

"Oh, Grandpa," she said, opening her eyes quickly.

"Don't worry, I'm here," Grandpa said gently. He stroked her hair. "Go to sleep now, honey."

When Amy awoke in the morning, Grandpa had left. As always, the first thought that flashed into her mind was the hot, quick hope that the last six weeks had never happened. But as she saw the pale morning light filtering through her curtains, reality hit her with an icy certainty — her mom was dead, and it was her fault.

Amy sat up, wrapping her arms around her knees. If she hadn't been so desperate to rescue Spartan, the bay stallion, from the barn where he'd been abandoned by thieves, then Mom would never have gone out in that storm, and the accident would never have happened. Amy was the one who had pleaded with her mom to go. She wanted to save Spartan, but in the end she had lost so much more. A sickening feeling of guilt gripped her heart.

Getting out of bed, Amy pulled on a pair of jeans and went to open the curtains. From her window she could see Heartland's front stable block and the patchwork of paddocks filled with horses grazing and dozing in the quiet of the early morning sun. Stepping over the clutter of clothes and magazines on her floor, Amy hurried downstairs. She decided to go ahead and start on the barn chores. She didn't want to think about Mom — just as she didn't want to think about what the day ahead held for her.

❧

Later that afternoon, Amy stood in one of the stalls in the stable block and shook a flake of straw onto a thick, fresh bed. Dust particles floated and danced in the shafts of warm sunlight that shone in over the half door. She thought about Spartan. Tomorrow he would be standing exactly where she was now. For a moment she almost wanted to be sick. Life felt so unfair.

"Almost done?" Ty, Heartland's seventeen-year-old stable hand, asked as he looked over the door. He must have noticed the look on Amy's face, because his expression suddenly softened with concern. "Amy? Are you OK?" he asked, walking in.

Amy nodded, not trusting herself to speak.

"Hey," Ty said softly. He looked around the stall. "Are you worried about Spartan?" Amy nodded again. "It'll be fine," he said, squeezing her arm sympathetically. "You'll see."

From down the yard came the sound of the farmhouse door opening. "Amy! Ty!" Grandpa called. "It's almost time to go."

Amy went to the door. "We're coming!"

"I'd better get cleaned up," Ty said. "I'll see you down at the house in a minute." Leaving the stall he hurried toward the tack room.

As Amy shut the half door she glanced around the stall one more time. The very next day Spartan would be there. He would look over this door, waiting to be fed, to be groomed, to be cared for, just like any of the other horses at Heartland. Amy shivered. She couldn't kid herself. Spartan would never be just another horse to her.

She walked slowly toward the white-painted farmhouse and let herself in through the back door. Grandpa and Lou were talking quietly in the kitchen. They were both dressed in dark clothes. On the table lay a big bunch of white lilies tied with a black ribbon. They filled the air with a sweet, heavy scent.

"We have to leave soon," Jack Bartlett said. "We said we'd meet Scott and Matt at five thirty."

Amy nodded. "I have to change out of my barn clothes," she said, heading for the stairs.

Reaching her bedroom, Amy grabbed a brush and ran it quickly through her light brown hair before twisting it up on top of her head with a clip. Leaving her jeans and T-shirt in a heap, she pulled on a long black sleeveless dress. She checked her reflection in the mirror on her desk. Her gray eyes looked large in her pale face.

Her gaze fell on the framed photograph of her mom that she kept by the mirror. She picked it up. It was one of her favorite pictures. Mom, standing by a pasture gate, laughing as she stroked Pegasus. It had been taken just a few weeks before the accident. Amy felt a stab of pain in her chest.

"Amy!" She heard Lou calling up the stairs.

Putting the photograph down, Amy picked up a piece of paper from her desk, folded it quickly, and put it in her pocket.

Lou was standing at the bottom of the staircase, her normally composed face showing signs of tension. "Ready?" she asked in her subtle accent, one of the obvious clues that Lou had attended boarding school and college in England before moving to New York.

Amy fiddled with the piece of paper in her pocket. "Yeah, I'm ready."

They went through to the kitchen.

Ty was by the door. His wavy dark hair was combed back, and he had put on a clean white shirt and black pants. His eyes met Amy's with a look of concern and support. She managed a faint smile in return.

Jack opened the back door. "Well then, let's go."

❧

They drove to the cemetery in silence. Scott Trewin, the local equine vet, and his younger brother, Matt, were waiting in the parking lot when they arrived.

"Hi," Matt said quietly as Amy got out of the car.

Matt and Amy went to the same high school and were good friends. In the past, Matt had suggested that he was interested in them becoming more than just friends, but today his face showed nothing but kind sympathy and concern. He smiled warmly. "How are you doing?"

Amy nodded. "Not so bad."

Walking across the memorial ground, Amy thought about the service. That morning her mother's headstone had been placed to mark her grave, and now Amy had the chance to say a proper good-bye. The official funeral had been held six weeks ago, a few days after the accident, while Amy was still lying unconscious in the hospital.

The group reached the shady corner where Marion's headstone had been placed. There was an older headstone to the left. Although it was weathered by the years, the plot had been carefully tended. Amy watched her grandpa's gaze fall on it. Walking up to it, he gently touched it and closed his eyes.

It was the grave of Jack's wife, Amy's grandmother, who had died even before Lou, who was twenty-three, had been born.

After a moment, Grandpa returned to the small group. He cleared his throat. "Well, thanks for coming. As you all know, we are here today to say a final farewell to Marion." He looked around at everyone. "A daughter, a mother, a friend. Each of us has our own special memories of her. She made us laugh, she dried our tears, she listened, she helped, she loved. She cared passionately for all the horses that she took in and healed at Heartland. Marion's love was boundless, and I am so proud that she was my daughter."

As Grandpa spoke, Amy focused on the light gray headstone, the soil around its base still fresh and slightly damp, flowers heaped on the grave. It felt as though Grandpa's words were washing over her — they weren't registering at all. She stared dry-eyed at the inscription on the stone and read her mom's name, the year she was born, and the year of her death, over and over again. She, Lou, and Grandpa had chosen the inscription together. It read:

Her spirit will live on at Heartland forever.

"Amy," Grandpa said softly, breaking through her thoughts. "Will you read the poem you have chosen to remember your mom?"

Amy walked forward, and kneeling, laid the lilies at the base of the headstone. Then she took her place again beside Lou, who squeezed her hand, tears welling in her eyes. Amy took the folded piece of paper from her pocket and opened it up.

"Mom loved this poem," she said quietly. "She had it pinned to the mirror in her bedroom. Daddy gave it to her when her first horse died. It's called 'The life that I have,' and it's by Leo Marks." Looking down at the creased piece of paper she started to read:

> "The life that I have
> Is all that I have
> And the life that I have
> Is yours."

As Amy read she noticed that Lou was fighting to stay composed, and her grandpa was brushing a hand across his eyes. Amy waited for her own tears to overwhelm her, but none came. She read on, her voice clear, her mind numb.

"The love that I have
Of the life that I have
Is yours and yours and yours.
A sleep I shall have
A rest I shall have
Yet death will be but a pause.
For the peace of my years,
In the long green grass
Will be yours and yours and yours."

As she folded up the paper, Amy heard a stifled sob come from Lou. Feelings of desperation welled up in her. Why wasn't she feeling anything? Why wasn't she crying? After she returned the poem to her pocket, she walked slowly forward. "Good-bye, Mom," she whispered, touching the headstone. "We'll take good care of Heartland. I promise."

Grandpa walked up behind her and put his hand on her shoulder. She turned, and he kissed her on the forehead. They stood silent for a moment.

As the little group moved slowly back to the parking lot, each one wrapped in his or her own thoughts and memories, Ty walked alongside Amy. "You OK?" he asked, his eyes looking deep into hers.

Amy knew that he must be surprised that she wasn't crying. It just wasn't her nature to keep her feelings to herself. But it wasn't a conscious decision. She felt all sorts of emotions whirling inside of her. She wanted to cry, she really did, but something was stopping her. "I'm fine," she replied. She smiled gratefully. "Thanks for coming, Ty."

"I wanted to come." Ty shook his head, his eyes dark and intense. "Your mom was an amazing person. She really made me believe that I had a special way of understanding horses. I dropped out of high school because I wanted to work with her. I knew that I could learn so much more from her than school would ever teach me. . . ." His voice echoed his confusion and loss. "I just can't believe she's gone."

Amy touched his arm. Quickly, he covered her hand with his own.

"Amy." Amy collected her thoughts and turned. Scott came up to her. "That poem was beautiful," he said, looking down at her. "I can see why it meant so much to Marion."

"I know," Amy said. Scott looked her full in the face and impulsively she changed the subject, hoping he wouldn't notice her lack of tears. "How . . . how's Spartan?" As the name left her lips her stomach tightened. *Spartan.* Scott had chosen the name. Spartan wasn't the easiest thing to think about just then.

"He's very unsettled," Scott replied. "Physically he's on the mend, but mentally he's still traumatized. He's extremely nervous and wary of people. The accident really got to him."

Guilt flooded through Amy.

Scott looked at her reassuringly. "But I think you'll be able to get through to him, Amy," he said. "If anyone can, it's you."

At three o'clock the next day, Amy waited for Scott to arrive with Spartan. Lou and Grandpa were out doing the grocery shopping, and it was Ty's day off, so Matt had come over to keep her company.

He kicked a stone down the drive as they waited for his brother. "Scott should get here soon," he said, glancing at his watch. "He said he'd be here before three."

"Yeah," Amy replied. Her heart was racing at the thought of seeing Spartan again. She was glad that Matt was there. He wasn't really into horses, and he couldn't fully understand how she was feeling, but just having him there made her feel better.

"Heard from Soraya lately?" Matt asked.

"I got a letter last week," Amy said. Soraya Martin was her best friend. She was away at a summer riding camp, and Amy was finding it hard not being able to speak to her on a regular basis. "She sounds like she's having fun."

"When's she coming back?"

"In three weeks," Amy replied. "I can't wait." She glanced at her watch nervously. Where was Scott? What was keeping him? He should have been here by now.

She walked over to the big gray horse in the end stall and stroked his nose. He nuzzled her affectionately. She smiled faintly. No matter how she was feeling, Pegasus always seemed to understand. He had been her father's horse — one of the finest show jumpers in the world. But a jumping accident in London twelve years before had left her father too injured to ever ride again, and Pegasus physically and emotionally damaged.

Amy kissed Pegasus's soft muzzle. It was through nursing Pegasus back to health that her mother had learned all about alternative therapies. Those methods had inspired her to move back to the United States and start Heartland — a horse sanctuary — after her marriage to Tim Fleming had broken up.

Matt walked over to Pegasus's stall. "It's twenty minutes past," he said with concern, looking at his watch. "I hope nothing's happened."

As Amy pulled away from Pegasus, her ears caught the faint chug of an engine coming up the drive. "That's probably him now," she said quickly.

A few seconds later, Scott's battered Jeep Cherokee came around the corner, a trailer swaying behind it. As it got closer, the sound of hooves crashing against metal could be heard. Matt and Amy exchanged nervous looks.

The Jeep stopped beside them. Scott cut the engine and jumped out. "What a journey!" he said. His face was strained as he nodded to the trailer. "I thought Spartan was going to burst out of the back at one point. He didn't stop kicking the whole way here."

There was a moment's silence, and then a high, whinnying scream rang out, full of rage and fury. Amy jumped as a hoof banged into the metal wall right next to her.

"Wow!" said Matt. "He sounds crazy!"

"He should calm down." Scott looked at Amy. "We'd better get him out. I'll go in and hold his halter while you two put the front ramp down." He disappeared through the side door. There was another series of thuds, and the trailer shook.

Amy's heart pounded in her chest as she moved around to unbolt the ramp. Any minute she'd see Spartan again. She remembered him as he had been the night she and her mom had rescued him — beautiful and trusting. And amazingly friendly considering he was a stallion and had been locked in a dark barn for days. He wasn't a stallion anymore. Scott had gelded him once it looked like he was going to recover and would be coming to Heartland to be rehabilitated and then rehomed. But even though he was no longer a stallion, he sounded wilder than ever.

"Let's go!" Scott shouted.

Amy and Matt let down the ramp, jumping aside just

in time as Spartan plunged forward with a screaming whinny.

"Easy now! Easy!" Scott shouted.

With a plunge, the horse clattered down the ramp. He stopped still and looked around at the fields and the fences, his bay coat gleaming with sweat, his eyes burning with fire.

Amy stood frozen. Spartan was unrecognizable. The trust and confidence that were in his eyes the first time she'd seen him had been replaced by fury and fear. Ugly scars stood out along his back and quarters. Guilt rushed through Amy as she looked at him. She felt a sudden desperate urge to turn and run away — far away.

Suddenly, Spartan's head whipped around as he caught her scent. With a sudden squeal of pure rage he lunged toward her, his mouth open, his ears flat against his head. Amy leaped back.

Scott struggled with the lead line to get the horse under control. "Are you all right?" he called anxiously to Amy.

"I'm fine," she replied breathlessly.

"We'd better get him into his stall," Scott said.

"I'll get the door," Matt said, edging cautiously past Spartan and then hurrying toward the barn.

Scott led Spartan after him. The horse sidestepped and shook his head as he jogged. He didn't seem to want to take his eyes off Amy, but Scott's voice and hand on his halter urged him onward.

Scott took him into the stall and secured the door behind him. "I'm sorry about what happened back there," he said to Amy. "I don't know what came over him. He's been difficult to handle, but he hasn't gone for anyone like that before."

"I guess it was probably just the shock of traveling in a trailer again," Amy reasoned. "It must have reminded him of the accident." She went to the door and looked over. She noticed Spartan stiffen as he saw her, and then, without warning, he plunged at the door, his snapping teeth missing her arm by inches.

"Whoa!" Scott shouted at the horse. Spartan shot to the back of his box again.

"Why'd he do that?" Matt asked Amy.

She looked quickly at Scott. "He hates me, doesn't he? He knows that it's my fault he was in the accident."

"He doesn't *hate* you," Scott said quickly. "Horses don't hold grudges. You know that. But he might associate you with the accident. He's probably attacking you because he's scared — scared that if he lets you get near, you'll put him through something similar again."

"So what's Amy supposed to do, Scott?" Matt asked, his voice full of concern.

"Rebuild his trust," Scott answered. His eyes met

Amy's. "It's going to be a long, slow process — but you've done it before."

Yes, Amy suddenly wanted to shout, *but not without Mom and never with a horse that was scared of me.*

Scott must have seen the doubt on her face. "You can do it, Amy — you might be the *only* person who can. If Spartan can come to trust and accept you, then he'll be able to trust anyone."

Amy swallowed. She would have to see Spartan every day, face his angry eyes, meet his resentment. She didn't know if she was up to it.

Scott studied her. "Look, if you really don't want to, then don't worry," he said. "I'll try to find somewhere else to take him."

Although Scott was hiding his disappointment, Amy knew that it wouldn't be easy to find someone else who would help Spartan. She swallowed. "No, I'll do it," she said.

Scott smiled. "That's great," he said, squeezing her shoulder. "It'll take time, Amy, but I know you can do it."

Amy glanced at Spartan's door, wishing she felt so sure.

Chapter Two

Leaving Spartan to calm down, Scott asked if he could take a look at Sugarfoot.

"Sure," Amy said. Sugarfoot was a Shetland pony that she had been nursing back to health.

As they walked up the yard, past the turnout paddocks, Amy stopped to pat a handsome buckskin pony that was looking over the fence. "Hi, there," she said. Sundance snorted in reply and thrust his head affectionately into her chest.

"He's looking good," Scott said.

"Yeah," Amy nodded. She fed Sundance a couple of mints. Although it was Heartland's mission to find new homes for all of the horses they rescued, Sundance was by nature too unpredictable and tempermental to be rehomed, so he was one of the few permanent equine residents there. Badly behaved with everyone else, he utterly adored Amy. Whenever there was time, she entered him in hunter-jumper classes in local shows.

"How's Sugarfoot's recovery coming along?" Scott asked as they entered the twelve-stall barn on the north side of the yard.

"He's getting much better," Amy said. "He's eating well now."

Sugarfoot had been brought to Heartland when he was discovered in his stable. He'd had no food for two weeks after his elderly owner, Mrs. Bell, had died. When Sugarfoot had first arrived at Heartland he was grief stricken and had refused to eat. He became very ill with bronchopneumonia. He had been so sick that they'd thought they were going to lose him up until a week ago — when he had turned a corner and started to recover.

Sugarfoot was standing by his hayrack. He gave a low, welcoming nicker and walked up to say hello.

"He's looking great," Scott said, stroking the Shetland's thick flaxen mane. "What remedies have you been using?"

Amy listed the herbs and aromatherapy oils she had been treating Sugarfoot with. "Diluted neroli oil for massage, then garlic, fenugreek seed, and nettles in his feed," she said. "They seem to be helping him get his appetite back."

"It seems like he's almost back to his old self," Scott said approvingly. He checked Sugarfoot's breathing and heart rate. "He's improving fast."

"Well, it's really Lou who's been looking after him," Amy explained.

"Lou?" Scott questioned.

It had been a surprise to Amy as well. Ever since their father's accident and the subsequent breakup of their parents' marriage, Lou had refused to have anything to do with horses. Even when she had come to Heartland after their mom's death she had avoided any contact with the horses at first. However, Sugarfoot had captured her heart, and she'd been moved to help nurse him back to health.

"She spends as much time as she can with him," Amy said.

"How long is she planning on staying?" Matt asked.

"Well, she's told her boss at work that she won't be back until the fall," Amy said. She patted Sugarfoot gratefully. If it hadn't been for Sugarfoot, Lou would *already* have gone back to her high-powered banking job in Manhattan.

"What will you do when she does go back?" Scott asked.

Amy shrugged. She didn't want to think about it. When she went back to school in the fall they would just have to find the money to hire another stable hand — or else they'd have to reduce the number of horses. "Maybe she'll change her mind," Amy said optimistically.

"You think there's a chance?" Scott said in surprise. "I thought she was really into city life."

"She is," Amy admitted. Lou *was* into her job in a big way — her job and her apartment and Carl, her boyfriend. "But she seems to like it here, too. I don't know . . . she *might* stay."

Just then, there was the sound of a car pulling up outside the house. "That's probably Lou and Grandpa now," Amy said.

They headed toward the house. Jack Bartlett's station wagon was parked outside, and he and Lou were getting out.

"Hi!" Amy called.

"Hi," Grandpa replied. "Spartan's here, is he?"

"Yes. In the stall at the end," Amy said.

Curious, Grandpa and Lou walked over. Amy glanced at Matt, who was drinking a soda by the back door, and then hurried after them. "Don't go too close," she warned.

Grandpa stopped. "Why?" A look of concern flickered in his eyes as he studied her face. "He's not *dangerous*, is he?"

"No, no, of course not," Amy said quickly. "He's just a bit upset after the journey."

"Well, he's a good-looking horse," Grandpa commented, looking over the door. "A Morgan by the looks of him."

Scott turned to Amy. "Look, I'd better be going now. Call me if you need any advice, otherwise I'll drop by in a few days." He smiled at her. "You'll do a great job with him." He turned to Matt. "Do you want a lift?"

"Yeah, sure," Matt nodded.

They said their good-byes and then walked down to Scott's Cherokee. The engine coughed to life, and then with a belch of exhaust fumes, the Jeep and trailer trundled away.

❧

That night, Amy sat up in bed reading until late. She didn't want to fall asleep for fear of facing a nightmare again. Forcing her eyes to stay open, she read and read, but as the night wore on, the print started to blur, and at last her eyes closed.

She was in the dark. But where? Four wooden walls pressed in on her. It was some sort of barn. Rain drummed down onto the tin roof above, and the wind howled outside. Amy wasn't sure why she was in this dark, enclosed space, but she had an unrelenting desire to escape. Uneasily she moved toward the door. There was a sudden crash of thunder followed by a creak as the door slowly opened. Her heart raced.

"Mom!" Amy gasped, seeing Marion standing there, her hair soaked with rain and plastered to her head, a halter in hand.

"Easy," Marion soothed. She seemed to be talking to Amy. Then she turned to someone behind her. "Stand back a bit now," she said, putting a hand in her pocket and taking out a tin.

With the next fork of lightning the two silhouettes were lit up, and Amy recognized her own figure hovering behind her mom. Suddenly, she realized what was happening. Everything was like the night of the accident, but she was seeing the events through Spartan's eyes. She was seeing her mom and herself as Spartan had seen them. She could feel his fear, his bewilderment!

Her mom stepped toward her, holding her hand out. There was a clap of thunder, a moment of total blackness, and then the scene changed. The dream jumped ahead. Amy heard a metal clang as a door shut fast behind her, echoing ominously like a prison door. She realized she was now inside the trailer. She could hear the engine of the pickup starting and felt the trailer rock as it began to move.

Panic gripped Amy. She knew what was coming next. "Let me out!" she screamed. Her head was tied so she couldn't get loose. She lashed out at the metal walls, rocking the trailer, but to no avail. She was trapped. She couldn't see where they were, but she knew where they were going. The rain hammered relentlessly against the roof. There was the sound of the fierce wind and of creaking branches, and then she heard it. The spine-chilling, cannon-loud crack of a tree trunk breaking, the sound of squealing brakes, a bang, and then nothing.

Amy opened her eyes and snapped her light on. She took in lungfuls of air, and her breathing gradually steadied. Her room seemed eerily quiet. Reaching out for her book, she opened it with shaking fingers. It was still dark outside and she was exhausted, but she couldn't face going back to sleep.

The minutes dragged by until it was an acceptable time to get up. Amy met Lou down in the kitchen, and after grabbing a coffee and a muffin they went outside to feed the horses. The sky was a cloudless blue, and the early morning air was clear and cool.

"What a beautiful day!" Lou said. "You know, on mornings like this Manhattan seems totally unreal. Sometimes I can't imagine getting up and going to work in an office again."

Just then, the peace was shattered as Spartan put his head over his door and let out a piercing whistle at the sight of Amy. He half reared in his stall.

Lou gasped in alarm. "What's the matter with him?"

"It's me," Amy admitted. "He's scared of me because of the accident." She ran a hand through her hair. "Look, it might be best if you feed him. Or we could wait till Ty gets here."

"I'll do it. There's no point waiting for Ty," Lou said as they entered the feed room. "I wonder what Carl will think of it here," she contemplated, unscrewing the lid of the cod liver oil tin as Amy started adding heaping scoops of grain to the buckets. "He'll be here in a couple of days."

Amy had met Carl only once when she had been visiting Lou in Manhattan. He hadn't seemed at all interested in hearing about Heartland, and Amy wasn't sure how she felt about him.

"I can't imagine it," Lou mused. "I've never been with him in the country." She started to stack the feeds up. "Still, maybe he'll have some ideas for how this place could make money."

"Make money?" Amy repeated.

"Yes," Lou replied, obviously noticing the doubt on Amy's face. "Well, we're going to have to raise some more money somehow — even *you* can appreciate that, Amy. Without Mom it's going to be a struggle to persuade customers to bring their horses here. I know Nick Halliwell said he would bring us some business. . . ."

"And he has," Amy interrupted.

Nick Halliwell was a famous show jumper. He had recently brought one of his best horses to Heartland so Amy could cure its fear of being loaded into a trailer. Star had been the first problem horse that Amy had attempted to heal without her mom. Within two days the horse was going in and out of the trailer with no problem. Nick Halliwell had been very impressed with Amy's work and had promised to recommend Heartland to all his friends. And two new horses — Raisin and Topper — had already arrived to be treated.

"But we can't *rely* on him," Lou pointed out. "We have to try to raise our profile in other ways as well. I've had some ideas that I'm going to work on this afternoon. I know she did her best, but Mom really didn't run this place in the most economical way. We simply *have* to make more money." She picked up the buckets for the front stable. "It may mean a few changes, but I'm sure we will manage."

Amy headed up to the back barn with the other pile of buckets. *A few changes.* She bit her lip. She didn't want changes. She wanted everything to stay just the way it had been before Mom died.

Ty arrived at seven thirty. He and Amy began their normal morning routine — turning horses out, cleaning stalls, filling water buckets. As Amy worked she became aware of Spartan watching her. She didn't want to look at him, and yet her gaze seemed irresistibly drawn to his stall. Time after time she would glance over to see what she thought was fear in his eyes. Every time she walked anywhere near his stall, his ears flattened and he snapped at the air.

She saw Ty coming out of Pegasus's loose box and went over to talk with him. "What do you think about Spartan?" she asked, trying to sound casual as she tickled Pegasus's muzzle.

Ty bolted the door. "You really want to know?"

Amy nodded.

"Well, I'm not sure about him," Ty said seriously. "Watch yourself, Amy."

Amy surprised herself by jumping to Spartan's defense. "He's not *really* bad," she said quickly. "You should have seen him before the accident when Mom and I went to get him. He was so gentle."

"I don't know." Ty shook his head. "He's got a lot of distrust in his eyes. He's been through some awful stuff. I just want you to be careful."

"He'll settle in," Amy said uneasily, looking up at Ty. "He'll get better." She said the words automatically, feeling a desperate need to believe them herself. If Spartan didn't get better, what would it mean for her? She knew she wouldn't be able to deal with him being put down. It wasn't his fault he couldn't trust anyone. She *had* to make him better.

Chapter Three

Amy was busy enough over the next few hours to keep her mind off Spartan. She brought Raisin, the younger of the two new show jumpers, out of the barn with a halter and longline on.

Raisin was a pretty, young chestnut who panicked and tried to bolt every time a rider attempted to mount her. In all other respects — being groomed, handled, and led — the mare was obedient and responsive. Amy was sure that her problem could be cured.

As she led the chestnut up to the circular ring by the turnout paddocks, Lou came jogging into the yard. "What are you doing with Raisin today?" she asked with interest.

"I'm going to join up with her," Amy said. Joining up was a way of establishing a relationship of trust and understanding with a horse. It was a technique Marion had taught Amy.

"May I watch?" Lou asked.

"Sure," Amy said.

When they reached the circular ring, Lou leaned against the fence. After shutting the gate behind them, Amy rubbed Raisin's forehead with the palm of her hand and then unclipped the longline. She tossed one end toward the horse's hindquarters. With a slight jump of surprise, Raisin trotted away. Moving quickly so that her shoulders were in line with Raisin's, Amy pitched the longline again. With a snort, the chestnut broke into a high-headed canter.

By keeping her shoulders square with Raisin's body and her eyes fixed on the mare's eyes, Amy urged the mare on. After seven circuits she stepped slightly into the horse's path, blocking her movement and sending her at a canter in the opposite direction.

"Look," she said to Lou after Raisin made a few more circuits. "See her ear?" Raisin's inside ear was pointing into the circle in Amy's direction. "It means she's ready."

She urged the mare to circle the ring a few more times, waiting patiently for the next signal. At last it came. Raisin slowed to a trot and started to lick and chew with her mouth. This was the way a horse showed that it wanted to be friends. Then came the final signal.

Raisin stretched out her head and neck so that her muzzle was almost on the floor.

In one swift movement, Amy turned her shoulders sideways so she wasn't facing the horse and dropped her eyes, concentrating entirely on Raisin and forgetting about Lou's steady gaze on her. Out of the corner of her eye she saw Raisin slow to a stop. The horse stared at Amy and then decisively walked into the middle of the circle up to Amy's back, stopping by her shoulder and snorting softly. It was the moment of the join up!

Amy slowly turned and rubbed Raisin's forehead. "Good girl," she murmured before walking away. Raisin's instinct told her that humans were predators, but now Amy was trying to tell Raisin that she wasn't a threat — by moving away with nonaggressive body language. For the join up to be a success, she wanted Raisin to voluntarily choose to be with her and to follow her. To Amy's delight, as she walked across the ring the young chestnut did exactly that — she followed, with her nose by Amy's shoulder, her warm breath on Amy's neck. When she was certain she had Raisin's trust, Amy stopped and rewarded her with another rub on the forehead.

"Now that we've got an understanding," Amy told Lou, "I can start working on getting her used to being ridden. She'll be much easier to handle now."

To prove her point, she ran her palms over Raisin's

back and then eased her weight onto her hands. Raisin didn't flinch. "See, Raisin, I'm not going to hurt you. You'll be just fine." Amy stroked her and gave her a pat. "That's enough for today," she said.

Lou's eyes shone as she opened the gate. "That was incredible!"

Amy smiled. She had watched her mom join up on numerous occasions and understood exactly how Lou was feeling. Mom always said that no matter how many times she did it, it never felt any less amazing.

"So, are you going to join up with Spartan?" Lou asked curiously as they led Raisin back to the barn.

Ty, who was walking past with a water bucket, stopped. "It would be crazy to try and join up now," he said, looking at Amy. "There's no telling what he might do."

"He's not *that* bad," Amy protested, but she knew deep down that Ty was right.

"He could be dangerous," Ty said, his dark eyes serious.

"He's not," Amy retorted, seeing the look of concern on her sister's face. She turned to Ty. "Look, relax. I wasn't thinking about joining up with him yet. He'd probably try to jump out of the ring at this point."

"Or worse," Ty said.

Amy ignored him. "I thought I'd just try to get him used to me first. Go into his stall, brush him." She swallowed. "I'm going to start this afternoon."

❧

After lunch, as Amy approached Spartan's stall, she realized that never before had she experienced such a reluctant feeling about working with a horse. Spartan stared warily at her, his head high, his long black forelock tumbling down over his handsome, dished face. Amy hesitated. Although she was nervous, her natural instinct was to walk straight up to his door. She needed to get close to him, to make him realize that he had nothing to fear.

She took a step forward.

Immediately, Spartan threw his head up and half reared. Amy stopped in her tracks, frozen by indecision.

Maybe, she thought, *if I just stand here, he'll calm down in a minute and let me get closer. But then, I might just make things worse.*

She waited, but Spartan didn't calm down. He paced from foot to foot, his head held high. After several long minutes, Amy fetched a chair from the tack room and placed it directly in front of the stall. Spartan moved ceaselessly, side to side, back and forth.

An hour passed. Amy stood up and tried to move the chair a little closer, but Spartan reared violently. Amy decided to give him a break — maybe she'd have more luck tomorrow. As she returned the chair to the tack room, she couldn't help worrying that she wouldn't have any luck at all. *Maybe I should just call Scott and tell him that this isn't going to work,* she thought. *But how can I, when he has so much faith in me?*

As she walked back to the stable block, Spartan was looking out over his door. She paused, downwind from him. He was looking out across the fields, unaware of her. His ears were pricked forward, and for one fleeting moment she saw the beautiful, intelligent horse that he had been before the accident.

Amy stepped forward. Spartan heard her footstep and swung his head around. His eyes fixed on her, and in that moment a terrible knowledge seemed to flow between them — a shared memory of that horrific night. With a snort, Spartan plunged back into his stall.

Amy stood rooted to the spot. Suddenly, she knew that she wasn't going to call Scott — she couldn't. Like it or not, she and Spartan were bound together. However much he hated her, she was the only one who could understand what he had been through. She was the only one who could make things OK again.

😘

That evening, while Amy and Lou were cleaning up after supper, the phone rang. Amy answered it and then handed it to Lou. "It's for you. It's Carl."

Lou took the phone eagerly. "Carl!"

Amy switched the TV on and collapsed into the easy

chair. In the background she heard Lou tell Carl everything that had been going on. After a bit there was a
pause. "Yes, I miss you, too," Lou said into the phone. "I
can't wait to see you again. Only two more days now."

Amy rolled her eyes.

Then Lou's tone changed slightly. "I can't come back
yet. You know I'm needed here, Carl." There was a
pause, and then her voice took on just the faintest tinge
of irritation. "I don't know when," she said. "Yes, I know
I said the end of the summer but . . ." She broke off. "Of
course, I want to be with you, but for now I have to stay
at Heartland." She looked around and saw Amy watching her. She lowered her voice. "Look, we can talk about
this when you get here."

Amy turned back to the television.

"How's Carl?" Grandpa asked as Lou put the phone
down.

"Fine, he's . . ."

"Hey, look! I don't believe it!" Amy sat up suddenly in
her chair, interrupting Lou. "There's a commercial for
Green Briar on TV!"

Green Briar was a large boarding and show-jumping
stable not far from Heartland. Val Grant, Green Briar's
owner, was standing in front a newly painted
eighteen-stall barn, smiling broadly at the camera.

Grandpa and Lou came over and stood behind the
easy chair.

"Want a perfect pony?" the voice-over on the TV asked as the camera shot changed to show a couple of beautiful ponies cantering around a course of jumps. "A pony that'll win you lots of ribbons?"

Amy scowled. She knew all about the forceful techniques that Val Grant used to make her ponies canter so correctly, heads poised, hooves snapping up precisely as they cleared a jump.

The camera zoomed in closer on one of the riders. "It's Ashley!" Amy exclaimed.

Ashley Grant was fifteen, and she and Amy were in the same class at high school. The large pony she was riding cantered smoothly toward a jump. Ashley's immaculate breeches clung to her slim legs, her sleek blond hair was pulled back neatly in a bun under her hunt cap, and her face was beautifully made up. Her pony jumped the fence perfectly, and she brought it to a halt and smiled straight into the camera.

"If you've ever dreamed of owning a perfect pony," the voice said as the camera cut to a shot of Val Grant petting a pony with a blue ribbon fluttering on his bridle, "then come to Green Briar. The place where dreams really *can* come true."

"Gross!" Amy exclaimed as the music faded out and the next commercial came on. She turned to Grandpa and Lou indignantly. "The whole thing's just aimed at people who want ribbon-winning, push-button ponies!"

Grandpa nodded in agreement, but Lou was looking at the TV thoughtfully. "You know, that's not a bad idea — making a commercial," she said. "Maybe we should consider it. Speaking of which . . ." She snapped off the TV. "Grandpa, Amy, it's time I told you about the plans I've been making for Heartland."

"Ah, yes, your plans to make us more profitable," Grandpa said, looking at the blank TV screen.

"Yes," Lou said briskly. "Now don't look at me like that, Amy," she said, seeing her sister's face cloud over. "When it comes to business, I know what I'm talking about. It's what I'm good at." She reached for a pile of papers. "First of all," she said, "it's obvious that we need better cash flow. Before the winter, the roof on the barn is going to need repairs and there'll be other expenses — blankets, extra hay, and straw. In addition, I feel that we need to maximize Heartland's potential."

"You sound like you're in a business meeting, Lou," Amy protested. "We're talking about Heartland — it's a horse sanctuary."

"But this place *is* a business." Before Amy had a chance to say anything more, Lou continued, "We have to think of it that way. Now, my first goal is to raise money for the winter. I thought that we could hold a barn dance."

"A barn dance?" Jack Bartlett questioned.

"Don't look like that, Grandpa," Lou chided. "A dance

is an ideal way to raise money. We can get a band, provide food and drinks, and then charge for the tickets and hold a raffle. This place is plenty big enough," she said.

"But who would come?" Amy blurted out.

"Mom's friends," Lou said. "It would be the ideal opportunity to invite them up here. I think they've been staying away to give us enough time. . . ." She trailed off for a moment. "It would be a way of breaking the ice — of showing them that we don't want them to stay away anymore. And it's a cause they'd support."

"But, Lou, are you sure it would work?" Jack Bartlett ran a hand through his hair. "It sounds expensive — a band, food, prizes for the raffle. How would we pay for all that?"

"Well, there would be the money from the tickets, and we could ask people to help out and donate things. Everyone has always been willing to help Heartland in the past, haven't they?" Grandpa nodded. "Well, they will again," Lou said. "The whole idea is that the event will cost us very little, but we'll make a substantial amount of money."

"What if people don't come?" Amy said. She was finding it hard to imagine their family's friends coming to a dance where they had to pay for tickets.

"But they will! It's for a good cause," Lou insisted. She looked around. "Well, what do you say?"

"OK, I guess," Grandpa said tentatively.

"Great!" Lou said. "I'll start organizing it — we'll aim to have it in two or three weeks. The sooner the better."

"Two weeks!" Amy said.

Lou waved a hand. "That gives me enough time, no problem. Carl will help out when he gets here. I'll start calling around right away."

Amy frowned. She didn't have a good feeling about this dance. It just didn't seem right to her.

Lou straightened her papers. Amy noticed that, for the first time in ages, she looked in her element — like she was excited and knew exactly what to do next. "Now let's look at some ways of increasing Heartland's profits. Obviously, the bulk of our income is from the paying horses — the nonresidents whose owners bring them here to have their problems solved. I think we need to market ourselves more effectively in order to get the maximum number of paying customers." She pulled out a piece of paper. "So, I propose that we have some sort of brochure that we can distribute in tack shops, to feed merchants — basically anywhere that horsey people go. Take a look at this outline."

Amy could see that the piece of paper she was holding was split into three sections. There was a column with the title HEARTLAND in big letters with suggestions for several photographs. The next column described Heartland's work, with quotes from a recent magazine article and AS RECOMMENDED BY NICK HALLIWELL in large letters across the top of it, and the final section detailed the services Heartland offered and the fees that were charged. Amy's heart sank. Lou just didn't understand what Heartland was about. Mom had never given estimates for how much treatments would cost! She had always had a flexible system for charging people, avoiding set fees because she believed that every horse was an individual and needed a different approach. A couple of lines on the page caught Amy's eye:

At Heartland we make a unique offer — for $50 we will assess your horse's needs and provide a detailed written evaluation.

"No," Amy said, shaking her head. "We can't do this." She pointed at the offending sentence.

"What's the matter?" Lou asked.

"We're not going to start evaluating horses and charging people for it. No way!"

"Why not?" Lou said. "It's perfectly normal. If you want someone to do some work for you, you have to get a quote first and then decide whether you want to pursue it."

"But how can we?" Amy exclaimed. "You can't tell

how long a horse is going to take to be cured until you start working with it — and even then you may have setbacks, or things might not go as planned. Mom *never* charged people until after treatment was complete."

"People expect a quote," Lou said. "It's a more professional approach."

"Well, I'm not doing it!" Amy interrupted. "I don't want to change things. Everything worked just fine for Mom."

"Everything could have worked *better*," Lou said. She shook her head, looking upset. "Amy, I'm only trying to help. We don't *have* to carry on doing things exactly the way Mom did. We can make changes to make things easier for ourselves."

"No, we can't!" Amy said, her voice rising as panic took hold of her. She didn't want any changes. She didn't even know how to give a quote before treatment. She wanted things to stay just the way Mom had left them. "You can forget it, Lou! Forget this whole stupid brochure idea!" She jumped to her feet.

"Come on, Amy," Grandpa suggested. "Sit down, and let's discuss it calmly."

"No!" Amy said. She stormed to the door and slammed it behind her.

Fighting a tide of anxiety, she hurried up to her bedroom. She couldn't let Lou change things! That just couldn't happen!

Opening her door, she immediately focused on the photograph of her mom on her dressing table. She walked over and picked it up. "Oh, Mom," she whispered desperately. "Why aren't you here?"

Chapter Four

The next morning the mood in the kitchen was tense. Amy had woken up with nightmares again. She felt groggy from the lack of sleep and depressed by the argument of the day before. She scowled at Lou as she sat down at the table.

"Can you pass the milk, please?" Lou asked.

Amy handed her the carton, banging it down on the table. She got up again, brushing past Lou to get to the teapot.

"Amy!" Lou said angrily as Amy knocked her arm.

"Oh, come on, you two," Jack Bartlett said with a sigh. "How about a compromise?" He paused. "We'll still consider the brochure idea, Lou, but maybe you can rework it and then discuss it again with Amy."

"But it doesn't need reworking, Grandpa!" Lou protested. "I really do think it's fine as it is . . ."

"Compromise," Grandpa said firmly.

"OK," Lou sighed. "I'll take another look at it." She looked at Amy. "But the dance *is* going ahead."

Grandpa nodded. "Yes. The dance can go ahead, and Amy and I will give you all the help you need." He threw Amy a warning glance as she opened her mouth to object. "Won't we, Amy?"

"I guess," she muttered.

"Good," said Grandpa with a smile. "Now can we just get along and be civilized with one another, *please*?"

℞

In the middle of the morning, Scott's old Cherokee came chugging up the drive. Amy hurried across the yard to meet him. "Hey," he said to her, getting out. "I was just passing and thought I'd stop by."

Lou was walking across the yard with an armful of fresh grass. She stopped and waited for them to catch up. "Hello, Scott."

Scott smiled, looking at the grass in her arms. "For Sugarfoot?"

"Yes," Lou said. "I gave him some yesterday, and he loved it. Do you want to see him?"

Scott joined her. As they walked toward the north

barn, Amy overheard Lou telling him about her plans for the barn dance.

"That sounds great!" Scott said, obviously impressed. "You can put me down for a ticket! I'll spread the word, too. After all, it's for a good cause."

"That's wonderful!" Lou said, her eyes shining. "Thanks, Scott."

Amy felt surprised — she wouldn't have thought Scott would be interested in something like a dance. Maybe she was just being unreasonable and it *was* a good idea after all. Yawning, she went into the tack room.

Ty was busy cleaning a bridle. He looked up as Amy grabbed a grooming bucket. "Who are you going to groom?"

"Spartan," Amy said.

"Are you sure?" Ty asked.

"It's now or never," Amy said resolutely.

She didn't even hesitate when she came to Spartan's stall. As she opened the door, he plunged forward. But Amy was quicker. She snatched his halter, quickly snapping a lead rope onto one of the rings. Feeling her hand near his face, Spartan panicked. He rose up on his back legs, and his front hooves came crashing down, but Amy held on, staying close beside him and moving her free hand to his head the second his hooves hit the ground. Eyes rolling, Spartan reluctantly submitted to the control of the halter and rope but he didn't relax.

"Easy now," Amy soothed, picking up a grooming brush.

Spartan started in alarm. His body language told her he didn't want her in his stall. He didn't want her holding his head, and he didn't want her trying to brush him. With determination, Amy lifted the brush to his coat. He flinched as if she had hit him.

Amy sighed. She knew she should keep trying to groom Spartan, be firm but kind with him, keep persisting, but she just couldn't bear to make him more nervous and afraid than he already was. She put the brush back in the bucket. Maybe she would just take him out to graze instead. That might help him feel more at home.

Keeping a watchful eye on him, she led him out of his stall and over to a large patch of grass in front of the house. He snorted, moving beside her with high, nervous steps. Amy stopped him where the grass was thickest, but he didn't lower his neck. Instead, he stood with every muscle tensed and his eyes fixed on her.

Ty came over.

"I was hoping he might relax and eat a little grass," Amy explained. "But it doesn't look like he's going to."

"Do you want me to hold him?" Ty offered.

"OK," Amy said.

Ty took the lead rope.

Once Spartan was satisfied that Amy was at a safe distance, he put his head down and jerkily started to snatch at the grass. Amy wiped the sweat off her forehead with the back of her hand.

Ty looked over. "Just give it time," he said quietly.

Amy nodded. Ty always seemed to understand how she was feeling when it came to horses. They worked really well together. Standing in silence, they watched Spartan graze.

After a while, Scott came around the barn with Lou. "How's Spartan doing?" he asked, looking at the bay horse.

Amy wondered what to say. How could she admit to Scott that she wasn't making any progress? What would he think? "He's OK," she said quickly.

"Good," Scott smiled. "Well, keep up the hard work."

As he turned and walked off toward his Cherokee, Amy caught Ty giving her a puzzled look, but to her relief he didn't say anything. She watched Scott drive away and then sighed. "I'd better put Spartan back in his stall now," she said. "We've still got a lot to do."

"Sure," Ty replied.

Amy took the lead rope from him, and Spartan pulled back in alarm. "Easy now," Amy soothed, but the horse threw his head up wildly. Amy moved in closer to him and tightened her grip. "Walk on," she said, clicking her tongue.

As Spartan reluctantly stepped forward beside her, Amy could sense fear pulsating through every muscle and nerve in his body.

Lou came over as Ty opened Spartan's stall door for Amy. "How is he?" she asked, looking apprehensively at the bay horse.

"Fine," Amy said curtly. She led Spartan into his stall and automatically unclipped his lead rope.

Free at last, he threw himself toward Amy, the full force of his body slamming into her and knocking her against the wall. She stumbled and heard Lou scream and Ty shout out her name as Spartan swung his hindquarters toward her. But Amy acted quickly. Scrambling to her feet, she flung herself toward his head, her fingers fumbling for the halter. Grasping the leather, she forced Spartan to lower his head and backed him into a corner until he was under control again. For a moment she stood there, clutching his halter, her heart pounding.

"Amy! Get out of the stall!" Lou cried.

Amy looked around to see Lou and Ty staring at her in shock.

Not wanting to turn her back on him, she led Spartan over to the door, only letting go of him when she could slip out safely. Then she let out a shaky breath.

Lou grabbed her by the shoulders. "Amy! What were you thinking? You could have been badly hurt."

"It was nothing." Amy pulled away, her hands still trembling slightly. She glanced back at the stall, not wanting either of them to blame Spartan. "It was stupid of me. I should never have unclipped his lead like that."

"But he tried to kick you!" Lou exclaimed.

"But he didn't," Amy protested. She shook her head, angry at herself. "I should have been more careful."

"More careful!" Lou exclaimed. "That horse is dangerous, Amy! He might need to be put down."

"What?" Amy gasped.

"He's not safe," Lou stated emphatically.

Anger surged through Amy. "What would you know?" she cried, drawing herself up. "You're an expert all of a sudden, are you?" She saw Lou's face stiffen but was too upset to stop herself. "You don't know what you're talking about, Lou! You don't know what he's been through," she shouted. "Just stay out of it!"

Lou went pale and then turned swiftly away.

There was a moment's pause, then Ty cleared his throat. "Amy, I hate to say it, but she has a point."

Amy swung around. "She shouldn't have said that!"

"She's just concerned about you," Ty said. "I am, too. I've never seen a horse turn on anyone like that."

Amy felt her cheeks flame with guilt and humiliation.

"You're not making things any better." Amy dropped her eyes to the ground and sighed. "Just keep out of it, Ty," she said under her breath.

"OK," Ty said shortly. "If that's how you feel, you're on your own." He turned and walked off.

As Amy watched him disappear out of sight, her temper suddenly faded as quickly as it had flared up. "*Great,*" she muttered, throwing down the lead rope. "Just great!"

From the end of the row of stalls there was a snort. Amy looked around and saw Pegasus watching her. "Oh, Pegasus," she groaned, walking over. Pegasus nuzzled her hair. Amy stroked his neck and felt her flurry of emotions gradually ebb. She sighed. She knew what she had to do.

Taking a deep breath, she walked across the yard. Ty was sweeping the aisle near the muck heap. Hearing her footsteps, he glanced up. But when he saw it was Amy, he concentrated on his sweeping again.

"I'm sorry, Ty," Amy said.

Ty leaned on the yard broom and looked at her.

"I shouldn't have said those things," Amy continued. "I — I just lost it."

"It's OK," Ty said with a shrug.

"It's not," Amy said quickly. "I didn't mean them." She rubbed her forehead. "Everything's just getting to me. I haven't been sleeping well. I'm sorry, Ty — really I am."

Ty's face softened. "Look, forget it."

Amy breathed a sigh of relief. She hated it when Ty was mad at her. "Thanks," she said gratefully.

He picked up the broom again. "So are you going to apologize to Lou?"

"After she said those things about Spartan?" Amy protested. "She doesn't know what she's talking about."

Ty shrugged. "Maybe not." He glanced up. "But she does care about you, and that's why she said those things, Amy."

"I don't think so!" she said, reading his expression. "I am *not* going to apologize to her." She saw Ty's eyebrows raise. "I don't want her to think putting Spartan down is even an option!"

Chapter Five

As the hours passed, Amy began to feel guilty about the way she had treated Lou — but she still couldn't bring herself to apologize. Every time she thought about Spartan being put down she felt like she wanted to be sick.

Amy avoided going into the farmhouse all day until she couldn't put it off any longer. She said good night to the horses and walked reluctantly to the back door.

Lou was setting the table.

As Amy walked in and their eyes met, she turned away and kicked off her sneakers. She waited for her sister to tell her to put them away, but Lou didn't say a word.

Amy poured some juice from the refrigerator and glanced across at Lou, who was placing the three sets of knives and forks down, each metal piece making a dull thud against the table. Her face was pale, her mouth rigid.

Amy suddenly couldn't bear the atmosphere any longer. "Lou . . ."

Lou looked up at her.

"I shouldn't have said those things," Amy said quickly. "I'm sorry. I didn't mean to hurt you."

Lou's face softened. "Oh, Amy," she said, stepping forward. "I was just so worried about you —"

Lou broke off quickly as Jack Bartlett came into the kitchen.

"Hi, honey," he said to Amy. Then he frowned. "I hear you had a bit of a problem with Spartan today."

Amy's eyes shot to Lou, who looked away — her cheeks flushing.

"Amy?" her grandpa prompted.

"Well, not really," Amy lied desperately, her mind racing. Why had Lou told Grandpa? If he thought Spartan was dangerous he would stop her from working with him. "He was kind of excitable," she said quickly. "But nothing really bad."

"He tried to attack you, Amy!" Lou said.

"He did not!" Amy exclaimed. "You're exaggerating!"

"You know I'm not!" Lou yelled back at her.

"That's enough!" Grandpa shouted, slamming his fist down on the kitchen table.

Amy and Lou glared at each other.

Jack looked from one granddaughter to the other. "If he's that dangerous, Amy . . ."

"He isn't!" Amy interrupted. "Grandpa, he just needs help!"

Her grandpa looked at her for a moment as if he was going to say something, and then to Amy's relief he let the matter drop and turned to deal with the stew bubbling on the top of the stove. Amy scowled at Lou and stomped past her to go get changed.

❧

The next morning, when Amy came downstairs, Lou was busy making out an invitation list for the dance.

"Morning, Grandpa," Amy yawned, shaking out a couple of aspirin from a bottle in the cabinet. She had been awake since four o'clock, and her head throbbed.

"Are you OK?" Jack asked, looking at her in concern.

Amy nodded.

Lou looked up from her notepad. "We need to decide on the food for the dance," she declared. "I thought we might have a barbecue. Then all we need to do is get a load of steaks, some chicken, and some corn on the cob, and that's most of the food done. What do you think?"

"Sounds great," Grandpa said. He turned. "What do you think, Amy?"

Amy shrugged. "Whatever."

"That leaves the desserts." Lou looked straight at Amy.

"But I won't bother telling you about those. You don't seem to be the least bit interested in trying to save Heartland."

"Stop it!" Grandpa said. "This arguing has gone on long enough." He looked from one to the other. "Now, listen. I know you both are under a huge amount of pressure, but I don't want you taking it out on each other. You are both too important to me. How about we take a trip to the movies on Sunday? It would do us all some good to get out for the day, and I'd like to see you two enjoy being together for a change. What do you say?"

"Sure," Amy shrugged.

"Fine," Lou said flippantly. "Carl might still be here, so he can come, too."

"Oh, great," Amy muttered under her breath.

Lou looked at her sharply. "What?"

Amy caught Grandpa's warning look. "Nothing," she sighed. She walked to the door. "I'm going to feed the horses."

✌

Right after breakfast, Lou set off to pick up Carl from the airport. After finishing the stalls with Ty, Amy went to see Spartan. She was attempting to groom him when a shadow fell across the door. Amy turned around.

Her grandpa was standing there. "Hey," he said.

"Hi," Amy said, her heart sinking. She was worried that Spartan might act up in front of her grandpa.

To her horror, he unbolted the door and came in. Spartan instinctively shrank back.

"It's OK," Amy murmured, stroking his neck.

But Spartan lashed out with his front hoof. The whites of his eyes flashed as he looked from Amy to her grandfather and back to her.

"Why did he do that?" Grandpa asked with a frown.

"He doesn't like me touching him," Amy said quietly.

Jack shook his head, looking at Spartan's flattened ears and rolling eyes. "I don't have a good feeling about him, Amy."

"He'll be fine," Amy insisted. "He's just traumatized. I'm going to help him. I'm going to make him better."

Her grandpa sighed. "Amy, honey, not every horse can be helped, even your mom used to admit that," he said, coming up close. "Sometimes, as hard as it is, it's best to just accept that there isn't — "

"No," Amy interrupted him, not wanting to hear what she knew he was going to say. She took a step toward her grandfather, preparing to plead her case. But with Amy's back turned, Spartan suddenly jerked his neck upward. Amy jumped away as she saw his head swing around. But Grandpa didn't react so fast. Spartan's teeth sank into his bare arm.

Amy's grandfather let out a yell of pain. Slowed by

shock, Amy grabbed at Spartan's halter, but it was too late.

"My arm!" Grandpa exclaimed. Spartan's teeth had left an ugly red welt on the skin.

"Grandpa, I'm sorry!" Amy gasped. Her eyes shot to Spartan. He was standing, unrepentant, with his ears still back. She followed her grandpa as he hurriedly let himself out of the stall. "It was a mistake," she said, her eyes filling with tears. "He didn't mean it." Behind her, Spartan's hooves crashed into the wall of his stall. "Please, Grandpa, he really didn't. He's just afraid."

But Jack Bartlett was silent as he strode down to the house, holding his arm. In the kitchen, Amy watched as he opened the first aid kit and cleansed the bite. She felt horribly guilty. "I'll get some arnica cream," she offered, desperate to find something she could do to help. "It will help reduce the bruising."

Amy hurried to the main barn and searched the cabinet in the feed room where all the natural remedies were kept. She returned to the house with the cream.

Grandpa applied it to his arm. His face was serious. As he screwed the top back on the jar he looked directly at Amy, speaking quietly but firmly. "This is a problem, Amy. He's going to really hurt somebody one of these days."

Amy swallowed. "He won't, Grandpa. He's going to get better. He just needs more time."

"I'd like to believe you, but I can't." Grandpa sighed. "I think . . ." But before he could say what he thought there was the sound of a car stopping outside the house.

Amy looked out of the window. "It's Lou and Carl!" Relief flooded through her as the car doors opened. She knew their arrival would distract Grandpa for the meantime.

"We'll talk about this later," Grandpa said, heading toward the door.

Carl was standing by the car looking around, his dark hair immaculate, his eyes hidden by designer sunglasses. To Amy's surprise he was wearing jeans, a leather belt with a big buckle, and sturdy boots. For some reason she had expected him to be wearing a suit like the one she had seen him in before. She took a longer look at his clothes — they looked new and expensive, but he'd obviously made an effort to dress casually.

Lou came around the front of the car. "You remember Grandpa and Amy, don't you, Carl?" she said happily.

"Of course I do." Carl smiled at Amy and then stepped forward holding out his hand to Grandpa. "Pleased to meet you again, Jack."

"Did you have a good flight?" Jack Bartlett asked.

Carl nodded. "Not bad." He looked around. "This place is great."

Jack smiled. "Well, we like it. Why don't you bring your stuff in, and Lou can show you around."

"Yeah, sure." Pulling out a green-and-tan overnight bag from the back of the car, he slung it over his shoulder and followed Grandpa and Lou into the house.

Amy didn't go with them. She was feeling confused. Carl actually seemed pretty nice. It wasn't how she remembered him at all. She walked up to Pegasus's box and stroked him thoughtfully.

After a bit, Carl and Lou came out of the house. "This is Pegasus," Lou said as they got close. "He was Daddy's horse. He was one of the top show jumpers in the world . . . before the accident." Carl stepped toward the horse. "He can be a bit nervous around strangers," Lou warned quickly. "You should be careful how you approach him."

Carl laughed confidently. "I know how to approach a horse. I used to spend hours playing with my cousin's pony when we were kids. Hello, big fella!" he said, his hand reaching out to pat Pegasus firmly on the forehead. "How you doing?"

Alarmed by the sudden movement around his head, Pegasus shot backward into his stall with a snort.

"Hey!" Carl exclaimed, looking startled.

Amy frowned. "You need to be a little more gentle when you approach a horse for the first time. Some of the horses here have been through a lot and are very skittish," Amy tried to explain politely.

"All I did was pet him," Carl said defensively. "That horse is just bad-tempered."

How would you like it if a stranger marched up to you and slapped you between the eyes? Amy wanted to ask Carl, but she held back.

Carl turned to Lou. "So, what can I do to help out? How about I give that horse a good brushing — he looks dirty." He walked toward Spartan. "Hi there, boy!"

Spartan snaked his head forward.

"I think we'll leave Spartan alone," Lou said, grabbing Carl's arm and steering him away. "But there's a pony in the other barn that I want you to meet."

"Take me to him," Carl said. "Just tell me how I can help."

Lou looked at Amy. "We'll do that, OK? We'll be up with Sugarfoot."

Amy nodded. As she watched them walk up the yard toward the back barn, she heard Carl say, "Oh, boy, this takes me back." She frowned to herself. Carl obviously didn't know anything about horses, so why was he pretending he did?

❧

That afternoon, Matt called. "Hi. How are you doing?"

"OK," Amy told him. "Carl's here."

"Oh, how's that going?" Matt asked.

Amy frowned. "I'm not sure. He really doesn't know anything about horses, but he's acting like he does. I think he's just trying to impress Lou."

"What's wrong with that?" Matt said, sounding mystified.

"I don't know . . ." Amy struggled to explain. "It's just that he's sort of trying too hard."

"Yeah," Matt said, not sounding like he understood. He paused. "Do you want to go and see a movie this week?"

Amy sighed. "I can't. It's really busy around this place with Carl here and Lou trying to get everything ready for the dance. Carl's taking us out for dinner tonight. But why don't you come by sometime?"

"Sure, OK," Matt said. "I'll see you soon."

As Amy put the phone down, the kitchen door opened. Lou and Carl came in, hand in hand. "Hi!" Lou said, her eyes shining. "I was hoping you'd be here. Carl's had some great ideas to make Heartland more profitable."

"What kind of ideas?" Amy said.

Carl sat down. "Just ways to help this place make money." He put his arms around Lou's waist and pulled her close.

Lou giggled and, bending down, kissed the top of his head. "It's great to have you here," she said to him.

Amy made a face and headed toward the door.

"Don't you want to hear what we have to say?" Lou

said, sounding hurt. "We thought that there could be an adopt-a-horse campaign. You know, people pay a certain amount and get a photo of a horse and a newsletter?"

Almost immediately, Amy shook her head. "It wouldn't work. We rehome all the horses we can. We don't have enough permanent residents for something like that."

"Oh," Lou said, the sparkle fading from her eyes.

"I mean, it's a good idea, but just not for us. I'm going back out to the yard, OK?" Amy said quickly, turning away to avoid any further discussion.

✇

Over dinner in the restaurant, Lou and Carl told Grandpa and Amy about the other ideas they had come up with. Jack listened and nodded while Amy felt the tension rising inside her, but she tried to suppress it. Lou was obviously really happy having Carl around, and Amy didn't want to ruin the evening. She was even beginning to think that maybe she should try to like Carl for Lou's sake. But when Lou explained Carl's suggestion of limiting the number of stalls kept for rescue horses to five, and using all the other stalls for horses whose owners paid to have them cured, Amy couldn't restrain herself any longer.

"What?" she exclaimed loudly. Some of the other people in the restaurant looked over. Amy lowered her voice. "What are you thinking, Lou?"

"It makes sense," Lou said. "The paying horses would

support the cost of looking after the rescued horses, and we'd make a profit."

"We're not reducing the number of rescue horses!" Amy said. "In fact, we're not making any changes." Her throat felt tight. She thought about her mom's devotion to saving horses and how that was always her first priority. "Everything's got to stay just as Mom left it. No changes." Her head was aching. She saw Grandpa staring at her. He looked like he was about to say something. "No changes!" she repeated. Suddenly, she couldn't bear to be at the table any longer. She got to her feet and hurried to the rest room. She was relieved it was empty.

Amy looked at herself in the mirror. Her face was pale, her gray eyes were ringed with purple shadows from lack of sleep. Thoughts whirled around in her head — Lou and Carl, Spartan, changes to Heartland, Mom . . .

Shutting her eyes, she leaned her forehead against the cold mirror, desperately wishing she could be somewhere — anywhere — else.

✦

As always, the nightmares came back that night. The creaking of the trees and the rain, the wind and the thunder ringing in her ears, and the sight of the tree steadily falling. When Amy switched on the light it was three thirty in the morning. She sat up, waiting for the feeling of panic to subside.

Taking a deep breath, she picked up a magazine from the floor. Pulling the blankets around her, she started leafing through it. She had been reading for about half an hour when her bedroom door creaked open. She glanced up. Grandpa was standing in the doorway, looking concerned.

"Amy?" he said in a low voice. "It's four o'clock in the morning. What's your light doing on?"

"I — I couldn't sleep," she said.

His face softened, and he came and sat down beside her. "Did you have that nightmare again?"

Amy nodded.

Jack looked at her for a moment and then stroked her hair. "Nighttime is always the worst, even without the dreams, isn't it?" he said softly. "I have nights when I lie awake wondering why I didn't stop you and your mom from going out in that storm. Those moments of that day just keep repeating in my mind."

Amy stared at him in surprise. "But it wasn't *your* fault, Grandpa!"

"I know," he said. "Deep down, I know that *nothing* could have stopped your mom going out that night once she'd decided to — just as nothing could have made her go if she didn't want to. But grief's like that." His eyes searched Amy's. "You always feel you could have done more. You always blame yourself."

Amy swallowed as Grandpa leaned over and hugged her. "It *will* get easier in time, honey," he said. "I promise you it will." He cradled her in his arms, rocking her back and forth.

Amy shut her eyes tightly. Her throat ached with unshed tears. *Was he right?* She knew he had no reason to blame himself, but did she? She had pleaded with Mom to go out that night. She wanted to save Spartan. But her grandpa's words ran around in her head: *Nothing could have made your mom go if she didn't want to.* She wished desperately that she could believe those words, *really* believe them.

🙠

Although Carl had only planned to come for an overnight visit, he decided to stay the following day as well. By the evening, Amy was longing for him to go. As far as she was concerned, his interest in everything about Heartland was obviously just an act. Amy couldn't believe that Lou didn't see through it, but Lou seemed oblivious; she was delighted to have someone around who would take her ideas seriously for a change.

When Amy came in from finishing with the horses for the night she found Carl and Lou in the kitchen, dressed up as if ready to go out. "Put your shoes away," Lou automatically reminded her.

Stubbornly, Amy kicked her sneakers into a corner. She was tired and didn't want to hear Lou's nagging. "We need some more feed, Lou," she said abruptly.

"I've ordered some," Lou said. "It's arriving on Monday."

Amy looked at her in surprise. "But McCullochs doesn't deliver on Monday."

"We're not using McCullochs anymore," Lou said. "They're really expensive. Carl and I were looking into it this afternoon. Rathmores makes an alfalfa cube for half the price, so I think it's best to use them in the future."

Amy stared at her in disbelief. "You what?" she asked.

"I decided that we should use Rathmores," Lou repeated. "They're delivering on Monday."

"It's a good idea," Carl said. "It'll be more economical."

"No, it won't!" Amy exclaimed. "You'll have to cancel the order, Lou. Rathmores' food is second-rate. Mom always made a big deal about it. We'd have to use twice as much of their feed! We won't save money, and the horses' health will suffer because their food isn't as high a quality. Not to mention the problems it would cause for the horses that have trouble digesting. They'll be far more likely to colic and to have allergic reactions. It's just not good feed."

"I had no idea," Lou said, her face suddenly falling.

"I would have told you if you had asked," Amy said in frustration.

"It seemed like such a good idea," Lou said defensively. "Anyway, you never have the time to listen to me, Amy! You just go on about how things can't change."

"Can't you can see why?" Amy exploded. "There's too much to do around here, and you can't even help by doing something as easy as ordering feed!"

❧

A little later, she heard the sound of the back door opening and, looking out of her bedroom window, saw Lou and Carl walking toward Lou's car. They were laughing together. Amy suddenly realized that she hadn't seen Lou laugh like that in ages. Doubt flickered in her mind. Was she wrong to dislike Carl so much? He obviously made Lou happy.

Amy struggled with her thoughts as she watched them get into the car. She wanted Lou to be happy, but she just couldn't repress the uncomfortable feelings she had about Carl. And she couldn't stop herself from yelling at Lou whenever she tried to change Heartland. She sighed. Maybe she should make more of an effort. After all, she wanted Lou to stay at Heartland more than just about anything. Even if she had to learn to compromise — even if she had to be nicer to Carl. She sighed again. It would not be easy, but she'd have to try.

❧

The next morning, Amy was drinking hot chocolate with Grandpa when Lou came down for breakfast alone.

"Hi," Amy greeted her sister, remembering the decision she had made the night before.

Lou smiled faintly.

"Did you have a good time last night?" Jack asked.

"Yes, thank you," Lou said, her voice subdued.

Jack looked closely at her. "Lou? Is there something the matter?"

"No," Lou replied. She sat down at the table and started fiddling with a pen, turning it around and around in her fingers. "Well, not *exactly*." She suddenly put the pen down and, taking a deep breath, looked at them both. "I guess you might as well know. Carl has been offered a new job in Chicago, and he's asked me to go with him."

Amy stared at her in astonishment. "But you're not going to, are you? Chicago's so far away!"

Lou didn't say anything.

"Lou?" Grandpa said.

"I've told him I'll think about it," Lou replied at last. "But I think — I think I might say yes."

Chapter Six

Amy followed Lou up to the feed room. Despite all their arguments she really wanted Lou to stay at Heartland. They had spent so much of their lives apart, since Lou had decided to stay at her English boarding school when Amy and her mom had moved to Virginia to live with Grandpa. Amy felt that she was just starting to get to know her older sister, and she didn't want her to leave.

"You're not really going to go to Chicago, are you?" she asked. "What would you do there?"

"I'd get a job," Lou said, setting out the feed buckets. "I might even be able to transfer with my present company."

"But you'd go there just to be with Carl?" Amy questioned.

"Yes." Lou looked suddenly serious. "I would."

"It's so far away," Amy stammered. "Please don't go, Lou. Stay here with us."

Lou straightened up, her blue eyes angry. "What would be the point?" she snapped. "You've made it perfectly clear that you don't want my help around here."

Amy felt torn. She didn't like the changes that Lou kept suggesting for Heartland, but she desperately wanted her sister to stay. "I do. I —"

"Stop it, Amy!" Lou interrupted bitterly. "I know what you think. Don't try and pretend otherwise."

"But, Lou . . ."

"I don't want to talk about it!" Lou raised her voice. "And that's the end of the discussion!" Banging the buckets down on to the floor, she turned and walked out of the feed room.

‒

After breakfast, Carl and Lou got ready to leave for the airport. "Thank you for having me," Carl said, shaking hands with Grandpa. "It's been great." He turned to Amy and winked. "See you later."

"Bye," Amy said curtly. She wished he had never come. If it wasn't for him, Lou wouldn't be thinking about going away.

Lou tucked her arm through his. "Come on, we don't

want you to miss your plane." She turned to Grandpa. "I'll be back by lunchtime."

"Remember we're all going to the movies this afternoon," he reminded her.

Lou nodded.

"Wish I could stay," Carl said. "But work calls."

Thank goodness! Amy thought to herself.

After Carl and Lou had driven off, Amy went to Spartan's stall. She had decided to take him out to graze again.

Spartan's eyes rolled angrily, and he pawed the ground as she led him out of his stall. His ears were back, but Amy barely noticed. She couldn't stop thinking about Lou going to Chicago. Reaching the patch of grass, lost in her own world, she forgot she was leading Spartan and loosened her grip on the lead rope.

Moving like a striking snake, Spartan pulled backward, half rearing as he jerked his head up and out of her reach. The rope slipped through Amy's hands, burning her skin as it went. She staggered back in surprise. "Spartan!" she gasped.

The horse swung around beside her, his heavy shoulder colliding with her and knocking her off balance. Amy felt herself falling and reached out too late. Her head crashed against a wooden fence post. Then she slid to the ground and lay there, dazed.

In front of her, Spartan rose up on his hind legs, his dark eyes glistened, and he shrieked savagely as his front legs thrashed out. Amy looked up and saw his flailing hooves above her. She screamed and closed her eyes.

"Stop it!" Jack Bartlett's voice shouted. Amy's eyes flew open. Red in the face and out of breath, her grandfather was grasping the end of the lead rope, frantically trying to pull the horse away. Distracted, Spartan shook his head wildly and turned to face Jack. Amy scrambled to her feet and, ignoring the wave of dizziness that swept over her, she flung herself at Spartan's head.

Spartan plunged backward at the touch of her hands on his halter, but she held on desperately. "Steady!" she cried. At last Spartan came to a stop, and he stood snorting, his body trembling with rage as he stared at her.

"Amy!" Grandpa exclaimed. "Are you OK?"

Amy nodded, not taking her eyes off Spartan for a second. "I'll put him back in his stall," she said. Not waiting for permission, she led Spartan toward the barn. Her legs felt weak with shock.

Quickly she put him in his stall and slipped out just in time before his hooves crashed defiantly into the wooden door.

The next moment Grandpa was beside her, his arms wrapping tightly around her. "Amy!" he exclaimed. "I thought he was going to kill you. I really did."

In the warmth and safety of his arms, the adrenaline left her and Amy's knees gave way. Grandpa supported her and helped her to the house. Then he gently checked her head. "You'll have a lump there in the morning, but I think it should be OK." He took her hand, his blue eyes shadowed with fear and relief. "When I looked out of the window and saw him knock you over, I could hardly watch. It was like my worst nightmare had come true."

"Thank goodness you were watching," Amy said with a cold shiver running down her spine at the thought of what might have happened if Grandpa hadn't been there.

Jack Bartlett stroked her hair. "That horse is vicious, Amy. I know it's hard, but we're going to have to put him down."

Amy stared at him. "Grandpa! We can't do that to him."

"Amy," her grandpa started, his voice firmer than she had ever heard it, "a horse like Spartan will never be cured. I know it's hard to accept, but he's just one of those horses that Heartland can't help. We need to talk to Scott." Amy opened her mouth to argue. But Grandpa wouldn't let her speak. "I'm sorry, but I'm not going to change my mind." He squeezed her shoulder. "You are far more precious to me than any horse."

Amy's voice rose desperately. "But, Grandpa . . ."

"No, Amy," Grandpa said sadly. "No buts. Not this time." He sighed. "Now, I think you should go lie down and rest for a while."

Amy walked numbly up the stairs. Pulling off her jeans, she got into bed. She couldn't stand by and watch Spartan be put down. She had to give him one more chance.

Then it came to her. *Join up!* She hadn't tried it before because she had been worried about what Spartan would do — but this was her last chance. It was *his* last chance. By joining up with him she might be able to win back his trust. Hope rushed through her. Spartan might try to escape, but it was a risk she was prepared to take if there was a chance that his life might be saved.

She sat up in bed. When could she do it? It had to be a time when no one was around. Grandpa would never let her anywhere near Spartan again.

Just then, there was a knock on her bedroom door, and her grandpa came in. "How are you feeling?" he asked.

"My head hurts a bit still," Amy replied. "But I'm OK."

"Looks like we shouldn't go to the movies this afternoon," Grandpa said.

The movies! Amy had forgotten about going to the movies. A plan quickly formed in her mind. Putting a hand to her head, she lay back down. "Well, my head hurts too much to go, but you should go with Lou," she said. "You could still go. I'll be fine here."

Grandpa shook his head. "I can't leave you after a knock like that."

"I'll phone Matt. He'll come over," Amy said.

Grandpa didn't look convinced.

"It would be good for you and Lou to spend the time together," Amy said. "You could talk to her about going to Chicago. She'll probably open up more if I'm not there." Amy looked at Grandpa. "You don't want her to go, do you?"

"Of course I don't, but it's up to her." Grandpa seemed lost in thought for a moment.

"If you don't let her know how much we need her, she'll never stay," Amy pleaded.

"It would be good to have a chance to talk with her, find out what's she's thinking." Grandpa stood up. "We'll see how you're feeling in a couple of hours."

By the afternoon, Amy had finally managed to convince Grandpa and Lou that she was quite happy to be left on her own. She'd given Matt a call. "I'll be fine," she said when Grandpa came to her room after lunch. "I called Matt," she said, but she didn't mention that Matt had been out playing basketball and that she'd told his mom that he didn't need to call back.

"OK," Grandpa said. "But we won't be long. Promise me you'll rest."

"I promise," Amy said.

Grandpa frowned. "Maybe we should wait for Matt to get here."

"No!" Amy said quickly. She saw his look of surprise. "If you don't leave now, you'll miss the movie."

"I guess you're right," Grandpa said reluctantly. He bent down and kissed her. "You take care."

Amy nodded and faked a yawn. "I think I'll go to sleep for a while."

Grandpa looked relieved. "Good girl. See you later."

Amy lay in her bed and listened to his footsteps going downstairs and then to the sounds of Grandpa and Lou getting into the car and the engine starting. Getting out of bed, she crept to the window and watched them driving off.

She waited a few minutes to make sure they were safely gone and then pulled on her jeans and ran down the stairs and out of the house. It was quiet in the yard. The air felt heavy and still and the horses were barely shifting in their stalls. In the distance, dark clouds were gathering. Amy felt sure a storm was brewing.

She fetched a longline from the tack room and then, with her heart thudding in her chest, she approached Spartan's stall. The quietness on the yard was so unusual that, for a moment, Amy felt a flicker of loneliness. She felt as though she was completely on her own. Alone with Spartan. She took a deep breath. It was the way it had to be.

She opened the stall door. Spartan leaped backward, his muscles gathered under his bay coat, his neck high. Adrenaline coursing through her, Amy slipped inside. "Easy, boy," she said.

Spartan snorted, the sound reverberating in the still air. Talking all the while, Amy approached him. The horse's hindquarters swung around, but Amy moved quickly, closing in on his head and taking hold of his halter before he could kick out. "Oh, Spartan," she said in desperation. "You don't need to be afraid of me."

Taking another deep breath, Amy clipped the longline to the halter and led him out. He pranced angrily beside her. A heavy drop of rain fell on Amy's arm and then another, but she ignored them. Rain or no rain, she only had this one chance with Spartan. In a couple of hours Grandpa and Lou would be back and her chance would be gone.

She led Spartan into the ring, securing the gate behind her. As she took him into the middle, she looked anxiously at the fence. It wasn't very high, just over four feet. He could probably clear it easily. Her fingers hesitated by the clip of the longline. What if he escaped? But what choice did she have? With one swift move she unhooked the line. It was a risk she would just have to take. She stepped back.

Spartan jerked his head and stopped, a look of surprise on his face. Realizing that he was free, he let out a wild snort and tossed his head in the air, wheeling around on his back legs. Then to Amy's horror he set off straight toward the fence.

"Stop!" she shouted, running after him.

Spartan jerked to a halt, his front feet stamping into the sand. He spun around and looked at her. Amy stopped in her tracks. She was caught in the savage glare of his eyes. For the first time *ever* in her life she realized that she felt afraid of a horse. And she was suddenly aware of how horribly vulnerable she was with only the longline in her hand. She took an uncertain step backward. There was a sudden roll of thunder, and with a screaming cry Spartan plunged toward her.

As he thundered over the sand, Amy's fear suddenly disappeared, drowned in the wave of blind fury that swept over her. How *dare* he attack her! After she had defended him, cared for him, believed in him! With every bit of strength in her body she flung the longline toward him. "*No!*" she shouted, almost incoherent with rage.

Startled by the flying rope, Spartan swerved and galloped past her. Amy grabbed the rope from the ground. "You can't blame me!" she screamed. "It wasn't my fault!" Stopping abruptly, Spartan turned and reared, his eyes gleaming with fury. His front legs flailed in the air. Amy slashed the rope toward him again. "It wasn't my fault!" she screamed, advancing on him. "It wasn't my fault!"

With a sudden snort of alarm Spartan came down and galloped away from her. There was a loud crash as a second clap of thunder burst overhead. The rain started to beat down with a new intensity, but Amy barely noticed it. Picking up the rope, she flung it after Spartan. "Go on!" she shouted. "Go on! Get away!"

Wherever he went she followed with the rope. White-hot anger coursed through her. Overhead a jagged fork of lightning blazed down through the sky. Water streamed down Amy's face, her tears mingling with the pouring rain. On and on Spartan galloped, his coat streaked with sweat and rain as she forced him on through the crashing of the storm.

She had no idea how long she drove him around the ring. But after many, many circles the rage seemed to start leaving Spartan's eyes. Amy saw his gallop steady and his inside ear flicker toward her. A shock ran through her. It was the *first signal* of a join up! Spartan's wild circles, his attempts to escape from her had led to the first stage of a join up. There was no mistaking it — his inside ear was fixed on her, his gallop was slowing to a steady canter.

Gasping for breath and soaked to the skin, she acted instinctively. She squared her shoulders with his and stepped slightly into his path. He picked up on the cue and turned. He started around in the opposite direction, his eyes fixed on her.

More circles. She hardly noticed that the thunder had passed. She wasn't satisfied yet. His acceptance of her had to be absolute. They had to have an understanding. And then it happened; he started to chew. Stretching his head down until his muzzle was almost on the ground, he trotted in circles, his mouth chewing at the air, his neck stretched long and low.

Amy took a step back and turned her body away, dropping her eyes to the ground. From the corner of her eye she could see Spartan stop. He looked at her. His ears pricked. There was a long pause. She blocked out the thought of what Spartan had done the last time she'd turned her back to him. She heard him take a step and chills ran down the back of her neck, but she forced herself to stay still, with her eyes looking down. The breath rasped in her throat, her heart pounded. What if he decided to attack her again? He was close now, getting closer. She could hear his hooves thudding softly into the wet sand, hear his heavy breathing.

Suddenly, she felt warm breath on the back of her neck, a muzzle on her shoulder. Hardly daring to breathe, she turned slowly around. Spartan stood there. His sides were heaving, his coat was streaked with rain and sweat, but the fire and fear had left his eyes. Very gently, Amy reached out and rubbed his face. For the first time since coming to Heartland, Spartan accepted her touch.

Amy felt her eyes filling with tears, and she suddenly realized it had stopped raining. Tears of relief and joy washed away the weeks of unrelenting guilt. "Spartan," she whispered. She caught the sob that rose in her throat. "It wasn't my fault," she whispered, leaning her head against his wet neck. "It really wasn't my fault."

As the tears on her face dripped onto Spartan's steaming neck, she suddenly knew that it was true — she wasn't to blame for the accident. As Grandpa had said, her mom would never have gone out that night if she hadn't wanted to. Fresh tears sprang to Amy's eyes, tears that welled from the very depth of her heart — tears of grief and loss, no longer held back by the crushing weight of guilt. Wrapping her arms around Spartan's neck, she sobbed into his mane and took comfort in their new understanding.

At long last her sobs softened and Spartan's breathing slowed. Amy drew back and realized that the clouds were parting. The sun was shining through, making the leaves on the trees surrounding the schooling ring shimmer and glow.

A new determination filled her, hot and fierce. She would never be able to bring her mom back, but she could help Spartan. She kissed him on the neck. "I promise I'll make you better, Spartan," she whispered as he turned and focused on her. "I promise." As she looked into his dark eyes, she knew that her mom would have approved. She knew her mom would have done the same thing.

Amy slowly led Spartan back to his stall where she fetched a hay net and rubbed him down. As she rubbed his back with the cloth she suddenly paused. Right by his withers he seemed to have a patch of white hairs coming through. It was the first time she had been close enough to see. She examined the area closely, parting the hair with her fingers. Her eyes widened. It was an old freeze mark. The fur over the freeze mark had been dyed brown to match his coat, but now the white hair was growing out. Amy thought that the people who had stolen him must have dyed the hair so Spartan couldn't be traced. Amy looked more closely. It was impossible to read the letters with the two colors of hair, but maybe if the area was clipped the letters would become more visible. Excitement surged through Amy. Maybe she could find Spartan's old owners. Maybe he could be reunited with them and lead a normal life again.

She finished rubbing him down and then sank into some straw by the feed bin. Spartan was pulling happily at the sweet-smelling hay. Amy watched him, marveling at the change in his eyes and demeanor. Relaxed and peaceful, he munched on his hay, occasionally swishing his tail.

He could do with a good brushing, Amy thought, but then she yawned, too exhausted to move. She could do it later. Leaning her head back, she closed her eyes. *Just two minutes' rest,* she thought. Her eyelashes flickered on her cheeks. Within seconds she was fast asleep.

Chapter Seven

"Amy! Oh, my God!"

Amy woke up with a jump at the sound of Lou's voice. Confused, she blinked and looked up.

Lou was staring down at her, her face pale. "Grandpa! Quick!" she shouted over her shoulder. "Amy's collapsed in Spartan's stall!"

"No, I'm OK," Amy said hastily, scrambling to her feet. "I just fell asleep."

Jack Bartlett came hurrying up to the door. "What on earth are you doing in there?" he demanded.

Amy saw the fear on his face. "I'm OK," she repeated. She hastened to explain. "Spartan's better." She moved toward the horse.

"Amy! Come out of there at once," Lou said, her voice piercing.

"No. Look!" Amy put her hand gently on Spartan's shoulder, hoping he would respond positively — that the join up really had been a success. He turned his head to her inquiringly. Amy was relieved to see that his eyes were calm. She moved around to the front of him and rubbed his forehead. "See," she said, turning to Grandpa and Lou, who were watching, openmouthed.

"What's happened to him?" Lou gasped.

"I joined up with him, and now he trusts me." As she spoke, Amy realized how inadequate the words seemed. She could never fully convey the experience she remembered — the explosion of fury and guilt, the anger, the fear. All mirrored in the violent storm that had reminded her of the night of the accident. She had never experienced anything like it and, amazing as it had been, she hoped to never have to go through anything like it again.

Lou and Grandpa looked at her with disbelief, but the evidence was there for them to see. As Amy stroked him, Spartan stood, gentle as little Sugarfoot.

Grandpa opened the stall door. "Amy Fleming," he said, running a despairing hand through his hair, "I didn't want you ever to go near Spartan again."

"I know. I'm sorry," Amy said. She grinned at him. "But aren't you glad I did?" She came out of the stall. "You know Mom would have done the same thing, Grandpa."

Jack Bartlett looked at her for a moment and then

swept her into his arms. "Yes, honey," he said, kissing her hair. "I know she would."

❧

Amy called Scott to let him know about the breakthrough and about the freeze mark she had found on Spartan's back. And then for the first time in a long time, she slept peacefully through the night.

Amy got up early the next morning. The sun was shining in through her window. Pulling on her clothes, she went outside.

The trees on the ridges of the hills that rose behind Heartland stood out dark green against the pale blue of the sky. She looked around, breathing in deeply, enjoying the cool of the morning air. She felt wonderfully refreshed and determined in her resolve to do everything she could to help Spartan.

As soon as Ty arrived she filled him in on the events of the day before and took him to see Spartan.

"I thought if we clipped the hair, the freeze mark might show up more clearly," she said.

"I'll get the clippers," Ty agreed. When he came back Spartan was nuzzling at Amy's shoulder. He shook his head. "I'm going to take days off more often!" he joked. "He's a different horse."

Amy patted Spartan. "He's not. He's just back to being the horse he was."

"Thanks to you," Ty said. "You believed in him, Amy. He wouldn't have had a chance without you."

Amy felt her cheeks turn pink.

Spartan moved beside them. "Well . . . I guess we'd better get this clipping done," Ty said, his voice suddenly brisk.

Amy moved to the side of Spartan's head. "Easy now," she murmured to the horse as Ty switched the clippers on. Spartan flinched but settled down as Amy stroked him.

It only took a minute. "All done," Ty said, turning the clippers off.

Amy looked eagerly at the rectangle of clipped hair. Six white numbers stood out clearly against Spartan's bay coat.

Ty pulled a pen and a piece of paper out of his pocket. He scribbled down the numbers. "Now all we need to do is call and ask Scott to have the number traced."

"I wonder what Spartan's owners are like," Amy said.

"I guess we'll find out," Ty said.

Amy took the piece of paper with the number on it and went down to the house to use the phone in the kitchen. She called Scott, and he explained how he'd make some calls to try to trace Spartan's owner. "Although," he warned her, "sometimes they don't have up-to-date information. I'll see what I can find out."

As Amy put the phone down she realized Lou had overheard the conversation.

"I hope he can find them," Lou said. "Especially now that you've cured him."

"Well, *started* curing him," Amy corrected her. She knew that Spartan wasn't completely better yet. He needed to build up his confidence with everyone. She was about to end the conversation and then hesitated. All their disagreements suddenly seemed so pointless. "So what are you up to?"

"Just running through the list of things that I still have to organize for this dance," Lou replied.

"Is there anything I can do to help?" Amy asked.

Lou looked up, her blue eyes showing her surprise. "But you think the whole thing's a stupid idea," she said. "Why would you want to help?"

Amy's cheeks flushed. "I don't think it's stupid. Well, maybe I did at first," she admitted, seeing Lou's expression. "But people want to come, and I . . . I hope it works." She smiled at Lou, suddenly realizing how much she meant it.

❧

After Amy did her chores and worked with Raisin for a while, she devoted the next couple of hours to bonding further with Spartan. She took him out in the circular ring and joined up with him again and then spent an hour grooming him, trying to brush out the dirt and grease that had built up in his coat over the past few weeks. Finally, she massaged diluted lavender oil around his nostrils to help soothe and relax him.

Ty looked over the door as she was finishing. "Lavender," he said, sniffing the air. "That's a good idea."

Amy nodded. "Can you think of anything else that might be helpful? He's been through so much, I want to help him feel really comfortable."

"How about some walnut-flower remedy?" Ty said. "Your mom used to use it on horses that were getting used to new situations. You could also give him a tablespoon of honey in his feed."

"Yeah," Amy said, pleased with the idea. She knew that honey was excellent for channeling energy. Her mom had said that it sometimes made difficult horses more manageable. It energized them and also made them willing to please.

Just then there was the sound of a car coming up the drive. "It's Matt and Scott," Ty said.

Amy came out of the stall.

"Hi!" she called as the Jeep came to a halt and Matt and Scott jumped out.

"Hi, Amy," Scott called. "Hi, Ty."

"Hey, guys," Ty said.

"That's great news about Spartan!" Matt said to Amy as they reached the stall. "Scott told me. You must be really happy."

"Spartan's like a different horse," Ty said. "You should see how he is with Amy."

Scott watched as Amy went into the stall and patted Spartan. She even picked his hooves. "You've had a real breakthrough," he said. "Well done!"

Amy's eyes sparkled as she came over to the door. "It was all because I joined up with him. I probably should have tried it sooner."

"Have you heard any news from the freeze-mark agency or from Spartan's owner?" Amy asked.

"Not yet," Scott replied. "If they make a match, they'll contact the owner."

"Bet you can't wait to hear," Matt said. "Then Spartan can go back to his real home."

"I guess," Amy said. She tried to sound more positive. "Yeah. It will be good."

"But it will be hard to say good-bye after all this, huh?" Scott said, looking sympathetically at her.

Amy nodded and caught Ty's eye. "Very."

"So you *don't* want him to go?" Matt said, sounding confused. "But I thought you wanted his owners to get in touch."

"I did — I do," Amy said. She saw the confusion on Matt's face. It was obvious he didn't understand. She sighed, wishing, not for the first time, that Matt understood her feelings about horses in the way Scott and Ty did. Maybe then, imagining him as a boyfriend wouldn't be so hard.

♌

After lunch, as Amy came out of the house, she heard a low whinny. She looked at the front stable block, expecting to see Pegasus's head over his stall door, but it wasn't Pegasus, it was Spartan. He whickered again. Amy smiled. "Hi there, boy." She walked over and stroked his face.

As she played with the whiskers on his lower lip, she thought about how she was going to rehabilitate him. Amy knew it wasn't enough for him simply to trust her — he had to learn to have confidence in other people as well. She would have to get as many people as possible to handle him — Grandpa, Lou, Ty, and Scott when he came by.

She smoothed his long forelock. And what about riding him? A thrill ran through her at the thought. When should she try that? She decided to ask Ty what he thought.

She found him filling the evening hay nets from the small stock of hay in the feed room. "Hi," he said, looking up as she came in.

"I was thinking," Amy blurted out her question, "when do you think I should try riding Spartan?" She felt the breath catch in her throat, anticipating Ty's answer. She respected his opinion and knew that as much as she wanted to ride Spartan, if Ty told her to wait a month then she would.

Ty shrugged. "The end of the week?" he suggested.

"That soon?" Amy said.

"Sure." Ty nodded. "If he continues to improve, then why put it off? It should help his confidence. You'll be able to take him out and see how he deals with new experiences."

Excitement flooded through Amy. The end of the week! She couldn't wait!

Over the next few days, Amy spent as much time as she could with Spartan, handling him, grooming him, lunging him, and getting other people to come into his stall and handle him, too. Gradually, the lingering nervousness started to leave his eyes. However, a certain reserve seemed to remain. Amy was puzzled by it. Spartan was affectionate and his confidence seemed to grow every day, but it was as if he was holding something back. Wondering whether she was imagining it all, she didn't mention it to anyone, and no one else — not even Ty — seemed to notice.

On Friday morning, she was grooming Spartan when

Ty looked over the door. "Thought any more about riding him?" he asked.

"Yeah, like always," Amy said. "I can't wait."

"So why not today?" Ty said.

"Today?" Amy said, her heart leaping with excitement. "You think he's ready?"

"Yeah," Ty replied. "Do you want me to get a saddle and bridle?"

Amy nodded eagerly. Her fingers trembled with anticipation as she quickly finished grooming Spartan. Thoughts whirled through her brain. She was going to get to ride Spartan! What would he be like? He looked fantastic to ride. Her heart raced as she remembered that she knew nothing about him before the accident. He might not even have been ridden before. He might throw her off. She ran her fingers through Spartan's mane and kissed his neck. She didn't care. She just wanted to try.

When Ty returned with the tack, Spartan sniffed at the bridle curiously but didn't seem to object when Amy took it and slipped it on over his head.

"Now for the saddle," she said, trying to keep her voice calm, although her stomach was fluttering nervously. Spartan's reaction to the saddle would give them a good indication if he had been ridden before. But he stood still as she placed the saddle and pad on his back and tightened the girth.

"So far, so good," Ty said, glancing at her. "He wouldn't be this calm if he hadn't been ridden before."

Amy nodded in relief. "Now, I've just got to get on."

"I'd lunge him first," Ty said. "Just to get him used to moving with the saddle and bridle on and give him a chance to get rid of some energy."

They led Spartan up to the training ring, and Amy started to lunge him. He bucked once as he first moved into a trot but then settled into a steady rhythm. After five minutes Amy brought him to a halt and looked at Ty.

"Here goes," she said, pulling the stirrups down.

Ty moved to Spartan's head and held the reins while Amy mounted. She felt Spartan move nervously as she sank lightly down into the saddle, but she patted his neck and soothed him until he settled.

Amy picked up his reins and gently squeezed with her legs. Spartan walked forward. He felt calm and relaxed, and after a few laps around the ring, Amy started to relax, too. She shortened her reins and squeezed him into a trot. With his long stride he seemed to float across the sand.

"He's perfect!" she said as she passed Ty.

After a while, Amy asked Spartan to canter, and he made the transition smoothly. She cantered three circles, grinning with delight. Riding Spartan was just as fantastic as she had imagined.

At last she drew him to a halt. "Wow!" she gasped,

patting his warm bay neck and smiling at Ty in delight. "He's the best!"

"He looked great," Ty said.

Amy took her feet out of the stirrups and dismounted. "I'd better make that do for today," she said.

"Something tells me you'll be riding him again tomorrow," Ty said with a grin.

"I think you might be right." She smiled back.

Ty opened the gate, and Amy led Spartan down the yard. Just as she finished cooling him, the phone rang. Leaving the tack outside the stall, Amy ran to the house. She reached the phone just before Lou, who had come in from collecting vegetables from the back garden.

"Heartland," Amy said breathlessly. "Amy Fleming speaking."

"Hi." The man's voice was deep. "My name's Larry Boswell. I've been contacted by the freeze-mark agency. I believe you are boarding a horse of mine — a bay with a white star. He was stolen a few months ago."

It was Spartan's owner!

"Hello . . . are you there?" the man said.

"Yes — yes, I am," Amy said quickly.

"And do you have my horse?" the man inquired.

"Yes," Amy said, her stomach seeming to flip over. "We do."

Chapter Eight

"That's fantastic news!" Larry Boswell said. "I can't believe you found him!" Amy could hear the emotion in his voice. "I never thought I'd see him again. He was stolen just over two months ago. How long have you had him?"

"Almost two weeks," Amy said. "But he was at the local vet's for six weeks before that."

"The vet's?"

Amy explained about the accident, and Larry Boswell listened intently. When she had finished, he whistled. "That's awful. I'm really sorry to hear about your mom. I can't thank you enough for taking Gerry in after all you've been through."

"Gerry?" Amy echoed.

"That's his name. Short for Geronimo. Full name Dancing Grass Geronimo," Larry Boswell told her. "He's

one of my best stallions. I have a stud farm — I breed
Morgans. Now, when would it be suitable for me to
come over and pick him up? My farm's about two hours
away."

Pick him up. Amy's mouth felt suddenly dry. "Well . . .
er . . . whenever you like," she stammered. After all she
had been through with Spartan the thought of losing
him was hard to grasp. *But you wanted to find his owners,*
she reminded herself. *You wanted Spartan to be happy.*

"Great!" said Larry Boswell. "I'll be over this afternoon, about three o'clock. Can you give me some directions?"

By the time she put the phone down, Amy was feeling
stunned. For a moment she was unable to move.

"What's wrong?" Lou asked.

"Spartan's owner is coming to collect him today."

"But that's great!" Lou exclaimed. She saw Amy's face
and frowned uncertainly. "Isn't it?"

Tears prickled at the back of Amy's eyes. She nodded.

"You're going to miss him, aren't you?" Lou said
softly.

Amy swallowed.

Lou put her arm around her. "It's the right thing,
Amy. He couldn't stay here. At least this way he'll go to
people he knows and who love him."

Amy knew she was right. Horses came to Heartland
to be healed so they could then go to new homes or back

to their owners. It was a rule their mom had insisted upon and Amy had grown up with. But somehow with Spartan it was different.

"I don't want him to go," she whispered.

"I know you don't," Lou said, hugging her. "But it's for the best. You know it is. We can't keep him here if he has the chance of a happy life with someone else."

Amy fought back her tears and nodded reluctantly.

❧

From two thirty on, Amy waited in the kitchen with Lou and Ty, watching the drive.

"What did he sound like?" Ty asked Amy.

"OK, I guess," she replied, pacing back and forth.

"It'll be fine," Lou said. "You'll see. Stop worrying." She looked down the drive. "Here's Scott."

Amy had been in touch with the vet soon after speaking to Larry Boswell to tell him the news.

Scott parked his Cherokee and came into the house. "Not here yet?"

Amy shook her head.

Ten minutes later, a pickup pulling a trailer came up the drive. "It's him!" Amy exclaimed, her stomach turning with anticipation.

The pickup stopped. A short, husky man with gray hair got out. "Hi," he said, as they came out of the farmhouse to meet him. "I'm Larry Boswell."

Lou took charge of the situation and introduced everyone. Larry shook hands. "I can't tell you how pleased I am." He looked at Amy. "Like I said on the phone, I own a stud farm — but Gerry, he's always been real special to me. "I hand-reared him as a foal." His eyes scanned the stalls eagerly. "Where is he?"

Amy swallowed. "I'll get him," she said.

Spartan was in his stall. As Amy entered, he pricked his ears and nickered a welcome. Amy thought he looked beautiful. He still had some scars — they would stay with him forever — but his bay coat gleamed, his tail hung below his hocks, soft and silky, and the star on his forehead stood out, snowy white. "Oh, Spartan," she whispered, her heart aching. "It's time to say good-bye."

As she untied the rope he nuzzled affectionately against her. Giving him a kiss, Amy led him out of the stall.

Larry Boswell was looking around eagerly. "Gerry!" he exclaimed as soon as he saw him.

Spartan stopped dead at the sound of Larry Boswell's voice. His head flew up. His ears pricked. A shrill whinny burst from him, and he plunged in the direction of Larry, pulling the lead rope right out of Amy's hands. The horse trotted over and stopped in front of his owner.

"Hey, Gerry, Gerry boy," Larry Boswell murmured, stroking the horse's ears and neck and face. "I never thought I'd see you again."

Amy stood, astonished, rooted to the spot where

Spartan had left her. She watched as the horse nuzzled Larry Boswell ecstatically. There was no mistaking the connection between the two.

Larry Boswell gently examined the scars along Spartan's side. "You're not going to be winning much in the showring from now on, are you, buddy?" he said ruefully, but then he patted the horse. "We'll have to leave winning those ribbons to your foals."

"Foals?" Amy said, eagerly stepping forward. "He's got foals?"

"Not yet," Larry Boswell said. "I'd just used him for conformation classes until he was stolen. But I'll put him to stud when I get him home. He should breed some good stock."

Amy's eyes widened. Larry Boswell obviously hadn't realized that Spartan had been gelded. "Um . . ." she said, glancing quickly at Scott for support. "You won't be able to use him for breeding."

Larry frowned. "Why not?"

Scott stepped forward. "He's been gelded, I'm afraid."

"What?" Larry replied in genuine astonishment.

Scott nodded. "It's the policy here at Heartland. Until last week there was no way of seeing his freeze mark or even knowing for sure that he had been stolen. It was assumed that he would be rehomed, so he had to be gelded."

"What!" Mr. Boswell exclaimed incredulously. "This horse is," he corrected himself, "*was* a valuable breeding animal." He glared at Amy. "How could you do this? He was my most valuable stallion."

"We had no idea," Amy stammered, taken aback by his sudden anger.

Larry Boswell's voice rose. "He's got some of the best bloodlines in my stock. His foals would have brought thousands of dollars!"

"I'm sorry," Amy said, feeling close to tears. "I really am, I —"

"You'll be hearing from my lawyers about this!" Larry shouted.

Lou stepped forward. "Now, Mr. Boswell, please . . ."

But he ignored her. Letting go of Spartan, he pushed past Amy and Lou and headed toward his car. Ty grabbed Spartan, who had tried to follow him.

"Mr. Boswell —" Lou cried. "What about your horse?"

"This horse here doesn't resemble any horse that I know!" Larry Boswell shouted.

Scott stepped out in front of the angry man. "I think you should consider carefully what you are saying, Mr. Boswell," he said, his voice calm but full of authority. Mr. Boswell pulled up short. There was no way he could push Scott's tall, broad-shouldered frame out of the way. "Amy and her family took in your horse," Scott continued, looking around at Amy and Lou. "Despite their own tragic loss, they looked after him, made every effort to trace you. In my opinion you should be thanking them, not threatening them with legal action."

"Yes — but —" Larry blustered, his face flushing a deep red.

"Thanks to them you still have a horse," Scott said firmly. "Believe me, Mr. Boswell, you have *every* reason to be grateful."

For a moment, Larry looked as if he was going to argue further, but then his shoulders suddenly seemed to sag. "You're right," he muttered.

Amy felt the breath leave her in a rush. She met Lou's eyes and saw her relief.

Larry shook his head. "I guess you did what you had to, and I appreciate all the heartbreak that you've been through on his behalf." He glanced at Spartan. "But Gerry being gelded changes everything."

Amy was astonished. "Why?"

Larry Boswell shrugged. "What use would he be? I have a business to run. I can't have a horse that won't pay it's way."

Amy couldn't believe what she was hearing. "But you can't just leave him here!" she exclaimed.

"Well, I'm not going to take him back with me," Larry said. "I'll pay your expenses for keeping him until you find him a new home. But that's the best I can offer."

Amy looked at Spartan who was now shaking his

head, trying to pull away from Ty. Spartan loved his owner — that was completely clear. Although she didn't want to have to say good-bye to him, she knew that he belonged with Larry Boswell.

She stepped toward him. "Take Spartan with you," she pleaded.

But Larry Boswell shook his head. "Sorry, young lady. That's the way it has to be." He walked slowly toward Spartan. "You know the rules, Gerry," he said softly. "I can't break them, not even for you." He reached up and gently stroked the horse's forehead. "No, not even for you." He turned to Amy. "I'll send you the ownership papers," he said. "Bill me for the boarding fees." Squaring his shoulders, he strode back to his car.

As Larry drove away, Spartan let out a high-pitched whinny and pulled forward. "Easy boy," Ty said hastily.

Amy looked at the distress on Spartan's face and had to fight back the tears welling in her eyes. She couldn't suppress a feeling of dislike for Larry Boswell. How could he do this to Spartan?

"Don't worry," Lou said calmly, her expression full of sympathy. "We'll find another home for him. You'll see."

"But he wants to be with his owner!" Amy cried.

"No, Lou's right, Amy," Scott said quickly. "There'll be other people who will want to give him a home. He's a fine horse."

Ty nodded in agreement and clicked his tongue. "Come on, fella, let's put you back in your stall."

As they followed Spartan to the barn, Lou looked gratefully at Scott. "Thanks for standing up to Mr. Boswell for us. I don't know what we'd have done if he had gone ahead and sued."

"He wouldn't have gotten anywhere," Scott said.

"Thanks anyway," Lou said. She patted Spartan's back as he went into his stall. "I'm just glad he's getting better." She turned to Scott. "I wanted to ask you about Sugarfoot. Would it be OK to put him out to graze in the field now? I've been cutting him fresh grass each day, but it's not really the same."

"Turning him out for a few hours each day should be fine," Scott said. "As long as the weather's good, of course. I'll just give him a quick checkup."

Scott grabbed his bag from the car and then went to Sugarfoot's stall with Amy and Lou. Sugarfoot was happily nibbling on the remains of grass that Lou had cut for him at lunchtime.

"How are you doing, boy?" Scott said to him, patting the Shetland's neck. He listened to Sugarfoot's heart and checked his breathing. "He's making fine progress," he said to Lou.

"Do you hear that, Sugarfoot? You're ready to go out in the paddock," Lou said. She turned to Amy. "Should we turn him out now? It's such a nice day."

"That would be great," Amy said, her heart lifting a little.

Lou put Sugarfoot's halter on and then led the Shetland out to the pasture just behind the back barn. The grass was lush, rich with clover, and dotted randomly with bright yellow buttercups. Sugarfoot's small ears pricked eagerly.

Amy opened the gate. The little pony trotted into the field, and putting his head down, he snorted.

"Look at him!" Lou said.

Suddenly, Sugarfoot sank down to his knees and rolled, sending two white butterflies fluttering up into the air. He jumped to his feet, shook, and then plunged his head down into the sweet grass and started to graze.

Lou smiled. "Isn't it incredible to see him like this?"

Amy nodded. She could vividly remember the shock of seeing Sugarfoot only a couple of weeks ago. Then he had been lying in his stall, breathing faintly, too weak to stand, half starved but too unhappy to eat. Now, here he was, grazing in the field. "It's so wonderful to see him happy again," she said.

"I know," said Lou, her eyes glowing. "I can't believe the change in him. There's nothing like seeing a sick animal recover. It's just such a good feeling!"

"I second that," Scott said softly.

"Better than clinching a deal at the bank?" Amy teased her as they started walking back to the house.

"Yes!" Lou said. "A million times better!"

Amy was surprised to see a black convertible Saab parked outside the farmhouse. The driver's door swung open as they approached.

"Carl!" Lou gasped. "What are you doing here?"

Chapter Nine

Carl stepped out of the car. "Well, that's a nice greet-ing," he said with a laugh.

Lou hurried forward. "You weren't supposed to be coming until tomorrow!"

"I took the day off." Carl put his arms around her. "I couldn't bear to be away from you another minute."

Lou pulled back. "Carl, this is Scott Trewin," she said, looking from one to the other, "our local vet. Scott, this is Carl Anderson."

Carl offered his hand to Scott. "Pleased to meet you."

Scott shook his hand. "Likewise," he said, but Amy noticed that his voice was cool. He turned to her. "I bet-ter go."

"Sure. Thanks for coming," she replied.

"Bye, Scott! Thanks again," Lou called after him.

Scott drove off in a cloud of exhaust fumes with the doors of his Cherokee rattling as usual.

Carl raised his eyebrows. "I would have thought a vet could afford an upgrade on that old Jeep model."

Before Amy could say anything, Lou leaped to Scott's defense. "Come on, Carl. Scott's a brilliant vet!" she said sharply. "Who cares if he doesn't have the newest Range Rover?"

Amy looked at her sister in surprise. It wasn't like Lou to sound so intense. Even though Lou had said it with a smile, she could tell her sister was serious.

As they went into the house, Lou started to tell Carl about Sugarfoot. "He's so much better," she said. "We just turned him out in the paddock, and it was so won-derful, he looked so happy!"

"Great," Carl said, sounding rather bored. He dumped his bag on the floor. "Any chance of a drink?"

Amy saw Lou's face fall in disappointment. He wasn't showing any interest in what she was saying to him. "Yeah, sure," Lou said flatly, and headed for the refrig-erator.

❧

Leaving Lou and Carl in the house, Amy went back outside. She was sweeping the yard in front of the stable block and thinking about what they could do to find Spar-tan a home when Lou and Carl came out. The horses

were all looking out over their stall doors. Lou walked
over to Spartan and offered him a mint. But the bay
horse ignored her as he stared down the drive, his ears
pricked, his head up.

Lou stroked his neck. "Poor thing," she murmured.
"Don't worry, we'll find you another home soon."

"You really think so?" Carl said. He scowled. "With
those scars?"

Amy stopped brushing and glared at him. "Some
people care about more than appearance!" she replied.

Carl frowned in genuine astonishment. "You mean
there are actually people who wouldn't mind?"

"Of course there are!" Amy said hotly.

Lou stepped in hastily. "I guess the most important
thing is that we find him the *right* home." She turned and
began to walk along the row of horses, feeding them
mints.

Carl followed her. "So how about Chicago?" he said,
putting his arm around her. "Have you decided yet?"

Amy looked up. To her relief she saw that Lou was
shaking her head. "No, not yet."

"I don't understand what the holdup is," Carl said.

"It's a big decision to make, Carl," Lou replied. "If I go
to Chicago, I'll be leaving everything here."

"Oh, come on, Lou," Carl said. "You can't seriously
want to go on playing country girl forever."

"Why not?" Lou said rather crossly.

"You love the city — you're great there," Carl replied.

"Don't try to tell me what I am!" Lou said.

Carl immediately backed off. "I'm sorry."

"Good," Lou said sharply. "Because I'm not going to be forced into anything. Going to Chicago is a decision I have to make on my own."

"I understand," Carl said. "You know I do, and I'd never interfere. I respect you far too much for that."

Lou looked slightly reassured and didn't seem to object when Carl slipped his arm around her shoulder again. "It's only because I want you to be with me so much," he said in a soft voice.

Amy didn't want to hear any more. She headed toward the paddock to get Sundance for a ride.

&

The next morning, Amy decided to ride Spartan again. He was just as good in the training ring as he had been the day before, so she decided to take him out on the trails behind the pasture.

Spartan jogged excitedly as they rode along the path behind Heartland and up the hillside. It was a warm day, and Amy chose a shady trail. The sun slanted down between the canopy of leaves, casting shadows on the sandy ground. Spartan pricked his ears as he stepped among the trees. Amy could feel him start to tense up. She patted him and he flinched. "What's the matter?" she said. "It's OK."

Spartan walked cautiously on, his nostrils blowing, his neck outstretched. As they rounded the corner the trees thickened, blocking out the sun overhead. Spartan stopped and stared. Amy felt her stomach turn as she saw the canopy of trees. The sight of the path covered by the lush limbs of the trees brought a tidal wave of emotion over her as memories of the night of the accident flooded back.

Spartan sensed her fear and stepped backward, his hoof landing on a dry branch that broke with a resounding crack. With a terrified snort, Spartan reared high into the air.

"Spartan!" Amy gasped, throwing herself forward just in time. Spartan's front legs thrashed out, his eyes wide with fear. He landed on all four feet but in an instant was up in the air again, higher this time, so high he seemed on the point of crashing over backward. Losing her stirrup, Amy let go of the reins and hung on to Spartan's mane. He stayed balanced there for what seemed to Amy like an eternity and then came down and set off at a wild gallop along the path.

Amy clutched his mane desperately, grabbing for the reins, trying to get her stirrup back. "Spartan! Whoa!" she cried. But by now the horse was in a blind panic. He swerved around a corner and into a clearing.

Amy lurched in the saddle, but the tight turn simultaneously swung the reins toward her. She grabbed them and threw her weight backward, pulling hard. "Steady! Steady, boy!"

Spartan came to a halt, his sides heaving and his neck damp with sweat. Amy petted him. Her hands were trembling. What had she just done? In one unthinking moment, had she just wrecked all her good work with Spartan? She glanced back at the tunnel of trees. Suddenly, she was gripped with Spartan's fear. She wanted to get away, as far away as possible, from the memory of that awful night.

Be calm. Amy suddenly heard her mom's voice clear in her mind. *To be the horse's strength,* the voice whispered, *you must control your own fear.*

Amy took a deep breath. Her hands stopped shaking.

"You're all right, boy," she said to Spartan, her voice steady apart from a slight tremor. "What was all that about?"

Spartan's ears flickered. It took immense resolve, but Amy knew what she had to do. She shortened her reins and turned him back toward the trees. "Don't be scared," she said. "Nothing's going to happen to you."

She knew that Spartan couldn't understand her words, but she hoped that the tone of her voice would reassure him. She also knew that she had to get him back through the tunnel of trees or else his fear would grow and grow. "Walk on," she commanded.

Spartan hesitated.

"Walk on!" Amy said more firmly, nudging him with her heel.

This time Spartan did as she directed. He took a step forward and then another. Forcing down her own fear, Amy patted his neck as he walked cautiously through the canopy of trees. "Good boy!" she praised, patting him.

At last they were out on the other side. It was then and only then that Amy allowed herself to dismount. She leaned against Spartan, her legs feeling weak with relief. She had done it — they had made it through. He nuzzled her, his eyes calm again.

"Oh, Spartan," she said, patting him. He put his head down to graze. Amy sighed. No matter how much he had come along, there was such a long way to go before he would be ready to be rehomed. And then they had to find someone who would fully understand him.

She picked up the reins. "Come on, boy," she said, shaking her head. "Let's go home."

As she rode into the yard, Ty was coming out of Pegasus's stall. "How was he?" he asked.

"Not so good," Amy replied. She was about to explain what had happened when the kitchen door opened and Lou came hurrying out.

"Amy!" She looked very excited. "I'm so glad you're back!"

"Why? What's the matter?" Amy said.

"The most amazing thing has just happened!" Lou said. "I've just had a call from a father looking for a horse for his thirteen-year-old daughter. She sounds absolutely ideal!"

"Ideal for what?" Amy said in confusion.

Lou's eyes glowed. "For *Spartan*, of course! They read about us in a magazine and were delighted when I said we had a horse ready for rehoming!"

Amy stared at Lou. "You're not serious?"

"But they sound perfect." Lou looked at her in confusion. "I thought you'd be pleased. I thought you wanted to find Spartan a good home, and you said he's wonderful to ride."

"Not yet!" Amy exclaimed. "He's nowhere near ready. He still needs to build his trust in me and other people. You'll just have to call them back and tell them that he's not available."

"But they'll have already left. I told them they could come and see him right away. I thought it would be fine. They're even bringing their trailer."

"Lou!" Amy said incredulously. "How could you? Why didn't you check with me first?"

Lou looked like she didn't know what to say. "I'm — I'm sorry," she stammered. "But you weren't here — I thought you'd be pleased."

"That's great!" Amy said. "Just great!" She shook

her head. "Well, they can't have him. *You* can tell them that when they arrive!" Grabbing Spartan's reins, she marched into his stall.

"Amy! Wait!" Ty said, following her.

"What?" Amy said.

"Maybe it's not as bad as it sounds. Maybe they'd be willing to wait until he's ready. You should at least talk to them."

Amy frowned at him. "You mean, you think I should let them see Spartan?"

"Yeah. Why not?" Ty said.

Spartan nuzzled Amy's hand. She patted him. "But he needs a really special home," she said quietly.

"You're right — but maybe this is the one," Ty said.

Amy had a gut feeling that it wouldn't be, but she gave in. "OK," she said. "I guess they can have a look at him."

🙠

The more Amy heard about the Satchwells from Lou, the more her reservations grew.

"Mr. Satchwell said that Melanie, his daughter, has been riding for three years," Lou explained as they waited for them to arrive after lunch. "She's just outgrown her old pony, and they want a horse that she can take to the local shows."

"They sound ideal," said Carl, who was waiting with them.

"They don't sound very experienced," Amy objected. "Where would they keep him?"

"At their boarding stable and riding school."

"But that would be all wrong for Spartan!" Amy exclaimed. "He needs a quiet home."

"Amy, it's OK — just give them a chance," Ty said in a reassuring voice.

Just then, a gleaming white BMW pulling a top-of-the-line trailer came slowly up the drive. The Satchwells got out.

"Max Satchwell," the father said, striding over toward Lou with his hand outstretched. "Pleased to meet you."

Lou introduced herself, Amy, Carl, and Ty.

"I'm Nancy," said Mrs. Satchwell, stepping gingerly over the gravel in her red open-toed sandals. "And this is Melanie, our daughter."

Amy looked Melanie Satchwell up and down. She was a couple of years younger than Amy, dressed in spotless breeches and tall black riding boots. She had red hair with tight curls. "Hi," she said brightly to Amy. "I read about you in a magazine. My friends couldn't believe it when I said I was coming here! They were *so* jealous!"

"Ever since she saw the article, Melanie's been wanting a horse from here," Max Satchwell said, smiling fondly at his daughter. "Haven't you, pumpkin?"

Melanie ignored her father and looked around impatiently. "Can I see the horse?" she said eagerly.

"He's over there," Amy said, pointing to where Spartan was looking out over his stall door.

"The bay with the star?" Melanie said. Amy nodded. "Wow! He's gorgeous!" Before Amy could stop her, Melanie had started running toward Spartan's door. Spartan snorted in alarm and shot backward into his stall. "He doesn't seem very friendly," Melanie exclaimed, stopping dead and looking surprised.

"It's because you were running!" Amy tried to explain. "He's a rescue horse. He's nervous. You need to be careful."

Melanie looked embarrassed. "I'm sorry. Piper doesn't mind me running. He isn't nervous about anything."

"Well, Spartan is," Amy said, a little too sharply. "He's been through a lot."

Melanie looked over the door. "He's got a lot of scars," she said. For a moment Amy wondered if it would stop her wanting him, but her hopes were dashed — Melanie turned around with a determined look on her face. "I want him, Daddy."

Max Satchwell reached in his pocket and got out his checkbook. He grinned at Lou. "Melanie always knows what she wants," he said. "Lucky we brought the trailer with us, eh? Now, you told me that you ask for a donation to Heartland. What sort of figure are we talking about?"

Amy couldn't stand it any longer. If Lou wouldn't say

anything, then she would. "You can't have him today!" she burst out. "He isn't ready yet . . ."

Max interrupted her. "Not ready?" He looked swiftly at Lou. "But you told me on the telephone that this horse needed a new home."

Lou flushed. "I'm sorry — it seems I spoke too soon."

Carl cut in smoothly. "It was a slight misunderstanding. However, if your daughter likes the horse, a deposit will secure him for her, Mr. Satchwell."

Amy stared at him in outrage. How *dare* he say that a deposit would secure Spartan! She swung around to Lou only to find that Lou was looking just as angry.

"A deposit will not secure him," Lou said in a controlled voice. "Spartan will only go when we are sure he's cured and that we've found him the right home." She turned to Mr. Satchwell and to Amy's astonishment apologized. "I am sorry, truly I am, that I didn't explain things fully on the telephone. But we have a policy of selecting new homes for our horses very, very carefully. People cannot just come and choose a horse, particularly a horse like Spartan who has been so badly traumatized. He needs a home with an experienced rider."

Max Satchwell looked outraged. "You mean you're not going to let my daughter have this horse?"

Lou shook her head. "No, I'm afraid not." She smiled quickly at Amy and then turned to Melanie, her eyes sympathetic. "Please try to understand, Melanie. We don't mean to be unfair. It's just that I don't think Spartan would be the right horse for you. We do have other horses you might be interested in though. There's —"

"You've already wasted enough of my time, Ms. Fleming," Max interrupted. "We'll be leaving right away!"

"Hold on, Daddy!" Melanie exclaimed suddenly. "I want to see the other horses."

The Satchwells and Amy looked at her in amazement. Amy had been sure that she would stalk off when she was told that she couldn't have Spartan, but it seemed she had been wrong about Melanie.

Melanie walked over to her father. "They're right, Daddy," she said calmly. "I probably don't want a horse that I have to be real careful around all the time. But maybe they have another horse that isn't so nervous."

"We have several actually," Lou said, looking as if she couldn't believe her ears. "Don't we, Amy?"

Amy nodded. "Do you want to come with me and have a look around?" she asked Melanie. "You might like Copper — he's not at all nervous, and he needs a good home with lots of activity."

"Can I see him?" Melanie asked eagerly.

"Sure," Amy replied. "Come on." She set off with Melanie toward the barn. As they walked, Amy told Melanie about Copper's history and told her that he had been abused, so she would need to be gentle with him, expecially around his head.

ž

An hour later, Melanie had completely fallen in love with Copper. Melanie had been very sweet when she tacked up Copper, and as Amy watched the younger girl ride him around the schooling ring, she smiled. Copper was a young horse that had been at Heartland for four months. He needed a fun, lively home, and Amy felt sure that Melanie would be good to him.

"What do you think?" Ty said to her in a low voice.

"They're perfect for each other," Amy told him.

"I think so, too," Ty agreed, smiling at her.

After Melanie had dismounted and helped Amy untack Copper, the Satchwells scheduled a time the following week for Ty to come by and check out the stable where Melanie kept her horse.

"Bye, Copper," Melanie said, kissing the chestnut on the nose. "See you soon."

Amy watched the Satchwells leave and then headed up to Spartan's stall. She stroked his bay head. She was really pleased for Copper, but she still wasn't any closer to finding the right home for Spartan.

ž

For the rest of the day, Lou seemed upset with Carl. She could not seem to forgive him for interfering with the Satchwells. However, when it came time for him to go back to Manhattan, Amy noticed that she had begun to relent.

"I'll miss you," Lou said as Carl put his bag in his car.

Carl put his arm around her shoulders. "Promise me you'll really think about Chicago this week?"

"Yes," Lou said, looking up at him. "I will."

They kissed and then Carl got into his car. "See you on Friday," he said as he started the engine. "Don't wear yourself out with all those dance preparations."

Amy watched Lou stand and wave until Carl's Saab disappeared down the drive.

She couldn't help feeling disappointed. After the way Lou had been so supportive that afternoon and positively angry with Carl over Copper, she had started to believe that Lou would turn down Carl's offer and stay at Heartland for good. However, looking at Lou's face, she didn't feel so sure anymore.

Chapter Ten

The next day, Amy took Spartan out for another trail ride, taking care to stay on the paths where he would feel confident. Enjoying the sand and grass beneath his feet, he pulled at his reins and pranced excitedly. The trail ahead was long and grassy, so Amy leaned forward and let him canter. Spartan's long strides seemed to eat up the ground. Ahead of them a fallen tree lay half across the path. Amy tightened her hold on the reins. "Easy now, boy," she said, intending to slow him down in order to walk around the tree trunk. Spartan tossed his head and would not slow his pace.

Amy felt excitement surge through her. He wanted to jump it. She knew she should take things slowly with him, but the tree trunk looked so tempting. Although no one was there, she glanced around almost guiltily and then shortened her reins, angling him toward the low end of the trunk.

Spartan steadied his stride. Amy dug her knees into the saddle. They were three strides away, two, one, and then with a surge of power Spartan leaped into the air, clearing the log by a good three feet.

"Wow!" Amy gasped, patting his neck. Spartan snorted and, putting his head down, bucked with sheer delight. Amy laughed and pulled his head up, stopping him. His jump had so much spring!

She patted him for a moment knowing she should keep to the trail, but instead she trotted him back around the tree trunk. This time when she turned Spartan, she headed him for the highest part. As he plunged eagerly forward her heart leaped into her throat. What was she doing? But then she felt his smooth, powerful canter and her doubts disappeared. She sat down deep in the saddle. The tree trunk loomed in front of them, and suddenly they were over.

"Good boy!" Amy cried ecstatically. She patted his neck over and over again, feeling excitement buzz through her. Spartan was a natural jumper!

Amy didn't stay on the trail for long. She couldn't wait to tell Ty about Spartan's jumping.

"He was so good!" she told Ty, having found him the moment she got back. "He just flew over it both times!"

"You should try him in the training ring tomorrow," Ty said.

"I can't wait for you to see him!" Amy said, exhilarated by the thought.

❧

The next day, after schooling Spartan on the flat, she hitched him to a post and put up a small jump. As she remounted she felt a shudder of nervousness. Maybe the day before had just been a fluke. But her worries melted when Spartan cleared the fence easily. Amy raised the jump just as Ty came to watch.

"Wow!" he said as Spartan cleared the jump by a couple of feet.

"He feels like he wants to go higher and higher," said Amy, her eyes shining. "I know he's overjumping a bit now, but he'll get over that with practice. He's incredible!"

From then on, every time that Amy rode Spartan she put up a jump. On Friday afternoon, she got Ty to help her set up an entire course of fences. "Here goes!" she called to him after she had warmed up Spartan.

Spartan threw his head up as she turned him into the first jump, but he soon settled into a perfect rhythm. He soared over jump after jump, evidently enjoying himself.

As they were approaching the last one, Amy suddenly realized that she had felt such sheer ability in only one other horse. And that was Pegasus. Excitement flooded through her. Spartan was smaller than Pegasus, but was there any reason why he couldn't one day be as good a jumper?

As they cleared the last jump, Ty clapped. "That was amazing!" he said.

"*He's* amazing!" Amy replied, her cheeks glowing. She looked around at the jumps. "I'd love to take him to a show — and do a long course of jumps. I bet he'd be fantastic!"

"Well, I guess he's not ready to compete yet, but there is a show at The Meadows on Sunday," Ty said. "You want to go? You could get him used to the atmosphere."

Amy stared at him. "Yes!" she said. "And they have a schooling ring there. You can pay to do warm-up courses. It would be a great experience for him!"

"Yeah," Ty said.

Amy's face suddenly fell. "But I bet Grandpa won't have time to drive me. It will be the day after the dance, and he'll be busy helping Lou with the cleanup."

"I'll take you if you want," Ty offered.

"Really?" Amy said. "But it's your day off."

Ty grinned. "I'd like to — it'll be fun. And if he jumps really well, we might find someone who would adopt him when he's ready."

Amy nodded, her thoughts reeling. She was going to take Spartan to a show! It seemed incredible that it was only a matter of days since he wouldn't even let her near him.

After Amy had put Spartan away in his stall, she went to the tack room to clean his tack. When she had finished, she went back to check on him. He was lying down in his stall, muzzle resting on the clean straw, legs curled underneath him. Amy smiled and quietly opened the door. Spartan looked at her but didn't get up.

"Taking a nap?" she murmured, kneeling down beside him in the straw and stroking his neck. Spartan snorted and rested his muzzle on her lap. Her fingers ran through his mane and he relaxed, his eyes half closed, his lower lip drooping slightly as he let her legs take the weight of his head.

Amy closed her eyes for a moment, letting her dreams play out in her head. She imagined Spartan clearing fence after fence at some big show, his scars not mattering, everyone cheering for him as he won class after class. He would be confident, happy. She let the most secret of her dreams come to the surface — Spartan living at Heartland, staying with her. She knew the horses that came to Heartland had to be rehomed, but Spartan was different. Mom had kept Pegasus after his accident because they had a special bond. Amy felt she was building that bond with Spartan, too. In her imagination, they galloped around an arena, a blue ribbon flying from

Spartan's bridle. Someday they might even become as good a team as Daddy and Pegasus had been.

She opened her eyes. "It could be," she whispered. "You and me, Spartan. I think we were meant to be together. I understand you better than anyone else ever could."

Spartan blew softly out through his nose.

"You'll be happy here," Amy said, kissing his head. "I'll *make* you happy." Feeling a great rush of affection, she put her arms around his neck and hugged him. As she did so she looked him in the eyes. His dark brown eyes were full of trust, but something was missing.

Amy's arms slackened their grip. People said that horses couldn't feel love, but she knew they were wrong. When she looked into Pegasus's or Sundance's eyes she could see love reflected there, welling deep and strong from the center of their being. But with Spartan, she couldn't sense the same connection. His eyes just held a sadness that hadn't gone away despite all her love for him.

He nuzzled her, but at that moment she realized that her dreams would always be just that — *dreams*. She could not bring the light back into his eyes. She couldn't make him love her. A lump formed in Amy's throat as she faced the bitter truth. Spartan was only hers for a little while — hers on loan, not hers to keep.

She stood up and walked slowly out of his stall.

"Amy! Amy!"

Amy looked up. There, jogging up the drive, her black curls bouncing, was Soraya!

"Soraya!" Amy gasped. She had been so busy thinking about Spartan that she had forgotten that Soraya came back from camp that day. Throwing away her worries, she raced down the yard to meet her friend. "You're home!"

"You noticed?" Soraya grinned. They hugged. As they pulled apart, Soraya looked around. "Gosh, it's good to be back." Her eyes sparkled. "Not that I didn't enjoy camp, of course."

Amy grinned. "It sounds like you enjoyed it a lot! So who's this Chris you keep going on about in your letters?"

"Chris?" Soraya questioned. "Amy, you're way behind! For the last two weeks it's been Kyle." She shook her head. "I can see we've got some serious catching up to do!"

One hour and a bag of chocolate-pecan cookies later, Amy and Soraya were almost caught up with each other's news. Soraya had started going out with a boy named Kyle after a bonfire one night at camp, but they had decided not to keep dating when camp was over because they lived hours apart.

"He was really nice, though," Soraya said wistfully as she showed Amy his picture. "He said he's going to write."

Amy hugged her. "You'll meet someone around here." She looked at Soraya's disbelieving face. "I know you will!"

"All the halfway decent boys around here are taken, or they're madly in love with someone else," Soraya said. She shook her head at Amy. "Which reminds me — what's going on with you and Matt?"

Amy shook her head. "Oh, the same as usual. We're just good friends."

"You know he'll start going out with someone else soon," Soraya warned.

"Maybe you," Amy teased her.

"Yeah, right!" Soraya said. "I was thinking more like Ashley Grant — she's had her eye on Matt for ages."

"Well, she'll be at the dance tomorrow," Amy said, making a face. "I think she's just coming because she knows he'll be here. I bet she wears a debutante gown or something," Amy joked.

"It'll probably be totally expensive, too," Soraya said, shifting into a more comfortable position on Amy's bed. "So, how are all the preparations for the dance going? Is there a lot left to do?"

"Tons," Amy said. "We had a whole bunch of stuff de- livered at lunchtime that needs organizing, and there's about a million napkins to be folded. Tomorrow is going to be just crazy!"

"I'll help with it all," Soraya offered. "I think it's a really cool idea — having the dance, I mean."

"Yeah, I do now," Amy admitted. "I didn't think so at first, but lots of people have been buying tickets. I guess Lou was right about it being a good way to raise money and get Mom's friends to come up here."

Soraya looked at her shrewdly. They had been friends since third grade and she knew all about Amy and Lou's stormy relationship. "How have you guys been getting along?"

Amy thought for a moment. "Better," she said. "We've been arguing on and off, but I think we're doing better."

"Your last letter said that Lou was thinking about moving to Chicago," Soraya said. "And by the way, can I remind you that we said we'd write at least three times a week? I only got one letter every ten days or so."

"I know — I'm sorry! It's just been crazy around here," Amy said. She shook her head. "Lou's still thinking about going to Chicago. I don't want her to, but she's just so into Carl that I think she might."

"And you still don't like him?"

Amy sighed. "I feel bad because I know he makes Lou happy, but there's just something about him. . . ." Amy heard a car outside and looked out the window. "Well that's the end of *that* discussion, here he is."

"Come on, I want to meet him," Soraya said, jumping up and heading for the door.

Amy followed her. "You don't. You really don't."

They went downstairs just as Carl came in. "I saw your mail had arrived," he said, handing a pile of letters to Jack. "So I thought I'd bring it in with me."

"Thanks, Carl," Grandpa said. "How was your trip?"

"Good, thanks," Carl replied. He nodded at Amy and Soraya. "Hi, kids."

"Hi," Soraya said politely, and then when Carl looked away she put a finger down her throat.

Amy rolled her eyes. *Kids! He's such a loser*, she thought.

Soraya smiled at her. "I'd better get back home. I promised Mom I wouldn't stay long. But I'll come over in the morning and help."

"OK," Amy said, walking to the door with her. "See you tomorrow. It's great to have you back!"

She watched Soraya disappear down the drive and then went into the kitchen. Carl had his arm around Lou.

"We've got so much to do!" Lou was saying to him. "I'm glad you're here."

"Don't worry. With you in charge it's bound to be a success," Carl said smoothly. "So how many people are coming?"

"Eighty-two at the last count," Lou said.

Carl looked casually at the mail. "And I guess a few more replies might have come today."

Lou picked up the pile to check. "Yes, it looks like it." Amy was about to go back upstairs when she heard Lou's voice change. "Hey, what's this?" Lou held up an envelope and frowned.

"Anything interesting?" Carl asked, looking over her shoulder.

"It's from Epstein and Webb," Lou said, holding an elegant cream envelope with an embossed crest in her hands. "Why are they writing to me?"

"Well, open it and see," said Carl.

Amy glanced at him. The slightest of smiles was playing at the corners of his lips.

Lou tore open the envelope and took out a letter. She read it, her eyes widening. Suddenly, she gasped. "They've offered me a job!" she cried, looking up. "An amazing one. And it's in Chicago." Lou flung her arms around Carl's neck. "It's actually in Chicago!"

"What? That's incredible!" Carl exclaimed. He hugged her. "It's fate, Lou. We were meant to be together in Chicago. Just think — we can get an apartment together, start a new life!"

"Oh, Carl!" Lou cried.

"That's great, Lou," Grandpa said quietly. Amy saw the sadness in his eyes.

Lou seemed to see it, too. She froze, the excitement fading quickly from her face. "Well, I'll have to decide if I should take it," she said hastily, stuffing the letter in her pocket and looking rather awkwardly from Grandpa to Amy.

"*If* you should take it?" Carl stared at her incredulously. "But Lou! This is the opportunity of a lifetime. You can't tell me you're thinking of turning it down?"

"It's a big move," Lou said defensively. "I'll have to call them and discuss the details."

"Lou!" Carl said in exasperation.

"Please, Carl," Lou said. "I need to think about it."

Carl stared at her for a moment, his face tightening. Suddenly, he picked up his bag. "I'm going to get changed," he said abruptly, striding out of the kitchen.

Lou sat down next to Jack at the table. "Oh, Grandpa," she sighed. As she looked up, Amy saw the confusion in her eyes. "What am I going to do?"

"What do you want to do?" Grandpa said, putting his arm gently on her shoulder.

"That's just it — I don't know."

"Don't take it, Lou. Stay here with us," Amy said softly, sitting down next to her.

"I *am* beginning to love it here. But I love Carl, too," Lou said. She shook her head. "And anyway, you don't really need me."

"Yes, we do!" Amy burst out.

"No, Amy. You don't," Lou said. "I make mistakes, like with the feed and trying to find homes for horses before they're ready. And you don't listen to my ideas, and that's hard for me. I'm used to being respected, I'm used to having my ideas really count."

"Lou, you can't know everything about Heartland right off the bat, but you've learned a lot. You just don't realize how much we need you," Amy said desperately.

Lou looked around distractedly. "Please, Grandpa," she groaned. "Tell me what to do."

"I can't do that, honey," he said, shaking his head. "You need to decide for yourself."

Lou sighed. "I know. But how?"

Grandpa leaned over and kissed her head. "Just follow your heart, Lou," he said softly. "Follow your heart."

Chapter Eleven

"If I see one more red napkin I am going to go crazy!" Soraya declared as she folded a fork and knife into the last napkin and put it down on the table with a bang. "What else do we need to do?"

Amy looked up from unpacking a crate of glasses. "The tablecloths need to be laid out," she said. "But there's one more table to be put up first."

As she spoke, Matt came through the doorway carrying a table. "Where do you want this?" he asked.

"Over there," Amy said, pointing to a gap. "Thanks, Matt."

"What about the food?" Matt asked as he set the table upright.

"Well, Grandpa picked up the meat for the barbecue yesterday, and he and Lou are making lots of salads and

279

desserts," Amy said. She had been put in charge of organizing the barn while Carl had been sent off to buy the drinks for the evening. She thought about the show the next day. She wasn't going to get a chance to give Spartan a bath. She'd just have to get up early in the morning despite the late night and give him a good brushing then.

"What next?" Matt said, coming over.

"If you unpack the plates," Amy said, pointing to the boxes of rented dishes, "I'll go and see if Carl has arrived with the drinks."

She went through to the kitchen. "Is Carl back?"

"Just," Lou said, looking up from slicing a tomato. "He's still outside."

Amy went out. Carl was leaning against the Heartland pickup with his back to her. Amy realized that he was talking on his cell phone, so she walked quietly toward the back of the truck to start unloading the drinks. She didn't want to disturb him.

She heard Carl laugh. "Of course, she doesn't know," he said. "She doesn't have any idea." Amy was trying not to listen, but his next words caught her off guard. "No, no. You've got it all wrong," he said. "Lou's not naive. She just trusts me." Amy froze at the mention of her sister's name. Carl shook his head. "The trouble with Lou is that she just doesn't know what will make her happy. All I've done is nudge her in the right direction, given fate a helping hand you could say."

Amy slowly started to back away. Her mind was reeling. She couldn't believe it! It sounded like Lou's job offer in Chicago was all a setup! Carl knew about it but was pretending he didn't. Amy suddenly remembered the way he had urged Lou to look at the mail the day before. She had to tell Lou what she had heard!

She tried to step backward toward the house, but then her foot caught on a stone and she tripped. Carl looked around. "Amy!" he said.

"Er — hi," Amy said. "I was just coming to help carry the drinks inside."

Carl's face visibly relaxed. "Oh, right." He spoke into his phone. "I'll talk to you later, Brett. Bye."

All the time Amy was helping Carl unload the drinks, she wished she could find Lou and tell her what she suspected. But after they had finished, she couldn't talk to her sister alone because Carl followed her into the kitchen.

Unfortunately, Lou was busy the rest of the day. Amy couldn't find a moment to talk to her without someone interrupting. In the end, she tried to push the bad news to the back of her mind, deciding it was best to tell Lou about it the next day, when things were quieter and her sister was less stressed.

By six o'clock, the barn was almost ready. The decorations were finished, the barbecue was lit, Grandpa had made his special punch, and the raffle tickets were stacked up and ready to be sold.

"Time to get changed!" Lou called, running through the kitchen. "It won't be long before people start arriving!"

Matt had gone home, but Soraya had brought her clothes over so that she could get changed with Amy.

"What do you think Ashley will be wearing?" she asked as she sat at Amy's mirror and brushed out her dark curls.

"Something revealing," Amy said. She looked over Soraya's shoulder and twisted her hair up. "What do you think, up or down?"

"Up!" Soraya said. She stood up and helped Amy knot her thick sun-streaked hair. "There!" she said, pulling down a few strands so that they framed Amy's face.

"Yeah. I like it," Amy said, pleased. She took out a pair of midnight blue cropped pants from her closet and pulled them on. Her mom had them bought them for her a year ago. She had hardly had a chance to wear them, but luckily they still fit, the slim cut making her look quite tall and elegant.

"Wow! Matt won't even recognize you in those!" Soraya giggled as Amy looked at herself in the mirror. Soraya pulled on a pair of black jeans and a strappy top made out of a silvery material. "What do you think?" she said, posing.

"You look marvelous!" Amy said dramatically. "Come on! Let's go!"

They hurried down the stairs and into the kitchen. Grandpa, Carl, and Ty were already there.

"You both look wonderful!" Grandpa said.

"Thank you," Soraya said.

Amy looked at Ty. He looked darkly handsome, his checked shirt emphasizing his broad shoulders.

"Wow!" he said, looking Amy up and down. "You look great!"

Amy raised her eyebrows teasingly. "You mean I don't normally?"

"Well, it's a change from your barn clothes," Ty commented. He grinned at her. "You really do look nice."

"Thanks." She smiled. "So do you." Their eyes met for a moment. Then Amy glanced away, feeling suddenly flustered.

Lou came into the kitchen from the barn. "I hope everyone shows up," she fretted.

Jack Bartlett opened the refrigerator and pulled out a jug of punch. "A toast!" he declared, getting out a tray of glasses. He filled the glasses and passed them around. "To the success of the dance!"

Amy looked at her sister. "To Lou!" she said impulsively.

"To Lou!" everyone echoed, clinking their glasses.

Lou smiled happily. "Thank you," she said.

"OK," Grandpa said. "We can't just stand around.

Someone needs to put out the appetizers and pour the drinks. Who's in charge of organizing the parking?"

Ty finished his glass and went outside to deal with the parking. Amy started opening bags of chips while Soraya went with Jack to the barn to help with the drinks.

Lou was just about to follow them when Carl caught her arm. "Here," he said, picking up their glasses and refilling them with punch. "Let's have another toast."

Amy glanced up.

"What to?" Lou asked.

Carl raised his glass. "To Chicago!"

Amy saw Lou falter, her glass stopping halfway to her mouth. "But, Carl, I haven't decided if I'm going yet."

Words leaped to Amy's lips, but she held them back.

"Come on, Lou," Carl exclaimed. "This is the perfect job, the perfect opportunity for us to be together. How can you still be undecided?"

"It's a hard decision to make," Lou said. "Surely you can see that. I need time to think about it."

"You don't have time!" Carl said, sounding irritated. "You have to schedule an interview by Tuesday."

"I know! I know!" Lou suddenly stopped. Amy saw her frown. "How do you know I need to have an interview by Tuesday?" she said to Carl. "I didn't tell you that."

For an instant, Carl looked horrified, but his expression

quickly smoothed. "Of course you did," he said quickly, putting a hand on her arm. "You must've forgotten."

"No, I didn't," Lou exclaimed. "I didn't want to tell you in case you started to pressure me. How did you know?" She suddenly took a step back, her eyes widening, her face going pale. *"You arranged it, didn't you?"* she whispered. "You *knew* about this job all along."

Carl looked for a moment as if he was going to deny it, but then he stepped forward. "Well, so what if I did?" he said. "Yes, OK, I arranged it, Lou. I want you to come with me — people *expect* you to come with me."

"You want me to come because of what our friends would think if I didn't?" Lou stared at him in horror.

"No — I —" Carl hastily changed his tone. "Lou, I only tried to get you a good job," he said, grabbing her hand. "Is that such a crime?"

"You tried to manipulate me! You deceived me!" Lou cried, snatching her hand away.

"Lou, listen —"

"No! You listen, Carl," Lou shouted. "I trusted you. How could you do this to me?"

Just then the back door opened and Scott and Matt walked in. Their greetings died on their lips as they took in the situation.

"Lou —" Carl moved forward.

Lou pushed him away. "Please don't," she pleaded. "I

can't go to Chicago with you. I'm going to need some time. Just go, and leave me alone."

"But —"

"Just go, Carl!" Lou said forcefully. "Go!" With that she ran out of the room, trying to stifle her tears.

Amy jumped to her feet, but before she could say anything Scott stepped forward. "You heard Lou," he said icily to Carl. "I think you'd better leave."

For a moment it looked as if Carl was about to hit him, but then he took a step back. "I'll get my things!" he snapped, and turning on his heel he stalked upstairs.

Scott looked out the window. "Amy, we've got to do something — the guests are arriving."

Amy looked at him in horror. "But what about Lou?"

"You should check on her," Scott said. "Matt and I will sort things out down here."

As Amy ran up the stairs, Carl came pushing past her, shoving things into his bag as he went.

"Bye to you, too," Amy muttered.

She hurried to Lou's bedroom. Her sister was lying facedown on the bed.

"Oh, Amy!" she sobbed, looking up. "What am I going to do?" She buried her head in her hands.

"You have to do what you think is right for you," Amy faltered. "Do you really want Carl to go to Chicago without you?"

Lou turned toward her sister. "All I know is, that after

all that's happened over the last few months, I definitely don't need anyone around whom I can't trust."

Amy knelt on the floor beside the bed and stroked Lou's hair. "Then I guess you're right," she said. "You're better off without him."

"How could he do that to me? I thought he respected me," Lou cried. "I thought he *loved* me."

Amy wrapped her arms around her sister. "Oh, Lou, we love you!" she said desperately. "Whatever you decide, Grandpa and I will always be here for you. No matter if you stay here or go back to New York, this will always be your home."

Lou started to sob even harder.

"And look, don't even worry about the dance," Amy consoled. "We can manage. Scott's greeting the guests. Everything is under control."

Lou sat up, tears running down her cheeks. "People are arriving already?"

Amy nodded. "But don't worry," she said quickly. "We can cope. You stay up here for as long as you want."

Lou brushed her tears away, "I organized it. I should be there."

"But Lou —"

"I'll be OK." With a sniff, Lou stood up and smoothed out her dress.

Amy felt her heart fill with admiration. *Lou is so strong,* she thought. She knew if their positions had been reversed she would have stayed in her room all night, cry-ing her eyes out. But Lou was already looking into the mirror and fixing her makeup.

When she finally turned toward the door, the only hint of her inner turmoil was the tear-washed brightness of her eyes. "Come on," she said, taking a deep breath and reaching for Amy's hand. "Our friends are waiting."

Amy hurried around, filling up glasses and saying hi. She tried to keep an eye on Lou to make sure she was OK. But there was no need to worry. With a bright smile on her face she greeted people, telling them about the program for the evening and steering them toward the table where Ty was selling raffle tickets.

The Grant family arrived, Ashley looking stunning in a short green dress that had virtually no back.

Very appropriate for a barn dance, Amy thought sarcasti-cally.

"Hello, Amy," Ashley said coolly.

"Hi," Amy replied, her voice curt.

Ashley looked around, her perfect eyebrows arching in surprise. "You've really got a lot of people here, haven't you?"

"That *was* the idea," Amy retorted, but Ashley wasn't listening. She had spotted Matt.

"Matt!" she called.

He looked around and came over. "Hi, Ashley," he said pleasantly.

"Hi," said Ashley, putting her hand on his arm. "I didn't know you were going to be here."

"Sure," Matt said in surprise. "I thought Scott had talked to your mom about it."

Ashley just raised her eyebrows and smiled coyly.

Shaking her head in amusement, Amy hurried away. Even Ashley's presence couldn't spoil the evening.

The barn filled up quickly. The noise level rose, glasses clinked, and as the band started up, people began moving onto the dance floor. Amy realized how right Lou had been all along. This was a terrific way to raise money! Everyone seemed to be having a wonderful time, and it was great to see all of Mom's friends. Amy thought about how proud Mom would have been of her oldest daughter.

She looked around for Lou and spotted her standing by the entrance to the barn with Grandpa and Scott. The earlier strain on her face had vanished completely. Scott said something and Lou laughed at him, her eyes sparkling. She looked genuinely happy and delighted as she watched all the guests having a good time.

Amy hurried over. "Lou! This is such a success — everyone's having a great time."

"They really are," Scott agreed. "Congratulations, Lou!"

"Thanks," Lou smiled. "And thanks for all your help."

"You're the one who pulled it together. I'm sorry I doubted you," Amy said decisively.

Lou looked slightly taken aback by her apology. "Thanks, Amy."

"And —" Amy struggled, finding the words difficult to say, "and — I think some of your other ideas for Heartland might work, too. You know, the brochure and things like that."

"Really?" Lou stared. "You'd really give them a chance?"

Amy nodded. "I've realized you know what you're doing when it comes to the business side of things." She looked at her sister, the words impulsively tumbling out of her. "Look, I was stupid not to listen to you before. Please say you'll stay, Lou. I promise I'll take your ideas seriously from now on. Don't go back to the city. Your home is here now and we *need* you."

Lou looked astonished and pleased. "Do you mean that?"

"Of course I do!" Amy exclaimed.

Lou looked at Grandpa, Scott, and Amy. "OK," she said, a smile suddenly spreading across her face. "I'll stay!"

Chapter Twelve

In the early hours of the morning, the last guests finally left the party, and Amy dragged herself to bed. She glanced at her alarm clock as she turned off her light. Two o'clock! In only four hours she had to be up again to get Spartan groomed and ready for the show. "Oh, great," she groaned, turning over and falling asleep.

At six o'clock, Amy pulled herself out of bed and staggered out to the yard. First she had to feed the other horses and then tend to Spartan. However, she gradually managed to wake herself up by drinking several cups of coffee. By the time Ty arrived at eight-thirty, she was beginning to feel more cheerful. "You're going to be so good today," she told Spartan as she bandaged his tail to protect it in the trailer. "We'll show everyone just how special you are."

Spartan looked around at her and snorted almost as though he understood.

When they arrived at the show, Ty parked the trailer near the edge of the show ground, well away from the main commotion of the showrings and spectator stands. Spartan backed down the ramp and looked around excitedly, his ears pricked, his nostrils dilated.

"It's OK," Amy told him. "It's just a show ground. Do you remember, boy?"

Ty bent down to remove Spartan's leg wraps. "I'd take him for a walk around," he said, throwing them in a pile and then removing the tail bandage. "It will help him settle."

Amy nodded. She'd been thinking the same thing. "Come on, boy," she said, clicking her tongue. "Let's go."

Spartan pranced beside her, his neck arched. Amy thought he probably remembered going to shows with his previous owner. "And you might be going to shows again soon," she told him. "But not to compete in boring conformation classes, but in jumping classes so that everyone can see how good you are."

Just then, a rider cantered straight across their path

only a few feet in front of them. Spartan shied back in surprise. "Steady, boy!" Amy exclaimed.

Amy swung around.

There was Ashley Grant sitting astride a bay pony, looking smug, her clothes perfect and her pony gleaming. Despite the late night, Ashley looked as fresh as a daisy. "So, he's still nervous!" she said.

"Any horse would shy away if you did that to it!" Amy exclaimed.

"Temper, temper," Ashley mocked.

Amy shook her head in disgust and walked Spartan on. She ran her hand up and down his neck to keep him calm.

But there was no escaping Ashley. She rode right alongside Spartan. "So what have you brought *him* here for?" she said. "I heard he was vicious."

"Well, he's not," Amy said through gritted teeth. "He's healed."

Ashley laughed as she looked at Spartan's sides. "His scars certainly aren't!"

"So?" Amy demanded.

"So, you're not exactly going to get far with him in the showring, are you?" Ashley said.

"I'm not planning to take him in conformation," Amy retorted. "And you know that in jumping classes scars don't matter."

"Like a judge is *really* going to pick a horse with scars like that," Ashley said. She shook her head. "You're wasting your time and your money, Amy — and from what *I've* heard, Heartland hasn't got too much cash to spare just now." With a snide smile she cantered off.

"Just you wait till you see him jump, Ashley," Amy muttered. She suddenly felt a strong desire to enter Spartan in a class just so that she could wipe the smile off Ashley's perfect face. But entries had closed a week ago. "Next time," she promised Spartan as she watched Ashley enter the collecting ring on the bay pony.

Amy took Spartan back to the trailer. "I think I'll get on," she said to Ty. "He seems fine."

They tacked Spartan up. Amy pulled off the sweats she had been wearing to keep her tan breeches clean and pulled on her long boots and navy jacket. It felt good to be in show clothes again.

"Just take it easy," Ty said, holding the opposite stirrup as she mounted. "You don't want to overdo it."

Amy nodded. But as she patted Spartan she felt sure that he was up for it. He felt excited but not wild. She entered the schooling area where the other horses and riders were warming up. There were trainers shouting instructions, horses rushing past. Amy took a breath. If Spartan could cope with this, then he could cope with anything!

At first he was a little high-strung, but after ten minutes or so he lowered his head and started to listen to her signals. Once he was settled, Amy tried him over a jump. He didn't even hesitate. After they had warmed up over several small fences, Amy decided it was time to take him over a course in the schooling ring.

Ty saw her heading for the entrance and walked over to meet her. "He looks good. You think he's ready?"

Amy nodded, excitement gathering in the pit of her stomach. This was the moment she had been waiting for.

At the gate to the training ring Ty paid an official the schooling fee. "Are the jumps OK at this height?" the official asked. Ty turned to Amy.

Amy looked around the elaborate course. The jumps were about three feet six, higher than she would have ideally liked. "They're fine," she said. When she was riding Spartan she felt as if she could jump anything!

"Good luck!" Ty called as she rode into the ring.

Shortening her reins, Amy patted Spartan's neck. "This is it, boy," she said, her excitement growing as she noticed a few spectators watching casually at the fence. "Let's show everyone what you can do."

Spartan's ears flickered. She gave him a squeeze with her legs, and he moved forward into a smooth canter. Amy circled once and then turned to the first jump — an imposing post and rails. Spartan's stride was even and perfect. He cleared the fence easily, his ears pricked forward as he headed to the second fence in the outside line.

Amy stayed with his steady rhythm as they cleared fence after fence. She could hardly believe what a great understanding they had. She cantered him toward the final jump — a tricky parallel spread — right next to the edge of the ring.

"Gerry?" she heard a girl's voice gasp from the ringside.

Amy felt Spartan's step falter. They were only three strides away from the fence and they had too much momentum to pull away. Amy closed her legs around his sides and pushed him on. "Come on, boy," Amy whispered.

Spartan responded. With an enormous surge of power he gathered himself and took off over the wide fence. It seemed like a minute had passed before they landed safely on the other side.

There was a smattering of applause from those watching.

"Good boy!" Amy cried, forgetting about the voice from the crowd in her sheer delight. Patting him constantly she trotted over to the gate. "Wasn't he great?" she cried to Ty.

"The best!" Ty called back.

"What a nice round," the official said to Amy. "You've got a horse with a lot of potential. You're sure to come away with lots of ribbons."

Amy just smiled as she slid off Spartan's back and flung her arms around his neck. "You were wonderful!" she said. Then, taking Spartan's reins she led him away with Ty.

"Um . . . excuse me," a voice said tentatively behind them.

Amy looked around. A girl about her own age with wavy dark hair was standing there. She was dressed in show clothes and her cheeks looked slightly flushed. "Is that Gerry . . . Geronimo?"

"Yes," Amy said in confusion, turning Spartan around. "At least he *was*. Who are you?"

Before the girl had a chance to reply, Spartan nickered and pulled Amy forward with a toss of his head.

"Oh, Gerry," the girl breathed in delight. "I thought I was never going to see you again."

Amy felt an ache of envy as Spartan nuzzled the girl's hands. Who was she? "Umm . . . sorry, but I don't know who you are," Amy said rather shortly.

The girl looked up at her, her brown eyes suddenly flustered. "Oh, I'm Hannah Boswell. Larry Boswell's my grandfather. I've known Gerry since he was born. I recognized him as soon as I saw you in the ring."

Amy's eyes widened in astonishment. "You're Mr. Boswell's granddaughter?"

Hannah nodded. "I live on the farm with him and Grandma. Are you Amy?" When Amy nodded, Hannah smiled. "Grandpa told me about you. About your rescue center and how you've been looking after Gerry."

"What are you doing here?" Amy said, still trying to get over the fact that she had met Larry Boswell's granddaughter.

"I'm here for the show," Hannah said. "I was supposed to be riding in an equitation class."

Ty frowned. "I thought I'd seen you before," he said. "Do you have a dapple-gray pony?"

"That's right," Hannah said. "We don't usually travel this far for a show, only when there's a big class like today."

"You're really good," Ty said. "I saw you at Middlebrook."

Amy felt a flash of jealousy as Hannah smiled at Ty.

"Thanks," the other girl said. "I'm just lucky I've got Sinbad." Her eyes glowed. "He'd make any rider look wonderful."

Amy's jealousy disappeared as she heard Hannah Boswell praising her pony, and she felt herself starting to like her. "What did you mean you were *supposed* to be in an equitation class?" she asked curiously.

"Sinbad's gone lame," Hannah said. "He must have knocked himself on the ride over. It's not too bad, but I'm not going to risk riding him. I'm just going to cancel my entry. It's typical though that it happened today when there's a big qualifying class." Although she smiled, Amy saw that her eyes looked sad. Hannah looked around. "I have to tell my Grandma that you're here. I know she'll want to say hello. Is that OK?" she asked.

"Yeah, sure," Amy said.

"I'll be back in a minute," Hannah promised, setting off across the show ground.

"She seems nice," Amy said, turning to Ty. Amy didn't compete in equitation herself; she preferred the hunter division where the emphasis was on the horse and not the rider. Still, she knew Hannah must be disappointed.

Ty nodded. "She's a really good rider," he said. "Whatever she says, her pony doesn't look that easy. I think she has real talent."

Amy patted Spartan thoughtfully.

Hannah came running back. "Grandma's coming!" she panted, her dark hair tousled. Spartan pulled toward her and nuzzled her.

"Umm . . ." Amy took a deep breath, the idea spilling out of her. "Hannah — would you like to ride Spartan — I mean *Gerry* — for your equitation class?"

She saw Ty turn and stare at her. Hannah's eyes widened. "Ride Gerry? But you don't even know if I can ride!" Hannah said.

"Well, Ty's seen you, and he says you're good," Amy said. She glanced at Ty. "That's enough for me."

"Well, I'd love to ride him!" Hannah said. She scanned Amy's face anxiously. "You really wouldn't mind?"

"No," Amy said slowly, watching as Spartan breathed on Hannah's hand. "No, I wouldn't mind."

Hannah smiled and then suddenly waved at someone over Amy's shoulder. "Grandma! I'm here!"

Mrs. Boswell had short gray hair and was dressed in jeans. Her face lit up as she saw Spartan. "Gerry!" she said.

Spartan nickered softly. Mrs. Boswell smiled and rubbed his head. "Well, hi, boy. It's sure good to see you looking so well." She turned to Amy and Ty, holding out her hand and smiling. "Hello, I'm Shelley Boswell."

They shook hands and introduced themselves. Hannah quickly told her grandma about taking Spartan in the equitation class. "I'd better get my hat and saddle," she said. "My class is next."

"I'll ride Spartan around," Amy said. "To get him warmed up for you."

"And I'll grab a brush and towel so we can go over him before you enter the ring," Ty said.

Amy rode Spartan into the schooling area. They trotted around, his strides long and smooth, his ears flickering as he followed Amy's signals. She asked him to canter and rode him in two neat figure eights. "Good boy," she whispered, stroking his neck.

Seeing Hannah outside the ring with her saddle, Amy brought Spartan back to a walk and rode over to where Hannah stood.

"Is it okay if I use my saddle?" Hannah asked.

Amy nodded and dismounted. Taking a deep breath, she ran up the stirrups, undid the girth, and then slid her saddle from Spartan's back.

"Are you still sure this is OK?" Hannah asked, looking at her.

Amy swallowed. "I'm sure."

Amy held tight on to Spartan's reins as Hannah lifted her own saddle onto Spartan's back. Spartan nuzzled her hands as Hannah tightened the girth. Amy quickly kissed his nose.

"I really appreciate it," Hannah said, standing back. "It's my last chance to qualify for the state finals."

Feeling her heart twist, Amy held out Spartan's reins. As Hannah took the reins, their eyes met.

"Good luck," Amy whispered, still holding on.

"Thank you," Hannah said softly.

Slowly, Amy let go.

🙢

After Hannah had ridden around for a bit, and had taken Spartan over a few jumps, she came over to Ty and Amy. Ty gave Spartan a quick brush over. "You look good on him," he said.

Amy nodded. She had been watching carefully as Hannah rode around. It was obvious that Ty was right. Hannah was a very talented rider — her hands were light and her seat was perfectly balanced. Spartan looked relaxed and happy.

"I always loved riding him when he was at Grandpa's, but I had never jumped him," Hannah said. She smiled. "He feels strange after Sinbad."

"How many hands is Sinbad?" Amy asked.

"Fourteen two. He's getting a bit too small for me now. Grandpa said he'll buy me a new horse. But I just can't find one I really like." She smiled. "I'll keep Sinbad, too, of course. I'd never sell him."

Shelley Boswell came over. "Hannah! You need to report to the announcer so they know you're here."

Hannah grinned nervously. "Well, here goes. Wish me luck!"

"Oh, Hannah?" Amy said. Hannah looked back. "If he seems to hesitate before a fence, give him a tiny nudge and he'll be fine. He just needs a little reassurance sometimes."

Hannah nodded. "Thanks," she said.

Ty and Amy went to watch at ringside. "Look, it's Ashley!" Amy said, elbowing Ty as Ashley trotted into the ring. She was on a different horse — a beautiful gray with a thick tail that floated behind it like a waterfall. Ashley asked the horse to canter and headed smoothly toward the first jump.

Amy watched carefully. When she competed with Sundance against Ashley, it was usually in the pony hunter classes where it was the pony that was judged and not the rider. But equitation was different. It was the rider's style and ability that mattered and Amy had to admit it — Ashley was good. She had perfect posture and her smile never left her face. "She doesn't seem to do anything wrong!" Amy said aloud.

"I don't know," Ty said critically. "She's a bit stiff in the shoulders."

At the next jump Ashley's horse took off too late, but Ashley recovered well.

"She'll lose points there," Ty commented.

"Not many," Amy said.

"But you can tell she doesn't have a real connection with the horse," Ty said. "I mean, her riding is technically precise, but there's no bond there. Some judges care about those things, too."

Ashley finished the course with a circle and rode out.

"Is Hannah next?" Amy asked.

But there was one competitor before her — a boy on a large chestnut pony.

Shelley Boswell came to join them. "It was really kind of you to let Hannah ride Gerry," she said to Amy.

"No problem," Amy said.

"Larry told me what happened on his visit to you. You must think he's not very devoted to his horses," Shelley Boswell said.

Amy wasn't sure what to say. "Well . . . um . . ."

"It's all right, honey," Shelley Boswell said, smiling. "I can imagine what he must have been like. But Larry's not a cruel man, despite what you might think. All his life he's had to work hard. He built his business from scratch, and he's always had the rule that each of his horses has to pay its way. That's what's made him successful. But I think it broke his heart to let Gerry go, and he sure does miss him. We all do."

"Hannah's up!" Ty said as the chestnut pony left the ring and Hannah trotted in.

Spartan's ears were pricked. He threw his head up for a moment when he saw the fences but then listened to Hannah's signals and lowered his head. They moved smoothly into a canter and then turned toward the first jump.

Amy held her breath. But Spartan sailed over it easily with a foot to spare.

"He jumps big, doesn't he?" Shelley Boswell said.

Amy nodded. She was full of admiration for Hannah's riding. It wasn't easy to stay in the perfect position on a horse that jumped as high as Spartan, but Hannah managed it. Her back was straight, her head up, and her heels down. "Hannah looks really good on him," she said.

Shelley Boswell nodded. "Hannah loves jumping — always has. She's going to look for a horse to compete in the jumper division next."

Amy nodded, concentrating on the ring. Hannah and Spartan were halfway around the course now.

As they cantered around the far side of the ring they made a perfect picture. There appeared to be a bond between them, a special connection. Amy suddenly felt her eyes blur with tears. She glanced at Ty. She was glad that she had listened to him and decided to let Hannah ride Spartan. She could see from his face that he felt the same.

"They look great together," he said softly.

Amy nodded. She couldn't help but think that Spartan really looked happy jumping with Hannah.

Ty touched her hand. "Thanks for trusting me — about Hannah's riding, I mean."

"I always trust you," Amy said, surprised by the words that sprang to her lips.

"Just one more fence to go!" she heard Shelley Boswell say.

With a start, Amy turned her eyes back to the ring. With perfect timing, Spartan cleared the last jump, and the audience burst into applause. Hannah circled him past the entrance and then, patting him as if she were never going to stop, brought him back to a walk.

Amy, Ty, and Shelley Boswell hurried over to meet her. "That was incredible!" Amy said.

"Great job!" Ty said, smiling at Hannah.

"He was perfect!" she said, jumping off. "Amy, thanks for the advice — I gave him a little nudge when he seemed nervous and he was fine." Hannah turned to Spartan and rubbed his face. "You were fabulous!"

Amy smiled. At that moment everything seemed really good. And then Amy saw Ashley and Val Grant walk past them, their faces set. They had obviously seen Hannah's round. "I guess Ashley won't be so quick to put Spartan down anymore," Amy said with a grin. She stroked the horse's nose, and he pushed against her hand.

It was a nerve-racking wait for the results, but at last the loudspeaker crackled into action. "Results of equitation over fences, 14- to 17-year-olds," it said.

Hannah looked nervously at Amy. "You know, I don't even care if I place. It's enough to have had such a great round."

Amy looked at Hannah as the announcer continued.

"In first place, number three-six-five — Hannah Boswell on Geronimo."

"You did it, Hannah!" Amy cried. "You qualified for state finals."

"Oh, my gosh!" Hannah gasped in astonishment. She hugged her grandmother and then turned to Spartan. "Gerry, we won!" Suddenly, Hannah was mounting Spartan. Mrs. Boswell brushed over her riding boots, and Amy hurried to check Spartan's girth.

"Go on. You're in!" Ty said, seeing the ringmaster waiting.

Grinning from ear to ear, Hannah rode into the ring.

It didn't take long for the ribbons to be given out. Ashley was in second place, and she looked thunderous, not even nodding a thank-you as she received her red ribbon.

As Hannah turned to lead Spartan out of the ring, Amy felt Ty's hand on her shoulder.

"You know, that was a really nice thing to do," he said softly.

Amy looked into his eyes. "Thanks," she replied.

❧

"Thank you so much for letting me ride Gerry. I mean Spartan," Hannah said a little while later as she and Amy took Spartan back to the Heartland trailer. "He really is wonderful — you are going to take him to lots more shows, aren't you?"

Amy's heart sank slightly. "Well, it depends when we find him a new home."

"But why don't you keep him?" Hannah said, sounding surprised.

Amy shook her head. "At Heartland it's our policy to try to rehome the horses that we care for."

Hannah looked sadly at the horse. "Poor Gerry. He seems so happy with you."

"Probably not as happy as he could be." Amy sighed. She decided to confide in Hannah. "I feel as if there's this bit of his heart that's locked away," she said. "The only time I've seen him look truly happy was when your grandfather came and just now, with you."

"I do think Gerry was happy with us before he was stolen. If only Grandpa would take him back or if I could have him." Hannah looked upset. "It's not fair," she said.

Amy stared at her, an idea leaping into her mind. "Well, why can't you? You said you were looking for a horse. You want one that can jump. Spartan would be perfect!"

Hannah looked startled. "Me have *Gerry* — but Grandpa would never agree. He gets upset whenever Gerry's name is mentioned."

Amy's flicker of hope died. "Oh." She sighed.

"But maybe it could work!" Hannah said, her face looking as if she was figuring out a difficult problem. "I can't tell Grandpa that I want Gerry because he'll say no. But if I call him and say that I've found an amazing jumper that I want to buy . . . and if I just show up with him —"

Amy stared at her. "But what would your grandpa say? Wouldn't he go crazy?"

Hannah shook her head. "I don't think so. Despite

what he says, he really misses Gerry, and I'm sure he would never be able to turn him away." She grabbed Amy's arm, her eyes suddenly shining with excitement. "Amy! This could work. This could really work! Let me ask Grandma and see what she says."

🐚

It took Hannah only a few minutes to persuade her grandmother that her plan could work. Amy called Lou on her cell phone to tell her the news.

"So he's going now?" Lou said in astonishment.

"Yes," Amy said. "The Boswells' trailer isn't big enough, but Ty said that he'll drive Spartan and me there in our trailer."

"But it's Ty's day off!" Lou said. "Look, ask him to bring the trailer back here, and I'll drive you and Spartan to the Boswells'."

"OK," Amy said. She switched off the phone and went to tell Ty.

Soon it was all arranged. Hannah and Shelley Boswell would go ahead with Sinbad and let Larry Boswell know about the "new" arrival.

"I'll get his old stall ready for him," Hannah said, giving Spartan a last pat before heading off with her grandma. "Now, you've got the directions?"

Amy nodded.

Hannah grinned at her. "Then we'll see you in a couple of hours."

❧

Ty drove Amy and Spartan back to Heartland. "Well, I guess this is good-bye, fella," he said, going into the trailer as Lou got her things together. He patted Spartan. "Be happy."

"He will," Amy said softly, looking at Spartan's handsome bay head.

Lou came out of the house. "Are we ready?"

Amy nodded. "See you tomorrow, Ty. Thanks for everything."

"No problem," Ty said smiling. He turned and walked off down the yard. Amy quickly got into the pickup.

Lou opened the door and jumped in beside her. "Okay, let's go!"

As the trailer bumped down the drive, Amy heard Spartan whinny. A sharp memory of a time, three months ago, when Spartan had been in the back of the trailer and Mom, not Lou, had been sitting beside her, leaped into her mind. Then, Amy and her mom had been trying to save Spartan. She glanced at her sister — now she and Lou were giving him a chance to be happy.

She swallowed as she thought about the last three months. She had lost so much, but looking at Lou now and remembering her decision to stay at Heartland, she suddenly realized she had gained something, too.

❧

Larry Boswell's stud farm was set deep in the rolling countryside south of Heartland. Amy watched as they drove past farm after farm. At last they reached Dancing Grass Stables. Dark wooden fences separated the paddocks from the road. A heavy wooden sign swung in the slight breeze.

"Looks like we're here," said Lou.

Amy felt a prickle of apprehension as they turned up the drive. What if Hannah was wrong? What if Larry wouldn't accept Spartan and they had to take him back again?

Lou drove up to the front of the farmhouse, and they got out and looked around. No one came out. "I'll go and knock," Lou said. But there was no reply at the front door, so Lou went around to the back.

Amy went to check on Spartan. Seeing her, he gave a little nicker. Amy stepped slowly through the side door of the trailer. Spartan's dark eyes looked at her calmly. She wondered what the future would hold for him. What would Mr. Boswell decide?

Just then she heard the sound of voices approaching from the back of the trailer. "That's the Heartland trailer!" she heard Larry say. His tone turned harsh. "What are *they* doing here?"

Amy froze and then she heard Hannah speak. "They're delivering the horse I rode at the show, Grandpa. The one I told you about."

Suddenly, she heard Lou's voice. "Hi," her sister said, coming from the direction of the house. "We finally got here. Hello, Mr. Boswell."

"Hi." Amy heard Larry say gruffly.

"So, are you ready to see him, Grandpa?" Hannah asked eagerly.

"Amy's in there with him," Lou said.

Hannah suddenly appeared at the side door. "Amy, hi! Are you ready to bring him out?" She must have seen the concern on Amy's face because she gave a reassuring smile. "Don't worry," she said in a low voice. "It'll be fine. Trust me."

She disappeared, and Amy heard the locks on the ramp being undone. She placed a hand on Spartan's bay neck and felt the warmth of his satin-smooth coat. *Is this finally good-bye?* she thought. After everything that had happened to them both, it seemed almost impossible to believe.

"Spartan, you're back at Dancing Grass Stables," Amy said. "We've been through so much since the last time you were here." She put her cheek against his graceful head. "I'm going to miss you, boy, but I think this is where you belong."

Amy heard the ramp being lowered and she steadily led Spartan out.

Larry Boswell stared at Spartan incredulously, but before he could speak, Spartan nickered and pulled at the lead rope. Amy let go of the halter and stood back. The horse walked briskly over to his owner. Lifting his muzzle to Larry's face, he snorted and then buried his head in Larry's shoulder.

"Gerry!" Larry Boswell said, reaching out and touching the horse's neck. Spartan pushed against Larry's chest and nuzzled him, his nostrils flaring as he breathed in his owner's scent. "Oh, Gerry," Larry murmured.

"Grandpa, Gerry's the horse that I won on at the show," Hannah said softly. "You wouldn't have believed it. He was amazing. He's the horse I want." She went up to her grandpa and took his hand. "Please say that I can keep him. Please say you'll let Gerry stay."

Amy held her breath as Larry hesitated. Then, she noticed a tear running down his cheek. "Yes," he said, brushing it quickly away and looking at Hannah. "Of course he can stay."

🐍

Soon Spartan was settled happily back in his old stall as if the immense trauma of the past few months had never happened.

"We should be going," Lou said to Shelley Boswell. "I'm glad it all worked out so well in the end."

"Me, too, honey." Shelley Boswell smiled.

Amy said good-bye to Hannah and then looked over to where Spartan was gazing out of his stall. He turned his head toward her, his ears pricked, his silky forelock tumbling down over his handsome face. The happiness in his eyes was unmistakable. Amy felt a lump of tears gather in her throat. At last, Spartan's heart was at home.

Amy bit her lip and thought of all she had promised Spartan, and how relieved she was to know he was now happy. She smiled through her tears and blew Spartan a kiss. She took one last look at him and turned away.

Swallowing painfully, she walked over to the pickup where Lou was waiting.

"I'll write!" Hannah called. "And send you photos."

As Amy opened the door and got in, she saw Larry Boswell walking over to Spartan's stall. Spartan whinnied softly, and Amy saw Larry's face crease into a delighted smile.

Suddenly, she felt Lou squeeze her hand. "You did the right thing, Amy," she said. "Everyone needs a home, and you know that Heartland would never have been Spartan's."

Amy looked at her sister. "But it is yours now, isn't it, Lou?" she asked, her words full of hope.

Lou smiled. "Yes," she replied. "It is." Her eyes met Amy's as she started the engine. "Come on," she said softly. "Let's go home."

Heartland

❧

Breaking Free

For Pippa le Quesne — who has made Heartland
a very special place, with thanks and love.

With special thanks to Linda Chapman

Chapter One

"Mom's not coming back, Pegasus," Amy said gently to the old gray horse. "She's never coming back." She knew that her words meant nothing to him, but she felt she had to say them — to try to explain.

In the weeks following the tragic accident, Pegasus had kept watch for Marion Fleming — standing expectantly at the door of his stall at Heartland, staring down the drive for hours until night eventually fell.

But now, in the past few days, Amy had noticed another change in her mother's favorite horse. Pegasus had become listless and quiet. Instead of looking out over the half door, he had taken to standing at the back of his stall, his head low, his eyes dull. It was as though he had given up looking for Mom and had lost all sense of hope.

Amy couldn't bear seeing him like this. She bent her face to his.

Pegasus snorted quietly and let his great head rest against her chest. Amy closed her eyes. Despite the sadness that hung over him, his huge presence still filled the stall — making her feel safe and at peace, just like it always had. It was the same presence that had once filled stadiums around the world and had made Pegasus and her father one of the most famous show-jumping partnerships ever known.

But that had been a long time ago; a time when she had lived in England and when her father still had been a part of her life; a time when Heartland hadn't even existed. Amy shook her head slightly. It was another person's life now.

Her thoughts were interrupted by the distant sound of a door opening. Giving Pegasus a kiss on his dark gray muzzle, Amy went to the half door of his stall. She could see the slim blond figure of her older sister, Lou, coming out of the weather-boarded farmhouse. Grandpa followed behind her, carrying a suitcase.

Amy opened the stall door and headed toward the house. "Are you leaving already, Grandpa?" she called.

Jack Bartlett stopped by the car and nodded. "Yes, honey. If I set off now, I can get there before dark."

Amy hurried to the car. "Give my love to Glen and

Sylvia." She put her arms around her grandpa's neck and hugged him hard, breathing in his familiar smell of old leather and soap.

"Don't forget to call when you get there," Lou said, giving Grandpa a kiss on the cheek.

Jack Bartlett looked from one sister to the other, his weathered face creasing in concern. "Are you sure you'll be OK? With all that's happened lately I'm not so sure I should go."

"We'll be fine," Lou said, her blue eyes meeting Amy's. "Won't we?"

"Of course we will," Amy replied. "And you can't *not* go, Grandpa. You know how much Glen and Sylvia look forward to seeing you."

Jack Bartlett didn't deny it. He always made a point of going to stay with his brother, Glen, and sister-in-law, Sylvia, for a month every fall. When Amy had been younger, she had gone with him to the Tennessee farm.

Grandpa was still looking worried. "Are you sure you can cope with the extra workload while I'm away?" he asked. "We're overstretched at the moment as it is."

"We've talked about this already, Grandpa," Lou said practically. "You know my friend Marnie's coming next week. She'll be able to help, and Ty's offered to put in some extra hours."

"Can we really afford that?" Jack Bartlett said. Amy

saw the wrinkles at the side of his eyes deepen as he thought about paying Ty, Heartland's stable hand, for the extra work.

"We'll find a way," Lou said, and then before he had the chance to speak again she interrupted him firmly. "Look, just go." She hugged him quickly and opened the car door.

"I'm starting to think you're trying to get rid of me," Grandpa said, throwing his suitcase into the trunk before getting into the car.

"You're absolutely right," Amy grinned. "We're planning wild parties while you're away, aren't we, Lou?"

Grandpa grinned back. "Sounds like fun. Maybe I'll stay after all." He saw Lou's expression. "OK, OK. I'm outta here!"

As he started the engine, Amy and Lou stepped back and waved frantically as he drove down the long, winding drive.

"Well," Lou said to Amy, watching the car disappear in a cloud of dust, "I guess it's just you and me now."

From inside the house came the sound of the telephone ringing. Lou's eyes lit up. "Maybe that's a new customer! I'll get it," she said, hurrying off.

Amy looked around the yard. To her left was the front stable block with its six stalls. White paint was peeling off the doors, and the wood around the door frames had been well chewed by the many different inhabitants over the years. Wisps of hay and straw were piling up under the water trough and scattered outside the stall doors. Amy sighed. The yard needed sweeping, and the mess around by the back barn was even worse.

She looked across the drive to the fields. Horses and ponies of all different colors and sizes grazed peacefully in the September sun. Amy's heart lifted at the sight. She knew that if it weren't for Heartland, most of those horses and ponies would have been put down — thanks to her mom's work they all had a second chance to live healthy and happy lives. Just seeing them looking so content made the hard work and long hours worthwhile.

Out of the fifteen horses that were currently at Heartland, twelve had been rescued from abuse and neglect; Amy and Ty were working to heal their mental scars so that they could be rehomed. Three horses were boarders whose owners had sent them to Heartland to have their behavioral problems cured — and then there was Pegasus. He had been Daddy's horse until the show-jumping accident that had led to Amy's father deserting his wife and family. After that, Pegasus had given his heart to Mom. Amy's eyes fell on the empty doorway of the end stall. Poor Pegasus — without Mom he seemed so lost.

The back door opened and Lou came out.

"Was it a new boarder?" Amy asked, but as she spoke she could tell from her sister's face what the answer was.

"No. Just a wrong number." Lou sighed, her eyes

scanning the yard. "We're going to have to fill those three stalls soon, you know, Amy. The boarders are our only source of regular income."

Amy nodded. The fees from the customers who sent their problem horses to Heartland helped pay for the rescue work.

"I just can't understand why there haven't been any more calls," Lou continued with a frown. "After Nick Halliwell started to recommend us we had a lot of interest. Now there's nothing."

"I could ring Nick and see if he knows of anyone who might need some help with their horses," Amy suggested. Nick Halliwell was a famous show jumper. Two months ago, Amy had cured one of his talented young horses of its fear of trailers. Since then Nick had been recommending Heartland to people he knew.

"It's worth a try," Lou agreed.

But when Amy phoned Nick Halliwell's barn, she discovered that he was out of the country, competing. "He won't be back for another three weeks," Nick's personal assistant explained.

Amy sighed as she put the phone down. "No luck," she said, turning to Lou, who was sitting at the kitchen table.

"It's just so weird," Lou frowned. "We haven't had one inquiry in more than a week now."

It *was* a bit strange, Amy admitted to herself. It *was*

unusual to not have any phone calls for an entire week. A feeling of unease ran through her, but she pushed it down. "Things will be OK," she said, trying to sound optimistic.

"I hope you're right," Lou replied. "We're going to run into difficulties if business doesn't pick up soon." She sighed and stood up. "Well, I guess we should go and get started on Mom's room."

The breath caught in Amy's throat. *Mom's room.* The words echoed in her head. Marion Fleming's bedroom had been untouched since the night she'd died, but now that Lou's friend Marnie Gordon was coming to stay for a few weeks, they needed the space. Lou had decided that the time had come to sort it out.

"It shouldn't take too long," Lou said as Amy followed her upstairs. "I thought we could divide the stuff into three piles: things to keep, things to donate to the Salvation Army, and things to throw away." She opened the door of the bedroom and walked in.

Amy stopped still in the doorway. She had tried to avoid the room since Mom's death, and now a sudden wave of emotion welled up inside her at the sight of the familiar objects and the faint smell of her mom's perfume. She struggled to control herself. It had been three months since the accident, and the unrelenting grief had subsided, but every so often the slightest thing would cause the pain and loss to come flooding back.

"OK," Lou said, walking over to a pile of cardboard boxes that she had brought in earlier. "Let's put the stuff we're keeping in this box and anything that's being thrown out or given away over there." She walked around the room and cleared her throat. "I guess we should start with the closet."

Feeling as if she was moving in a dream, Amy stepped into the room. The photographs of horses on the walls, the barn jacket on the back of the chair, the slightly crooked bedclothes, the hairbrush with a few strands of hair still caught in between the bristles — it was as if Mom were still alive, as if she were going to come walking into the room any second.

Lou opened the oak closet and for a moment even she was overcome by the row of familiar clothes hanging there. She reached out and touched the fabric of a skirt, and Amy saw her swallow. But when she spoke, her voice was still practical. "Well, shall we go through these first?" She hesitated again and then pulled out a couple of blouses. "Anything that's in OK condition can go to the Salvation Army, and I guess we should get rid of the rest."

"We can't throw out Mom's clothes," Amy said quickly. She caught her sister's eye.

Lou frowned. "But we have to make room for Marnie's stuff. Besides, Amy, it's something we need to do."

Amy couldn't bear the thought of getting rid of her

mother's clothes just yet. "Can't we just keep them somewhere else?" She walked to the closet and took out a pair of green riding breeches. Her stomach clenched. She could remember Mom wearing them just a few days before she died.

Lou gave way. "OK, for now," she said, sighing. "I'm sure there's room in the basement."

It didn't take long to pack away the clothes. Amy folded up breeches and shirts and sweaters from the shelves while Lou took down the few dressy outfits that Mom had owned and packed them quickly and methodically into boxes. When she reached the last item, she paused.

"Mom's jacket," she said almost in a whisper, looking at the navy riding jacket with its deep crimson lining.

Amy saw Lou's eyes suddenly fill with emotion and felt her own chest tighten. Mom had given up her own show-jumping career after the accident that twelve years before had injured Pegasus and Daddy so badly. Amy had only been three and didn't really remember anything about her life then. Her memories started after she and Mom had moved to northeastern Virginia to live with Grandpa. But she knew that Lou, eleven years old at the time of the accident, had many more memories of their life in England, memories that the jacket obviously brought flooding back.

Blinking quickly, Lou folded the jacket tenderly and

placed it on top of the other clothes. Then she started to clear out the bottom of the closet, the shoe boxes, the bits and pieces of makeup and jars of skin cream. "Look at this," she said, her voice tight.

Amy silently took out a jumble of shoes. Under them she found a wooden box. She opened it. "Photographs!" she said, looking at two faded blue-and-gold albums and several envelopes of loose photographs. She opened the pages of the first album. "Lou! It's you!" There was no mistaking the golden-haired toddler who looked out of almost every photograph, cornflower blue eyes wide and curious in her heart-shaped face.

Lou looked over Amy's shoulder. "Yeah, it is."

"And Daddy and Mom." There were photographs of their parents looking strangely young. Their father, tall with dark, curly hair. Mom, smiling up at him, small and slender with the same blue eyes and fair hair as Lou.

Amy turned the pages. There were pictures of their parents' show-jumping stable in England, the horses looking out from around a smart square courtyard with dark timber stables. There were pictures of their dad and mom riding in competitions, pictures of Mom's beautiful bay mare, Delilah, and Daddy on Pegasus. There were even pictures of Lou at just five years old, jumping around a course of jumps on a small pinto pony.

"That was Minnie," Lou said, kneeling down beside Amy with a smile. "Daddy bought her for me when I was three. Then when you were old enough to learn, you always wanted to ride her, so Dad bought me Nugget." She opened the second photograph album. "Hey, look! Here's when you were first born."

Amy looked at herself as a baby and leafed through the pages of the album until she found pictures of herself as a two-year-old — a skinny toddler with light brown hair and gray eyes. In almost every picture she was either by a horse or on a horse. She looked so different from Lou, more like her father.

Lou pointed to a picture of the whole family, all smiling, sitting on a beach by a huge sand castle. "That was when we went to Spain. You were just three, and I was eleven."

Amy turned the pages, eager to see more, but suddenly the photographs stopped. The rest of the book was blank. She looked at her sister.

"Daddy's accident," Lou said quietly.

Amy pulled out the envelopes and tipped the photographs onto the floor. They showed Amy and Mom with Grandpa at Heartland. Amy had grown by about a year, and Mom looked different, too, her face serious, her eyes quiet.

"That's me," Lou said, pulling out a photograph. It showed her standing outside the entrance of her English boarding school. She, too, was looking very serious, wearing a smart school uniform, schoolbag in hand.

Amy glanced at her sister. "Why didn't you come with us, Lou?" Mom had tried to explain it to her, but she had never been able to understand why Lou had wanted to stay in England at boarding school.

"Because I thought that Daddy would come back," Lou said.

"But Mom waited for months," Amy said, remembering Marion's words. "She said that after Daddy left she waited and waited but nothing happened." She frowned. "He deserted us, Lou."

Lou's eyes flashed. "He was trying to come to terms with never being able to ride competitively again. Showing was his life," she said fiercely. "He would have come back for us, but Mom just took off and left the country."

"Of course she did!" Amy exclaimed, memories filling her mind of the months when they'd first arrived in Virginia and Mom had been so distraught. "There's no way she could have stayed in England — it reminded her too much of him."

"If she *had* stayed in England, then maybe she'd have been there when he did come back, and then they could have gotten back together!" Lou said.

But he never did come back! Amy bit back the words. She knew that she had only been told her mom's side of the story, but she didn't see that there *was* another side. And she'd never understand how Lou could still support their father. Amy felt her mother did the only thing she could have done. After months of anxious waiting, Marion had sold all of the horses apart from Pegasus, who had been badly injured in the accident, and moved back to her family home in Virginia. There she concentrated on healing Pegasus and then started the equine sanctuary at Heartland. Through healing horses that had nowhere else to go, she gradually restored her own emotional well-being.

"I couldn't have lived here anyway," Lou said. "Mom would have wanted me to help and get involved, and I just couldn't handle being around horses after what had happened with Daddy."

Amy thought about the long years of growing up when she had hardly seen her sister and about the occasions when Lou had visited and there'd been arguments over her refusal to have anything to do with Mom's work. It was different now. Since Mom had died, Lou had rediscovered her love of horses. Amy fingered a photograph of Lou dressed in a long black university gown, taken on her graduation day in Oxford, England. Standing next to her were Mom and Amy herself.

Lou looked over her shoulder and smiled. "I couldn't believe you and Mom came all that way for my graduation."

"Mom was really proud when you were accepted at Oxford University," Amy said. "And when you called to say how well you'd done in your finals, she said that we *had* to be there to see you graduate. Not even Heartland was more important to her than that."

Lou looked surprised. "She actually said that?"

Amy nodded.

"I never knew," Lou said softly.

Amy squeezed her arm. "Mom really missed you, Lou. She was so glad when you got a job in New York."

Lou bit her lip. "But I still didn't come and visit much, did I? Oh, Amy, if only things had been different. . . ." Her voice trailed off. Suddenly she seemed to pull herself together. "It's pointless, thinking like this," she said briskly. "You can't live a life of regret. You have to move on." She started putting things into boxes again. "Come on. Let's finish up."

Amy put the photographs back in the envelope and put the albums carefully away. She carried the box over to the window. Mom's window, like the one in her own bedroom, looked out over the yard. Pegasus was still at the back of his stall, nowhere to be seen.

"I'm worried about Pegasus," Amy said, turning to help Lou, who was now clearing out the drawers of the dresser.

"You mentioned that he hasn't been himself lately," Lou said.

Amy nodded. "You know how he used to look out over the stall door for Mom after she died?"

"Like he was waiting for her to come home?" Lou said.

"Mmm," Amy replied. "Well, he's stopped doing it now. The last few days he's just been standing in the back of his stall, looking depressed. Something's wrong with him, Lou."

"I'm sure he'll be OK," Lou said, putting the lid on a box.

Amy glanced out the window, wishing she could feel so certain. "Mom meant everything to him. He must be really confused. Without a warning she's gone, and he doesn't understand why. I'm sure that's why he's so listless."

"Can you do anything to help?" Lou asked.

Amy thought about the herbal and other natural remedies that her mom had taught her how to use. She knew several different treatments for grief and loss. "I'll try," she replied. "I'll see what I can do."

Lou smiled at her reassuringly and opened another drawer. "I'm sure he'll perk up in a while."

They worked in silence for a few minutes. "I think we can throw these out," Lou said, opening the last drawer and pulling out a pile of letters and cards. She flicked through them quickly. "They're just old birthday cards and . . ." Suddenly she stopped. She pulled out an envelope from the pile.

"What is it?" Amy asked, seeing Lou's eyes widen.

Her sister didn't answer. Amy looked over Lou's shoulder. The letter was addressed to Marion at Heartland. "What is it?" Amy said again, not sure why Lou was looking at the letter so strangely.

"It was sent five years ago," said Lou, looking at the postmark.

"So?" Amy said.

Lou looked up, her face pale. "It's from Daddy," she said.

Chapter Two

"It *can't* be!" Amy exclaimed, staring at the envelope in Lou's hands. "Mom never heard from him after he left."

"Well, it's his handwriting," said Lou. Amy saw her eyes glance at the address. "He sent it from England. *England!*" Lou swallowed. "He was there all along — I knew it!" She opened the top of the envelope, her fingers trembling, and took out a letter written on plain white paper.

"What does it say?" Amy demanded as Lou unfolded the letter and skimmed the contents.

There was a pause. "I was in England then," Lou whispered, her hand dropping to her knees. "Why didn't he contact me?"

"What does it say?" Amy repeated. Impatiently, she

snatched the letter from Lou. "Darling Marion," she read out loud. Her voice faded as she read on.

Please write to me, just a note, a card — anything other than this silence. I know I did a truly dreadful thing, and I have blamed myself every day for seven long years. But please, please, find it in your heart to forgive me. We could start again together — just think how much we could do as a team. We were so good together once — weren't we? I know we could be again. I won't write any more now. Please tell the girls I love them and miss them. All I want is for us to be a family once again.

I have never stopped loving you,

Tim

Amy's arm seemed to go numb, and the letter fell to the floor. As Lou picked it up and started to read, thoughts began reeling through Amy's head. Mom had lied to her. Mom had told her that her father had never been in touch. And yet here was a letter from him, pleading for forgiveness, asking her if they could get back together.

She looked at Lou. Her sister's face was pale. "Why didn't he try to reach me?" she whispered. "I was the one who waited. *I* was there."

Amy shrugged helplessly. She couldn't believe it. Daddy had tried to persuade Mom to get back together with him. And what had been Mom's response? Had she written back? She pushed a hand through her hair, feeling her whole life and all it was based on disappearing like quicksand beneath her. Everything that she had thought she knew suddenly seemed less certain. What other things had Mom not told her? How should she feel about her father, now that she had read this letter?

"Do you mind if I keep it?" Lou's voice broke through Amy's thoughts. She was folding up the letter, her chin set at a determined angle.

Amy shook her head, hardly able to bring herself to speak. "No . . . I don't want it." She looked at her sister. The expression in Lou's eyes was unfathomable. "She never told me," she said to Lou.

"She never told either of us," Lou said. She put the envelope in the pocket of her shirt and then turned to the boxes, her voice suddenly brisk and practical again. "OK, let's go through the chest and then take some of this stuff downstairs." They continued to work in silence.

After clearing out Mom's bedroom, Amy left Lou to vacuum and dust and went outside to see to the horses. It was Ty's day off, and there was still plenty to do. Five stalls in the back barn needed cleaning, all the water buckets and hay nets needed refilling, and the horses still had to be brought in from the fields. Amy hurried around, using the chores as an excuse not to think about the letter. Just knowing that five years ago her father had sat down and written to Mom was weird enough without thinking about the content of the letter.

She set to work grooming and working the three boarded horses, Swallow, Charlie, and Whisper. She rode Charlie and Whisper in the schooling ring and then concentrated on Swallow. He was a bay gelding who had come to Heartland to have his fear of traffic cured. He'd been working well in the schooling ring that week, and Amy had planned to take him out on the roads for the first time that day. But with one thing and another, it looked as if he was going to have to wait. She glanced at her watch. There just wasn't time. She would have to put off working him on the roads until the next day. Maybe she and Ty could take a ride together when she got in from school.

As Amy led Swallow up to the exercise ring, she thought about how much she missed Ty on the rare occasions when he took his days off. He had started working part-time at Heartland when he was fifteen and then, a year later, had left school to train with Marion full-time. He had been amazing in the last few months since the accident. In fact, Amy wasn't sure how they would have coped without him. He worked tirelessly and knew as much about natural remedies and working with problem horses as she did.

At feed time, Lou came out to help her. "The yard is such a mess!" she said as they filled the last of the water buckets.

Amy looked around. The yard looked even worse than usual — loose handfuls of hay and straw littered the ground, and feed buckets were piled haphazardly outside stall doors.

"It's no big deal," Amy said. "We can clean everthing up tomorrow."

"You'll be at school," Lou reminded her.

"I'll do it before I go," Amy replied. As far as she was concerned, a few misplaced feed buckets didn't matter — what mattered was that the horses were exercised, watered, and fed. She brushed off her jeans. "I think I'll spend some time with Pegasus," she said.

Lou looked at her. "Have you done all your homework?"

"Almost." Amy saw Lou's face. "I just have a little more to do, that's all."

"You're sure?" Lou said suspiciously.

"Positive," Amy lied quickly.

She headed for the tack room where the medicine cabinet was. Her homework would have to wait. Finding something to help Pegasus was far more important. Lou went back into the house, leaving Amy to decide which aromatherapy oils to use. Selecting three different oils that could help treat depression, she carried them over to Pegasus's stall, where she noticed that the feed in his manger had hardly been touched.

Putting down the unopened bottles of oil, Amy started to gently massage the horse's head, making small, light circles with her fingers. It was a treatment called T-touch that her mom had taught her. Her fingers moved over his ears and down his face, sensing where her touch was needed. Gradually she felt him relax.

Giving him a kiss, Amy stopped massaging him and unscrewed the top of the first bottle, offering him the oil to smell. She watched Pegasus's reaction carefully. He put his ears back and turned his head away. She was surprised. It was neroli oil, the remedy that was most effective with horses suffering from sadness and loss. But Marion had always said that horses must be allowed to choose their own remedies, and so Amy accepted the gray horse's reaction and offered him the next bottle — yarrow. Again he turned his head away. Frowning slightly, she offered him the third bottle. Pegasus sniffed at it and then lifted his upper lip as if he were laughing. He reached for the bottle with his lips.

"No, you don't," Amy said, quickly closing her fingers around the bottle. The oil had to be diluted before it was used. She checked the label — bergamot oil. It was good for balancing and uplifting emotions and was a stimulant for the immune system. It wasn't necessarily an oil for helping to deal with grief. However, if that was what Pegasus had chosen, then that was what she would use.

She returned the bottles to the tack room and took a larger bottle of diluted oil back to Pegasus's stall. Putting a few drops on her hand, she started to massage his nostrils. "You've got to start getting better," she told him. "You can't stay depressed like this." She looked at his aging body. His once dappled coat was now snow-white, his ribs showed slightly. He sighed deeply and her heart ached for him. All her life Pegasus had been there. Whenever she was miserable and upset she would talk to him, and he would always listen and seem to understand. Now he was suffering and she had to try to help him — just as Mom had done all those years ago following the accident. "I'll make it better for you, Pegasus," she whispered. "I promise."

▬

The next morning, Amy sat at the kitchen table trying to eat a muffin and do her math and history assignments at the same time. She had meant to finish them the night before, but almost as soon as she had sat down at her desk her eyes had closed, and she had fallen asleep on her books.

"Amy! I thought you said you were done with

your schoolwork!" Lou exclaimed, coming into the kitchen.

"I've just got a bit to finish here," Amy said defensively.

Lou looked at the half-written page. "A fairly large bit by the looks of it!" she said. "And the bus will be here in ten minutes. Oh, Amy, when will you . . ."

She was interrupted by Ty coming into the kitchen. "Hey, guys. What's up for today?" he asked, leaning against the door frame, his dark hair falling down over his face as he looked at Amy.

"I don't know," Amy said, scribbling another few sentences. "Swallow was really good yesterday, he's ready to go —" she was about to say *out on the road*, but she broke off as the second part of the history assignment caught her eye. "Help! Ty, do you know anything about revolutions in medicine in the late nineteenth century?"

"Sorry," Ty said. "Can't help you there. So Swallow's OK now? What about Charlie and Whisper?"

"Amy! You're going to miss the bus if you don't get a move on!" Lou insisted.

Amy swallowed the last piece of muffin and shoved her books into her backpack. "Just do what you want with them," she said quickly to Ty, her mind on her assignment. Maybe she could finish it on the bus. Matt and Soraya could help her.

"OK," Ty said as she rushed out past him. "Bye."

🙙

Amy got to the end of the drive just in time to stop the bus. Seeing Soraya sitting near the back, she made her way there. "Hi!" she gasped, collapsing onto the seat beside her best friend. "How was your weekend?"

"Good," Soraya said, shifting in her seat to make more room. "How about yours?"

"Not great," Amy admitted. "And I still haven't finished that history assignment."

Soraya shook her head. "One day you're going to surprise me and actually do your homework on time." She rummaged in her bag. "Here. Take a look at mine."

"Thanks," Amy said gratefully, getting out her own book.

"So what was wrong with the weekend?" Soraya asked, as Amy found a pen.

"Oh, you know — just things." Amy looked up and saw Soraya's concerned brown eyes. "Pegasus isn't eating," she sighed. "We haven't had any calls about boarders for more than a week now. Grandpa's gone to Tennessee, which means extra work for Ty and me, and then yesterday when Lou and I cleaned out Mom's room, we found a letter that my dad had written to Mom five years ago."

"But I thought your mom hadn't heard from him since he left!" Soraya exclaimed in surprise.

"So did I," Amy replied. "And he said in the letter that he wanted to get back together with her."

"Get out of here!" Soraya gasped. "Are you OK?" she asked curiously.

Amy wished she could find the right words to express the confusion she had been feeling since reading the letter. "I'm not sure," she said at last. She paused. "I always thought that he'd just abandoned us without another thought, but that's not true and — and —"

"And it makes you feel different about him?" Soraya said.

Amy nodded. "I think so. And Mom, too," she added, glancing quickly at her friend.

Soraya squeezed her hand. She didn't say anything — she didn't need to. Amy knew that she understood. Suddenly, not wanting to think about the letter anymore, she looked down at the history worksheet. "Did you understand the second part of this?" she asked.

Soraya accepted the change of subject. "Yeah. Take a look."

Amy read through Soraya's notes and quickly started scribbling her own answer.

"Have you got anything else to do?" Soraya asked.

"Yeah, math," Amy replied. "But I was sort of hoping that Matt might help me with that."

"I'm sure he will," Soraya said, giving her a sideways grin. "Matt would do *anything* for you, Amy."

Amy feigned innocence. "I don't know what you mean."

"Sure you don't," Soraya said sarcastically. She shook her head. "Poor Matt. Every other girl in the school would jump at the chance to date him, and he goes and decides that he likes you."

Amy grinned and bent her head over her work.

A few stops later, Matt Trewin got on the bus. He sat down in the seat in front of them and grinned. "Still doing your homework, Amy?" he said. "How unusual."

"I need help, Matt," Amy pleaded, looking up from the last line of the history assignment. "I've still got the math homework to do."

"OK," Matt sighed. "Where is it?"

Amy handed him her book. He scanned down the page. "This doesn't look too bad," he commented. Matt was a straight-A student who wanted to be a doctor. Amy's report cards were more likely to be covered with Cs and comments like "has ability and could achieve more than her current grades suggest." She didn't mind school — it was just that studying always came second to Heartland and the horses.

By the time the bus reached Jefferson High, both of her weekend assignments were finished. "Thanks, Matt," Amy said as they got off the bus and headed for their lockers.

Matt gave a wry smile. "Anytime." He left Amy and

Soraya to go to his own locker around the corner from theirs.

"Oh, no," Soraya said in a low voice, her eyes suddenly fixing on a point over Amy's left shoulder. "Look who's coming."

Amy glanced around. Walking toward them were three girls, all with meticulously applied makeup and shiny, perfectly cut hair. They all looked somewhat alike, dressed in the very latest designer labels. The girl in the center paused. Seeing Amy and Soraya, she raised her carefully plucked eyebrows into an arch and walked over, her pale blond hair bouncing on her shoulders. Amy couldn't help but think of a shampoo commercial.

"Well, hello, Amy," the girl said, stopping in front of her and tilting her head to one side.

"Hi, Ashley," Amy acknowledged her stonily.

"So how's business at . . ." Ashley paused. "Heartland?" The way she said it made Heartland sound like some small, run-down, four-stall affair.

"Fine," Amy said, lifting her chin defiantly. "In fact, we're very busy."

Ashley's lips curved into a smile. "That's not what *I've* heard." Ashley Grant's family owned an upscale riding stable called Green Briar. Her mom, Val Grant, specialized in producing push-button horses and ponies for hunter jumping, but she also offered a service curing problem horses. Her methods, however, were very different from those used at Heartland.

Amy frowned. "What do you mean?"

Ashley looked around at her two friends, Brittany and Jade, who had moved up to join her. "Should I tell her?" It wasn't a question that required an answer. They smiled at one another.

Amy stepped forward, refusing to be intimidated. "Tell me what?" She felt Soraya move closer to her and put a hand on her arm. Soraya hated confrontations, but Amy's anger was rising swiftly. "What are you talking about, Ashley?" she demanded.

"Oh, just that people are saying that Heartland's days are numbered," Ashley said. Her voice was airy, but her green eyes never left Amy's face. "And that with your mom gone there isn't anyone who can cure the horses."

"But that's not true!" Amy burst out indignantly.

Ashley laughed. "Come on, Amy. There's you, your sister from New York, and Ty. You can't believe people are still going to bring valuable horses to Heartland." She tossed her hair back. "Come on, get real."

"They are!" Amy cried. From the corner of her eye she saw Matt come up beside her. "They'll still come. How would you even know, Ashley?"

"Oh, I've heard the rumors," Ashley said. "They're going around like wildfire. You might as well face it,

Amy. You should sell Heartland. Daddy would buy the land from you." A catlike smile curved up her lips. "After all, our business is doing just great. *Our* barn has never been so full." She smiled at Matt. "Oh, hi, Matt." And with that she turned and walked away.

Amy made a move to follow her.

"Leave it, Amy," Matt said, grabbing her arm. "You know what Ashley's like. She's just doing it to get to you."

"And she's succeeding," Soraya said. "Just ignore her."

But Ashley's words had hit a raw nerve. Amy stared down the hallway. What if people *were* staying away from Heartland because they doubted if it had a future without Mom? They needed the chance to work with new horses to prove that she and Ty were good enough to continue her mom's work. If the boarders stopped coming, if there were no problem horses to cure, then what would happen to Heartland?

As soon as Amy got back to Heartland that afternoon, she went to find Lou to tell her what Ashley Grant had said. Lou was sitting at the kitchen table writing an address on an envelope. She jumped guiltily as Amy came in and quickly slipped the envelope under a pile of papers.

"What was that?" Amy asked.

Lou seemed to hesitate for a moment, and then she shook her head. "Oh, just a bill," she said. She stood up and quickly started to clear her papers away. "So . . . how was school?"

Forgetting about the letter, Amy launched into a tirade about Ashley.

Lou listened intently. "So she says that people have been staying away on purpose?"

Amy nodded. "If it's true, what are we going to do? We can't have people believing that we can't cure horses anymore."

"Hmm," Lou said, frowning. "Well, we'll just have to come up with something."

The kitchen door opened and Ty came in. "Hey," he said. "Can I get your help?"

"Sure." Amy hurried upstairs to get changed. It took her less than a minute to pull on her work jeans and a T-shirt. Ty waited for her in the kitchen. "How much else is there to do?" she said, slipping on her boots.

"A good bit." Amy noticed that Ty's normally calm face looked unnerved. "I haven't groomed anyone yet, and three still need working. It hit me today just how much your grandpa normally does around here."

"It should be easier when Marnie arrives," Lou said. "She's coming on Saturday and she wants to help. She used to ride when she was a kid."

Ty nodded. "And having one horse less will help — but not with money, I guess," he added, glancing at Lou.

"One horse less?" Amy said in surprise, wondering what he meant.

"Swallow went home," Lou said. "His owner, Mrs. Roche, called this morning and asked if he was ready. She picked him up a couple of hours ago." She must have seen the confusion on Amy's face. "You said he was OK to go," she continued uncertainly. "This morning when Ty asked you, you said he was ready."

"No, I didn't!" Amy exclaimed, staring at her. Suddenly she remembered the half-finished conversation they'd had that morning. Her hand flew to her mouth. "I meant that he was ready to start going out on the roads, *not* ready to go home!"

Lou stared. "So he's not safe on the roads yet?"

"Of course he's not!" Amy cried, jumping to her feet in horror. "I haven't ridden him on them at all. What are we going to do?" She saw the look of shock on Lou's face and swung around to Ty. "Ty!" she exclaimed. "How could you let Swallow leave? You must have *known* he wasn't ready."

"But you said he was," Ty replied. "I guessed you'd worked him over the weekend."

Amy almost stamped her foot in frustration and worry. "I didn't have time!"

"Listen," Lou broke in quickly. "Let's just call Mrs.

Roche right now and explain." She ran to the phone. "Quick, find me the number."

Amy grabbed the client book and started to leaf frantically through it. What if Mrs. Roche had taken Swallow out on the roads? He was better than he had been but nowhere near cured. *Anything* could have happened.

"Here it is!" she cried, holding the book up.

But just then they heard the sound of car tires crunching to a halt on the gravel outside. Amy swung around and looked out of the kitchen window. "Oh, no!" she gasped, seeing a well-built, red-faced woman get out of the car. "It's Mrs. Roche, and she looks really mad!"

Chapter Three

Amy, Lou, and Ty hurried to the door. "Mrs. Roche," Lou began, "I was just about to telephone you, there's been a —" She didn't have a chance to finish. Mrs. Roche bore down on her.

"I want a word with you, Louise Fleming!" she demanded, her eyes furious.

"Mrs. Roche," Lou said quickly, "if you'll just give me a chance to explain."

But Mrs. Roche seemed in no mood to listen to explanations. "I picked up Swallow this afternoon because I was assured that he was cured of his fear of traffic. I took him out on the road as soon as I got home, only to be almost thrown under a bus. That may be your idea of a cured horse, but it's certainly not mine!"

"Mrs. Roche, you don't understand —" Lou began, but once again she was interrupted.

"I understand perfectly!" Mrs. Roche snapped. Amy could see the veins standing out on her forehead. "You've been making a living by trading on your mother's reputation without having the experience to deal with the problems you promise to cure."

"That's not fair!" Amy burst out. "It was a mistake! Swallow should never have left. We were about to call you."

"Amy's right," Lou said. "We're very sorry. If you'll just bring Swallow back we'll continue his treatment free of charge." She tried smiling at Mrs. Roche, but the woman was obviously too worked up for it to have any effect.

"Bring him back!" she exclaimed. "No way! I'm going to take him somewhere where they know about horses." She stalked off toward her car. "And you'd better watch out for yourselves," she shouted over her shoulder as she yanked open the car door. "I'm not going to keep quiet about this, and once I've spread the word you can say good-bye to anyone bringing their horses here anymore!"

"But, Mrs. Roche —" Lou cried.

The angry woman slammed her car into reverse and, revving the engine, turned around in a shower of gravel and disappeared down the drive.

Lou put her head in her hands. "Oh, this is not good!" she groaned.

"What are we going to do?" Amy cried.

"There isn't much we can do," Lou said, looking up. "We just have to accept it. I'll write her a letter of apology, of course. I could try to call her, but I doubt it'll change her mind. I just can't believe it — this is the last thing we needed."

Amy bit back her anger as she saw her sister's shoulders sag. "Don't worry, Lou," she said quickly. "It was just one customer."

"I'm really sorry, Lou," Ty said, pushing a hand through his dark hair. "I should have waited."

Amy shot a look at him — frustration at the stupidity of the situation and worry about what it could mean for Heartland flashing hotly in her eyes. *Of course he should have waited.* "I can't believe you let Swallow go!" she said accusingly.

She saw Ty's face stiffen.

"Oh, come on, it's not Ty's fault, Amy," Lou spoke up quickly. "I was the one who spoke to Mrs. Roche on the phone. And this morning you did say that Swallow was ready."

But Amy couldn't help herself. "You knew Swallow wasn't ready. Why didn't you think it through?" she cried to Ty. "You've worked here long enough!"

As soon as the words came out Amy wanted to grab them back. They had made Ty sound like he was just a hired hand. She made a move toward him, but he was already turning away from her, his mouth clenched.

"I'll be in the back barn if you need me," he said, his voice flat.

"Ty —" Amy's heart sank as she watched him leave. *What had she done?*

With her mind immersed in Heartland's financial problems again, Lou hadn't noticed what had just happened. She sighed. "Look, we can't just stand around wishing Swallow was still here. We need to think about what we can do to make things better. Let's go inside, make some tea, and talk about it."

"I'll just be a minute," Amy said. Leaving her sister to go into the farmhouse, she hurried after Ty.

She caught up with him by the tack room. "Ty, I'm sorry," she blurted out, putting a hand on his arm. "I shouldn't have shouted at you like that."

Ty's eyes were expressionless. "I'll live."

"But I didn't mean what I said," Amy said quickly. "I really didn't. I was just upset. I'm sorry." She waited, expecting him to smile his familiar grin at her, tell her that all was forgiven. But he didn't — he just shrugged.

"Whatever."

An awkward silence hung between them. Amy suddenly became conscious that she was still holding on to his arm. She loosened her grip and let her hand fall to her side.

"I'll be in the barn grooming Jasmine," Ty said flatly. With that he turned and continued to the back barn.

Amy stared after him in confusion. She had lost her temper with him before, but usually he accepted her apology. He knew what she was like. She said things she didn't mean when she was upset. So why was this time different? Maybe it was because she had never treated him like a hired hand before, like someone who was just paid to do a job. Feeling uncomfortable, she returned to the house.

Lou was sitting at the kitchen table, making some notes on a piece of scrap paper.

"What are we going to do, Lou?" Amy said, sitting down next to her.

Lou looked up. "If people are staying away because they think we aren't experienced enough, then having Mrs. Roche going around telling her story will only make things worse," she said. "However, what happened can't be undone, so I guess we should just try to weather the storm and prove them wrong. But I think we are going to have to make some changes."

"What kind of changes?" Amy asked doubtfully. Lou, with her practical business mind, had tried to suggest alterations to the running of Heartland before, but Amy had fought against them. She wanted things to stay like they were when her mother was alive. *Still,* Amy reminded herself, thinking about the success of the fund-raising dance that her sister had organized that summer, *some of Lou's ideas worked.*

"Well, first of all I would suggest that we need to make the place look more professional," Lou said. She must have seen the confusion on Amy's face. "Come on, Amy, admit it — the place is a mess. There's hay and straw all over the yard, pitchforks and rakes just thrown in a corner, and the manure pile seems to have a life of its own! It doesn't give a good impression to clients who come and look around."

"It's only because Grandpa is away," Amy said. "Ty and I are just so busy with everything else."

"OK, I agree it's worse at the moment," Lou said. "But even when Grandpa's here the place never looks as neat as it should." She shook her head. "I think we need to give the place a makeover—repaint the stall doors, fix the fences, organize the tack room, and then make an effort to keep everything tidy."

Amy frowned. She liked the yard the way it was. But after the dance she had promised to listen to Lou's ideas. "I guess," she said, rather reluctantly.

"Great!" Lou said. "We'll start this weekend. Marnie can pitch in. Of course, having a clean yard isn't much use if we don't have clients to come and see it, so I think we should consider advertising." She turned to Amy. "You remember my idea about the brochure? Well, I'm going to work on that. Maybe it will bring in a few more boarders." Her face brightened. "If we get enough business we might be able to hire another stable hand. Just part-time — but it would help."

"It would have to be the right person, though," Amy said quickly. "Someone who's into alternative therapies and our way of doing things." As far as Amy was concerned, it would be out of the question to employ someone at Heartland who didn't believe in their mom's ideals.

"Of course," Lou said, sounding surprised. "But I'm sure that won't be a problem." Picking up her pen, she started scribbling a few more notes.

Amy frowned slightly. She had a feeling that finding the right person to work at Heartland wouldn't be as easy as Lou thought. A lot of people in the horse world were traditionalists who dismissed people who used alternative methods as crazy faith healers. She sighed. Right now, however, the problem wasn't about finding someone else to employ, it was about finding some new customers and managing all the work with just her and Ty. She stood up. "I'd better go and help outside," she said.

Amy headed up the yard, wondering whether Ty had forgiven her yet. She found him in the feed room making up the evening hay nets.

"Hi!" she said, looking hopefully at his face.

Ty nodded a brief greeting and then bent his head over the hay again.

Amy hesitated uncomfortably by the door. He was obviously still not over it. She wondered what to do. Finally she picked up a hay net and started to fill it. "Lou's been coming up with some ideas to help us get more customers," she said. Ty didn't respond. Amy persevered. "She's going to put together a brochure and drop it off at all the feed merchants and tack stores and places like that." She was aware that she was talking faster than normal, her voice unnaturally high. Ty continued to shake out the flakes of hay and stuff them into a net, his head bent. "She also thought that we could straighten up the yard a bit. She thinks it's a mess." She grinned, attempting a joke. "How can she possibly think that?"

Ty looked up at her, his mouth set in an angry line. "I've been busy," he said. "There are sixteen horses here and only so many hours in the day. I'll clean up after I'm done with the other stuff."

"Ty, I didn't mean — I wasn't criticizing you," Amy stammered. "Anyway, *I'm* usually the one who makes all the mess!"

Ty dumped the hay net he had been filling in the pile with the others. "OK. I'll go and start sweeping now," he said.

"Ty!" Amy exclaimed as he brushed past her.

For a brief moment she hesitated. Should she just let him go? But she couldn't. "Wait!" she said, leaping after him.

Ty stopped, his back still turned to her.

"I'm sorry." The words tumbled out of Amy. "I didn't mean what I said earlier. I really didn't. I should have talked to you about Swallow this morning, but I was thinking about my homework." She caught his arm. "Please . . . I don't want us to argue. You're too important to me." She saw Ty's shoulders stiffen and realized what she had just said. "Too important to Heartland," she stammered, adjusting her words.

Ty turned and looked at her. Amy hastily let go of his arm and tried to hide her confusion by laughing awkwardly. "I can't seem to keep my hands off you today."

Ty's lips flickered in a faint grin. "I seem to have that affect on girls."

Amy felt a rush of relief as she realized that he had forgiven her. "Whatever, in your dreams!" she responded. She saw Ty's face relax. "I really am sorry about before," she said more quietly. "It was my fault. I wasn't paying attention this morning. I had no idea that I made it sound like Swallow was OK."

"It's OK," Ty said. He shrugged and walked back to the hay nets with her. "It's not all your fault. I guess I overreacted. It's just difficult." He glanced at her. "You know, this place, now that your mom isn't here."

Amy nodded. It was a huge responsibility. She felt it as well.

"Hey, don't look like that," Ty said softly. "We'll make it."

She lifted her eyes to his. "We have to," she whispered, seeing in Ty's eyes the same mixture of uncertainty, hope, and fear that she felt in her own heart.

🖎

At feed time Amy brought Pegasus in from his field. He walked slowly up the drive beside her, his seventeenhand frame looking gaunt, his ears flopping listlessly. The bergamot oil appeared to not be of much help. However, Amy knew she couldn't expect a miracle cure. Natural remedies often took time to work. She got the bottle and offered him a few drops on the back of her hand.

Pegasus licked them off, his tongue rasping against Amy's skin. She looked at his ribs, showing more clearly than ever, and bit her lip.

"I think I'll give Pegasus a bran mash," she said, going to the feed room, where Ty was scooping grain into yellow buckets. "I need to tempt him into eating something."

"Try adding a banana and some honey to it," Ty suggested. "They're good for energy."

Amy nodded. However, even with the addition of

some dried mint powder that Pegasus normally adored, he only picked at the hot mash. She stroked him as he rested his muzzle on the manger. The hollows under his ears were pronounced, and his eyes looked sunken. "What am I going to do with you, Pegasus?" she said softly.

He snorted. Putting an arm around his neck, she leaned her cheek against his rough mane. She couldn't bear seeing him so depressed. Leaving the stall, she went to find Ty.

"I'm going to call Scott," she said.

"Yeah, I would," Ty agreed.

Amy went down to the house. Scott Trewin, her friend Matt's brother, was the local equine vet. He was a young doctor who believed in using alternative therapies alongside conventional medicine. Through sharing an interest in Marion's work, he had become good friends with her before she died. Amy phoned him at his office. He asked a few questions and said he'd stop by later to check on Pegasus.

"It's not urgent, Scott," Amy said to him, not wanting to cut into his evening. "We're just a bit worried."

"I'll come over tonight. It's not a problem," Scott said, his deep voice reassuring. "I haven't got anything else on, and I'll be passing your place anyway."

"Thanks," Amy said gratefully.

✿

At six thirty, Scott's battered Jeep came bumping up Heartland's drive. "So Pegasus hasn't been eating?" he asked, taking his black bag out of the car and walking toward the barn with Amy. Scott was fair and tall, with a broad-shouldered frame.

"No," Amy replied. "And he's been very quiet. I think he really misses Mom."

In the stall, Scott patted the old gray horse and then listened to Pegasus's heart and breathing before taking his temperature.

"Well, there doesn't seem to be anything obviously wrong," he said at last. "Although he's lost some weight. It could be a virus — have any of the other horses shown similar signs?"

Amy shook her head.

"I'll take a blood test," Scott said, taking out a syringe from his bag.

Amy watched the deep red blood filling up the tube. "Do you think it could be because of Mom?"

Scott considered the question as he removed the needle. "Maybe. Some people would disagree with me, but I think horses can feel grief and loneliness when they lose a close companion — whether it's another horse or a human. Pegasus's symptoms are pretty general. That could be a sign it's emotional — but these symptoms could also be from a physical illness like a virus or possibly something more serious."

"Something more serious?" Amy echoed in alarm. She hadn't considered the possibility of Pegasus being really ill.

"I'm sure it's nothing to worry about," Scott said. "He'll probably perk up in a day or two."

Amy patted Pegasus. "I hope so."

Just then Lou looked over the stall door. "Hi, Scott."

"Hey," Scott said, his eyes lighting up. "How's it going?"

"Fine," Lou said. "Have you found anything wrong with Pegasus?"

"Nothing obvious," Scott replied. He repeated what he had told Amy and then packed his things away in his bag. "Well, I guess I'd better be off," he said, straightening up.

Lou opened the stall door for him. "Would you . . . would you like some coffee?" Her voice, usually so confident, caught hesitantly.

Amy looked at her sister and saw a faint blush creeping along Lou's cheekbones.

"Yeah," Scott said with a smile. "That would be great." He walked out of the stall and then, suddenly seeming to remember that Amy was there, he turned to her. "You coming, Amy?"

"I think I'll stay with Pegasus a while," Amy said. She watched as Lou and Scott walked to the house together, a thought suddenly forming in her brain. What if Lou and Scott liked each other? Until recently Lou had been going out with Carl Anderson, a guy she knew from Manhattan. But that was over now. Amy put her arms around Pegasus's neck. "They'd be just perfect together, wouldn't they?" she said to the old, gray horse.

Pegasus lifted his head as though nodding. Amy smiled. She knew it was only because a passing fly had happened to settle on his muzzle, but it seemed he understood.

"I love you," she whispered, kissing the side of his face.

Pegasus snorted softly in reply.

Chapter Four

The next morning when Amy came into the house to get changed for school, she found Lou putting the phone down, her face worried.

"That was Laura Greene," she told Amy.

"Whisper's owner?" Amy said.

Lou nodded. Whisper was one of the two remaining livery horses. "She wants to take him away. She's coming with her trailer this afternoon."

"But why?" Amy demanded. "Things are going really well." Whisper had come to Heartland to be gently introduced to being ridden. After several weeks of carefully building up his confidence and trust, Amy and Ty had decided to get on him for the first time that weekend.

"She's been talking to Mrs. Roche," Lou said. "Guess where she's taking him?"

Amy knew from Lou's face what the answer would be. "Not Green Briar?" she said. Lou nodded. "But that's not fair!" Amy exclaimed. "They'll get all the credit, and we'll have done all the work."

"I know," Lou sighed. "But there's not much we can do."

Seething with rage at the unfairness of it all, Amy marched up the stairs. It was bad enough that Swallow left, but now Whisper, too. And Green Briar would get all the thanks, all the recognition.

❧

Her frustration flared up again when Ashley came over to her in the cafeteria that day at school. Amy was sitting at a table with Soraya when she walked up.

"Hi, Amy," Ashley said, crossing her arms and smirking. "I hear you're losing another boarder."

Amy glared at her.

"Oh, go away, Ashley," Soraya said.

Ashley ignored her. She was evidently on a mission. "You know," she commented, "some people might say it's a bit careless to lose two clients in one week. What *are* you doing to them?"

Amy's fingers clenched her fork as she felt her temper starting to rise.

"Just so you know, Mrs. Roche is delighted with the progress Swallow has made at Green Briar," Ashley said. "I rode him out on the roads yesterday, and he didn't even flinch. Of course, as my mom explained to Mrs. Roche, that's because *we* have the experience to deal with problem horses."

It was the last straw. Unable to bear the thought of Ashley riding Swallow, Amy jumped to her feet. "Experience!" she snapped, not caring that everyone around them was staring curiously at her and Ashley. "He was practically cured. You didn't have to do anything!"

Ashley had a ferocious smile on her face. "What a shame Mrs. Roche doesn't seem to agree with you." As she turned to go, she suddenly stopped. "Oh, by the way," she said. "Did you hear about my latest success? I took home two champion ribbons from the Meadowville show — First-year Green Hunter and Small Junior Hunter. It's a pity you don't have time to compete anymore. You used to be good." Smiling smugly, Ashley walked away.

That night when Amy got back to Heartland she found Lou talking on the phone. Her sister was frowning.

"No," she was saying, shaking her head. "No. We're not interested." There was a pause. "Yes, I appreciate that it *is* a good offer, Ted, but like I said, we're really not interested in selling." There was another pause. "Yes, of course I'll let you know if we change our mind. OK. Good-bye."

"Who was that?" Amy asked curiously as Lou put the phone down.

"Ted Grant," Lou replied. "He wanted to know whether we were interested in selling Heartland's land. Apparently they want to extend Green Briar." She must have seen the shock on Amy's face, because she added quickly, "I said no, of course."

"I can't believe that family!" Amy exclaimed, dumping her backpack on the floor. "Why can't they just leave us alone?"

"It was a very generous offer," Lou said.

"But we don't want to sell!" Amy said.

"Hey," Lou said, changing the subject. "We've had *some* good news today. I had an inquiry from a potential customer. A Mrs. Garcia. She's got a horse that won't load into a trailer. She's going to come by Saturday to have a look around."

"Great," Amy said.

Lou nodded, her blue eyes shining with relief. "I gave her a quote. She was very pleased — apparently it was fifty dollars less than Green Briar's."

Amy stared. "You gave her a quote?" Her voice rose. "But we don't give quotes!"

"Well, she asked for one," Lou said defensively.

"What else could I do? It normally only takes you about a week, doesn't it? I gave her a quote based on that."

Amy couldn't believe what she was hearing. "But we don't know what this horse is like. It might take a month!" she exclaimed. "You'll have to tell her that the quote can't stand. Tell her that we won't know until we've had the horse for at least a few days."

"I can't do that, it's not professional!" Lou objected. "We should have rates and stick to them. Everywhere else does."

"But we're not *like* everywhere else!" Amy cried, her frustration mounting. "That's the whole point of Heartland. Mom always treated each horse that came here as an individual."

"But, Amy —"

"No!" Amy said fiercely. "That's not changing, Lou. Not for anything!"

"OK, OK," Lou said, running a hand through her hair. "I'll guess I'll have to make it clear to Mrs. Garcia when she comes on Saturday."

Seeing the worry lines on Lou's face reappearing, Amy felt bad, but this was something she was determined never to give in about. It was one of the things that made Heartland so special — the belief that each horse was different and should be treated according to its needs. She wasn't about to let that change.

❧

On Saturday morning, Mrs. Garcia arrived. She was a tall, thin woman who looked immediately put out when Lou explained that the price she had been given was liable to change. "But you told me a price on the telephone," she said, standing in the kitchen.

Lou looked distinctly embarrassed. "I know. I'm sorry."

Amy tried to help her sister. "You see, we don't know how much it will cost until we've had the horse for a few days. All horses take a different amount of time."

"I see," Mrs. Garcia said coolly. She turned again to Lou. "So you're telling me that the price might change?"

"Yes, according to how long the process takes," Lou said. "But it might take only three days."

"Well, three days for an initial cure," Amy put in quickly, "but then another couple of days to make sure that the problem behavior has really gone."

Mrs. Garcia ignored her, obviously thinking of her as Lou's little sister and of no consequence. "Three or four days?" she said to Lou, sounding surprised. "At Green Briar they told me it would take at least ten."

Amy had seen her mom cure horses in even less — it was generally easy if you approached the problem with understanding and respect for the horse. However, she wanted to make things clear to Mrs. Garcia. Horses came to Heartland strictly on the understanding that Heartland decided on the type and length of treatment needed. "Sometimes, of course, they can take much longer — up to a month," she said, ignoring Lou's horrified stare, "or even six weeks."

"Six weeks!" Mrs. Garcia echoed, her eyes widening.

"Of course, I'm sure that wouldn't be the case with your horse, Mrs. Garcia," Lou said hastily.

"But you can't guarantee it," Mrs. Garcia said, stepping back, shaking her head. "No, I'm sorry. I think I'll take my horse elsewhere."

"But, really, Mrs. Garcia, like I said, it might take only three days," Lou said desperately.

But Mrs. Garcia was already walking out of the kitchen toward her car.

Lou turned on Amy. "Amy!" she said in frustration. "How *could* you? Now she'll go back to Green Briar, and we've still got an empty stable!"

"I only told her the truth," Amy said defensively.

Lou's eyes flashed. "The truth! You did your best to put her off."

"I did not!" Amy protested.

Lou shook her head. "Don't you understand? We're running out of money. If we don't get some paying clients soon, we're going to be in serious trouble. How are we going to feed the horses? How are we going to pay Ty? I can't write checks if we don't have any money in the bank." She took a deep breath. "Look, if we're going to survive, you may have to ease up on your principles for a bit."

Amy stared at her. "No!"

"Hi," a voice said tentatively. They both swung around. A tall, slim woman in her early twenties with blond hair falling to her shoulders in a mass of corkscrew curls was standing behind them, a worried frown creasing her forehead.

"Marnie!" Lou exclaimed.

Marnie looked from Amy to Lou. "Have I arrived at a bad time?"

"No," Lou exclaimed, hurrying forward. "Don't be silly! It's great to see you!"

"You, too," Marnie said, hugging her. "I parked in front and, er —" she raised her eyebrows quizzically, "heard the sound of voices in here."

Lou grinned. "I guess you couldn't exactly miss us." She turned quickly. "This is my sister, Amy."

Amy stepped forward. "Hello."

"Hi," Marnie said with a warm smile. "I've heard so much about you — and this place."

"Come on, we'll show you around," Lou said. She looked at Marnie's smart pantsuit. "Or do you want to get changed first?" she asked. "You might get a bit dirty."

"Who cares?" Marnie grinned. "Clothes can be cleaned. Come on. Show me the way."

Amy followed Lou and Marnie up the yard. She already had the feeling that she was going to like her sister's friend.

They met Ty in the back barn. "Good to meet you, Ty," Marnie said, shaking hands. Suddenly she caught sight of Sugarfoot, the tiny Shetland in one of the stalls, and gave a gasp of delight. "Isn't he the cutest thing!" The next second she was crouching down, saying hello to the little pony. The Shetland nuzzled her face, reveling as he always did in any attention. She looked up at Amy. "You're so lucky to live here. This place is great!"

Amy grinned at her, delighted by her enthusiasm.

"I always wanted to live somewhere like this when I was a kid," Marnie said as they walked around the rest of the yard.

"Where did you live?" Amy asked her curiously.

"New Jersey," Marnie replied. When they reached the front stable block, she looked into Pegasus's stall. "Hey, this fella doesn't look too happy," she said softly.

"He's not," Amy said, joining her at the door. There had been no improvement in Pegasus's condition. He was still not eating much.

"What's wrong with him?" Marnie asked curiously.

"We don't know," Lou said.

"He's had a blood test, but it didn't show anything,"

Amy said. Scott had called her the day after his visit to tell her that the results were inconclusive. "I think he's just missing Mom. He really loved her."

"Poor thing," Marnie said. "But he is going to get better?"

Get better? Amy felt her heart skip a beat as she looked at Marnie. Of course, Pegasus would get better. She hadn't even considered the possibility that he might not. "Yes — yes, he is," she said, nodding. She turned and looked at Pegasus. He had to. The thought of losing Pegasus was just too much to bear.

Amy and Lou helped Marnie unload her car, and then Lou showed her to their mom's old room. As she unpacked her two large suitcases, Marnie shook her head. "I've brought all these clothes," she said as she hauled one of the suitcases into the house, "but only one pair of jeans and a pair of shorts — I guess I'll be living in those."

"Don't worry," Lou said. "We can always find things for you to borrow."

Leaving Marnie to unpack and change, Amy and Lou went downstairs. A little while later, she joined them in the kitchen. "This is going to be so much fun," she said happily. She was dressed far more casually in a pair of cutoffs, a T-shirt, and sneakers, her wild hair tied back in a ponytail.

"I don't know about fun." Lou grinned. "There's lots of work to be done."

"Lou's got plans," Amy said warningly to Marnie.

Marnie raised her eyebrows. "Sounds scary."

"Oh, very," Lou teased her. She opened the fridge. "Do you want a cold drink?"

Soon they were all sitting around the table, drinking cans of soda. "So, come on," Marnie said to Lou. "Out with it, then. How about this change of lifestyle? It's so totally different from living in the rat race. How are you *really* coping?"

"Oh, you know," Lou said with a shrug. "I'm coping fine, though I guess I do miss some things."

"I should hope you do!" Marnie said. "All your friends miss you."

Amy felt a bit peculiar. She never really gave a thought to Lou's life in the city now. Lou seemed so much a part of Heartland that it was hard to remember that only three months ago she hadn't been to visit in more than two years and had lived her own separate life — with an apartment, boyfriend, and job — that Amy hadn't been a part of at all.

"And having the responsibility of things here is difficult," Lou continued. "I guess it's particularly bad right now, with Grandpa away."

"But there must be some positive aspects about living here," Marnie said.

Amy wondered what Lou would say.

"Oh, yes," Lou said. "There are lots of good things. I've rediscovered my love of horses and having a home like this and, well, just being here in the country is great."

Marnie grinned. "And what about the guys? Come on, what are *they* like around here?"

Lou blushed. "Oh, you know."

"I want more than that!" Marnie exclaimed. "Tell me all the gossip." She looked closely at Lou. "There must be someone or you wouldn't be turning that color." She turned to Amy. "Come on, Amy. You'll have to fill me in. Is there a new man in your sister's life since she dumped Carl?"

"I've been too busy, Marnie!" Lou protested.

"Amy?" Marnie questioned.

Lou jumped to her feet. "We should be helping Ty, not sitting around and gossiping."

"OK, then, you escape this time," Marnie said, getting up reluctantly. "But I'll find out," she warned as Lou headed for the door. "Just see if I don't."

In the afternoon, Amy went down to the field to bring Pegasus in. As usual, he was standing by the gate. She called his name, but his ears didn't even flicker. Her heart sank. He seemed to be getting worse instead of better with every day that passed. The remedies just didn't seem to be working. Patting his neck, she snapped the lead rope onto his halter. "Come on, then," she said softly. "Let's get you into your stable."

She clicked her tongue, but Pegasus didn't move. "Come on, boy."

With a deep sigh, Pegasus took a slow step forward and then another, the tips of his hooves dragging in the dirt. But then, suddenly, he stumbled, his feet slipping away beneath him. With a horrifying thud, his huge body crashed to the ground. He landed on his knees and fell almost immediately onto his side.

Amy felt as though the world had stopped. "Pegasus!" she gasped, throwing herself down beside him. He lifted his head.

Relief flooded through her. He was still alive.

"Pegasus! Come on! Up!" Amy urged, pulling his halter. "Come on, boy!"

The great horse looked at her. *No*, his eyes seemed to say, *I can't*. His head sank to the ground again.

Fear stabbed through Amy. She dropped the lead rope and raced up the drive.

"Lou!" she screamed. "Come quick!"

Chapter Five

Amy crouched by Pegasus's head, stroking him and talking to him softly. Marnie stood anxiously beside her. She and Lou had come running as soon as they heard her call.

Lou came hurrying down the drive toward them. "I called Scott," she said. "He's coming right away."

Amy looked frantically at her. "I can't find any bleeding, but he might have broken something. I can't tell with him lying down."

Lou took the lead rope. "Come on, Pegasus. Get up." But Pegasus didn't move. His eyes were half closed, his muzzle resting on the ground.

"Lou! What are we going to do?" Amy exclaimed, desperately wishing that Ty was there. But it was his half day, and he had left Heartland after lunch. "He might have broken something."

"Stay calm," Lou said, putting a hand on Amy's shoulder, utterly practical and efficient as always. "You won't help Pegasus by getting worked up."

"But I can't stay calm!" Amy burst out. Her breath was short in her throat, and her eyes filled with tears. "Pegasus! Please get up!" she pleaded.

"Look, I'll get some food," Lou said. "That might encourage him." She hurried off, returning a few minutes later with a bucket of pony cubes. She shook them, but Pegasus's eyes barely flickered in her direction.

"It's like he's frozen there," Marnie said, looking at Lou anxiously.

"It could just be shock after falling," Lou said. "Maybe he hasn't broken anything at all. Amy, what would Mom have used for shock?"

"Rescue remedy," Amy said.

"Can you go find some? I'll get a blanket. If he's in shock, it'll be important to keep him warm."

Through her panic, Amy saw the sense in Lou's words. Jumping to her feet, she raced to the medicine cabinet in the tack room. She pulled the dark brown bottle of rescue remedy from the shelf and ran back to Pegasus.

Crouching down beside him, she placed a few drops on the back of her hand and offered them to him. His nostrils flared slightly at the scent, and then he lifted his head and licked the drops off her hand. "Good boy," Amy murmured, delighted to see him move.

"What are you giving him?" Marnie asked.

"Bach Flower Rescue Remedy," Amy told her. "It's a mixture of different flower essences. Mom always used it for sudden trauma or shock."

Lou returned with a blanket and laid it over Pegasus's body. She glanced at her watch. "I wonder how long Scott will be?"

They watched Pegasus anxiously, each second dragging by. After five minutes, Amy was sure his eyes were looking clearer. He lifted his head slightly and his ears flickered. "The rescue remedy's working!" Amy cried to Marnie and Lou. She jumped to her feet and pulled on the lead rope. "Good boy! Come on, Pegasus! Up!"

With a huge groan of effort, Pegasus staggered to his feet. His head hung down, his knees were scraped and bleeding, and there was a gash on his right hock, but Amy was relieved that he didn't seem to have broken anything. She'd had a horrible image that when he stood up one of his legs would be dangling uselessly, but he was standing fairly evenly on all four legs.

Just as she started to check him over, there was the sound of a car tearing up the drive. Amy looked around. "It's Scott!" she said in relief, as the vet's battered Jeep pulled up outside the farmhouse. Throwing the door open, Scott jumped out and raced toward them.

✖

Half an hour later, Pegasus was back in his stall. It had been a slow process, but once there, Scott checked him over thoroughly, cleaned up his wounds, and gave him a shot of antibiotics to combat any infection. Amy watched from the door with Lou and Marnie. As Scott started to pack his equipment away, all the questions that she had been biting back while he treated Pegasus came surging to the surface.

"What's wrong? Why did he fall over?" Her voice rose. "Will he be OK, Scott?"

"He's weak because he hasn't eaten," Scott replied. "I think that's why he tripped and didn't get up. His injuries from the fall aren't serious." He frowned. "What really worries me is his lack of appetite."

"Do you have any idea why he's not eating?" Lou asked.

Scott looked serious. "It could be any one of a number of things." He looked at Amy. "Remember, he is an old horse."

"What do you mean?" Amy said quickly.

"Well, I'll have to do some tests. When I get the results, we'll have a better idea."

Amy couldn't speak. She felt hot tears well in her eyes.

"He'll be OK, won't he, Scott?" Lou said, her face pale.

There was an awful second of silence. "We'll have to wait and see," Scott said. He shook his head gravely, then looked at Amy. "He's getting older, and he's more prone to viruses now. What he's fighting is probably more serious than depression. I know this is hard to hear. You've got to consider the possibility —"

"No, I can't, Scott. I just can't," Amy sobbed. Pushing past Scott, she flung her arms around Pegasus's neck and started to cry as if her heart would break.

She heard Scott turn to Lou. "I think we just have to wait and see what happens over the next few weeks," he said. "We can see if anything shows up on the test results."

Amy sobbed loudly. What if Pegasus was really sick? How could she bear living without him? The straw rustled behind her and then she felt Lou's arm around her shoulders.

"It's OK, Amy," Lou said. "We can continue to treat him. Scott's not saying he won't get better."

"It's still too early to tell anything," Scott said slowly. "If the depression eases and he gets his spirit back, then he might be fine. We just have to keep an eye on him and see if he develops other symptoms."

Amy's heart lifted slightly. Maybe Pegasus would make a full recovery. She sniffed and looked up. "What can I do to help him?"

"Try anything you can think of," Scott told her. "You never know, something might work."

Amy nodded. "I'll try everything." She hugged Pegasus's neck. "I'll make you better, boy," she told him confidently. "I promise I will."

"Come on," Lou said softly, squeezing her shoulder. "We should let him rest."

❧

Back in the kitchen, Lou properly introduced Marnie and Scott.

"Nice to meet you." Marnie smiled at the vet.

"You, too," Scott said politely, and then seeing Lou trying to carry four cans over from the fridge, jumped to his feet. "Here," he said, "let me."

"Thanks," Lou replied, smiling.

As he took two of the cans from her, their hands brushed. Lou's cheeks flushed pink and Amy glanced at Marnie to see if she had noticed, but she had gone to the sink to wash her hands.

"So how's business?" Scott asked as Lou brought over some potato chips. "Any sign of things picking up?"

"None," Lou admitted.

"Well, I have some good news," Scott informed her. "I

think I might just have found you a new client, and not just any old client — Lisa Stillman."

"The one with the Arabians?" Amy said, feeling suddenly interested. There was a Lisa Stillman who owned a large Arabian farm about an hour away. Her horses were known throughout the state as superb show horses.

"That's the one," Scott replied. "I started treating her horses a few months back. Anyway, she's got a young mare who's recently become highly aggressive. She won't let anyone tack her up. I've checked her over and there's nothing physically wrong, so it has to be a behavioral problem of some sort. I suggested that she send her here."

"That's great!" Amy said. She turned to Lou in excitement. "Lisa Stillman's place is huge! If she likes us then we could get loads of work."

"The horse has been to two other stables already," Scott said, "including Green Briar. No one's been able to do a thing with her. Lisa's at her wit's end."

"Hey, Lou," Marnie said, "this could be your big break. Sounds like if you get in with this woman then you've got it made."

Lou's eyes lit up. "Is she going to phone us?" she asked Scott.

"Well, I said I'd talk to you and arrange a time for you to go over there so she can meet you," Scott replied.

"She's extremely particular about who she lets her horses go to. Most of them are very valuable animals." He scratched his head. "You know, I could give her a call and take you over there now, if you want. I've got to go anyway to see a horse I'm treating."

"That sounds great!" Lou said, but her face fell suddenly. "Oh, what about Pegasus? We shouldn't leave him."

"I'll stay," Amy said immediately.

Scott shook his head. "Lisa will want to talk to you about how you would go about treating Promise — her horse."

"Would you like me to stay with him?" Marnie offered.

"Thanks, Marnie," Lou said, "but it might be better if I stay. Pegasus will be happier with someone he knows."

Amy looked at Scott. She was sure she could see a hint of disappointment in his eyes, but he nodded understandingly. "Yes, I guess that would be best," he said. "Amy and I'll go."

"Can I tag along, too, then?" Marnie asked him. "I'd love to see this place."

"Sure," Scott said. "I'll call Lisa right now."

❧

Ten minutes later, Amy, Marnie, and Scott got into his car. Amy sat in the back, sharing the seat with Scott's big coat, a trunk of veterinary equipment, and a heavy flashlight. She pushed several map books and a box of medical supplies under the front seat so that she had room for her feet.

"Sorry it's such a mess back there," Scott said over his shoulder.

"I don't mind," Amy replied.

"So how long have you been a vet?" Marnie asked Scott as they drove off.

"Well, I got out of school six years ago," Scott replied. "And then I started specializing in equine work about three years ago."

Marnie smiled at him. "It must be a fascinating job." She twisted a strand of curly blond hair around in her fingers. "What do you like best about it?"

As Scott talked, Marnie nodded and smiled and laughed. It suddenly dawned on Amy that Marnie obviously hadn't realized that Lou liked Scott. Amy's eyes widened. She was flirting with him!

"So how long have you known Lou?" Scott asked Marnie.

"From when she moved to Manhattan," Marnie replied. "We worked for the same company. I —"

"I guess you know her ex-boyfriend then," Scott broke in.

"Carl?" Marnie said. "Yes. He's working in Chicago now."

"So, are they still in touch?" Scott's words sounded casual, but Amy picked up the slight edge to his voice.

"Not as far as I know. I think it's definitely over," Marnie said, looking a bit surprised.

"She hasn't spoken to him since they broke up," Amy put in. Lou and Carl's relationship had ended in a furious fight when Lou had discovered that Carl had set up a job for her in Chicago behind her back. It was a scheme to persuade her to move there with him.

Scott shook his head. "She's been going through a pretty tough time recently, hasn't she?" he said. "What with everything that's happened and deciding to give up her job and stay at Heartland. She's had to deal with some major life changes. But she seems to be coping really well."

Amy saw Marnie shoot him a sideways glance. Realization suddenly dawned on the older girl's face. "Yeah," she said, after a short pause. "Lou's great." Her hands dropped to her lap. "I couldn't ask for a better friend."

❧

Lisa Stillman's farm was called Fairfield. It was set at the end of a long, straight drive bordered on each side by tall trees. Behind the trees, Amy could just catch tantalizing glimpses of Arabian horses grazing in lush fields.

They drove past an impressive white house and stopped. The barns were set up around a brick courtyard. Purple and pink flowers cascaded from large hanging baskets. Each dark wood stall door had a shining brass nameplate. Stable hands were bustling about, each wearing a green shirt with the Fairfield crest embroidered in purple on the pocket. It was the very picture of an old Virginia horse farm.

"Oh, wow!" Amy gasped, getting out of the car and spotting several beautiful Arabian horses looking out over the stall doors, their ears pricked and dished faces curious. "This place is amazing!"

Scott grinned. "I thought you'd be impressed." He shut his car door. "I'll go find out where Lisa is."

He walked over to speak to one of the stable hands. The second he was out of hearing range, Marnie turned to Amy. "You know what? I think he likes Lou!"

Amy nodded.

"You already knew!" Marnie groaned. She put her head in her hands. "And there I was, flirting like an idiot! But he's so cute!" She glanced up at Amy. "Lou likes him, doesn't she?" Marnie said, her voice hopeful.

"I'm pretty sure she does," Amy said.

"Oh, well, there goes my chance!" Marnie said with a laugh. "I guess that's life. So how come they haven't gotten together yet?" she asked curiously.

"I think it was a hard decision for Lou, breaking up with Carl," Amy replied. "And Lou and Scott have been getting to know each other slowly."

Marnie grinned. "Well, now that I'm here, we'll soon get things moving."

Scott headed back toward them, and Marnie stopped talking.

"Lisa's over in the office, apparently," Scott said. As they walked over to the redbrick building at the far end of the courtyard he said in a low voice, "She can be a bit odd — so be warned."

They walked into the office where a woman in her mid-forties was sitting behind a desk. She jumped up as soon as she saw them. "Scott!" she said, with an attractive, husky rasp to her voice. She had highlighted blond hair that fell onto her shoulders and a slim figure shown off by fitted cream breeches and an open-necked silk shirt. Amy stared. She didn't know what she had been expecting Lisa Stillman to look like, but certainly not anyone this glamorous!"

"How *are* you, darling?" Lisa said, coming around the desk, her arms outstretched. She kissed Scott on both cheeks.

"Fine." Scott turned quickly. "Let me introduce you. This is Amy Fleming from Heartland and a family friend, Marnie . . ." He paused.

"Gordon," Marnie said swiftly.

"Marnie Gordon," Scott repeated. "Amy's sister, Lou, had to stay with one of the horses — but I'm sure Amy will be able to answer all your questions."

Lisa looked at Amy. Her eyes were narrowed and skeptical. "How old are you?"

"Fifteen," Amy replied.

"Don't be put off," Scott said quickly. "Amy knows what she's doing, and Heartland has an excellent record."

Lisa turned to him. "Promise is a valuable horse. I'm not letting her go to a fifteen-year-old!"

"Lisa, Amy's got more experience than most people twice her age," Scott began.

"I have dealt with valuable horses before," Amy put in. There was a pause, and then Lisa looked at her. "I cured one of Nick Halliwell's best young horses of its fear of trailering recently," Amy said quickly, now that she had her attention. "And I am familiar with all the techniques my mom used at Heartland. She taught me everything she knew."

"And what sort of techniques are those?" Lisa demanded.

"Treating horses with kindness, respect, and understanding," Amy said, refusing to let herself be intimidated by this imposing woman. "Using rewards instead of punishments. Never bullying, never frightening." She put her chin up and met Lisa's eyes squarely. "Listening to the horse, mostly."

There was a moment's silence. Lisa raised her eyebrows thoughtfully and then suddenly, she nodded.

"OK," she said. "I like your attitude. You can treat Promise."

Amy felt an enormous rush of relief. For a moment she had been half expecting to be asked to leave.

"Come and see her," Lisa said.

Amy followed her out of the office, and Lisa pointed to a stall a few doors away. "That's her — the palomino."

An exceptionally pretty Arabian was looking over the stall door. A long creamy-white fringe fell over her face, her eyes were bright, her dark gray nostrils delicate and refined. Amy frowned. Everything about the mare's head suggested intelligence, softness, and sensitivity. "She doesn't look aggressive," she commented.

"She isn't," Lisa Stillman said, "until you try to ride her. Last week we got her tack on and took her in a show and she threw the rider and tried to bite the judge."

Amy walked forward slowly. Promise turned to look at her. Her ears pricked curiously, but Amy noticed that her eyes seemed reserved. Reaching the door, Amy stopped and gently stroked her. "What's her history?" she asked.

"I bought her six months ago from an elderly friend of mine," Lisa said. "She was selling her stock, and I was looking for a palomino. Promise had the perfect blood-lines and the perfect temperament — or so I thought," she added ruefully. "The first few days she was fine. But then one morning when a stable hand was saddling her up, he scolded her for fidgeting, and she turned and took a chunk out of his shoulder. When he smacked her she began kicking out. And things have gotten gradually worse since then. Whenever a saddle or bridle is brought close to her, she attacks anyone standing nearby, and if you try to mount, well, she bucks like crazy."

"But she was OK in her last home?" Amy said.

"Sure," Lisa said. "Half the time she was ridden by my friend's partially blind grandson. Apparently she never did anything wrong."

Amy looked at the palomino. She was standing, slightly aloof. "And she's been to other stables?" she asked. "What did they do with her?"

Lisa shrugged. "Tried to show her who's boss, I guess, but it didn't work. She's got some temper. And crops just seem to make her worse. The other stables sent her back in the end, telling me she's a rogue horse." She frowned. "But somehow I just don't believe it."

Looking at Promise's intelligent head, Amy didn't believe such words, either. Her mom had always insisted that rogue horses were virtually a myth. Yes, maybe there was the odd one who really couldn't be helped, but generally fear was at the root of all behavioral problems — and if that fear was dealt with, treated, and resolved, the attitude problems would go away, too.

"So, what do you think?" Lisa asked. "Can you help her?"

Amy nodded. Following her mom's reasoning meant that if she found the cause of Promise's fear, then stopping the aggression should be no problem at all. "Sure," she said honestly. "But I don't know how long it will take."

"You can have all the time you need," Lisa said firmly. "I just want her to be all right."

ℚ

"Hi, there!" Lou said, coming eagerly out of the house as Scott stopped the car. "How did it go?"

"Really well!" said Amy. "How's Pegasus?"

"No change," Lou said. "He ate a couple of carrots I offered him, but otherwise nothing to report."

"You should have seen this place, Lou," Marnie enthused. "It was amazing. Lisa Stillman has all these attractive stables set around a courtyard."

"And what about the horse?" Lou demanded.

"She's coming tomorrow!" Amy said.

"Really?" gasped Lou, her face lighting up. She turned to Scott. "That's wonderful!" For a moment Amy thought that Lou was going to throw her arms around his neck, but she seemed to control herself just in time. "Thank you so much for arranging it," she said to him.

"You've got Amy to thank," Scott said. "I just put the idea to Lisa; it was your sister who convinced her." He smiled. "But I'm glad that it's worked out," he said warmly. Their eyes met for a moment. Lou turned away, her face slightly pink.

Marnie nudged Amy and grinned.

After checking on Pegasus, Scott left. As soon as his car had disappeared around the first bend, Marnie couldn't contain herself any longer. She grabbed Lou's arm. "Lou!" she exclaimed. "That guy's crazy about you!"

Lou looked shocked. "What? Scott?"

"Yes! Who else?" Marnie grinned in delight. "Lou! He's gorgeous!" She shook her head. "I can't believe you didn't tell me about him!"

Lou didn't seem to know what to say. Her face turned crimson. "I — I didn't think there was anything to tell," she stammered.

"Hello, Lou!" Marnie exclaimed, throwing her hands up in the air. "This is *me* you're talking to. It couldn't be more obvious! All he did in the car was talk about you, didn't he, Amy?"

Amy nodded eagerly. "Yes, and he kept asking about Carl — if you were still seeing him."

"And, boy, did he seem pleased when we said that you weren't!" Marnie said. She grinned at Lou. "You're not going to tell me that you don't feel the same. I saw you just now, looking deep into his eyes." She mimicked Lou's voice. "'*Thank you, Scott. Oh, you're so wonderful, Scott!*'"

Lou burst out laughing. "I didn't do that!"

"Not much!" Marnie teased. *"'Oh, Scott, I really don't know what we'd have done without you!'"*

Lou buried her face in her hands. "OK! OK!" she cried. "So maybe I do like him." Her blue eyes shone as she looked at Amy and Marnie. "And you really think he might be interested in me?"

"Trust me," Marnie said. "I *know* he is."

Chapter Six

As soon as Amy woke up the next morning she hurried down to see Pegasus. He wasn't looking much better than the day before. "Good boy," she murmured, checking his cuts and scrapes. They had bled slightly in the night, so she got some hot water and carefully cleaned away the dried blood. Then she applied some comfrey ointment to help speed the healing process.

"Now let's get you something to eat," she said. "You have to build up your strength."

Seeing her walking up the yard toward the feed room, the other horses started to nicker hopefully. "In a minute," she told them. On this occasion, Pegasus had to have her undivided attention.

She chopped up three apples and, adding them to a small amount of bran and barley, mixed the food in a bucket with some beet juice and a spoonful of molasses. Then she hurried back to Pegasus's stall. He stared listlessly at the food and made no attempt to eat, so she took a handful and offered it to him. His lips grazed over her palm, taking up a bit of apple and some bran. "Good boy," she praised. She fed him a bit more and then a bit more. After twenty minutes he had just about finished the bucket. Feeling more hopeful, Amy patted him and then went to feed the other horses.

Just as she started filling the water buckets, Ty arrived. "Morning," he called, getting out of his car.

"What are you doing here?" Amy asked in surprise. It was Sunday, his day off.

"I thought you'd need a hand with the painting," he said, joining her at the tap. "I told Lou I'd come and help."

With everything that had happened the day before, it had slipped Amy's mind that today they were supposed to start painting and sprucing the place up.

"You forgot, didn't you?" Ty said, looking at her face.

"Kind of," she admitted. "But so much has been happening." She realized that Ty didn't know about the events of the day before. As the water buckets filled, she told him about Pegasus's fall and then about Lisa Stillman and Promise. It was a relief to be able to talk. That was the good thing about Ty, he always listened to her and understood.

When she had finished, Ty helped her take the water buckets to the stalls, and then they went to the house to talk to Lou about her plans. She and Marnie were in the kitchen, washing the breakfast dishes.

"So what do you want us to do?" Amy asked, opening the cookie jar and offering it to Ty before taking one herself.

"I thought if you two worked on the stalls and turning out the horses, then I could go pick up the paint and some brushes," Lou said.

"I'll help with the horses, too," Marnie offered.

Lou nodded. "When I get back we can paint the stable doors and then start cleaning out the tack and blanket rooms."

"If you get some wood, I could make storage trunks for the blankets, brushes, and extra tack," Ty said.

"Super," Lou said. "That will help things look better. Then I might get some new feed buckets and hay nets. They're not too expensive, and they'll look a lot better to new clients."

"How about some hanging baskets?" Marnie said. "Just two maybe, at each end of the front barn. You can put together really pretty ones, even with cheap plants."

Amy started to feel quite enthusiastic. She had thought that she didn't want any changes, but all these ideas would make Heartland look much better. "I'll call Soraya and Matt," she said. "I bet they'll come and help. We can give the yard a good sweep and straighten up all the pitch-forks and brooms. It's going to look great!"

❧

By lunchtime Heartland was a hive of activity. Amy and Soraya were busy painting the stall doors white while Lou and Matt freshened up the unpainted wood in the two barns with dark brown creosote. The tack room had been cleaned out and swept, and Ty was busy making large trunks to hold all the stuff that ended up in a pile on the tack room floor — polo wraps, bits, hoof picks. Marnie had filled two hanging baskets with red and yellow flowers and was sorting out the grooming kits, washing the brushes, and removing old caked hair from the currycombs.

Amy put a last brushful of paint on the stall door she was working on and then stood back to admire her work. "One more finished!"

"Everything is looking so much better," Soraya said, putting her brush down. She looked at Amy. "Which is more than can be said for you!"

Amy grinned. She had started off applying the paint carefully but had soon gotten bored and began to slap it on. Her jeans and T-shirt were covered with white splashes, and she was sure there must be some paint in her hair.

"It doesn't come off, you know," Soraya pointed out.

"Who cares?" Amy shrugged. "These jeans are old anyway."

Soraya shook her head and, picking up her brush, started to finish the last section of the door she was painting. "So, what was Fairfield like?" She was as crazy about horses as Amy and knew all about Lisa Stillman and her prizewinning Arabians.

"Very stylish," Amy said, and she told Soraya about the stable hands with their matching uniform shirts, the beautiful horses, and how glamorous Lisa Stillman was.

"Do you think she'll bring the horse here herself?" Soraya asked.

"She didn't say," Amy said. She wondered what Lisa would think of Heartland if she did come. Promise was supposed to arrive about four o'clock. She hoped they would have finished working on the yard by then.

"And this horse has a bad temper?" Soraya asked.

"Just when she's being ridden," Amy explained. "I think it's because something's frightened her in the past. She didn't look like a naturally aggressive horse." She saw that Soraya's door was just about done. "Should we start on the blanket room? There's a lot to go through in there."

〰

By four o'clock the paint was almost dry, the blankets were sorted, and the tack had been put neatly away.

New trunks lined the back wall of the tack room, the bridles hung neatly on their correct pegs, and the halters were untangled, with their lead ropes tightly coiled. There were still a few things to do — the manure pile needed attention and the feed room still hadn't been swept or de-cobwebbed — but overall there was a huge improvement.

Amy stood drinking a soda with the others by the farmhouse and admired the bright white doors set against the dark wood, the hanging baskets filled with fresh flowers, and a yard that for once was almost free of hay and straw.

"Now we've just got to keep it like this," Lou said with a sigh of relief.

"Yeah, right, not with Amy around!" Matt joked.

Amy hit him. "Hey!"

There was the sound of a vehicle coming up the drive. They all turned to see a good-looking trailer with green-and-purple stripes heading toward them. "That must be Promise!" Amy said.

The trailer stopped just in front of them. The driver's door of the pickup opened and out jumped a tall, blond-haired boy. "Hey!" he said, looking a bit surprised to see such a crowd.

"Hi," Amy said. She felt slightly disappointed to see that the boy was alone. After all their work, she would have liked Lisa Stillman to see Heartland. She stepped forward. "I'm Amy."

The boy smiled. "Pleased to meet you, Amy," he said, holding out his hand. "I'm Ben Stillman. I'm delivering Promise for my aunt."

So that was why he looked a little familiar! Amy shook his hand and introduced everyone else. "We've been painting," she explained, suddenly realizing how messy she must look.

"I sort of figured," Ben said with a grin. He moved toward the trailer. "Should I unload Promise here?"

Amy nodded. "Yeah, that would be fine."

"Do you want a hand?" Ty offered.

"Thanks," Ben replied.

"He's cute!" Soraya whispered to Amy as Ben and Ty walked around the trailer to unbolt the ramp.

"I guess," Amy said, looking at Ben and feeling slightly surprised.

"Very cute!" Soraya said with a giggle as he disappeared into the trailer.

There was a clatter of hooves and Ben came out of the trailer, leading Promise. Amy caught her breath, all thoughts of Ben far from her mind. The mare pranced down the ramp with the grace of a ballet dancer. Her neck was arched, her golden coat gleamed, and her creamy white tail floated behind her. Reaching the ground, she stopped and snorted, wide nostrils flaring, soft dark eyes staring in surprise.

"She's gorgeous!" Amy breathed.

She glanced at Ty to see his reaction. He was nodding in agreement.

The mare whinnied loudly and then tossed her head and swung her hindquarters around. "Easy now," Ben said, patting her neck. He turned to Amy. "Where should I put her?"

"Over here," Amy said, leading the way to one of the empty stalls in the front block. Promise pranced in after him.

"High-spirited," Ty commented.

"Most Arabians are," Ben said, unclipping her lead rope. "She's OK — as long as you don't bring a saddle or bridle anywhere near her."

Promise looked over the stall door. Amy stroked her nose, admiring her sculpted face.

"I hope you can do something with her," Ben said. "You may be her last chance."

❧

After seeing Promise settle in, Ben left. Ty was going home and offered Soraya and Matt a ride.

"Thanks for all your help!" Amy called as they got into Ty's car. "See you tomorrow."

"Well, I could do with a long bath and a change of

clothes," Marnie said, looking down at her filthy jeans as they drove off.

"Me, too," Lou said. She looked at Amy. "But do you want a hand feeding the horses?"

"No, I'll be fine," Amy said. Ty had found time in the afternoon to make up the hay nets, so she just had to deal with the grain.

"I'll get dinner together, then," Lou said. "Coming, Marnie?"

They walked off into the house, and Amy made her way up the yard, enjoying the peace and quiet. It had been a hectic day. She stopped to check on Promise. The mare was standing at the back of her stall, pulling hay from the net. Hearing Amy's footsteps, she looked around.

"Hey, there, girl," Amy said, letting herself into the stall.

Promise looked at her for a moment and then continued to eat. Amy stood back, studying the mare. Her mom had always believed that a horse's personality could be read in its face. Amy looked at the mare's eyes. They were large, soft, and slightly triangular — thoughtful eyes, highly intelligent eyes. In fact, she thought, everything about Promise suggested intelligence. Her gaze wandered over Promise's delicate, fluted nostrils, shapely ears, and dished face with a slight moose nose. All of those features suggested that she was a horse that was alert, sensitive, proud.

A horse that would be fabulous to ride. One thing was for sure; she certainly did *not* look naturally aggressive.

It had to be fear that was causing her to act so out of character, Amy thought. When a horse was scared there were only three things it could do: flee, freeze, or fight. Looking at the pride and self-awareness mirrored in every line of Promise's beautiful head, it wasn't hard to believe that she had chosen to fight.

"Well, there's no need to fight me," Amy said, patting the mare's shoulder. "I won't hurt you or make you scared."

She left the stall feeling the first flicker of excitement that she always felt when facing the challenge of a new horse. She would make Promise ridable and show everyone that Heartland could run just as it always had, curing the horses that the rest of the world had given up on.

Suddenly feeling optimistic, she went to the feed room and began to fill the buckets. Maybe things were finally getting better, she thought as she added handfuls of soaked beet pulp to the grain. The yard was looking wonderful. If she cured Promise, then Lisa Stillman was bound to bring Heartland more customers. Best of all, she and Lou were getting along just fine. Yes, life at Heartland was looking up at last.

Amy started to pile the buckets up and then remembered Pegasus. Her newfound optimism faded slightly when she thought about the old gray horse.

She fed the other horses and then took Pegasus's bucket to his stall. He was standing quietly, his head low, his eyes depressed.

"Hey, boy," she said, looking over the door.

Hearing her voice, Pegasus lifted his head slightly. "I've brought you some supper," she said, letting herself into the stall.

Pegasus looked at the bucket, nudged his lips uninterestedly over the metal handle, and then dropped his head to the straw again.

"Come on. Eat," Amy urged, holding a handful of the feed by his nose.

With a sigh, Pegasus's lips moved over her hand, taking up some of the grain. Again, Amy fed him handful by slow handful. Pegasus ate listlessly, appearing to eat more to please her than out of any real sense of hunger. Amy consoled herself with the thought that at least he *was* eating something.

She kissed his forehead, willing him to recover, desperately searching in her mind for something more that she could do.

When he had finished the last handful of feed she began to massage his head and neck with T-touch circles. Pegasus rested his muzzle on his manger by the window and half closed his eyes.

"You like this, don't you?" Amy murmured. She swallowed as she remembered how Mom used to stand in the exact place, massaging Pegasus in the same way. Through the stall window she could see the evening shadows lengthening, and as she worked she thought of all the times when she had come out and watched Mom work her magic.

The minutes passed, her fingers moved over Pegasus's neck, and she felt herself relaxing. As the light in the stall began to fade it was as if the rest of the world had slipped away, leaving her and Pegasus alone — like it had once been just Mom and Pegasus. In the sweet-smelling stall, the past and the present seemed to merge into one.

Suddenly every muscle in Pegasus's body tensed. His head shot up and he stared out the window.

"What's the matter?" Amy said, following his gaze into the dusk.

She gasped, her heart standing still.

Amy didn't know if she could trust what her eyes were seeing. There, walking up the yard, hands in her barn jacket pockets, was a familiar figure. And the leap of Amy's heart made her believe that it really was her mom.

Chapter Seven

"Mom," Amy whispered, her insides felt numb as the figure walked toward her through the dusk. Then, without thinking, she flew to the stall door. *Could it be?*

Wrenching the bolt back with her trembling fingers, she stumbled out.

"Amy?"

Amy stopped in her tracks, feeling as if someone had just tipped a bucket of cold water over her. It was Marnie, hurrying toward her. Her hair was tied back, and she was wearing Marion's old barn jacket.

"Are you OK?" the older girl asked, looking at her shocked face in surprise. She followed Amy's gaze and looked down at the jacket. "Is it the jacket? Lou said I could borrow it."

Amy's mouth opened but she couldn't speak.

Marnie moved swiftly to her side. "I'll take it off if it upsets you. I'm really, really sorry."

"You looked so much like Mom." The words came out of Amy before she could stop them. She stared at Marnie, tears filling her eyes. For a moment, she had almost let herself believe. . . . She started to shake uncontrollably.

Marnie quickly put her arms around her. "Hey, it's OK," she soothed.

"In the dusk you looked just like her," Amy sobbed, overwhelmed by the rush of emotion. It was so real.

Just then there was a low whicker. Amy swung around. Pegasus had come to his stall door. His ears were pricked, and he was looking at Marnie. He tossed his head up and down.

"Pegasus?" Amy said, forgetting her own distress in her astonishment at seeing him look so alive. He pushed against the door.

"He doesn't think I'm your mom, does he?" Marnie asked.

Amy's eyes widened with sudden realization. "It's the jacket!" she exclaimed. "It must smell like Mom."

Pegasus whinnied again.

Marnie walked slowly up to his stall. Lowering his head, Pegasus rubbed against the jacket with his muzzle, breathing in and out in sharp, eager bursts. Marnie reached out and stroked his face. "I think you're right," she said to Amy. "He must remember."

"He looks almost happy again," Amy said, full of wonder. It was true. As Pegasus nuzzled the jacket, a kind of peace seemed to creep into his eyes. The tears dried on Amy's face. Suddenly she didn't care that Marnie was wearing her mom's jacket. Nothing mattered except the fact that Pegasus was looking like himself again.

✇

Lying in bed that night, Amy found it difficult to get to sleep. She kept thinking of the moment when she thought it was her mother walking across the yard and of Pegasus's reaction. Her hopes rose. When she and Marnie had left his stall he was looking much happier. Maybe this was the breakthrough that she had been so desperately hoping for. Maybe now he would start to eat properly and get better.

She hurried out to feed the horses the next morning. However, even though Pegasus's eyes looked brighter, she found him as reluctant to eat as ever.

Her heart sank. "Come on, boy," she encouraged him, holding out a handful of feed. But instead of eating he simply nudged at the grain with his lips, spilling it into the straw.

In the end Amy had to give up. Time was passing, and

she had to get ready for school. But still she kept hoping. "Can you keep an eye on Pegasus today?" she asked Ty before she went to catch the bus. "I think he might start eating again."

"Sure," Ty nodded. "Have fun at school."

"Yeah, whatever," Amy replied, making a face. She threw her backpack onto her shoulder. "See you later."

As Amy walked along the corridor to her first class, she saw Ashley coming in the opposite direction. Amy tried to ignore her but Ashley stepped into her path, platinum hair falling glossily to her shoulders.

"So I hear you have one of Lisa Stillman's horses?" she demanded, crossing her arms. "Is it true?"

"Yeah," Amy replied, lifting her chin. "What's it to you?"

Ashley's green eyes were ablaze. "Lisa Stillman must have gone crazy. Why's she sending one of her horses to Heartland?"

"She's heard that we actually cure horses," Amy snapped, infuriated by Ashley's attitude. "Which is more than *you* apparently managed when Promise came to you."

Ashley's arched eyebrows rose. "So, it's that palomino?" Her perfectly made-up face suddenly creased into a smile. "OK," she said, nodding. "Now I get it."

"What do you mean?" Amy demanded.

"Well," Ashley replied. "It's not as if Lisa Stillman's letting you have one of her *valuable* horses. Everyone knows that palomino is a hopeless case. She's savage. Mom tried everything with her, but she never gave in, she just fought like crazy. What she needs is a bullet through her head."

"She does not!" Amy exclaimed furiously. "No horse deserves that."

"We'll see what happens to her when you can't cure her."

"I will cure her."

Ashley laughed mockingly. "In your dreams, Amy."

Feeling the anger inside her reaching boiling point, Amy pushed past Ashley.

"You'll never do it," Ashley called after her, her voice amused. "You haven't got the experience to cure any horse, let alone one like that."

Amy marched along the corridor, determined not to listen to Ashley any longer. Her words weren't true. She *was* going to cure Promise. She had never felt so determined about anything in her life.

As soon as Amy got home from school that afternoon she went to find Ty. He was cleaning the bridles in the tack room. "How's Pegasus been?" Amy asked.

"No change, really," Ty replied. He looked at her curiously. "What made you think he'd be different?"

Amy told him about what happened with the jacket the evening before. "I thought it might make him start eating again." She sighed. "But obviously not."

They were silent for a minute or two. "Are you going to work Promise this afternoon?" Ty asked.

Amy nodded. "I thought I'd join up with her first and then see how she reacts to the saddle and bridle," she said. Join up was a technique used to build a horse's trust. Marion had always used it as the first step in the rehabilitation of a horse, and she had taught it to Amy. "What do you think? I'm sure she's unmanageable just because she's scared. If I join up with her, hopefully she'll trust me enough to let me get the tack on."

"Sounds good. I can give you a hand, if you want," Ty offered.

"I'd like that," Amy said with a grateful smile.

Twenty minutes later she led Promise into the circular schooling ring at the top of the yard. The mare walked eagerly beside Amy, her steps short and fast, her eyes swiveling from side to side as she took in the unfamiliar surroundings.

Ty followed some distance behind with the saddle and bridle. Shutting the gate, Amy unclipped the longline from Promise's halter. Feeling herself free, the Arabian shied away, then cantered a few paces, and stopped dead a few yards from Amy. She sniffed at the sand.

With the longline coiled in her hand, Amy clicked her tongue and swept the lead toward the mare's hindquarters. Snorting wildly, Promise leaped into a high-headed canter. Amy moved quickly to the center of the ring and stood facing the mare. By pitching the longline toward the mare's rump, she urged her on at a canter. She knew that a horse's basic instinct was to see humans as predators and to try to escape if there was space to run. What Promise would learn through the join up was that Amy was a human who could understand her body language and be trusted.

After Promise had cantered around for several minutes, Amy stepped forward so that she was slightly in front of the horse. Immediately, Promise jerked to a halt and then swirled around and took off in the opposite direction. Amy's eyes were fixed on the mare's. Soon she saw the palomino's head starting to lower slightly and her muscles relax as her canter became smoother, the strides more rhythmical.

Still urging her on, Amy watched for the first signals of trust from the mare. After five or six circles the first one came. Promise's inside ear stopped moving; it seemed to stay fixed on Amy. It was a signal that the horse was getting tired and wanted to slow down. But for the moment

Amy kept her going, watching for the next sign. With most horses it took a while, but almost immediately Promise's head began to tilt so it was angled toward the center of the circle — closer to Amy. After a few more steps Promise lowered her head and neck, opening her mouth and looking as if she were chewing. It was her way of saying that she would like to stop, that she didn't want to run away from Amy anymore.

Quickly coiling in the line, Amy dropped her eyes from Promise's and turned her shoulders around. She stood and waited, trying not to tense up. She heard the soft thud of hooves on the sand behind her and the sound of the mare's breathing. She took a step and then paused. Suddenly she felt Promise's nose on her shoulder and warm breath on the back of her neck. It was join up!

Turning slowly and keeping her eyes lowered, because only predators stare, Amy rubbed the palomino between the eyes. Then, turning away, she walked across the ring. She listened closely. Would Promise follow her? If she didn't, then she would have to put her back to work and try again. But there was no need for a second try. After the slightest hesitation the mare followed her. Amy walked in a circle and changed direction several times with the mare following her every footstep. At last she stopped and rubbed Promise's head again.

"Good girl," she praised. The mare pushed her nose gently against Amy and then lifted her muzzle to Amy's face, snorting inquisitively. Amy smiled and rubbed her golden neck before turning to Ty, who was standing at the gate. "She was very quick to respond."

"She's very smart," Ty said. "She knew what to do right away."

"That's what I thought!" Amy said.

They exchanged smiles. Amy felt a warm glow of happiness spread through her.

Turning back to Promise, she started on the next stage of her plan. She ran her hands over the mare's neck, withers, back, hips, and flanks, all the vulnerable areas that a horse would be uneasy about letting a predator near. Promise stood rock solid.

Feeling confident, Amy snapped the longline onto Promise's halter and called to Ty to bring the tack into the ring. Now that Promise trusted her, she was sure that the mare would let her put the saddle and bridle on her.

But as Amy stepped forward to take the saddle from Ty, Promise suddenly exploded. Pulling back, she reared up on her hind legs, her front hooves lashing angrily through the air. Amy leaped back just in time. Dropping the saddle on the ground, she moved quickly to the mare's shoulder, closing in on her head as soon as her hooves touched the ground. "Easy now," she said. "Easy." For a moment Promise's eyes seemed to flash and she fought Amy's hold on her halter, but then she settled.

Glancing around, Amy was relieved to see that Ty had acted quickly and whisked the saddle away. Balancing it over the gate, he now headed back toward her. "That was close!" he said breathlessly.

Amy nodded, feeling confused. She was certain that the join up had gone well and that Promise wasn't afraid of her, so why did she react so violently to the saddle?

"I'll send her around again," she said, unclipping the longline.

Ty moved to the side, and Amy sent Promise around the ring once more. The join up went even quicker this time. Within two circuits Promise was licking her lips and lowering her head, asking permission to stop. As soon as Amy coiled the longline and turned around, Promise joined her and followed her trustingly around the ring.

Ty brought the saddle over. But almost immediately, Promise was on her back legs, rearing and striking out. Ty hastily backed off.

"I can't understand it," Amy said when Promise was standing still beside her again.

"Maybe it's something else," Ty said, joining her without the saddle this time. Promise bent her head toward him. "Maybe the saddle hurts her."

Amy shook her head. "Scott said that he's checked her over thoroughly and there's nothing wrong. It has to be fear." She frowned. "So what do we do now?"

"We could leave an old saddle in her stall," Ty suggested. "That way she'll see it all the time and get used to it."

"Good idea," Amy said, nodding quickly. "If we leave it there overnight, then we can try again tomorrow."

"Let's put some powdered valerian in her feed," Ty said. "That should help her relax."

Amy started to lead Promise toward the gate. "It's funny," she said, looking at the mare's intelligent head. "She doesn't look like the fearful type, and she seems confident about everything else."

"Fear's like that, though," Ty commented. "Horses can be afraid of some crazy things, just like people."

Amy nodded. She guessed he was right, and yet something about the way the mare had reared bothered her. She went over the moment in her mind. As the mare had struck out, Amy had caught a glimpse of her eyes and they hadn't looked scared.

Amy pushed the thought away. Of course it was fear — fear was at the root of nearly all behavior problems. That's what Mom had always said. She had also said that you shouldn't rush a horse. Amy knew they just had to be patient. They would work Promise slowly, and eventually she would get over her fear.

🙖

Before going into the house for the night, Amy put an old saddle in the palomino's stall. As she walked in with the saddle over her arm, Promise shied away, flattening her ears and throwing her head in the air.

"It's OK," Amy said, dropping the saddle to the floor. "I'm not going to put it on you." She waited outside to see how long it would take Promise to leave the back of her stall.

To her surprise, before she had even bolted the door, Promise walked over to the saddle and began sniffing it curiously. Then with apparent disinterest, Promise turned to her hay net and continued to munch her hay. She didn't seem bothered by the saddle at all.

Strange, Amy thought. Usually a horse took quite a while to get used to an object that scared it. Apart from when Amy had been carrying the saddle, Promise had shown no hint of fear or unease. She guessed the valerian might have kicked in. But to have such a change, so soon? It wasn't normal. Not knowing what to think, Amy went into the farmhouse.

Lou and Marnie were sitting at the kitchen table, talking and poring over a page of figures. Their faces were serious.

"Hi!" Amy said.

"Hi," Lou replied.

Marnie smiled quickly at Amy and then turned back to the papers and continued the conversation. "There has to be something we can do."

"What are you talking about?" Amy said, looking over their shoulders.

Lou shuffled the papers together. "Nothing."

Amy looked from one to the other. "What's going on?"

Marnie sighed. "You should tell her, Lou."

"It's OK," Lou said quickly to Amy. "Just some financial worries."

"Oh," Amy said, feeling slightly relieved that it wasn't anything serious. They always had money problems. She opened the cookie jar and took out a couple of cookies. She turned and found Lou looking at her.

"You're not concerned, are you?" Lou said slowly.

Amy shrugged. "We always have money problems. We'll manage. We always do."

"Amy, we've got to face the facts!" Frustration showed clearly on Lou's face. "We really need to get some more clients."

"We've got Promise," Amy retorted.

"One horse?" Lou shook her head. "Amy, we can't run this place on the fees from one horse!"

"So what are you saying?" Amy demanded. "We just give up?"

Lou's response was swift. "No, but we have to think of something. And fast." Lou put her head in her hands. "I didn't want to tell you," she said hopelessly. "I know how worried you've been about Pegasus and how pleased you were to get Promise but, yes — unless we get some new clients very soon, we could have a real problem."

"It's really that bad?" Amy asked.

There was a horrible silence.

Marnie looked at her. "Lou and I have been trying to think of something, looking over the figures, looking at the assets. But she's right, Amy. It's not a good situation."

Amy took a step back, horrified. "But it can't be. What about the brochure and the advertising?"

"They haven't brought us any new business yet." Lou stood up. "Amy, we can't pretend any longer. If things don't get better fast, we'll have to close the place down."

Chapter Eight

Amy hardly slept that night. She tossed and turned, thinking over and over what Lou had said. Heartland couldn't close. There had to be something they could do to keep it open. At five thirty she gave up trying to sleep and, pulling on her jeans, went outside.

The early light was pale, and the only sounds were the birds singing in the trees. Feeling sick with worry, Amy carried a saddle up to the circular training ring and then got Promise's halter. The only plan that she had been able to come up with was to cure Promise as quickly as possible in the hope that Lisa Stillman would send them more horses.

Amy led the palomino up to the ring and went through the process of joining up again. As the sun rose and the light brightened, Amy tried putting a saddle on the palomino's back, but as soon as she had lifted the saddle off the gate the mare reared and fought. Eventually Amy gave up and took Promise back to her stall.

Before returning the halter to the tack room, Amy looked over Pegasus's door. He was lying down, his muzzle resting on the straw, his breathing labored. "Pegasus?" Amy said in alarm.

Pegasus staggered to his feet. His ribs were sticking out, and the hollows in his sides moved in and out as he breathed. Amy went into his stall and checked him over. His breathing seemed to steady a bit. But he still didn't look well. Putting an arm over his back, Amy laid her face against the swell of his shoulders and felt tears well in her eyes. What else could she do?

"Amy?"

She jumped and swung around. Ty had arrived and was leaning on the half door. "You OK?" he asked in concern.

"Yeah," she said quickly, brushing her eyes with her hand. "I'm fine." But as she met Ty's concerned look a sob leaped into her throat. "I don't know what to do, Ty," she burst out helplessly. "I've tried everything. Nothing's working." She looked at him desperately. "What else can I do? There must be *something*!" Amy said in frustration. "*Mom* would have thought of something!"

She saw a muscle in Ty's jaw tighten.

"If only she were here!" Amy murmured, looking down to the ground.

"If only," Ty said quietly. With a sigh, he straightened his shoulders. "Look, you stay here. I'll go start the feeds."

Amy watched him leave and, burying her face in Pegasus's mane, she tried to fight back her tears.

✲

As Amy walked down the drive to catch the school bus, a turmoil of thoughts ran through her head — Pegasus, Promise, Heartland's future. Then as she passed Pegasus's empty paddock she felt overwhelmed with sickness.

On the bus, she hardly said a word. Soraya and Matt seemed to sense that she didn't want to talk and left her alone. Several times she caught them exchanging worried looks.

"I'll see you guys later," Matt said quickly as they got off the bus. "I . . . I need to check the roster for tonight's game." Shooting a look at Soraya, he hurried away.

"So what's up?" Soraya asked as she and Amy walked to their lockers.

Amy didn't answer. She didn't know what to say or where to start.

"Is it Pegasus?" Soraya asked.

"Yes. Well, partly," Amy said. She hugged her backpack to her chest. "He's worse."

"Oh, Amy, I'm really sorry," Soraya said, her eyes filling with sympathy.

"Nothing I do seems to make a difference," Amy said. "I just can't seem to cure him."

"I'm not surprised," Ashley's voice drawled.

Amy swung around. Ashley was standing behind her with Jade.

"So the healing hands aren't working?" Ashley prodded, her green eyes dancing at Amy's discomfort. Jade smirked. "A healer who can't even heal her own horse. That's just too bad."

"Give it a break, Ashley," Soraya snapped with unusual force. She put her hand on Amy's arm. "Come on, Amy, let's go."

Feeling too drained to cope with Ashley's taunts, Amy turned away.

"When are you going to face it, Amy?" Ashley called after her. "You and your sister are never going to make Heartland work without your mom."

Amy stiffened, but just as she was about to retaliate she was struck by the painful realization that Ashley's words might be true.

"Come *on*," Soraya hissed, pulling her arm.

Amy followed Soraya dumbly. For the first time in her life, she was doubting herself and her own abilities.

Maybe I'm not good enough to save Heartland, she thought. *After all, Promise won't let me near her with a saddle, and Pegasus is getting worse.* She started to feel sick again. She wouldn't let Ashley be right.

🐚

By the time Amy got home from school and started the long walk up the drive, she was feeling intensely depressed. Instead of the leap that her heart normally made on coming home again, she felt it sink at the thought of all the problems awaiting her.

To her surprise, as she reached the house the back door flew open. "Amy!" Lou said, her eyes shining. "We've been waiting for you to get home! Marnie and I have had an idea!"

"An idea," Amy echoed, following her into the kitchen.

Marnie was standing by the sink. "A way of getting new customers for Heartland," she said, excitement lighting up her face.

Amy's hopes leaped. "What is it?"

"We can organize an open-house day," Lou declared. "But not just for people to come and look around; one where we actually *show* people what we do. You could demonstrate joining up with a horse, and Ty could explain the treatments we use, you know, the aromatherapy and the herbs and the . . ."

"I don't think it will work," Amy responded.

Lou stared at her. "Why not? It would definitely get us customers. Most of them have never seen a join-up demonstration before — it's a magical experience!"

Amy shook her head desperately. After Ashley's words that afternoon the last thing she wanted was people coming out to Heartland. What would she say if they asked her about Promise? What would they think when they saw Pegasus? Ashley's words echoed in her head — who would want to send a horse to Heartland when she couldn't even cure her own horse?

"But, Amy," Lou said, looking at her in surprise. "Don't you see? This could be the answer to our problems."

"Lou's right, Amy," Marnie said. "I'm sure that if people actually see how you work they will be really interested in sending problem horses here."

"I can't do it," Amy said firmly.

"But . . ." Lou began.

"Lou, I just can't. Please don't make me, not now," Amy said in almost a pleading tone.

Lou's temper suddenly seemed to snap. "Oh, for goodness' sake, Amy! What's the matter?" she shouted angrily. "Don't you realize that this is our last chance? You can't just say no!"

"But, Lou," Amy shouted back, "you don't understand. There's just too much going on. Everything's going wrong!" Flinging her backpack down, she ran out of the house.

She headed for the stable block, overwhelmed with emotion. It felt like her world was collapsing. Seeking comfort, she went into Pegasus's stall and threw her arms around his neck. "Oh, Pegasus, what are we going to do?" Burying her face in his mane, she breathed in his sweet smell and wished that everything could be different.

A few minutes later there was a faint knock behind her. "Amy?"

She turned. Marnie was standing in the doorway.

Pegasus whickered softly. Ever since the evening when Marnie had been wearing the jacket, he seemed to have taken a liking to her. He stretched out his nose. "Hi, big fella," Marnie said, stroking him.

Amy swallowed her tears.

"Um . . ." Marnie said hesitantly. "Lou's a little upset, Amy."

Amy didn't say anything.

"The open house is a really good idea," Marnie said. "Why don't you want to do it?"

Amy looked at Pegasus. His ribs were poking out, his white coat looked stark and dull. "How can we have people here?" she said hopelessly. "When I can't even cure Pegasus, my own horse?" A lump of tears swelled painfully in her throat. "It's no good," she said, shaking her head. "I'm no good."

Marnie looked at her in genuine astonishment. "But that's crazy. Lou's told me about all the horses you've cured — little Sugarfoot, and Nick Halliwell's horse, and the horse that was in the accident."

"But I'm not Mom," Amy whispered, hot tears in her eyes. "She would have cured Pegasus. She would have known what to do with Promise."

Marnie's blue eyes searched Amy's face. "But your mom had years and years of experience. Do you think she got it right all the time when she was first starting? She would have made mistakes, had failures. But she didn't let that stop her." She took Amy by the shoulder. "Anyway, for all you know, the vet said Pegasus could have a sickness you can't cure — something that even your mom wouldn't have been able to cure."

Amy bit her lip.

"Amy," Marnie said softly. "Stop being so hard on yourself. You can't be Marion. All you can do is be yourself and listen to your own instincts."

There was a deep moment of silence. "Mom used to say that," Amy whispered. "She always used to say that I had to trust my instincts."

"So *do* it!" Marnie said. "Look, Heartland can be a success, I'm sure of it. But only if you run it in your own way and for your own reasons, and only if you and Lou work together as a team. You are both very talented, in different ways. You're great with the horses, and Lou knows what she's doing with the books and business side of things. You have to find a way to use those talents together to really help Heartland."

Slowly, Amy nodded and then took a deep breath. "I'll — I'll think about the open house."

Marnie smiled. "Good. I really think it could work." She hugged Amy. "And remember what your mom said — trust your instincts."

Amy watched her leave the stall. *Trust my instincts.*

As she stroked Pegasus's neck the truth hit her. She had been so busy thinking about what Mom would have done that she had forgotten to listen to her own instincts. Not only that. She had also forgotten her mother's absolute rule — *listen to the horse.*

That evening when the last of the work had been done and Ty had left, Amy led Promise to the schooling ring. Following the pattern of her previous sessions with the horse, she joined up with her and then picked up the saddle from the gate. However, this time as Promise backed up defensively, Amy watched her eyes.

It was hard to believe, but Amy was certain that she saw no fear.

Dropping the saddle, Amy quickly moved Promise

away, talking to her and leading her around until she was calm again. Then she stopped and thought.

At the sight of the saddle coming near her, Promise's eyes had filled with anger and — Amy struggled to find the right word. *Resentment.* Yes, Promise had looked resentful.

For a moment, Amy looked at the horse. *Why?* She thought about everything she had heard about Promise. As she remembered the details of Promise's life prior to belonging to Lisa Stillman, Amy suddenly had a feeling that she was close to finding what was at the root of the problem.

Unclipping the longline, she set Promise loose in the empty field next to the training ring and secured the gate before hurrying across the yard to the house. To her relief, there was no one in the kitchen. She picked up the phone.

A quick call to Scott gave her the telephone number that she wanted. She punched the numbers and waited, still not totally sure what it was that she was trying to find out.

When the phone was picked up, an older woman answered. "Eliza Chittick speaking," she said briskly.

"Hi," Amy said. "This is Amy Fleming from Heartland Sanctuary. I have a horse you once owned — Promise, a palomino. I'm working with her for Lisa Stillman, and I was wondering if you could help me with some details about her background."

"Promise?" Mrs. Chittick said, her voice immediately softening. "Why, sure, I can help. Fire away."

Amy explained about Promise's reaction to the saddle and bridle.

"I'd heard from Lisa she was being difficult," Mrs. Chittick said, sounding worried. "But I had no idea it was this bad. She was perfect when she was here. A horse in a million. Did Lisa tell you that my grandson used to ride her? He's almost blind, and she's the only horse I would have trusted with him."

"Yes, she told me about that," Amy said, still not quite sure what information she was hoping to get from Mrs. Chittick but feeling sure that the key to Promise's behavior was somehow connected to her past. "So she was good with him?"

"Wonderful," Mrs. Chittick said. "We trusted her completely, and she seemed to understand that she needed to take special care of him. He'd ride her bareback with just a halter. I've never known a more intelligent horse. She acted more like a human than a horse, really." Amy heard her smile. "And I guess that's how we treated her. Somehow, when you were doing things with her, you almost felt that you had to ask her permission."

Something in Amy's brain suddenly seemed to click

into place. *That was it!* Her fingers gripped the receiver in excitement. She was sure that she had figured it out.

"Like I said, she was a horse in a million," Mrs. Chittick continued. "I just can't believe that Lisa's having these problems with her. The horses are treated well at Fairfield. I can't understand what's gone wrong."

Amy thanked Mrs. Chittick for the information and promised to call her with news about Promise's progress. Putting the receiver down, she leaned against the wall. Yes, at Fairfield the horses were undoubtedly treated well — but they were treated like horses. And that wasn't what Promise had been used to.

Amy hurried back to the field. Promise was grazing in the fading light, but as Amy undid the gate, she walked over, her head outstretched, her delicate ears pricked. Amy rubbed her forehead and tried to imagine what it must have been like for Promise. All her life she had been treated as an individual, trusted, respected — *loved* — and then suddenly she had been uprooted from everything she knew and placed in a yard where she was treated like any other horse.

Amy remembered what Lisa Stillman had said about the first day that Promise had been tacked up. Amy could picture how it happened when the tack was thrown swiftly onto Promise's back — she tried to object to what she felt was rough handling but she was slapped by the stable hand. Then Promise retaliated by biting and was punished further.

Amy studied Promise's head — confident, intelligent, bold. Whereas most horses would have submitted to the discipline, Promise had chosen to fight the firm handling with aggression. It was her way of saying that she wanted to be treated better, but the stronger people got with her, the more aggressive she had become. Arabians were a proud breed, and every line of Promise's body, every contour of her head suggested that she had an extreme sense of pride. She was a horse that would never give in to harsh treatment.

"But I wasn't strong with you," Amy whispered to the golden horse. "So why fight me?"

Think like the horse, she thought to herself. She looked at the saddle and imagined it from Promise's point of view. After the first time when she kicked at the stable hand, the staff at Fairfield would have approached saddling her with firm words and ready slaps. And each time Promise would react aggressively. Maybe now the sight of someone carrying a saddle was enough to make Promise go wild. Even though joining up was powerful, it had not been enough to show Promise that she was respected and trusted. Somehow Amy had to break Promise's negative feelings. She needed to show Promise that the sight of the saddle didn't mean she'd be mistreated.

So what do I do? Amy thought.

She stood for a moment, looking at the horse, and then, all of a sudden, she knew. She clipped the longline onto Promise's halter and stroked the mare's neck. Then she moved her hands and pressed experimentally on the mare's back.

Promise turned and looked at her.

"May I?" Amy whispered.

Promise turned her head back to the front. Taking a deep breath, Amy took hold of the long, creamy mane and vaulted onto Promise's back. As she landed she tensed, half expecting her theory to be wrong and the mare to explode with a defiant rear, but nothing happened. Promise stood still and steady.

Amy relaxed. "Walk on," she said, squeezing with her legs. Promise moved forward, her body warm under Amy's legs.

Amy guided her around the field, using the halter and pressure from her knees. Promise seemed calm and happy, striding out, her action smooth and effortless, her ears pricked. After a few circuits Amy gave her a pat and asked the mare to trot. Her stride was bouncy, but Amy relaxed into it, letting her body absorb the bounces.

She stroked Promise's neck. After a few moments she couldn't resist it any longer — leaning forward she urged the mare into a canter. Promise leaped forward, her ears pricked. Amy grasped the mane, her body forward, her eyes alight. She could feel the energy surging through Promise's muscles, feel her quarters gather and push.

"Faster," she whispered.

With a surge, Promise's stride lengthened. Her mane whipped back into Amy's face, the wind dragging tears from Amy's eyes. Bending low over her neck, Amy lost herself in the thunder of hooves and the power and speed of the golden horse beneath her.

At long last, she slowed Promise down, eased her to a trot, a walk, and finally to a halt. Leaning forward, she kissed Promise's neck and then slid off. Promise nuzzled Amy's shoulder and then, lifting her muzzle to Amy's face, blew in and out. For the first time since she had come to Heartland, her eyes looked genuinely happy.

"Now let's see about the saddle," Amy said. She hitched Promise to the fence and got the saddle from the schooling ring. Walking back through the gate, she watched Promise's reaction carefully. Promise turned and looked but did nothing else. Amy could feel her heart speeding up in her chest. She approached the horse. She reached Promise's side.

"May I?" Amy asked, offering the saddle to the mare. Promise snorted but did not move.

Holding her breath, Amy lifted it up and gently slid it onto the mare's back.

Promise stayed still.

Fingers trembling, Amy did up the girth. The saddle was on. She pulled down the stirrups and, not bothering with a bridle, mounted Promise.

Nothing happened.

Amy stroked Promise's neck in delight. "Walk on."

After several times around the field, Amy halted Promise by the gate. Dusk had fallen, but Amy was so elated that she hardly noticed. Promise had let Amy saddle and ride her! She knew that it wasn't enough for Promise to trust just one person to tack her up, but that could be worked on. Amy dismounted and hugged the mare.

The breakthrough had been made.

Chapter Nine

The following morning, Amy woke early again and hurried out of the house. If she was quick she would have time to work Promise before school. She hadn't told Lou and Marnie about the previous night's success. It had all felt somehow unreal, and she decided to ride Promise one more time before she told anyone.

The palomino was looking out over her stall door. She whinnied softly when she saw Amy, her eyes shining. Amy felt a warm glow of happiness. Suddenly she just knew that Promise was going to be OK, and she knew she wanted to help Lou with the open house. Amy wanted to do whatever she could to save Heartland and help more horses like Promise.

She got the mare's halter, but before returning went to check over Pegasus's door.

Her heart stopped.

Pegasus was lying on his side, his head and neck stretched out in the straw. For an awful moment Amy thought he was dead, but then she saw his side rise and fall.

Dropping the halter she fumbled with the bolt and ran into his stall. "Pegasus?" she gasped.

The great horse lifted his head slightly. His nostrils quivered in a faint whicker, and then his head fell to the straw again.

An icy feeling closed in on Amy's heart. She stood undecided for a moment and then turned and raced to the house. "Lou!" she screamed, flinging the door open. "Lou! Quick!"

A few seconds later, Lou came stumbling into the kitchen, her eyes blinking, her hair uncombed. "Amy, what's the matter? It's only six o'clock."

"It's Pegasus!" The words left Amy in gasps. "He's down in his stall. I don't think he's going to get up again."

The sleepiness left Lou's face in an instant. "I'll call Scott. You go back to Pegasus. I'll be out as soon as I'm dressed."

Amy ran back to Pegasus's stall. He was lying there, motionless. Amy knelt by his head. His eyelids flickered, and lifting his head slightly, he rested his muzzle against her knees. He groaned quietly. Bending over, Amy cradled his huge head in her arms, kissing his ears, his eyelids, the soft skin above his nostrils. Her fingers rubbed his head and neck frantically. "It's OK, boy," she said. "It's going to be OK." She repeated the words over and over again, desperate to believe them, to somehow make them true. But deep down she knew the awful truth. It was the end — Pegasus was dying.

There was the sound of running footsteps. Marnie appeared in the stall doorway. "Lou's talking to Scott now."

At the sound of her voice, Pegasus lifted his head, and for one brief second his eyes seemed to brighten. But then he sighed and his head sank to the ground again.

"Is there anything I can get you?" Marnie said to Amy.

Amy shook her head, tears blurring her eyes. "I don't think so." Looking at Pegasus's side, she saw that his breathing was getting shallower. She stroked his cheek. His half-closed eyes were dull. It was as if the spark inside him that had started to fade when Marion died had finally gone out. Amy suddenly looked at Marnie. "The jacket!" she said.

Marnie's eyes widened with realization. "You mean your mom's barn jacket?"

"Yes," Amy said quickly. "Where is it?"

"In my room."

"Can you get it, please?" Amy whispered. "I think it might help."

Marnie hurried back to the house.

Amy stroked Pegasus's head. "There, boy, it's going to be just fine. You'll see."

Lou arrived at the stall. "Scott's on his way," she said. She knelt down beside Pegasus. "Hey, boy," she said softly.

Just then, Marnie came back with the jacket. "What do you want me to do with it?"

"Hand it to me," Amy said. As she reached for it, Pegasus caught its scent. Lifting his head, he whinnied hoarsely and, making a great effort, reached toward the jacket. All three of them said nothing, their eyes fixed on his face.

Pegasus breathed in and then out for a long moment.

Then, seeing his head about to fall, Amy folded the jacket onto her knee and Pegasus lowered his head so it rested gently in her lap. Blinking back the tears, Amy stroked his face as he nuzzled the worn fabric. He looked more at ease, but his breathing was growing more shallow. And then his eyes closed and he sighed.

Amy started to sob. "Oh, Pegasus, please don't die! *Please!*"

Lou put an arm around her shoulders. "His body is old," she said softly. "He's lived a long, full life."

Just then there was the sound of footsteps coming up to the stall. Amy glanced around. It was Scott. One look at his face was enough.

"Scott, there has to be something we can do," Amy sobbed.

Scott shook his head sadly as he looked at the horse. "Amy, you've given him a wonderful home, an ideal life. But life doesn't last forever."

"But Mom, Mom would want us to try," Amy cried in anguish.

"Your mom would understand, Amy," Scott said as he crouched down beside her and ran his hand over Pegasus's shoulder and chest. "I didn't want to worry you, but you see these swellings?" he said, pointing out a number of small fluid-filled lumps on the underside of Pegasus's chest. Amy nodded. "They suggest he has a kind of internal tumor, a lymphosarcoma, I'd guess," Scott told her.

"A tumor . . . *cancer*?" Amy stammered.

Scott nodded. "I suspected it last time I saw him." His eyes sought hers. "And the last batch of tests came back late last night. They were positive. Amy, there isn't anything we can do to cure him. Some diseases simply can't be healed." He paused. "We can't let him suffer, Amy," he said solemnly. "It wouldn't be fair."

Amy bit hard on her lower lip, desperately struggling to hold back the sobs that were threatening to shake her body. Part of her wanted to cling to every last moment she had with Pegasus. But Scott was right, she couldn't let him go through this any longer. However painful it would be, she had to do what was best for the horse she loved.

"Amy?" Scott said softly.

Amy looked up at him. She knew he was asking permission to put down her beloved Pegasus. Everything was blurred. All she could see was Pegasus's head in her lap, his eyes flickering. With tears streaming down her face, she nodded.

"It won't take long," Scott said, opening his black bag and taking out a needle. "He won't feel a thing. I promise. You're doing what is best for him."

For the last time, Amy bent her head to Pegasus's. His eyelids blinked. "I love you, Pegasus. I always will," she whispered, hot tears falling on his face. "Good-bye, boy."

She kissed his muzzle, and then looked to Scott, her eyes foggy with tears. She cradled Pegasus's head as Scott administered the injection.

A few long seconds later, Pegasus's breathing had stopped.

"That's it," Scott said softly. "He's in a better place now."

Amy gasped, staring first at Pegasus and then up to Lou.

"It was the right choice, Amy," Lou said, tears streaming down her face. She put an arm around her sister. "It was the only choice. Now he'll be with Mom again."

In that moment, Amy suddenly realized how much

she needed her sister. "Oh, Lou," she sobbed against her shoulder. "I'm so glad you're here."

"And I always will be," Lou said softly. "I'll always be here for you, Amy, and you'll be here for me."

"Yes, Lou, always," Amy replied. "Always."

Chapter Ten

That night, Amy called Grandpa to tell him about Pegasus. At first, Grandpa wanted to return immediately.

"No, it's OK. Stay," she told him.

"But I feel so bad," he protested. "I should have been there."

"There wasn't anything you could have done," Amy replied. "There was nothing anyone could have done." The tears gathered in her throat, but she felt inwardly calm. She knew that she had done the right thing. Pegasus's suffering was over.

"And what about a burial?"

"Scott and Ty dug a grave in his favorite field," Amy said quietly. "And we planted an oak sapling beside it." She glanced out the kitchen window. It was getting dark now, but she could still make out the field and the slim young tree, silhouetted against the evening sky. "You don't have to come home early, Grandpa. We'll be OK."

"Well, I'll stay until next Sunday, then, like I planned," Grandpa said. "But if you need me, promise you'll call."

"I promise," Amy said. Then she launched into a new topic. "You wouldn't believe the idea Lou came up with to get more customers," Amy exclaimed.

Just then Lou came into the kitchen. "Is that Grandpa?" she asked.

Amy nodded. "Here's Lou, Grandpa. I'll let her tell you all about her idea," she said, handing over the phone.

As Lou spoke to Grandpa, telling him about the open house they were planning, Amy leaned against the sink and stared out at Pegasus's tree. She found it almost impossible to believe that he wasn't in his stall and that when she went out to feed the next morning he wouldn't be there. But looking up at the gray sky she knew that she had to accept it — Pegasus was gone and life had to move on. Still, there was something about the tree just being there that would keep Pegasus alive for her.

"It's all settled, then," Lou said, putting the phone down. "We're going to have the open house next Sunday — Marnie's last day. Grandpa thinks it's a great idea." She looked at Amy. "You know, this is going to be one busy week."

⚞

Lou was right. There was a lot to be done — posters to be made, ads to be placed, food to be planned, and the final touches made to the stables. Marnie worked like crazy — she was so enthusiastic and really wanted the open house to be a huge success. Soraya and Matt helped as much as they could, and Amy found the days passing in a whirl of activity — going to school, helping with the open-house preparations, doing her normal chores, working Promise in the mornings and evenings. At night, when she fell into her bed, she was too exhausted to think, too tired even to dream.

On Thursday, Scott dropped by. Amy was sweeping the yard with Ty, Marnie was pruning the flowers in the hanging baskets, and Lou was attaching the nameplates to the horses' doors.

"Hi, guys," Scott called, as he was getting out of the car. "I just thought I'd stop by and see how you're getting along."

"We're doing fine," Lou said, going to meet him. "Almost ready for the big day."

"I've been spreading the word," Scott said. "So, I hope you're expecting a big crowd?"

"That's the plan," Lou said.

They stopped a few feet away from each other. "How are you?" Lou asked, her cheeks flushing slightly pink.

Amy and Marnie exchanged knowing looks.

"Fine," Scott replied to Lou. "Listen, do you need any help on Sunday? I'd be happy to lend a hand."

"Thanks," Lou said. "That would be really great." She smiled up at him.

There was a pause as they looked at each other. Suddenly seeming to become aware that they were being watched, Scott cleared his throat and turned to Amy. "So — how's it going with Promise?" he asked. "Have you made any progress?"

"You won't believe it!" Ty said, leaning on his broom.

"She's behaving herself?" Scott said to Amy.

Amy grinned at him. "You want to see?"

Getting Promise's halter, Amy led the palomino to the training ring on the longline, the saddle and bridle over her arm.

"What have you been doing with her?" Scott asked, opening the gate. "Lunging? Long-reining?"

"Riding," Amy replied, leading Promise into the ring. She grinned at his astonished face. "Watch."

She patted Promise and then vaulted lightly onto her, bareback. After riding the mare several times around the ring she halted.

"That's great," Scott said, looking impressed. He glanced at the tack. "What about with the saddle and bridle?"

"Oh, I can ride with those as well," Amy said. Her

voice was casual, but inwardly she was bubbling with delight.

Swinging her leg over Promise's back, she dismounted and got the saddle. She offered it to Promise to sniff, and when Promise had turned away, lifted it carefully onto the mare's golden back. The horse stood without moving as Amy did up the girth and then slipped on the bridle. Putting her foot in the stirrup, she mounted and rode in a circle.

"Well," she said, stopping Promise by the gate as the sweet sensation of success flowed through her, "what do you think?"

"Wow, that's amazing!" Scott exclaimed. He ran a hand through his hair. "How did you do it?"

"By listening," Amy said simply. "And respecting her."

"And she's OK for other people to ride?" Scott asked.

"She's getting there," Amy said. Only the day before, Promise had let Ty tack her up and ride her. She was still a little sensitive about the saddle being lifted near her, but with careful handling, Amy was sure that Promise would become less defensive and learn to trust other people as well.

"No one's going to believe this," Scott said, shaking his head. "Have you told Lisa yet?"

"I was going to call her tonight," Amy said.

"She'll be thrilled," Scott said. His blue eyes looked suddenly thoughtful. "You know, you should ask her permission to use Promise at the open house. People around here have heard of her. If they see that you've cured a supposedly rogue horse, they're bound to be impressed."

Amy thought for a moment. Why not? She knew Lou wanted her to do a display of joining up with a horse for the visitors to see. Why not use Promise, if Lisa Stillman thought it was OK? After all, it would have an impact on those people who had heard about the palomino, and if people hadn't, well, she was a very pretty, healthy horse and would look good in the ring. But she wouldn't do it unless Lisa agreed.

❧

After Scott had left, Amy phoned Fairfield. Lisa Stillman sounded astonished to hear that Promise was already ridable. "But you've only had her for a week!" she said. "And you're telling me she's cured?"

"Well, not completely," Amy replied. "But she's definitely improving. I can ride her and saddle her up, no problem. I just want her to get more confident with other people."

"But other stables had her for months at a time, and not one of them ever made a difference," Lisa Stillman said. "What on earth did you do?"

Amy told Lisa about her phone call to Eliza Chittick and about how Promise's behavior had changed when she had started trusting her and treating her with respect.

"This is amazing!" Lisa Stillman said as she listened to Amy's tale. "I have to see her!"

"Well, I was calling to ask if we could use Promise in a demonstration on Sunday. We're having an open house at Heartland." Amy explained the idea behind the day and how she needed a horse to join up with. "Promise would be ideal — if you'll give your permission, of course," she added politely.

"Sure, you can use her," Lisa Stillman said. "I'll even come along myself to see how she's doing. What time does it start?"

"Eleven o'clock," Amy said. "And the demonstration will be around twelve."

"I'll see you then," Lisa Stillman said.

Amy put the phone down, feeling excited but nervous. She knew that Ty was carefully preparing his talk about the alternative remedies they used at Heartland. His part of the demonstration was bound to go well. But the join up? It was normally such a private, intense experience. How would she feel doing it in front of a lot of strangers? What if it didn't work?

She pushed those thoughts away. It had to work. After all, Heartland's future depended on the demonstration being a success. And she would do *anything* to keep Heartland going. She had made a promise to Mom and a promise to herself.

🐎

The final few days before the open house seemed to race by, but by quarter to eleven on Sunday morning Heartland was finally ready for the visitors to arrive. Amy, Lou, Marnie, Ty, and Soraya stood in the middle of the yard.

"We're ready!" Lou said, looking around in relief.

"And it's looking good!" Marnie said, gazing at the front stable block and the spotless yard.

"It sure is," Amy agreed. She looked at the horses that had their heads over their stall doors, their coats gleaming and their eyes shining. They all looked so healthy and happy. The hanging baskets provided a splash of cheerful color against the dark wood of the stables. Around the yard, Ty had put up signs to show visitors where to go. "It all looks so neat and clean!" Amy exclaimed.

"Well, everything except you!" Lou grinned.

Amy looked down at her filthy jeans. She had started work at five thirty that morning and hadn't had a second even to brush her hair. "I guess I'd better change," she admitted.

"Me, too," said Soraya.

They hurried upstairs to Amy's bedroom and changed

into jodhpurs and clean T-shirts. "I hope everything goes OK," Amy said, feeling butterflies starting to flutter in her stomach.

"It will," Soraya said, pulling her dark curls back into a ponytail. She glanced out the window. "We'd better hurry! I think the first people are arriving!"

They raced downstairs to find Ty directing a carload of visitors into the field they were using as a temporary parking lot. Just then, Scott's Jeep came up the drive. He stopped it near the house, and he and Matt jumped out.

"Hi, there!" Lou said, coming out of the house with a carton of sodas for the refreshments stall that Marnie was in charge of.

"Sorry we're late," Scott said. "I was called out first thing." He saw her with the big box and walked over. "Hey, do you want a hand?"

"Thanks," Lou said gratefully, letting him take the box from her. "There's a couple more cartons inside."

"No problem," Scott said. "I can take care of that."

"Hey, guys," Matt said, going over to Amy and Soraya. "What do you need me to do?"

"Could you take over the parking from Ty?" Amy suggested. "Soraya and I are going to show people around, and Ty's supposed to be giving out brochures and talking about what we do here."

"Sure. No problem," said Matt, jogging off.

The first group of visitors headed toward the yard.

Soraya glanced at Amy. "Well, here we go," she muttered as they drew closer. "Get ready to smile."

Amy nodded and, taking a deep breath, stepped forward. "Hi," she said brightly. "I'm Amy Fleming. Welcome to Heartland."

❧

Soon the place was teeming with people. Although most of them were really friendly and interested in Heartland's work, there were some who clearly doubted the effectiveness of the methods used. Amy struggled to keep control of her frustration. She couldn't fathom how close-minded some people were.

"If one more person tells me that aromatherapy or herbal remedies won't work with horses, I'm going to scream," she muttered to Ty as she stopped to get some brochures from him.

Farther up the yard she could see Soraya telling a group of visitors the history of each horse.

"Relax," Ty said to her. He shrugged. "You know the folks around here. Not everyone's going to get it. We'll be lucky if we can convince a couple of people that our ways work."

But Amy couldn't think like that. She knew the methods they used at Heartland worked, and she desperately wanted *all* the visitors to realize that — to see what a unique and special place it really was.

"But why did they bother to come?" she demanded, thinking of a man she had talked to who refused to believe alternative remedies could have an effect. "Some of them just want to criticize."

"Yeah," Ty said easily. His eyes suddenly fixed on a point behind Amy's shoulder. "Speaking of which —"

Amy looked around. Ashley Grant was sauntering up the yard. Beside her was her mom, a tall, broad-shouldered woman with short blond hair.

"What are they doing here?" Amy hissed.

Val Grant caught sight of her and came over. "Hello, Amy," she said, her smile revealing a mouthful of perfect white teeth. "We thought we'd pop by and offer you our support."

Like that's true, Amy thought to herself. But she forced herself to smile back. "Thanks so much. It's nice to see you."

Val Grant's eyes flashed. "You've sure cleaned this place up."

"Hi, Ty," Ashley said, virtually ignoring Amy. She flicked her hair back. "How are you?"

"Fine." Ty coughed and started to shuffle the brochures.

"Can I have a brochure?" Ashley asked. Amy saw her gingerly take the sheet from Ty and smile.

Feeling a wave of irritation, she turned to excuse herself. "I'd better be going," she said to Val Grant. "There are so many people to see."

"Sure thing," Val Grant said. "We'll just have a look around. We're looking forward to seeing the demonstration later. Good luck." She laughed. At least her mouth did; her eyes stayed hard. "You never know, we may learn something."

Amy smiled briefly and then hurried away. Now, more than ever, she was determined that the join up would succeed.

🙚

At twelve o'clock, Scott, Lou, and Marnie started to encourage people to go to the schooling ring. Amy put Promise's saddle and bridle on the fence and then went to get the palomino.

"This is it, girl," she said, rubbing Promise's golden neck. "Please be good." Suddenly she realized that she hadn't seen Lisa Stillman. She felt a flash of disappointment but quickly pushed it down. There were more than enough people out there to impress.

She led Promise up to the training ring. At the sight of people clustered two deep around the fence, her stomach knotted with fear.

Ty had already started his talk.

To demonstrate the use of aromatherapy oils, Soraya led Sugarfoot into the ring, and Ty showed the crowd how the Shetland turned away from certain oils but sniffed long and hard at two of the bottles. "Horses know what will help them," he told the crowd. "Sugarfoot came to Heartland after his owner died. At that time, he liked the neroli oil; it helps with grief and depression. But now that he is getting better, he is drawn to the smells of bergamot and yarrow oils. Bergamot is an energizing oil, and yarrow relaxes. Sugarfoot's instincts help him choose the oils that will help him most."

Ty then started to work on the Shetland with T-touch circles and again pointed out to the audience how the Shetland moved himself to place certain parts of his head and body under his fingers.

Amy noticed the growing interest of the crowd as they began to murmur to one another.

"He's telling me how to help him," Ty told them. Leaving Sugarfoot he walked around the ring. "Horses try to communicate with us, but time after time humans just don't listen," he said. He looked around, and his dark eyes were serious and convincing. "Well, at Heartland we believe in listening. We don't whisper things to horses. We let *them* speak to *us*."

As he finished there was a burst of applause.

Promise started at the sudden noise. "It's OK," Amy quickly soothed her.

Soraya led Sugarfoot out of the ring, and Ty held up his hand for quiet. "Amy is now going to show you another way that we communicate with the horse. It is called the join up." There was another round of applause, and he walked over to the gate where Amy was waiting. He opened the gate. "It's all yours," he said to Amy. "Good luck."

Their eyes met.

Ty squeezed her shoulder. "Go on. You can do this. I know."

Taking a deep breath, Amy braced herself and led Promise into the ring.

The clapping died down and an expectant hush descended.

Horribly aware of the eyes watching her, Amy unclipped the lead rope and let Promise go. As the palomino trotted off around the ring, Amy heard a few murmurs and gasps from the people in the crowd who recognized Promise as Lisa Stillman's rogue horse. Amy knew she had to speak, to explain what she was doing, but for a moment her courage failed her. Suddenly she caught sight of Lou in the crowd. Her sister nodded and smiled at her, and Amy felt her confidence return.

"Promise is a horse that came to us with a behavior problem," she told the crowd. "For months she had been considered virtually unridable, refusing to be saddled or bridled. But then she came to Heartland. She has been here for two weeks, and her problem is pretty much cured — as I will show you at the end of this demonstration," she said, motioning to the saddle and bridle on the fence. "But first of all I will show you the technique we use to establish a relationship with a horse. Not a traditional relationship based on fear, but a relationship based on trust and understanding."

Moving to the center of the ring, she began.

The join up worked like a dream. Amy explained to the audience every signal that Promise gave. She could feel the tension in the crowd when she dropped her eyes and turned her back on the mare. And then she heard the universal gasp as Promise walked confidently over and rested her muzzle on Amy's shoulder. The audience's astonishment was obvious as she walked around the ring with the palomino following wherever she went.

To end the demonstration, Amy picked up the saddle and offered it to Promise. "I'm now asking her if I can saddle her up," she told the crowd. "By asking her permission I am showing that I respect her. Promise is a highly intelligent, proud horse — too proud to ever be bullied into obedience. She responds to respect, not reprimands."

After Promise had sniffed the saddle, Amy tacked her up, mounted, and then rode around the ring. She trotted the palomino in two serpentines and then cantered her in a perfect figure eight.

Drawing Promise to a halt in the middle of the ring, she dismounted. "In two weeks Promise has changed from an unridable rogue into the perfect pleasure horse." She smiled at the crowd. "And it's all because, here at Heartland, we listen to the horse."

The applause broke out. It went on and on. Patting Promise, Amy smiled happily. They had done it! She and Promise had shown them all!

Ty came back into the ring. "So, are there any questions?"

There was a murmur in the crowd, and then a man raised his hand. It was the same man Amy had been talking to earlier who seemed determined to believe that Heartland's methods would never work.

"How do we know that the horse really was unridable?" he demanded. "We only have your word for it."

"You're right," Ty replied. "But there are enough people here who know or who have heard of this horse to back us up. Ask your neighbors."

Amy heard the crowd murmur an assent. But then she noticed movement near the gate.

"It's my belief that horse was drugged!" The voice was loud and strident. Amy swung around to see Val Grant pushing her way to the front of the fence. "It's the oldest trick in the book," the blond woman announced. "Get a rogue horse, sedate it, and then make it look like you've worked a miracle. If you come back tomorrow, I think you'll see a very different horse."

To Amy's horror, people in the crowd started to nod. "That's not true!" she exclaimed. "I'd never drug a horse."

"Well, of course you'd say that," the first man spoke up again. "You want our business."

"Not if it means drugging a horse!" Amy said. "That's against everything Heartland stands for."

Val Grant spoke up again. "Well, these people just don't seem to believe you."

"I believe you." The crowd turned. A woman pushed open the gate and walked into the ring. With her long blond hair and elegant jodhpurs, Lisa Stillman was instantly recognizable to all who followed the show circuit.

"Lisa!" Amy gasped.

Lisa Stillman walked to the center of the ring. "What some of you may not realize," she explained, "is that this horse is one of mine. I can vouch for the fact that she was as unridable as Amy Fleming says. Although," she shot caustic looks at the man who had spoken out and at Val Grant, "you may of course choose to doubt my word as well." She looked around at the rest of the audience. "The fact is, it's true. This was the horse's last chance, and as far as I'm concerned Heartland has worked nothing less than a miracle. She isn't drugged, anyone can see that by looking into her eyes." She patted Promise. "When I first agreed to let Promise come here, I was as skeptical as many of you," she announced. "But not anymore. After what I've seen, I realize that this is the way of the future. From now on," Lisa turned and smiled at Amy, "any problem horse of mine will be coming to Heartland."

"Thank you!" Amy gasped.

"And now," Lisa Stillman said, "I think we should give our hosts a round of applause."

This time the applause was deafening. People clapped their hands and whistled. Sensing Promise tense up, Amy quickly led her away from the noisy ring and back to the peaceful sanctuary of her stall.

"Thank you," she whispered to the mare.

Promise snorted and nuzzled her shoulder.

Suddenly the stall door flew open. It was Matt and Soraya. "That was fantastic!" Soraya gasped.

"The way that Lisa Stillman just marched into the ring was so cool!" Matt almost shouted.

"Val Grant didn't know what to do!" Soraya grinned. "We saw her storming back to her car with Ashley, looking really angry." She hugged Amy. "And you were great! You seemed so cool and confident."

Amy grinned. "I was terrified!"

"You should see all the people by the ring now," Matt said. "Everyone's trying to talk to Lou and Ty about bringing their horses here. You're going to have so much business. You're going to have a waiting list."

Amy could hardly believe it, but when she returned to the ring with Soraya and Matt, it was clear they were right. People were crowding around Lou and Ty. Amy's eyes widened. It was wonderful, just what they'd wanted, but how were they ever going to cope with the extra work?

Her sister suddenly spotted her. "Amy!" she called, waving.

Amy made her way through the crowd, with people patting her on the back and congratulating her. "Hi!" she exclaimed, reaching Lou. "Isn't this amazing?"

"Yeah," Lou said. "Look at this!" She waved a piece of paper under Amy's nose that was filled with names and addresses. "And Ty has more. After today we'll be able to fill the barns three times over."

"How will we deal with it all?" Amy cried, half in delight, half in despair.

"That's the best part of all," Lou said. "Lisa Stillman asked if we'll take her nephew Ben as a stable hand. She wants him to learn everything we do so that he can return to her barn and practice the same therapies we use. Even better, she's going to pay us to train him!"

"I can't believe it, Lou!" Amy gasped, flinging her arms around her sister's neck. "It's going to be so much better."

Lou hugged her back joyfully.

"I know you said you'd have wild parties when I was gone," a much-loved voice said behind them. "But isn't this a bit much?"

Amy and Lou turned. "Grandpa!" they both cried in delight.

Jack Bartlett smiled at them. "Yes," he said, "I'm home."

🐎

That evening, after the horses had been fed and the yard cleared, Amy walked down the drive to Pegasus's favorite field. The air was still and peaceful. Amy leaned over the wooden gate and watched the shadows lengthening across the grass.

Ty, Soraya, Matt, and Scott had gone home, and Marnie was in her bedroom, packing for her trip back to the city the next day. Amy knew she was going to miss her. After all, it was Marnie who had helped her realize that she had to run Heartland in her own way and follow her own instincts, and that she and Lou had to work together as a team.

A cool breeze shivered across Amy's skin. After the commotion of the open house, everything seemed twice as quiet. It had been a wonderful day. For the moment, at least, Heartland's financial worries were over, and with Ben Stillman as an additional stable hand there would be more time to spend with the horses. *Maybe I'll even get a chance to enter some jumping classes*, Amy thought.

She looked at the freshly planted oak tree and her heart twisted. There was just one thing missing from her life — Pegasus.

"Why did you have to go?" she whispered painfully.

But even as she spoke, she knew the answer. Life moves on. Nothing lasts forever.

The light faded and the evening shadows covered the tree. A last, lone bird sang out.

"Amy?"

She looked around. Grandpa and Lou were walking toward her through the October dusk.

"We saw you from the kitchen window," Lou said.

"May we join you?" Grandpa asked quietly.

Amy nodded her head.

For a moment all three of them stood by the gate in silence. "Today was a good day," Lou said at last.

"Yeah," Amy said. "It was."

Grandpa put a hand lightly on their shoulders. "I think tomorrow will be a good day, too," he said. "I'm proud of you, and your mom would have been proud, too. Now Heartland has a future, and you've made it your own."

Amy looked at her Grandpa and at Lou, and then her gaze fell on the slender young oak. Life was about the future, not about clinging to the past. Staring at the tree, her lips moved silently. *"Good-bye, Pegasus."*

Despite the shadows of the night, the bird sang on.